AN

UNWIZARDLY

SILENCE

AN UNWIZARDLY SILENCE

THE WIZARD'S DIARY
BOOK TWO
(PARTS III & IV)

ROBERT J. BRADSHAW

BEAUPORT BOOKS

A special thank you to my family (Lori, Reid, and Sarah) for countless hours of workshopping, editing, and proofreading every aspect of the story. *The Wizard's Diary* wouldn't exist without your love of reading, invaluable insight, and boundless creativity. Thank you also to my parents, Joan and Bruce, and the many people who assisted in publishing this edition.

THE WIZARD'S DIARY: BOOK TWO (PARTS III & IV)
Written and Illustrated by Robert J. Bradshaw
Cover photography and design by Robert J. Bradshaw
Copyright © 2024 by Robert J. Bradshaw
ALL RIGHTS RESERVED

Publication date: May 1, 2024
eBook ISBN: 979-8-9906096-9-3
Paperback ISBN: 979-8-9906096-8-6
Hardcover ISBN: 979-8-9906096-7-9

BEAUPORT BOOKS
P.O. Box 551
Gloucester, MA 01931
www.wizardsdiary.com

Dedicated to
Lori, Reid, and Sarah
for the year that never was.

TABLE OF CONTENTS

PART III 1

1   SURROUNDED BY STONE.................................3

2   A NARROW ESCAPE 5

3   MISCHIEF AFOOT 17

4   THE COTTAGE IN THE WOODS 33

5   THE MEETING PLACE...................................42

6   KEE-EEEEE-ARR! 55

7   HEADING SOUTH...69

8   OF TWO MINDS 75

9   THEY'RE BACK!..93

10   BRING YOUR OWN ROPE 101

11   A PUFF OF AIR...109

12   CALM BEFORE THE STORM 121

13   THERE MAY NOT BE ONE TRUE ROOT 131

14   JUSTICE IS NEVER BLIND 143

15   A SPARK OF TRUTH 152

16   THE ONCE-GREAT MARBLE HOUSE 157

17   A MYSTERIOUS VISIT 170

18   A WHITE BELL OF EATHĒSIUM 174

19   TOGETHER, WE STAND..............................191

20   A RIVER OF MAGIC....................................196

21   DAWN OF A NEW DAY................................209

22   OIL AND WATER...213

23   THE POWER OF SILENCE............................226

24   HISTORY IS WRITTEN BY THE VICTORS 238

25 LIGHT AT THE END OF THE TUNNEL 246

26 PAWNS ARE THE SOUL OF THE GAME..............................259

PART IV **273**

1 THE OLIPHAUNT IN THE ROOM 275

2 THE NIGHT BEFORE..279

3 A WIZARDLY RETURN..289

4 AN EARLY MORNING MEETING....................................300

5 DARK CORNERS AND WICKER BASKETS 307

6 WILLOW BRANCHES SWAY 314

7 KNIGHTY KNIGHT 325

8 BACK BY LUNCH 337

9 A BRIEF DETOUR 346

10 TWO CAN PLAY AT THAT GAME..................................352

11 THE MOTHER OF ALL DESSERTS.................................358

12 THE END OF THE ROAD 370

13 OLD EASTIE SOWTOWN..376

14 WHEN ONE DOOR CLOSES..384

15 AHÎKEHNN-DEHLN..394

16 ONE PICKUP PENNY..404

17 PRIVATE SPIRE GARDEN...416

18 A RIVER OF RATS..428

19 IT'S ALL FUN AND GAMES UNTIL…............................433

20 CAPTAIN AT THE HELM 442

21 A TERRIBLE REALIZATION...447

22 ONE HAND FOR THE BOAT..456

23 BROKEN 464

24 BRINDLEWISE THE REMARKABLE...............................473

25 PITCHFORKS AND SHOVELS..483

26 THE WORLD BETWEEN 493

27 WINTER IS COMING 500

REFERENCE...507

CALENDAR 509

DAYS OF THE WEEK 510

EVENTS AND HOLIDAYS 511

MAP: ARDILAKK VALLEY..512

MAP: GEMINI CITY 514

MAP: WIZARDING SCHOOL GROUNDS 516

MAP: MARBLE HOUSE..518

MAP: ANCIENT QUADROPOLIS 522

PART III

THE WIZARDS' UNDERGROUND

CHAPTER 1

SURROUNDED BY STONE
AARGHATHLAIN

TO7, 3-333

Dear Diary,
 They're coming for us. I must get Holly-Mine to safety.

Toodlesday of the 7th week
Year Three Hundred and Thirty-Three of the Modern Age
Early Morning: The Dark Hours

CHAPTER 2

A NARROW ESCAPE
AARGHATHLAIN

Guildebrande's steely voice sliced its way into Aargh's dreams. "Wake up, Wizard Aarghathlain! We must get out of the cottage!"

Overhead, flames poured in through the room's shattered windows, making everything shimmer. Aargh stumbled over his once-favorite chair and landed hard on the floor.

Half-asleep and delirious from the thick smell of carriage fuel, he panicked, convinced he was reliving the Great Fire. "No! I can't lose you again, Mother Tree! Wrudge, I need you!"

"It's not the forest," Guildebrande yelled over the crackling wood. "It's our trees. Someone means to do us harm. Hurry Aarghathlain. Save Holly-Mine!"

Coming to his senses, Aargh hastily gathered his belongings and hurried across the living room toward the bower he'd grown for his daughter. "Holly-Mine, are you okay?"

Much to his relief, she responded.

"I'm here, Papa. Hurry! Guildebrande is calling!"

Aargh saw her toss any hope of stewed berries and biscuits for breakfast out the window along with the bag she'd packed for their return trip to the Spire. Not wasting any time, she grabbed the short green cloak Dram had given her and threw herself out, too.

Before following, Aargh took one last look at the cottage. So many memories. So many wonderful memories. Then, he tucked his spellbooks (as Holly-Mine called them) into his robes and climbed through the window after her.

Their glassy eyes met when Aargh landed on the dry autumn grass, but neither spoke. Language contained no words sad enough to express how they felt. Nearby, a person coughed, and they reflexively bolted for the forest, only to find themselves running toward danger instead of away from it.

A shrouded figure cursed as he tried to light what appeared to be a mass of cloth wrapped around the end of a long stick. Aargh almost rushed the man before realizing they'd escaped because his torch hadn't lit...but Aargh had no time to be thankful for small mercies.

Whoosh! The torch burst into flame.

Fearing the flickering light would give him away, Aargh stumbled deeper into the underbrush after his daughter. He had no desire to watch what the wizard did next.

Disoriented from being woken up in the middle of the night, Aargh flopped behind the carcass of a long-departed oak to catch his breath. It offered little shelter from the agony he felt inside.

"Hurry, Papa! Hurry!" Holly-Mine yelled, but the tree's cries drowned out her voice.

Burning and cracking!

Tumbling and crashing!

Aargh grabbed his head, overcome by the tree's agony as their cottage north of the Once-Great Wall succumbed to the fire's insatiable appetite.

Minutes before, he'd been sleeping comfortably on his favorite rug—a handwoven piece he'd brought back from the port city of Ondlingstad. Though it had been five seasons since they'd traveled the river aboard the *Prosperity*, he still treasured the keepsakes and memories they'd brought back with them.

The daily routines of the Spire were a distant memory, and, truth be told, Aargh didn't miss it all that much. He'd had his fill of cantankerous wizards grumbling about the cafeteria serving chicken noodle soup again instead of sautéed cabbage with lemon and garlic. Or the never-ending stream of irate Geminians lodging complaints about odors emanating from experiments that had gone off. Although these things had once held great import to him, they felt trivial compared to building a life in the woods with his daughter.

The only wizard he saw with any regularity was Dramwitch, his former mentee. That was nice, but neither of them ever wanted to talk about the famed Gemini City School of Wizarding. Mostly, they whiled away the hours trimming the verge, weeding the garden, or sipping tea. Still, being forced out had hurt…a lot…and Aargh wondered how the school was getting on without him. He even hoped to return someday. But that was the realm of the future–something neither he nor any wizard could see any more. The burning of the forest had brought significant and irrevocable changes to the art of wizarding and Ardilakk Valley. Now, he was forced to take the slow road like everyone else.

Most wizards struggled with this, but not Aargh. He focused on more important things, such as taking long walks, sharing a cup of cocoa with his daughter, and telling stories to Wrudge's Tree. Deep inside, he'd always known their sylvan utopia wouldn't shield them from his past forever. And, as he watched flames leap into the sky, he knew it was gone.

A loud wrenching sound pierced the fiery din. Straining to see what was happening, he wiped his forehead with his robes. The delay proved to be a mistake.

"Run, Aarghathlain, run!" Guildebrande's voice yelled in his mind, but the blast knocked him to the ground before he could take action.

Aargh covered his head as a shower of sizzling embers fell around him. When it was safe, he peeked between his arms. About twenty paces away, Holly-Mine was pressed against a monolithic stand of granite protruding from the forest floor. She had one arm in front of her mouth and was gesturing to him with the other.

"Papa...we need to go!"

He got to his feet and staggered over to her, collapsing against the rock. She immediately took hold of his arm and pulled.

"We can't stay here!" she said, insisting they keep moving.

Aargh resisted. "You...go," he sputtered. "Get...out...of here! Don't wait for me!"

"I won't leave you, Papa."

No, she wouldn't. He knew that. So he took her hand, and they plunged deeper into the thicket.

As they navigated the forest's understory, Aargh muttered words of encouragement to himself. "Over those mushrooms. Under that branch. Don't let it snap back! You'd better grab a stick to warn snakes you're coming. Careful! Don't get tangled in those briars."

Distracted by a sound nearby, he tripped over a log and landed on all fours. His mind instantly vanished into a memory brought to the surface by his fall and the screams of the trees burning around them.

"Get up, Papa! We have to hide. They're coming," Holly-Mine pleaded, but Aargh's bloodshot eyes stared vacantly into the void of the past.

Tenderly leaning him against the log he'd fallen over, she brushed the hair away from his forehead. Then, positioning herself so they were sitting face to face, she peered into his eyes, saying, "Papa, tell me what you see."

"Fire...the barn...Aldenthwaine...I have to help... Nooooo!" Young Aargh cried from his memories.

"There, there, Aarghathlain," a familiar voice soothed.

"Mother Tree? Is that you? But I thought you were... I must have been remembering the fire."

"Yes, you were. There's no fire here. It's a beautiful autumn day."

Even as a postulant, Aargh often visited Mother Tree, effortlessly falling into conversation with the Heart of the Forest.

"You're safe. Rest in my arms," she said, cradling the boy between her strong roots.

Young Aargh relaxed, leaning back against her trunk.

As her leaves rustled in the wind, dappled light speckled the ground around him while songbirds perched on her oaken arms called to friends.

"The cardinals have come back," Young Aargh observed.

"Yes, they've come to watch over you. You're their pride and joy."

"Me?" he asked, unable to hide his astonishment.

"Oh yes. You're special to all creatures who live in Ardilakk Valley."

"But why?"

"They love you," Mother Tree responded.

"*I love them, too,*" the young boy sighed, watching birds hop from branch to branch.

A brilliant red papa cardinal called out, "*Cheer! Cheer, cheer!*"

"*Birdie! Birdie, birdie!*" came another's response carried by the wind.

Most people liked the papa reds, but not Aargh. He enjoyed watching the mama cardinals, with their rustic browns and reddish tinges on their wings and tails. They appeared regal to him, especially when they raised their tall crests.

"*Aarghathlain,*" Mother Tree said. "*I'm sure you didn't come here today to watch the birds.*"

"*No, Mother Tree.*"

"*Tell me your story. I'll keep it for you, and you will no longer be troubled by it.*"

Aargh's mind flowed farther into the past. The barn was burning, and the fire had spread to the house!

"*Papa, wait! Don't go in there!*" Tears streamed from his eyes as he watched the barn's roof collapse with his father still inside. "*Nooooo!*" he howled.

A tall man wearing embroidered purple robes materialized out of the flames and walked over to him, offering him an acorn.

"*Head Wizard Aldenthwaine is here,*" Young Aargh told Mother Tree. "*He's taking me to the Spire.*"

The boy's arms reached over the memory of Aldenthwaine's shoulders, trying to hold onto the past.

"*Papa's gone,*" he sobbed.

"*I remember it well. Such a terrible day,*" Mother Tree consoled. "*The memory of it will live in your heart, as all joys and sorrows do, but the memory will no longer burn as brightly as it once did.*"

Aargh dried his eyes as images of the day he'd left the forest faded and years sped by. Now, he was a student at the Gemini City School of Wizarding.

"Sister Wind says you're becoming quite the wizard. Is this true?" *Mother Tree asked.* "My Aarghathlain isn't little anymore, is he?"

Gone was the angelic voice of his boyish youth. "I've finished my Seconds."

"Ah, so you're no longer a novice," *she observed.*

The young man standing before her beamed with pride. "That's correct. I'm beginning my seventh year and have been elevated to Wizard of the Third Circle."

"An impressive achievement, Aarghathlain!" *Mother Tree complimented.*

"It is. I'm to begin my mentorship with the Head Wizard next week."

"The Head Wizard, no less? You're certainly on your way. And you did this on your own?"

"Oh no, Wrudge helped me. He's a clever rat!"

"He certainly is. I can't imagine a more trustworthy familiar. Where is your furry friend today?"

"Off finding a snack, I imagine. He enjoys coming to the forest as much as I do."

Images of Wrudge rummaging under the fallen leaves—his nose poking through here and there to get his bearings—made Aargh chuckle.

Time continued to pass, and an older Aargh stood before Mother Tree, wearing beautiful embroidered wizard's robes that matched his striking sapphire-blue eyes. The rich cloth surrounded him like the ocean's flowing waters, and its gold threads glinted like sea pennies at sunset.

"I'll be graduating soon," Aargh said. "The last three years have gone by too quickly, but I'm excited to start my job as Spire Historian."

"Indeed," Mother Tree said, but she sensed anxiety growing in Aargh as memories of the Great Fire surfaced in his mind.

He rubbed the soot from his eyes. "I can't find her! Holly-Mine? There's too much smoke. Mother Tree? If only Wrudge were here. Dearest Wrudge…"

"I'm here, Aarghathlain," Mother Tree said. "You slipped away again. Don't you remember? You saved the forest."

"Oh yes," he said but didn't relax. He remembered the destruction the Wizard of the Council had wrought on Gemini City, Wrudge sacrificing himself to save the forest, Bram and Doros on the Prosperity, and so much more.

Still more time passed, and a careworn Aargh stood with Guildebrande hanging by his side, weary from the weight of his burdens. Gone were the oversized robes he'd worn. Now, Aargh dressed in less ostentatious, close-fitting, bespoke robes that were practical. Sensible.

Mother Tree's voice also changed, as mothers speak with many voices. "You've shared your memories with me, Wizard Aarghathlain: Greatest of all Wizards. Although no one can take them from you, I will be the bearer of your pain. Let the fires of your life fade. Be strong. The future will test you in ways you cannot imagine. She is your future. Together, you will heal Ardilakk Valley and save the world."

Aarghathlain the Renewed gazed upon Mother Tree, but no, something wasn't right. She'd changed. Mother Tree was–

"I release you!"

Aargh coughed. "Holly-Mine, you'll never believe the dream I had. Mother Tree spoke to me and…and…Holly-Mine? Oh, no! Sweet Girl. What's wrong? Come here. Papa's got you."

Curled into a fetal position at his feet, Holly-Mine shook as tremors of fear wracked her body.

Aargh lifted his daughter into his lap, holding her tightly and rocking back and forth as he quietly sang part of what she called *The Weeping Song*.

Its real name was *The Ode of Arkorar*, but few remembered that.

There, as he lay in the sparkling dew
of the tears she'd shed 'neath the sky of blue.
Ilyaana wept. Ilyaana cried.
Nevermore, her father standing by her side.

Sacrifice is given by a heart that's true,
and the earth rewards souls where love once grew.
There above the river. There above the sea.
Arkorar returned his life to thee.

Holly-Mine turned over, and Aargh stopped singing. "There, there. Papa's here. Everything will be all right," he said, looking into her chocolatey brown eyes.

But would it? The fire destroying their home illuminated the forest, and Aargh winced. Flames had always plagued his nightmares, but as he sat there holding his daughter, the memories felt a little farther away, and he could almost put the pain aside. He didn't know if he'd ever be comfortable calling on fire as he did with Sisters Wind and Water, but that was a challenge for another day. Right now, Holly-Mine needed him.

A sound floating on the air caressed the hairs on the back of his neck.

"They're coming closer," he whispered. "Too close."

A bush nearby offered meager cover, but the chance to find a better hiding place had passed. Parting the branches, he snuck inside, placing Holly-Mine gingerly on the ground.

"Earth Mother?" he asked. "We're in grave danger. Please make a safe place for us to hide. We have nowhere else to go."

Holly-Mine's hand brushed Aargh's cheek. "She hears you, Papa. She is coming."

"Are you feeling any better, my Sweet Girl?"

Holly-Mine moved closer, hiding her face in his robes.

Aargh's heart cracked like the Mounts of Ardilakk. He understood her suffering, and it pained him to see her this way.

"We'll make it through this. I promise," he whispered in her ear. "You and me."

"Me and you," she responded.

"Together," they said at the same time.

The Earth Mother had indeed heard Aargh's plea, and as they watched, the seasons passed before their eyes.

Seedlings sprouted, their pale arms stretching and yawning as they grew taller and taller, concealing them from view. Aargh wished the plant's lush green leaves didn't have to go away, but they looked out of place for this time of year (being the seventh week after the Fall of Autumn), and few things other than the tall pines were green. The world had begun its preparations for the long dark of winter. Therefore, as he expected, the leaves changed into an array of rustic colors, blending in perfectly, if not a little fuller than the surrounding foliage.

"Thank you," Aargh said, grateful for the Earth Mother's help.

Only a few hours before, he and Holly-Mine had discussed replanting the garden beds with chrysanthemums they'd collected. But that was before they'd been woken by Guildebrande's warnings to get out of the house. Now, they were attempting to evade mysterious pursuers by hiding in a bush.

Sharp voices shouted from several directions.

"Over here!"

"They went this way!"

"How did they make it past you?"

"Try over there!"

"Spread out!"

Holly-Mine stiffened. "They're close."

"Yes, I hear them," Aargh whispered.

An angry voice yelled, "They can't have gotten far."

Aargh and Holly-Mine held their breath when a twig cracked nearby. Another crack. Closer.

Then, a hoarse voice lifted above the others. "What are you doing?"

"I–," the twig cracker started to say but must have thought better of it. Instead, he closed his mouth and ran off to rejoin the others.

Aargh let out a sigh of relief.

"Why are those men trying to hurt us?" Holly-Mine asked.

"I'm not sure, but I'm going to find out," he said, stifling a cough.

"They felt wrong."

"Can you explain it to me?"

"It was…"

"Yes, Sweet Girl? What did you feel?"

Early on, Aargh had learned to pay attention to Holly-Mine's feelings, and he listened intently to what she had to say.

"Glee, possibly," she said. "As if they enjoyed it."

This troubled Aargh. He could understand lashing out in anger or losing control of one's emotions. Everyone flew off the handle now and then, but enjoying being angry or mean? That spoke of something more profound. Something malevolent.

Aargh blinked. His eyes burned from the smoke and ash billowing out of the living trees he'd once called home. "Oh, the trees. I must help them."

"How?" Holly-Mine asked, sitting up.

"I'm sure Sister Water would put the fire out if I asked."

"Of course she would, but you mustn't. They'll find us."

Aargh hung his head. "But how can I let the trees burn when it's within my power to save them?"

"It's okay, Papa. The forest weeps with you, but the trees understand. They say there's evil in the woods tonight, and we must leave."

He nodded. She was right, but that didn't make it easier.

"Forgive me, wood of the forest. Please, please forgive me," he pleaded.

Aargh didn't know what to do. How could he? He didn't understand why they'd been chased from their home in the first place.

The forest had always been his sanctuary…his refuge. Sadly, that wasn't the case anymore, and he knew their lives would never be the same.

The bushes rustled, and Aargh's heart skipped a beat. He guided Holly-Mine behind him with one hand and unsheathed Guildebrande with the other.

Much to his surprise, a group of rats appeared from under a bed of fallen leaves. A sleek rat with carefully tended hair sat on his hind feet, sniffed the air, and bowed.

CHAPTER 3

MISCHIEF AFOOT

THE WIZARDS' UNDERGROUND

Alantus hummed a tune to himself as he repotted an ailing *Hyoscyamus niger* plant. He refused to call the plant by its common name, stinking nightshade, because its healing properties were far too valuable to refer to it in such an unfortunate way.

Several of the older wizards suffered from muscle tremors, so he regularly extracted henbane oil from the plant to soothe their troubled limbs. Although deadly if mishandled, this didn't trouble Lan. He was an expert, having learned his trade from skilled teachers from beyond the wizarding school's hallowed halls.

Ever since his postulant days, Lan enjoyed working in the dirt. This made him a bit of a pariah—not because he didn't mind getting his hands dirty, per se, but because he spent most of his time studying with non-wizarding folk. Most wizards referred to people outside the wizarding community as commoners, but Lan found the term vulgar. In his estimation, wizarding was a vocation no different than learning to be a smithy or a cooper. At the time, he didn't know he was part of a vanguard that would dramatically alter the perception of wizarding in Ardilakk Valley. He just loved nurturing things to grow.

After Groundsman Grimms passed, and to absolutely no one's surprise, Lan was appointed *Deputy Assistant Spire Groundskeeper.* He didn't report to a *Head Spire Groundskeeper,* though, because the school didn't have one. In their infinite wisdom, the Board of Regents had decided it would be inappropriate for a Spire Wizard to hold such a lowly title; therefore, they'd made him assistant instead. It seemed backwards to Lan, but whatever. Either way, he got to spend time with his beloved plants.

After loosening the dirt a little, Lan lifted the sick *Hyoscyamus niger* plant out of its old home and paused. Two wizards had slipped in a side door near the other end of the greenhouse. They must have assumed they were alone because neither bothered to check if anyone else was there.

"How presumptuous of them," Lan thought, picking an errant rock out of the plant's roots.

Lan was a detail-oriented person. His skill at identifying the slightest color variation came in handy when tending to the herbage. It's also why, even though he hadn't met every wizard at the spire, he usually recognized people's faces or the color of their robes.

Unfortunately, his keen observation skills were of no use this evening. The wizards were clothed in dark, hooded robes that covered their faces. This wasn't unusual for wizards, but skulking around a greenhouse during the wee hours of the morning certainly merited a raised eyebrow or, at the very least, a second glance.

Lan almost shrugged it off as wizardly eccentricity, but the uncomfortable knot in his stomach made him change his mind. As he moved to put the plant on the table, a clump of dirt clinging to its rootball fell onto his round belly.

"*Carpinus betulus!* I almost made it a whole day without getting my robes dirty."

Shocked by the sound of his voice, Lan cupped a hand over his mouth and ducked under the closest table. Inching forward, he suspiciously peered between a *bacopa's* dainty pink flowers cascading out of their planter.

They hadn't heard him. Whew.

Lan wobbled. He had a tightness in his chest, and the room appeared to be undulating. Had he mishandled the plant? No, he'd been careful. Then, the cause dawned on him. He was still holding his breath, so he let go of his face and inhaled.

"How foolish of you, Alantus. You should be more careful where you put your hands!" he scolded himself.

Once the room stopped spinning, he brushed the dirt from his face and robes, not that it made much difference. Lan's hunter-green robes were right at home with a dirt spot or two complimenting the blue aster embroidery. In general conversation, he referred to the thread as pond blue, but a wizard had to be accurate when shopping for these things. There were two hundred and sixty different types of blue to choose from, and Lan could identify every single one.

Satisfied his robes were in order, he tiptoed behind one of his prized possessions: a miracle fruit tree. The tree's luscious red berries had no flavor, but if a person chewed one, other foods tasted sweet, no matter how tart they were. At any rate, that was the hypothesis Lan was currently testing. He looked forward to checking off every food on the list he'd copied from *Tempting, Tingling, and Titillating: A Compendium of All Things Tart*.

As he watched the figures talking in hushed tones, Lan absently picked a plump berry off the tree and put it into his mouth. The sensation of biting into the fleshy fruit calmed his nerves as he chewed.

The wizard on the right bowed his head while the other urged him to make a decision.

"We've waited long enough!" the urger hissed.

That didn't sound good! Lan stopped chewing and leaned forward to hear better.

"Let me ask you this," the pensive wizard said. "If Aargh is dangerous, why hasn't he attacked the Spire?"

"How should I know? Tarth says he's dangerous, so he's dangerous. What more explanation do you need?"

"I guess, but it seems odd."

"We don't have time to stand around discussing this. Are you in, or are you out?"

The pensive wizard looked up. "I'm in."

"Good. Tell the others. We go tonight!"

The hooded figures clasped each other's arms in the usual way and headed for different exits.

Lan apologized to the *Hyoscyamus niger* for not being able to finish his work before sneaking out of the greenhouse, too, but not before spitting out the miracle fruit's seed and placing it on a clean scrap of cloth. He'd let it dry and plant it next season. You could never have too many miracle fruit trees.

As he quietly closed the door behind him, he heard another door clap shut.

"Strange. The wind must have caught it," Lan said absently before hurrying off to the school.

Along the way, he met Onaveris, who responded to his account of the *tête-à-tête* with a flurry of unwizardly exclamations. It took a while, but when O finally finished his tirade, they set about gathering the other members of The Wizards' Underground to discuss what Lan had witnessed.

After what seemed like hours of discussion, the group still hadn't decided what to do, as coming to a consensus had never been a common wizardly trait. As the night dragged on, the suggestions became increasingly outlandish...bizarre even...until Dram inserted a well-placed *ahem!* and the gathering of wizards fell silent.

"Why don't we spread out and make sure no wizards leave the grounds?" he suggested.

This sounded reasonable, and since no one offered a valid reason why they shouldn't, they adjourned the meeting and dispersed.

• • •

On the eastern side of the grounds, near the West 78th Street entrance, Paladand threw his hands over his head in frustration. "This cursed fog makes it impossible to see. I wouldn't notice even if someone passed right by me!"

Attempting to peer down the road, he saw Gemini City's streetlamps stretched into the distance. They were reduced to nothing more than mystical hazy balls. On any other night, the youngest Wizard of the Third Circle in more than a century might have considered how beautiful they were, appearing to magically float in the air, but not tonight. They merely served to reinforce what he already knew: if a person had a predilection for sneaking around, this would be the night to do it!

A light flashed in the carriage park behind him.

"What's going on over there?" Paladand asked, removing his half-moon glasses and rubbing them on his robes. "The last thing I need is to be run over by a steam carriage. I better check it out."

He hooked the glasses' wire temples back over his ears and headed along the driveway to the lot. One by one, he peeked into the carriages parked neatly in a long row.

Nothing.

Frustrated by his lack of success, Paladand turned to head back to his post when a blinding light made him shield his eyes. "Who's there? Show yourself!"

"Oh…uh…sorry, Paladand. I didn't mean to startle you," the other wizard said, shuttering the lantern.

"Is that you, Afynn? Has to be with those orange robes."

"Yeah, it's me," he said, climbing out of the steam carriage and placing his iguana familiar, Sprocket, on the ground next to him.

"What are you doing?" Paladand asked, the shadows making his long face look even more severe than usual.

"Um…let me show you. Come, look at this strike plate," Afynn said, pointing to the lantern.

Afynn's mind sped along far too fast for any tongue. Therefore, he'd devised a kind of shorthand to have conversations with himself that was efficient enough to keep up with his racing thoughts. Unfortunately, when it came to speaking his contemplations out loud, he had to force himself to slow down and organize the words into something other people understood. This resulted in a stilted, um-filled delivery that many Geminians mistook for ineptitude. Of course, they couldn't have been further from the truth and, likely, had never stood that close to someone that brilliant in their entire life.

"And here," he continued. "Uh…the flint is so worn that when I pull the lever…it barely makes a spark. It's not… um…enough to ignite the lantern."

Not being the most patient wizard, Paladand interrupted. "What does that have to do with shining a light in my face?"

"I had to go to the back of the carriage to find a new flint. That's probably why you didn't notice me. And when I came back, you were…uh…standing…um…here, I mean, over there, in front of the light."

"Yes, I get it, but why are you messing with the carriages instead of guarding your post?"

"I'm turning on lights to help with the search because it's so foggy!"

"Larix laricina," Paladand hissed. "That won't help. The fog reflects the light. See? Shouldn't you be the one telling me this? You're the engineer."

"Yes, well, um…" Afynn said, pushing the bottle glasses he wore back into place. "I've studied a great deal about the inner workings of lamps, lanterns, searchlights, diya, etcetera, but haven't yet examined the effect of said lights on atmospheric phenomena."

"Look for yourself!" Paladand said irritably, pointing at the white wall of fog.

"Yes, I understand. I'll…um…uh…shut it off right away."

"I'm returning to my post, and I suggest you do the same."

"I will, as soon as I put away this extra flint. I got two just in case."

As Paladand walked back to the entrance, he heard Afynn still talking about flints and shook his head. "He's a bright one but doesn't have much common sense, that's for sure. Then again, not many wizards do."

With each step, the young wizard grew more concerned about standing alone in the fog. Out of an abundance of caution, he put two fingers to his mouth and whistled. "Nerah, come! We'd better stick together tonight."

• • •

High above the grounds in the Spire's Observation Lounge, Fizzbain kicked a nearby chair. It briefly hopped up, folded flat, and crashed to the floor with a metal clang. Shocked by the sound, he lifted the chair, unfolded it, and put it back in place as if nothing had happened.

"Why is it always me who draws the short straw?" he asked glumly, sitting on the rescued chair and pulling his robes around him.

Antithetical to the common practice, Fizz regularly changed the color of his wizarding robes, generally favoring muted hues such as burnt sienna, asparagus, or his current choice, mulberry. His robes changed, yes, but his socks always stayed the same.

Fizzbain differed from his school friends because one of his legs stood shorter than the other, and he had a stiff knee. This didn't bother him, but people couldn't seem to let him forget about it. One might say his leg drew people's attention with more interest than a garble rooting out a patch of rutabagas.

He especially disapproved of when people called his short leg bad. There was nothing bad about it, thank you very much! And when a doctor instructed him to climb stairs by going up with the good and down with the bad, it really set him off! Right then and there, he'd decided to devise a new way to refer to his legs—one that didn't involve insulting them. He remembered that moment in his life as if it had happened yesterday...

Determined to find a solution to his problem, Fizz limped the entire length of Middling Street, looking for a vendor. What kind of vendor, he had no idea, but there had to be one that could help him if he looked hard enough.

Didn't everyone have something different about them? Of course, they did! That's what made people unique. But no matter how many carts he visited, no answer presented itself.

"I guess I'll have to get used to people talking about my leg," he told his pocket.

Bit, Fizzbain's toad familiar, voiced his displeasure with a deep-throated croak.

"You said it."

Thankfully, when Fizz finally returned to the school, he had his dorm room to himself. He didn't bunk with his friends, Garth, Bee, or Aargh (not by choice, mind you, but by assignment). For some inexplicable reason, he always found himself paired with the one person in class who teased him the most.

Fizz didn't understand why adults did this—likely out of some misguided belief that sticking enemies together would result in instant friendship, but that never happened. It only meant the bully had unfettered access.

Fizz had repeatedly explained this to his teachers, but they never listened, blaming him for Drinitor hiding his towel for the umpteenth time. He'd probably left it back in his room by mistake. Sure, he had.

Everyone liked Drinitor with his flowing dirty blond hair and that wink and a smile he gave the teachers. Whatever. Behind closed doors, there were no smiles, only torment.

Fizz dejectedly plopped onto his bed in such a way that his feet didn't touch anything. He hated being messy, but dirt, in its many forms, was unavoidable when walking Middling Street. So, he set about changing out of his soiled clothes.

Left sock off. No problem. Next came the tricky part. His right knee didn't bend much, so he used the bed to help. Out of the corner of his eye, he noticed his laundry bag sitting crumpled by the door.

"Oh, no. I forgot to send my bag to be washed. Everything's dirty!"

Fizz frantically rummaged through his trunk, looking for clean socks, but he only found one bright red knee-high and a short lemon-yellow crew—their mates lost to the steamy wilderness known as the Gemini City School of Wizarding's washroom.

"I guess I have to work with what I have." Pulling them on, he yelled, "That's it!" and jumped off the bed.

Bit chirped as if to ask, What's it?

"Up with the yellow, down with the red! Don't you see? The solution was right here, in my trunk the whole time. How about that?"

Bit trilled a long, happy sound, celebrating his wizard's discovery.

Not only had it solved the problem, but it also made walking, climbing, and pretty much everything else involving locomotion less stressful. As what kid doesn't revel in a pair of mismatched socks? Not Fizzbain, that was for sure.

But that revelation happened a long time ago, and his socks didn't bring him much joy as he sat alone in the Observation Lounge…

Slumped in the chair with his yellow and red feet jutting out of the bottom of his mulberry robes, Fizz moped at being stuck alone at the top of the Spire. With fog thick on the ground, he knew he wouldn't be of any help to the search, and he didn't like being left out. He'd had enough of that in his life.

The murky mist had pushed its way uptown until it shrouded the entire city, but it hadn't invaded the forest yet. The winds drifting from the Mounts of Ardilakk had kept it at bay, at least for the time being. The fog stopped right at the Once-Great Wall as if that had anything to do with it, which it didn't.

Fizz wondered which would be victorious, the wind or the fog. Only time would tell, but he didn't plan to wait around. He was about to rejoin his friends when an enormous plume of fire leapt out of the forest, far away, past the Congregational House on the city's eastern side.

"What in the world? Oh no! Aargh's cottage grows there! We're too late!" he shrieked, limping around the room. "They're at Aargh's house already! What do I do? What do I do?"

Overcome by panic, Fizz forgot about the chair, tripped over it, and landed on the floor. A muffled squeak came from his pocket.

"Bit. You're not hurt, are you?"

The toad chirped in response. It sounded like, *Yes, I'm okay,* and *Don't do that again,* rolled into one.

"Sorry. I lost my head for a minute," he said, getting back to his feet. "Right. The uplifter."

Fizz stamped on the machine's button with his yellow leg. A loud *clank!* reverberated off the windows as its gears engaged, and the uplifter's many cables started moving. He peered through the metal cage that encircled the hole in the floor, trying to see it.

"It's probably sitting in the rotunda!" he grumbled.

Under normal circumstances, he enjoyed watching the uplifter's complex inner workings–especially its famed *worm gear reducer system.*

Fizz had graduated long before Areas of Study were offered, but he enjoyed listening to the engineering students talk about their lessons. He'd learned that the machine's clever design allowed for the maximum speed reduction in the smallest package, but he didn't know what that meant. Hopefully, he'd have the opportunity to attend an engineering class or two and possibly help figure out how to make the blasted thing move faster!

As he waited for the uplifter to appear, Fizz fidgeted. Soon, the fidgeting escalated to jumping, which, in turn, elevated to yelling.

"Let's go!" he shouted at the cage. "No, no, no! This won't do. You're taking too long. There must be a quicker way to warn them."

Then, an idea came to him: the maintenance ladder.

There it rose, bolted to the only wall in the Observation Lounge not made entirely of glass. Ladders had never been his thing, but he had no other choice.

"Are you out of your mind, Fizz? Climb onto the roof?" he asked himself.

"I can't see any other way," he replied.

No wizard ever wanted to get near it, and why would they? Wizards didn't climb ladders onto roofs; maintenance people did, and Fizz hadn't crossed paths with one of their kind since Groundsman Grimms had passed.

Wizards and students used to shuffle past Grimms' office, hoping he didn't speak to them or, worse, come out. They'd peer around the corner to see if the coast was clear and then tiptoe by, trying not to make a sound. But there came a day when being quiet didn't matter anymore because Grimms would never leave his office again except with the expert guidance of the undertaker.

That day, there he'd been, sitting with a sour expression etched into his face. Of course, that's what everyone had expected to see, so that's what they saw. And since no wizard ever went into Grimms' office unless they had to, no one realized he'd surreptitiously shuffled off the mortal coil. Even so, *The Grimms Affair*, as it had come to be known, didn't hold a candle to what Fizzbain was about to do.[1]

"Time's a-wasting, Fizz," he told himself.

"Yes, yes. I know."

Spurred into action by a rather huffy *chirp!* from Bit, Fizz reached out a trembling hand and grabbed a rung.

He pulled back, surprised by how cold it felt, but it also felt good. Strong. Resolute, even. Fizz did, too.

With new-found confidence, he said, "Up with the yellow."

He put his left foot on the lowest rung. It held his weight.

"That's a good sign."

Fizz climbed one rung at a time: yellow, red. Next rung: yellow, red. When he reached the ceiling, he undid the latch and pushed, but it didn't budge. Had someone locked it? No. That would be unnecessary. Wizards didn't climb on roofs.

---

[1] There has never been a time when wizards were comfortable with folks hanging around who didn't perform magic themselves, and Grimms' passing ended an era of commoners living and working at the Spire. Unfortunately, this resulted in a great many things breaking with no one around to fix them. That's the way it remained until Aargh came along. His curriculum changes offered a wealth of opportunities to utilize the students' newly learned knowledge—one of which involved having engineering novices practice their craft on broken items from around the school. Long lines of wizards stood outside their classrooms at the beginning of each term, holding all manner of things they hoped to have repaired by the students. Major projects even included reseating the dumbwaiter and reviving the steam rotavator. Everyone agreed this arrangement provided excellent real-world experience for the students (with the added benefit of being both inexpensive and not having to seek help outside of the Spire's compound).

"Well, this one's going to," Fizz told himself. "It must be stuck. I just need to get better purchase."

Fizz got into position, leaned his head to the side, and threw his shoulder at the hatch. The door flew open with a bang, and he burst through the opening. The cold, damp air shocked the breath out of his lungs, and he slid down the ladder. Thankfully, his arm caught on the top rung before he fell to the floor.

When his faculties returned, he tried again.

"Better calm yourself, Fizz, or you'll hyperventilate. The air's thin up here."

Even on calm nights, the wind whipped around the Spire, and he had to hold on tightly as he inched his way onto the roof.

"So far, so good."

Next, he dragged himself away from the opening and rolled onto his back.

"We're on the roof of the Observation Lounge, Bit. Can you believe it? What would Professor Snoodlebood say if he saw us now? Are you okay in there? Not too high for you?"

A muffled *croak!* told him Bit was fine.

"Then, here we go," he said, crawling over to the edge.

A safety rail ran around the structure's rim, which he used to pull himself to his feet. It wobbled under the strain, which didn't instill confidence, but what could he do? It was the only thing to hold on to.

Bit let out another chirp, confirming that he, too, agreed the railing was a good idea.

Fizz moved his foot. "That's funny," he said, turning more.

The slope of the roof matched the length of his legs perfectly, and Fizz realized that, for the first time in his life, standing didn't feel awkward.

"How about that! I'm made for walking on roofs. Pretty darn cool!"

Bit trilled in agreement.

"I guess it's time to do what we came here for," he told his pocket.

Straightening his robes, he sucked the cool night air into his lungs and yelled as loudly as possible to his friends below.

No luck. The wind swept his voice away long before it reached the ground.

"It was worth a try. It's time for Plan B."

Fizz knew what he had to do but hesitated. He'd never tried anything so wizardly before. Bit, however, was ready for action!

Although toads have a variety of vocalizations, they're most well-known for a warbling trill that can travel great distances, especially on a still night. Aargh had often encouraged Fizz and Bit to practice together. That way, if the need arose, Fizz could access Bit's extraordinary voice. But not being the most social wizard at the Spire, Fizz had only tested his and Bit's newfound skill in a quiet part of the gardens.

To do this, Fizz had been forced to write a spell. It shouldn't have taken as long to perfect as it did, but he might have been procrastinating a little. Okay, he'd procrastinated a lot, concocting a bevy of reasons to put it off. Now, as he surveyed the ground far below, Fizz wished he'd listened to Aargh and tried a little harder.

"What do you say, Bit? Want to give it a try?"

Bit moved into position as if to say, *No time like the present!*

In response, and in a very un-Fizz-like fashion, he threw caution to the wind and let go of the railing.

Terror gripped him as he swayed with the tower. But then, the fear faded, revealing something unexpected: excitement. Fizz had never felt so alive in his entire life! Ardilakk Valley spread gloriously below him in every direction, and he took it in.

Bit trilled.

"You're right! Enough playing around, though. Time to get to work."

The toad let out a deep croak.

"Then, let's do this!"

Fizzbain closed his eyes and prepared himself.

Calm Your Heart;

"You've got this, Fizz."

Clear Your Mind;

"Deep breaths."

and above all else, Concentration is Key.

"Wow!" Fizz gasped as a new magical door opened in his mind.

Aargh had often spoken about his connection with Wrudge, but Fizz had never experienced it himself.

"It's beautiful!" Fizz told the world. "Can you feel it, Bit?"

The long trill coming from his pocket told Fizz, yes, Bit felt it, too.

"Here we go!"

This time, when Fizzbain opened his mouth, his warbling voice crashed down the Spire with the force of avalanches tumbling from the high mounts.

• • •

Far below, Paladand and the others stopped, looked up, and ran toward the forest.

CHAPTER 4

THE COTTAGE IN THE WOODS
TARTHANABELLE

The sweet sting of carriage fuel hung in the air, mingling with the fragrant aroma of fallen leaves and pine sap. For much of the night, the winds of the mount had kept the fog at bay. Now that they'd died down, the air had become dense and motionless. Bugs had stopped singing their nighttime songs, and the entire forest had grown quiet with anticipation.

Odaraphrim inhaled the stillness. "Things are about to change in Ardilakk Valley."

He was a brooding figure who stood tall against the shrubs at his feet. He'd given up his bright green robes for dark ones, more appropriately suiting his demeanor. The boy who'd entered the Gemini City School of Wizarding years ago had been replaced by someone who wanted more from magic in the valley than talking to trees.

"After tonight, Tarth won't be able to ignore me anymore."

Silhouetted by ghostly moonlight, a line of shadowy figures crept into their assigned positions. Together, they formed a wide circle that stretched out of sight.

Covering his mouth, Phrim hooted a doleful sound reminiscent of a mourning dove. "Hoo. Hoo, hooooo."

Immediately, flint striking on steel disturbed the night, followed by bursts of flames.

WHOOSH! Whoosh, whoosh.

One by one, the menacing light of torches appeared, encircling Aargh's cottage north of the Once-Great Wall.

Seconds later, the fiery missiles gracefully arced through the air, leaving pixie dust-like trails hanging in the night sky. When the torches reached the apex of their trajectory, they changed direction, converging on the cottage made of living trees–a fitting end to the abomination grown by Aargh.

The carriage fuel fumes ignited before the flames touched the ground, sending a billowing plume of smoke into the air and shattering the home's windows. Animals burst out of the undergrowth, scrambling to safety as flames engulfed the trees. To Phrim, their branches appeared to be reaching out for help, but he paid no attention to their woeful cries. Trees were home to animals, not refined Spire Wizards!

Phrim used to speak with the trees, but not anymore. He considered them babbling and foolish, unable to share anything of value, let alone foretell the future. Soon, he'd possess real magic. Magic that didn't need intricate spells. Magic that was infinitely more powerful than asking trees what color an arrogant lord's curtains should be.

"So self-important," he mumbled to himself. "Wizards have become a shadow of what they once were. For generations, we've groveled at the feet of the rich elite, hoping for scraps. Now, when real magic is within our grasp, Aargh has us behaving like commoners, performing menial tasks meant for those not worthy of Spire ascension. If it weren't for a spark of magic here and there, the Gemini City School of Wizarding would be no different from any other institution of learning. Mundane. Why not eliminate the wizarding part altogether? That seems more appropriate these days."

Yelling voices interrupted Phrim's ruminations.

"Over here!"

"They went this way!"

"How did they make it past you?"

"Try over there!"

"Spread out!"

"They can't have gotten far."

"*Endothia parasitica!*" Phrim cursed. "If they get away, everything will have been for naught!"

Then, the unthinkable happened.

A hoarse voice lifted above the others. "What are you doing?"

Tarth's anger shocked Phrim, stopping him in his tracks. Things went from bad to worse when Flinghower appeared at Tarth's side with a wicked look in his eyes. It didn't escape Phrim's notice that Fling had also traded in his old robes for dark ones. Apparently, he too, wanted to move around without being seen. Alone, that wasn't concerning. But knowing Fling, he'd probably been snooping around, and there was no telling what he might have heard…and shared with Tarth.

"We'll find them," Phrim assured his master. "It's simply a matter of time."

"Find who? Aargh? No, you won't," Tarth corrected. "None of you will."

Phrim's voice caught in his throat. Did Tarth sound relieved that Aargh had escaped? That didn't make sense.

"What were you thinking?" Tarth asked, standing nose to nose with Phrim.

"I was…removing Aarghathlain from the equation," he stuttered. "Isn't that what you told us we needed to do?'"

"Not by killing him!" Tarth thundered. "We aren't drunken deckhands brawling on the piers. We're dignified wizards! I've known Aargh since we were boys…and you've been his student and worked alongside him for years. Have you lost your mind?"

Tarth took a few steps away from the wizards. After what appeared to be a contentious discussion with himself, he returned a little calmer.

"Listen to me. Our power comes from working behind the scenes. Aarghathlain is the most famous wizard in Gemini City, probably the entire River Wide, and this kind of behavior risks mobilizing the valley against us. Don't you understand? The right opportunity will present itself if we're patient."

With anger smoldering in his eyes, Tarth again stepped toward Phrim, staring him down.

Don't do it, Phrim! Don't look away. Be strong. Show him that you deserve his respect. This might be your last chance!

Sweat dripped from Phrim's temples. Every muscle in his body tensed. One...second...more...but his strength failed, and he yielded.

Tarth smiled at the small victory and turned to the others. "Are you sure he got away?"

Hoods nodded and mumbled, but no one dared to say a word out loud.

"And he didn't identify any of you? You never took off your cloaks, right?"

More nods.

"Good. This might not be a total loss."

Unable to stop himself, Phrim muttered, "If we can find Aarghathlain, we can send him away or hide him."

"No!" Tarth's raised voice burst out of the clearing, and the forest grew silent again. "We'll do no such thing! We're returning to the school, and no one—not a single one of you—is going to breathe a word about this to anyone. We have business there, and I don't want anything getting in the way. This never happened. Understand? Who cares if Aargh's house burned? He was probably playing with fire, right? We all know how unpredictable elemental magic can be. He won't ever let us forget! That's what we'll tell the good people of the Spire, and they'll never be the wiser."

"I seriously doubt that," Paladand said, stepping from behind a tree.

Tarth's contorted face changed from an expression of frustration to fury at Paladand's untimely arrival. "Ah, Paladand. Good," he said. "There's been an accident at Aargh's cottage, and I haven't been able to locate him or Holly-Mine. Have you–"

"Nice try," Paladand said, cutting him off.

"This is how you speak to your Head Wizard?" Tarth snapped back, too frustrated to continue the charade.

"*Interim* Head Wizard," Paladand corrected. "And, if I'm not mistaken, we can add *Former* to that after tonight. Especially after I bring word of what you've done to the Spire."

Tarth sneered, sucking in air between his clenched teeth. "Self-righteous Paladand, always pointing out everyone's flaws. Teacher's little pet. I can't imagine anyone being able to satisfy the expectations you espouse. Come to think of it, how do you live with yourself?"

"Perfectly well, thank you. The real question is: Will you be able to live with yourself after what you've done here tonight?"

Tarth moved toward the young wizard, but Paladand stood his ground.

"You're evil, Tarth," the young wizard said. "Trying to kill people who disagree with you is incomprehensible. There's no place for this kind of behavior in wizarding."

"What? You blindly follow Aargh as he destroys everything wizarding has meant to Ardilakk Valley for centuries, and you have the gall to call me evil? Watching you bow to him as if he's some kind of benevolent idol to be worshipped makes me sick! If you want to talk about evil, talk about him!"

"Aargh is trying to make the world a better place," Paladand tried to interject, but Tarth wasn't done yet.

"Better? By making himself all-powerful with elemental magic while we fumble around with cumbersome spells that only work half of the time? Your arrogance is only trumped by your ignorance, my young friend! It's time you saw Aarghathlain for who he is: a tyrant!"

Tarth would have been wise not to consider Paladand so naive. Although the young wizard recognized the modicum of truth hidden in Tarth's words, he had nothing but respect for Aargh. He'd seen how tirelessly Aargh worked on behalf of wizards and Geminians. Most importantly, Paladand understood the line between right and wrong, and Tarth hadn't crossed it; he'd leapt over it and sped off into the distance.

"Tarth, you can keep talking, but it isn't going to make any difference. You and your followers are no better than the Marauders who used to prowl these woods. Besides, I'm not challenging you. I'm telling you. Your time at the Spire has come to an end."

"Exactly how will you prevent me from returning?" Tarth asked with more than a note of condescension. "And, what's more, why would any Wizards Regent take your word over mine...a lowly Wizard of the Third Circle? This is why I put them in place, to prevent rogue wizards–you and Aargh, for example–from ruining what we've achieved."

"You call this an achievement?" Paladand yelled, his outstretched hand illuminated by the burning trees. The young wizard rarely lost his temper, but he'd make an exception this time.

However, it had no effect on Tarth. The ex-Interim Head Wizard nonchalantly waved off Paladand's interruption the way a cow swats bothersome flies with its tail. "Besides, you have no one to support your story. Did any of you see anything?"

The hooded wizards shook their heads as they gathered around their master.

"And thanks to your beloved Aargh, you can't even use magic. So, standing there alone, how do you plan to stop me?" Tarth asked, his lips curling into a triumphant sneer.

Paladand scratched his head. "It's true. I'm a healer. Even if I wanted to, my magic couldn't be used to prevent you from returning to the school. Truthfully, I wouldn't be tempted to use magic that way even if I could. That being said, you're overlooking one vital point."

"Yes? Young Paladand the Oh-So-Wise, enlighten me."

Instead of answering, the young wizard turned and stepped toward the forest. Two sparkling emerald-green eyes peered out of the gloom. Paladand placed his wizarding fingers over his indexing fingers and moved both hands in front of his body.

In response, the eyes nodded.

"Well?" Tarth asked in a snide tone. "What vital piece of information have I carelessly overlooked?"

"Nerah doesn't need magic," Paladand said threateningly as his familiar sauntered out of the underbrush.

The panther's sleek black fur glistened in the firelight. She purred loudly as she nuzzled Paladand's leg before rounding on Tarth and baring her teeth. Her menacing growl made the hair on the back of everyone's neck stand on end.

"Oh. And one more point of clarification, Former Interim Head Wizard," Paladand said.

"What's that?"

Tarth's voice contained more than anger. Frustration? Definitely, but also a note of fear, and Paladand seized the opportunity to keep him off balance.

"We're not alone," the young wizard explained, inclining his head toward the trees.

With that, The Wizards' Underground stepped into the light.

Tarth could barely contain the horror welling inside him. Paladand's actions proved what he'd known all along: Aargh's followers had abandoned the moral and ethical rules governing Ardilakk Valley and those who practiced magic within the arms of its mountainous embrace.

Unable to hide the shock in his voice, Tarth asked, "You'd risk using your familiar as a weapon? The greatest gift the Earth Mother ever gave a wizard? I guess, to you, Nerah's nothing more than a tool to help you get what you want. You disgust me! What kind of a wizard are you? And what would Aargh say if he saw you behaving this way?"

Paladand shook his head. "You may have known Aargh longer than me, but you don't understand him. He's the one who taught us what being remarkable means. If Aargh were here, he wouldn't hesitate to put himself in harm's way to protect the city and the Spire."

As much as he wanted to, Tarth couldn't argue the point. Lists and plans or not, Aargh always jumped right in with both feet. Even so, Paladand's words unsettled the older wizard. There's an ocean of difference between placing yourself in danger and commanding your familiar to take the risk for you. But he hadn't chosen the circumstances of their meeting, and now he was faced with an impossible decision: play along or risk everything.

Left with no other option, Tarth pulled back the sleeve of his crimson robes, revealing a leather guard strapped to his arm.

Griff plummeted from the branches above, uttering a piercing cry. He landed on the wizard's arm, deftly snatching a small piece of meat from Tarth's gloved hand.

Nerah hissed at the red-tailed hawk, but Paladand uncrossed his open hands and moved them down, telling her to *be calm.*

Flinghower's familiar, Renfir, also appeared, baring his teeth and growling. Tarth pointed at them, commanding *hold,* and Flinghower placed his hand on the gray wolf's back.

Both groups of wizards stood silently as Aargh's cottage burned, a mixture of anger and fear keeping their bodies perfectly still. Neither wanted to make the first move. Even Paladand held some doubt behind his brave face.

The inevitability of their predicament weighed on Tarth. They'd gone far beyond finding a reasonable way to defuse the situation, but being hauled back to the Spire by this lot wasn't part of his plan.

Ultimately, what Tarth, Paladand, or any of the other wizards wanted didn't figure into it because before either side spoke another word, the familiars attacked.

CHAPTER 5

THE MEETING PLACE
RATS & AARGHATHLAIN

Rats from all four corners of the city descended into the Underoof, filling the tunnels with as many of their numbers as possible. The Trust, an ever-changing consortium of representatives that loosely served as a governing body for the Underoof Collective, had summoned their community to return at once, and the risk of gathering this way weighed heavily on their minds. A person might ignore a rat here and there, but tens of thousands clamoring out of every conceivable dark space and heading under the streets drew a great deal of unwanted attention, but it had to be done. Aarghathlain had saved their community from starvation, and rats don't take loyalty lightly.

Throughout the maze of tunnels that ran south to north (from the river to the forest) and west to east (from the wastes to the highlands), rats puffed themselves up, glowing with a soft golden light. They did their best to put images of being corralled and forced to illuminate musty cellars or being hung in cages by people's front doors out of their minds. This had never happened before, but that might have been because no one knew rats glowed...until the night of the Great Fire. Fortunately, the Mischief had nothing to worry about because these things couldn't have been further from Geminians' thoughts.

Above ground, those who were still awake or had to clock in at work far too early in the morning found themselves surrounded by an eerie glow emanating from the sewer drains. Alarmed that the Wizard of the Council had returned, everyone clapped their shutters and slammed their doors. The people of Gemini City accepted magic, but only as long as it stayed in its lane.

Who cared if the idle rich wanted to hem and haw about what color drapes to hang in the nursery? Let them do as they please. And if a street wizard offered to help make light of a tedious job for a coin or two, great—one less chore to worry about. But magic powerful enough to light the entire city from beneath their feet was way outside their comfort zone.

This is why rats weren't on anyone's mind. After all, the world was undoubtedly ending, and it was probably best if they closed the shutters and brought in the cat (which happened to be the one thing both people and rats agreed upon).

Back in the Underoof, the Mischief expected Aarghathlain to seek refuge in the tunnels. Search parties were formed when he didn't appear, but no sightings had been reported.

"Where are they?"

"There's been no sign…"

"…of them anywhere."

"Do you think…"

"…they've left the valley?"

"What if…"

"…something has happened…"

"…to them?"

"That would be…"

"terrible!"

"Holly-Mine is so kind."

Outside the city, an uptown rat named Parsifal sat on a log, contemplating the situation. He was an inquisitive rat by nature with a penchant for finding things. More than that, he had a keen understanding of the workings of the world of rats and their place in Ardilakk Valley.[2]

Parsifal reasoned that if Aarghathlain hadn't been found by exploring the usual places, he should focus on unusual ones, and it paid off.

As he sat there tapping his pointy chin, a dense bush caught his eye. It appeared slightly out of place against the other bushes, which had already gone to sleep for the winter.

"Hmm. Isn't it a tad late in the season to be holding onto your leaves, dear bush?" he asked. "I think we should have a look."

After getting Werff and Mooble's attention (they'd gotten distracted by a pile of seeds that looked perfect for the Collective's stores), off the trio went.

Parsifal poked his head through the forest's floor of fallen leaves, sniffed, and bowed. They'd found what they were looking for, and, with a quick salute, he sent his companions back to the tunnels to report the good news: Wizard Aarghathlain and his daughter had been found.

• • •

Aargh lowered Guildebrande when the rats emerged from the leaves.

---

[2] The story of Parsifal (meaning pure fool) is a legend dating back to what is known as the Prehistoric Era. He was thought to be an innocent young man forced to overcome trials during which people attempted to take advantage of his naivety. Over time, he grew bitter and disillusioned but was ultimately redeemed when he realized that happiness could only be achieved by living an authentic life serving the greater good.

"Hello, friends," he said in a hushed tone. "Holly-Mine and I need your help. Do you know where we can find safe shelter?"

"I do," a particularly well-groomed rat said with a formal air. "If you would do the honor of accompanying me, Great Wizard Aarghathlain, I'll show you to The Meeting Place, where we have prepared for your return."

"Thank you…uh…um," Aargh stuttered.

"Parsifal, sir," the rat said, bowing again.

Aargh almost chuckled but caught himself.

"Yes, it's a silly name. Had I listened more carefully to Wrudge's parables as a pup, I might have been spared the epithet. I assure you, I am no fool, but I am pure of heart, having chosen to devote my life to caring for the welfare of the Underoof Collective."

"I have no doubt, honorable Parsifal. I meant no offense and apologize. I didn't realize that tale was known to both people and rats," Aargh explained.

"Please, there's no need to apologize. I am not offended. Rats tell many stories, but we don't recite them for entertainment like people do. They're used for teaching. That being said, I've always considered *Parsifal's Quest* to be more than a cautionary tale. It exemplifies our way of life, sharing the same streets with people but being ignorant of their motivations. That is, until you and Wrudge taught us, of course."

The corner of Wrudge's Diary pressed against Aargh's side, and he imagined his friend sharing their stories with the Mischief. It must have been exciting listening to him recount their adventures. Then a funny thought popped into his head: Wrudge must have told the stories from his perspective. How interesting! Aargh wished he'd been there to hear that.

Parsifal cleared his throat to get Aargh's attention. "It's not safe to stay here. Follow me, please, and I'll show you to the tunnels."

Holly-Mine smiled and whispered, "I like him, Papa."

"Me, too," Aargh agreed. "He doesn't speak the way most rats do. He…uses more words."

"Lots more!" Holly-Mine whispered.

Aargh remembered the day his daughter taught him to speak with all living things. That night, like this one, had also been filled with fire and rats. Although taught might not be the most accurate way to describe what she'd done. She'd unlocked a door that had already existed in his mind, and when it opened, an entirely new world of magic had been revealed.

"I wish I'd learned how to communicate with rats sooner," he thought, imagining himself and his familiar chatting away as they watched the hustle and bustle of Lower Middling Street from their apartment balcony.

Holly-Mine touched his hand and said, "Wrudge would have enjoyed that, too."

"This way," Parsifal said, scurrying ahead.

Aargh and Holly-Mine followed their guide into an abandoned service shaft: a large metal pipe that led directly into the Underoof's maze of tunnels. They tried to be as quiet as possible, but the dry autumn ground crunched under their feet, and they cringed with each step, often pausing to listen for their pursuers. Even moving in such a stilted way, it didn't take long before they once again disappeared into the secret world of rats.

Once inside the tunnels, they walked along a rat-lit path toward the juncture where they'd first met the Underoof Collective. In the time since their visit, the rats had renamed the space *The Meeting Place.* Rats were practical creatures, and the practicality of their names didn't surprise Aargh. He found it reassuring.

This was also how he'd describe Holly-Mine. Every decision needed a reason, and every reason needed to be analyzed, questioned, and understood—especially at bedtime. Therefore, every night, after they'd read a book or three, she'd inevitably ask a long list of insightful questions that had no answer known to wizard or tree.

She was particularly fascinated by sayings that contradicted themselves, such as *pretty ugly* or *old news*. Aargh struggled to explain these kinds of linguistic oddities. They didn't make sense to him either. Most of the time, the conversation ended with him saying, that's just how people speak.

"That might be, Papa, but it's still peculiar," she said as if they'd been carrying on a conversation.

Even at the most difficult of times, she made him smile.

As soon as they reached The Meeting Place, Aargh got to work. "I need to speak with the cleverest rat in the Mischief." But his request was met with an awkward silence.

Rats are clever, and, for the most part, they view each other as equals. Only one rat had ever been raised up the way Aargh was suggesting, and Wrudge had sacrificed himself to save the forest.

"They don't view themselves in that way, Papa. Their minds are filled with images of Wrudge."

Aargh's shoulders sagged. "Mine, too." He removed Guildebrande from his scabbard. "Will you help me?" he asked the sword.

"Always," the blade responded.

The rats' eyes grew wide, awed by the sword's light. Never before had they seen another magical being glow, and they didn't know how to react. As far as they were concerned, glowing had been unique to the Collective.

Holly-Mine reached out to them, saying, "Open your hearts and minds to Guildebrande. He is *Protector of the Wizard Aarghathlain* and my father's new familiar."

A change came over the Mischief, and the rats moved closer, trying to get a better look at the sword. Many had served as Aargh's familiar through Wrudge, so they were accustomed to the flow of magic, and it didn't hurt that the metal was shiny.

Aargh sensed a shift in his connection to the rats and knew he needed to act quickly. But first, he took a few seconds to collect his thoughts to avoid a wizardly misstep. "Remember your *C's*, Aarghathlain. Remember your *C's*."

Holly-Mine whispered, "They're listening."

With Guildebrande's added strength, Aargh opened his mouth and spoke to the entire Underoof Collective at once, his voice weaving through the lines of glowing rats covering the stone pathways. "Friends of *Wrudge the Trustworthy*, I ask you to offer one of your own to help me. If there is a rat among you whom Wrudge would have chosen for this task, have them step forward."

Aargh's voice boomed, making the ground shudder. Dust slipped from treasures stowed away in forgotten attiks and bottles rattled in underground wine cellars.

For the second time that night, something strange was transpiring beneath Gemini City's unswerving streets, and frayed nerves were wearing thin. Geminians from every corner of the city quivered with fright. No one wanted to peek out of their windows, content to wait until the sun dispelled the oppressive darkness. Hopefully, by then, the frightening events occurring under their feet would have faded into memory.

The rats heard Aargh's voice in their ears and in their minds, but only one rat heard his voice in her heart.

"Is he speaking to me?" an unusually small rat named Mnoonge asked.

She stood on her hind legs to get a better look. A sea of rats filled the tunnel. They were glowing with every ounce of energy they could muster, but none were moving.

Mnoonge sat back down. "He can't be calling to me. Get a hold of yourself. You're a rat from the lower blocks...and a small one at that. Don't get ideas above your station. The great Wizard Aarghathlain doesn't need you."

She risked another peek above the others again. Rows of rats sat motionless on the tunnel floor. Mnoonge tried to convince herself that another rat must have already answered the wizard's call, but no. She could tell. No other rats were moving in the Underoof. How did she know that?

Mnoonge pushed on her belly. It felt hollow, like she hadn't eaten, but that didn't make sense. She'd had a snack while they waited for Aarghathlain's return. Wait a minute. It wasn't hollow. More twisted. Yes, that was it: twisted in knots. That fish might have been a little too rotten.

As she sat there contemplating the strange feeling in her stomach, her body lurched, and she felt the urge to stand up again. Only this time, she also took a step.

"That's better," she thought, taking a few more steps. "Yes, that's much better. I just need to walk it off."

As she moved along the tunnel floor, the knots faded, replaced by a new sensation. It was sort of a ringing in her ears. But it wasn't just a ringing. There were words. Whispers on the wind. Each step brought her closer to understanding.

"Yes," Mnoonge said breathlessly. "I'm here."

She crawled over another rat and onto a ledge.

Come to me. Come in the name of Wrudge.

She weaved between the rows of glowing rats, scurrying through a pipe to a higher level. When she reached the top, she turned left...left again...and then right. She ran as fast as she could, bounding over the other rats, and they watched her with joy in their hearts, cheering her on.

It was low at first, but the sound grew as rats scratched the stone floor and clicked their teeth. Then, the entire Underoof Collective screeched, hissed, and chattered. A clamorous *raterwauling* burst out of storm drains and streethole covers, echoing off the stone facades lining Gemini City's wide streets and narrow sidestreets.[3]

The sound emanating from beneath the streets set everyone's teeth on edge, from the piers to the 11Blocks. Apprehension took hold, making Geminians more suspicious. Then, as suddenly as it began, the cacophonous sound stopped, and the silence that overtook the world was even more deafening than the noise had been.

From that day forward, Geminians locked their doors, walked a few steps, and went back to double-check. Mothers took their daughters' hands and crossed the street whenever they saw someone they didn't recognize, and the ominous silence from the Norters, who had not contacted the Congregational House yet, made everyone uneasy. Gemini City had descended into a panic not seen since the night the Wizard of the Council destroyed most of Middling Street, and it was steadily getting worse.

---

[3] As a general rule, rats don't talk about members of the Felis genus, so they change the word cat to rat whenever possible. For example, *catwalk* becomes *ratwalk*, or *caterwauling* becomes *raterwauling*. It's an elegant solution to their problem.

Lit by the soft glow of hundreds of rats, the chosen one introduced herself, bowing before the wizard and placing her head between her tiny hands.

"No, no. You don't bow to me," Aargh said. "It is I who should bow to you. I am grateful you have answered my call."

Mnoonge lifted her head, and much to her surprise, the Great Wizard Aarghathlain was bent at the waist! She was out of her depth. Oh, how she missed her mother. If Mama were here, she'd know what to do.

"I must ask you," Aargh said, rising again. "Will you help us? The road will be dangerous, and I have no idea where it will lead. If you choose this path, you must do so without reservation. And above all else, you must be willing to be remarkable. Unless I'm much mistaken, every one of us will have to face that challenge before this is done."

Mnoonge studied the wizard. The first time Aargh and the little girl had visited the Underoof, she'd squeezed in next to them. Rats are excellent at relating stories without embellishing them, but Mnoonge wanted to hear what they said first-hand. She'd been surprised when Holly-Mine had stroked her fur. No person had ever shown her kindness before, and she wondered if the little girl remembered.

"Yes, Mnoonge. I remember you," Holly-Mine said, kneeling.

Mnoonge raised her eyes to meet the girl's, and she realized Holly-Mine wasn't entirely as she appeared. The girl with the straw-like hair that poked out in every direction felt old—much older than her silly giggles, sparkling chocolatey brown eyes, and kind smile revealed. She was wiser, too, and much sadder. Mnoonge didn't understand why or how she knew these things. She just did.

"That will remain our secret," Holly-Mine's gentle voice spoke in Mnoonge's mind.

The small rat's face filled with wonder, and she nodded her head. Then she noticed Wizard Aarghathlain whispering in long, slow tones to a faint breeze wafting through the Underoof. The Mischief lifted their noses to sniff the air. It carried with it the smell of the river, the forest, and drops of oil from Gemini City's many steam carriages and other machines.

"Why are you speaking to Sister Wind, Papa?" Holly-Mine asked.

"I'm calling an old friend."

Holly-Mine was thrilled by the possibility. "Will he come?"

"I hope so, but I can't be certain that he heard me. Mnoonge, you look familiar to me. Have we met before?"

"In a way, Wizard Aarghathlain. I sat beside you the first time you and Holly-Mine entered the Underoof. It's also possible that you recognize my resemblance to Wrudge. I am his third cousin, thirteen times removed."

"Fascinating. I wish we had more time to talk. Unfortunately, we are in a race against time. Will you assist us, friend Mnoonge? Can you be remarkable?"

"Yes, Wizard Aarghathlain, I will help you," she squeaked, using rat speech. "Tell me what to do."

Aargh sheathed Guildebrande, thanking the weapon for its help.

"Until you require my services again," the sword responded, his voice growing distant as the blade's glow faded.

Aargh lifted Mnoonge off of the ground and spoke to her in quiet tones.

Holly-Mine realized what her father planned to do and grabbed his arm. "No, Papa! You mustn't!"

"I'm sorry, but I have no choice. I'm needed in more than one place at the same time. Maybe Mnoonge can help me with that."

"There must be another way. She won't be able to return your voice, and you can't take it from her."

"Of course not. I'd never use magic that way."

"But Papa, if you do this, you won't be able to speak to the Earth Mother."

"It's a risk I have to take. What comes next will require more than whispers on the wind. Besides, it isn't safe for us out there. If Wrudge taught me anything, it's that rats are clever, fast, and, most importantly, small. That means she'll be able to travel through the city unnoticed."

"I don't think it's a good idea."

"I know, but I can't think of another way. Once it's done, will you help me communicate here in the Underoof?"

"Of course."

"Come here," Aargh said, hugging Holly-Mine with his free arm before turning his attention back to the small rat. "Are you ready, Mnoonge?"

"Yes, Wizard Aarghathlain. I am ready."

Aargh breathed a long breath over the rat, doing his best to present an air of confidence, but inside, he wasn't convinced it would work.

Elemental magic offered a world of possibilities, free from the strictures that guided the intellectual magic performed at the Spire. Instead of following carefully crafted potions, incantations, and spells, it was unbound, guided by a wizard's emotions–a risky business, to be sure!

As the spell took effect, magic flowed into the small rat. Aargh wondered if he'd thought of everything this time, but experience had taught him not to get his hopes up.

The Collective sensed the magic, too, and the rats reverently lowered their heads between their hands.

When Mnoonge opened her mouth, the strength of Aargh's voice reverberated in every word she spoke. "The *Great Wiz-*

ard Aarghathlain, Wielder of the Sword Guildebrande and Keeper of the Precious Child, has entrusted me with a vital mission. I require two companions. Who amongst you will assist me?"

One of Wrudge and Mnoonge's many cousins stepped forward.

"Wrulde, what are you doing?" a nearby rat whispered.

"I'm answering my cousin's call." Ever since he'd first heard the *Parables*, Wrulde had longed for the opportunity to walk in his elder cousin's footsteps.

Another rat stepped forward, too: Buck, Head of Lower Block Security. Mnoonge was glad he volunteered.

Now that the party was complete, Aargh placed the small rat back on the ground.

As he did, Mnoonge heard herself say, "Thank you," in Aargh's voice.

"How odd," she thought. "This lends new meaning to the idea of speaking to oneself."

The trio wasted no time, as rats rarely waste time dithering the way people do. As they scurried away, the glow subsided, returning the Underoof to its customary darkness.

Mnoonge heard the rats around them chanting as they passed.

"Secrecy is security."

"Secrecy is security."

"Secrecy is security!"

CHAPTER 6

KEE-EEEEE-ARR!

THE WIZARDS' UNDERGROUND

Paladand flailed his arms, desperately trying to prevent Griff's beak and talons from latching onto anything important. With a ferocious flutter of wings, the bird's razor-sharp claws grasped his glasses and tore them from his face, leaving the young wizard blinded and disoriented.

"Nerah, help! I need you!"

The panther heard his call, but Renfir prevented her from coming to her wizard's aid. The animals collided in a blur of fangs and growls as Aargh's cottage collapsed.

The air around them filled with fiery debris, forcing everyone to the ground. Luckily, Paladand's hand landed on his broken glasses, and he put them back on, only to see Tarth running into the woods.

"It's a feint! They're getting away! Hurry!" he yelled, but he wouldn't leave Nerah, who was still fighting with Renfir.

Just as Paladand was about to jump onto the wolf, an arm grabbed him about the waist.

"Are you crazy?" Bartlebee said, doing his best to restrain the young wizard.

"Let me go!" Paladand hollered, threshing the air with his arms and legs. "Nerah needs me."

Bee pointed across the clearing. "Wait, Pal. Look!"

A sleek red fox sprinted toward the fighting animals.

"Be careful, Ember!" Pud yelled, running after his familiar.

Quick as a flash, Ember jumped onto Renfir's back, biting the scruff of the wolf's neck. As Renfir ran in circles, trying to shake off the fox, Nerah stealthily bided her time, waiting for the right moment to pounce.

"Isn't there anything we can do?" Paladand asked.

"Yes," Bee said, reaching into his robes. "I'm sorry, Ermy. This isn't how I wanted our journey to begin, but we need you."

A small brown and white stoat wriggled out of Bee's pocket, down his leg, and under the thick bed of leaves carpeting the forest floor.

"Wait, no! Come back!" he called after her. "Don't run away!"

But Ermy wasn't running away. She reappeared directly under the wolf and, after a glance at Bee, scampered up Renfir's hind leg. Flinghower's familiar howled in pain as the stoat sank her sharp teeth into a place no wolf should ever be bitten.

It was the opportunity Nerah had been waiting for, but Renfir anticipated the attack, deftly rolling to the side. With one last shake, he cast off Ember and Ermy and darted into the undergrowth.

Griff circled in the sky high above the melee, watching and waiting. When Renfir escaped into the woods, the hawk changed course, making a graceful turn in the air. Then, the bird of prey pulled in his wings and plummeted toward the ground, screeching, "Kee-eeeee-arr! KEE-EEEEE-ARR!"

Faster and faster, he flew, locking his eyes on the panther. Usually, red-tail hawks were born with amber eyes that turned brown as they aged, but not Griff's. Since he'd bonded with Tarth at such a young age, they'd kept their piercing color, lending more intensity to the bird's angry visage.

Nerah heard Griff's call, and she knew it was for her. That was okay. They had unfinished business. No one attacked her wizard and flew away. No one.

The panther locked eyes with the hawk speeding toward her. Nerah knew those eyes. The lion that had separated her from her mother had that color of eyes. Amber eyes…

When the pride attacked, Nerah was lying in her mother's arms, enjoying her morning bath. Kasih tried to push her daughter out of harm's way, but Nerah rolled right to the feet of the Pride Male. He had a bountiful mane circling his head and shoulders that resembled a king's royal mantle.

The panther cub froze in terror, staring into the lion's intense amber eyes, but he didn't move. He just kept licking his paws that were crossed in front of him. Then, yawning, he stood and nonchalantly strode away. Although Nerah searched and searched for Kasih, she never found her mother.

Alone and hungry, Nerah hid in a tree throw, trying to figure out what to do. When night came, she did her best to sleep, but the sounds of the forest–sounds she used to find comforting–frightened her. By morning, she couldn't keep her head up, but she still wouldn't close her eyes.

Thump!

A piece of something fell out of the sky and rolled into her throw. It smelled good, so she licked it. It tasted good, too, so she ate it. Another landed nearby, and she cautiously pulled herself from between the tree's roots and snapped that one up, too.

Her stomach growled.

One flew through the air, and she jumped to grab it, not considering where she might land. Not accomplished in leaping yet, she tumbled over the edge of a steep slope and right into Paladand. Standing upright and hairless, the boy looked peculiar to her, but he'd fed and cared for her, and they'd become close friends in no time.

Paladand!

Nerah blinked, and her thoughts returned to the Northern Forest. How could she have let herself get distracted? It was those amber eyes! Before she could react, Nerah felt Griff's talons sink into the side of her face, and she roared in pain, batting the hawk away with her paw.

"Nerah!" Paladand shouted, running toward her without paying attention to the chaos unfolding around them. He watched as she tried to claw her way to the safety of the trees, but she didn't make it.

A long red gash split her black fur, and when Paladand tried to inspect the injury, she growled and jerked away.

"Steady. I won't hurt you. You're safe," he said, uncrossing his fists.

Nerah purred and moved closer to her wizard.

"That's a good girl. You need to trust me. This is going to hurt a little," he said, crossing his open hands and closing them into fists.

Nerah watched him intently, nodded, and laid her head on the ground.

Paladand pulled out a vial from a small leather folio that he carried. He placed a tiny drop of its contents on his palm and rubbed the potent healer's potion between his hands. Then, he moved them over Nerah's wound and recited the *Spell of Wondrous Healing.*

Nerah growled again.

"I'm sorry. Do you remember the time you got a thorn stuck in your paw?" he asked, making a motion similar to pulling something out of his hand.

She shook her head, *no.*

"Oh yes, you do. I took care of you then, and I'll take care of you now, too."

Nerah relented, and Paladand continued.

She let out a blood-curdling scream as the spell repaired her injured face. Everyone's breath caught in their breasts, but in no time, she was on her feet again, nuzzling Paladand.

Bee sighed with relief as he picked up Ermy. "You had me going for a minute there, but I'm proud of you. Thank you for helping Nerah." Once she was safely back in her pocket, he turned his attention to their group. "Is everyone accounted for? Where's Alantus? Garth, have you seen him?"

"No. I thought he was with you." He often stood hunched over in thought, but Garth's face looked more drawn than quizzical today. "Wait a second. Do you hear that?"

In the distance, Bee heard the baleful cry of a tree squirrel. The sound tore at his heart.

"Paladand, hurry. Lan needs you!" he cried, recklessly tearing through the thicket to locate his friend.

He found Alantus propped against a tree with Pip next to him, screaming as loudly as she could.

When Bee saw the state of Lan's leg, he almost passed out. "Oh, Buddy. Are you okay?"

The ridiculousness of the question embarrassed Bee, but he couldn't think of anything else to say.

Pale from the loss of blood, Lan's round face almost glowed in the moonlight. "I'm sorry," the horticulturalist said, barely managing a whisper. "I let you down. I tried, but I couldn't stop him. Please forgive me. I'll do better next time."

"Are you kidding? You were amazing," Bee said, taking a few breaths to calm himself.

Lan coughed.

"Save your strength, Buddy. We're going to help you," but the gash in Alantus' leg did its best to shake Bee's confidence.

The other members of The Wizards' Underground emerged from between the trees. They stared at their friend lying on the ground as the seriousness of the situation sank in. No one had to be told what had happened. Lan had blocked Renfir's escape and paid a heavy price.

"What are you waiting for?" Pud said irritably, his whole body shaking. "Help him!"

"I-I don't know if I can," Paladand said, staring at his hands.

"I know it's a lot to ask," Bee said. "Do what you can. Others can finish the job once we get him home."

Garthelwaite sat down and leaned against the tree next to Lan. "We're here for you," he said, taking his friend's hand.

Alantus was younger than Aargh and his school friends, Bee, Garth, and Fizz, but that didn't matter. They were a tight-knit group that watched out for each other, as did their familiars. That's why Pip and Ermy crawled on Lan's lap, and Ember laid his sleek fox nose on the wizard's uninjured leg.

Paladand pulled the leather folio out of his robes for the second time that evening. If a person didn't look closely, they might have mistaken it for a journal, but when he unclasped the buckle, it revealed a neat row of thin glass tubes, each held in place by a small leather strap protruding from the maroon felt inside. They appeared innocuous enough: a series of small glass vials with corks in their tops. The liquid inside didn't shimmer or glow. It wasn't particularly viscous or an interesting color. In fact, the potion was so thoroughly nondescript that it might have been mistaken for sips of water.

That's why Paladand had visited a pyrographer on Lower Middling Street to have a skull and crossbones seared into the case's cover. Several wizards had scolded him for being so vulgar, but the pictogram got the point across.

He hesitantly removed a vial from the case and studied it. This one had slightly less liquid in it than the others. A casual observer might not have noticed, but Paladand could tell. Minutes before, he'd used potion from this container to heal Nerah. He had no choice but to use this one again because he didn't want to mix potions from different vials on his hands. No one knew why, but combining different batches often resulted in fiery explosions; therefore, he used one vial at a time until it was empty and then moved on to the next.

With a small *pop!*, he removed the cork and placed two drops on the palm of his hand. It burned, and he winced at the pain. The healing arts professors would have called him *foolish* or *arrogant* for trying to control that much magic. Then again, they were safely back at the school and not sitting in the forest trying to save a wizard's life.

Bee gripped Paladand's shoulder so tightly that his knuckles turned white. "You've got this, Pal."

The young healer gritted his teeth and leaned against him for support. Paladand's muscles tensed as he thought about the endless hours he and his colleagues had hovered over the vials, enchanting them with as much knowledge and power as they could impart. He hoped it would be enough to save Lan, but not so much that it overwhelmed them.

That many wizards combining their magic created powerful potions not to be trifled with, even if you were an accomplished healer (which wasn't a thing yet, seeing as the healing arts were so new to the Spire).

"Wait!" Alantus cried.

Paladand panicked. "I haven't done anything yet!"

"What is it, Lan? What's wrong?" Bee asked.

"It's not me. It's the *Agalinis acuta*."

"I don't understand," Bee said, looking around. "Is that an ailment?"

"No. The flower there. It's a sandplain gerardia," Lan explained between coughs. "It's rare in these woods. Please, don't kneel on it."

A plant with delicate pink-purple flowers at the ends of its spindly arms poked out of the ground a few inches from his leg. The other wizards hadn't even noticed it.

"Are you kidding me?" Bee asked. "Paladand is trying to heal you, and you're worried about a flower? It's not even that pretty!"

"Please, Bee. It's special."

"Okay, okay. Paladand isn't going to smush it. Right, Pal?" Bee asked, exasperated with his friend, the situation, and just about everything else in the world. It wasn't wizardly to lose control of his emotions this way, but he couldn't help it.

The young healer tried to speak, but only a squeak came out.

That was enough for Alantus. He muttered, "Thanks," and promptly passed out.

"Lan," Garth whispered, gripping his friend's hand. "Come back, please!"

"You'd better hurry, Pal," Bee said, kneeling beside him.

The wizards gathered around their friend, watching with bated breath. Tassior, who always kept an eye out for people who needed support, put an arm around Illbrahss because the violist looked as if he might chew through his lower lip.

"*Concentration is Key,*" Paladand recited as he laid his hands on Alantus' wounds.

A soft purple glow enveloped the leg.

Although no magic was considered harder or easier than another, healing occupied a class by itself. If a musician made a mistake during a performance–say, by playing the wrong augmented sixth chord–the music might sound awful for a brief instant. However, the faux pas wouldn't keep the concert from continuing. If an engineer miscalculated the vertex where two planes intersected in an architectural design, skilled stonemasons were there to correct the problem.

However, if a healer made a mistake when tending to a patient, it meant further injuring the person. No one at the school took that risk lightly, healer or patient. That's why few wizards chose it as their focus. Those who did practiced their craft reluctantly, if at all.

Worry lines appeared on Paladand's furrowed brow. What if he lacked the strength to control the magic flowing through him? A single drop took a tremendous amount of focus, but two? He'd never tried to use that much before. No one had.

A strange warmth crept into his fingers. It moved along his arm like a clutter of spiders. Soon, the prickly feeling entered his shoulder and neck. This was what he'd feared might happen: the magic was searching for a way to slip into his mind. From there, it could control him instead of the other way around.

The light under his hands grew brighter and brighter, and Paladand struggled to hold on. An instant before the magic overtook him, he wrenched himself away from the leg, dispelling the incantation. All living things felt the release of energy, and trees nearby shuddered.

Usually supremely confident in everything he did, Paladand scrunched his eyes closed as tightly as possible. Had he lost control of the magic? Did he hurt Alantus? It had been a mistake to try! Wizards of the Third Circle were warned that a little knowledge could be dangerous. Plus, he'd never healed such a severe wound before. And to do it without the aid of other healers? What in the world possessed him to try something so foolish? He'd overstepped his bounds, and the school would reprimand him. Maybe expel him—

"Enough napping, Pal," Bartlebee said in his good-natured way.

"Excuse me?"

"Time to go, Lazybones."

Paladand heard the smile in Bee's voice, but he still asked, "Is Alantus okay?"

"See for yourself."

He squinted to prevent himself from having to view the full extent of the damage he'd done to poor Lan. With a heartfelt sigh, he exclaimed, *"Carya cordiformis!* What a relief."

The tension in Paladand's shoulders released as he watched Garthelwaite and Tassior help Lan to his feet. The herbalist leaned heavily on the wizards, favoring the injured leg, but he looked well enough to make the journey home.

"I'm not fond of being called nicknames," Paladand grumbled as Bee helped the young wizard off the ground.

"Sorry," Bartlebee said, laughing. "I forgot. It won't happen again."

"Yeah, right," the young healer mumbled, knowing full well Bee wouldn't stop. He hated being called Pal. Why was that so hard for people to understand?

"Why don't you and Pud give poor Fizzbain a hand," Bee suggested, slapping him on the back. "He's going to need a shoulder to hold onto. Oh no! There he goes again!"

"And what are you going to do, Bartlebee?" Paladand asked, emphasizing Bee's full name.

"Dram's wandered off again. I'd better fetch him."

• • •

Dramwitch stood as close as he dared to Aargh's cottage. He'd just finished talking to several trees, and although their stories were jumbled, he'd gleaned that Aargh and Holly-Mine had escaped into the forest. Where they'd gone remained a mystery, but at least they'd made it safely out of the house.

The clearing had always been a restful place for Dram–an oasis, far away from the stresses of Spire life. Many a day, he'd played in the brook with Holly-Mine or whiled away the hours chatting with Aargh as they weeded the garden. One time, he'd found himself snowed in for several days and wound up being recruited to play the part of a knight from a far-off land visiting from the Queen's Palace in Arkorar.

Now, that had all been taken away...destroyed by Tarth and his followers.

Crack! An old pine crashed to the ground after succumbing to the inferno, and Dram threw himself to the side, tumbling to safety. He wasted no time brushing off the bits of smoldering bark and dirt from his earthy brown robes.

"Cleanliness is next to wizardliness," he murmured, giving them a pat.

Feeling exhausted and sad, he sat there watching fireflies dance against the black night sky, only they weren't fireflies. They were embers.

"How awful is it that your death should be, in a way, so beautiful? Or, I guess, maybe that's how it should be. At least the wind has dropped off."

He hoped this would keep the fire from spreading to the surrounding forest. If only he could speak to water the way Aargh did–

Bee grabbed Dram under his arms and lifted him off the ground. "I almost didn't notice you there. You blend in pretty well."

"Hi, Bee. You startled me."

"Sorry about that," the older wizard said, waving off the smoke surrounding them. "This is awful."

Dram agreed, stifling a cough as he picked up the messenger bag he'd dropped when he fell to the ground.

Bee looked at Aargh's former assistant. "Hey, I've been meaning to ask, aren't you tired of wearing brown? I mean, it does go rather well with that shock of red hair of yours, but don't you want some color?"

"Not really. I'll pick my wizard colors when I'm ready, I guess," Dram answered, touching the coat of arms embroidered on his shoulder. It was a shield with a dove holding an oak leaf, representing strength in peace.

"You doing all right?" Bee asked, concerned at the distant sound in Dram's voice.

"No, not really. It's a terrible sight, there's no doubt, but we can be thankful that Aargh and Holly-Mine got away."

"Finally, some good news! Did you see them?"

"No. The trees told me," Dram said, pointing to where he'd spoken with the forest.

Bee shook his head. "I wouldn't put much stock in that. The forest hasn't grown into its wisdom yet, and you may not have heard the whole story. Not many wizards are willing to ask the trees much of anything these days."

"I'd like to think it's the truth. Jumbled or not, I've never known a tree to lie."

"I'll take your word for it. Might be a sign that things will be okay."

"I'm not sure about that, Bee. It wasn't the easiest conversation I've ever had with a tree, but I have to keep trying."

"You and Aargh are cut from the same cloth," the older wizard said, brushing a leaf off Dram's robes.

"Thank you. That might be the nicest thing you've ever said to me."

The two wizards stood in silence, watching the cottage burn.

"Can I ask you a question?" Dram asked over the crackling.

Bee did his best to look away from the mesmerizing fire. "Of course."

"What drives people to do bad things? I mean, this is beyond the pale."

"Gosh, Dram. I can't answer that. People have their reasons, but I doubt we'd understand, even if they explained them to us."

"I guess, but it saddens me that people–Spire wizards!– would do such a terrible thing."

"Me, too, my friend. Me, too. Listen, if you're done here, we should rejoin the others. We need to get Lan to the infirmary. He's been hurt."

"Oh no! What can I do?"

"Whoa, there. Hold your horses. The situation is under control."

"But, Lan!"

"Don't worry. Paladand worked his magic. It was elegant. That young man is going places if you ask me."

"That's a relief," Dram said, rubbing his temples. "I can't take any more scares today."

At precisely that instant, Aargh's voice interrupted their conversation. "Dramwitch!"

Dram's legs wobbled uncontrollably, and Bee steadied him.

"Mentor! Thank the trees. You're safe. Where are you?"

"Down here," Aargh's voice directed.

Shocked at the sight of three rats–one of whom spoke with Aargh's voice–Dram whimpered, *"Tsuga canadensis!* The Head Wizard's been turned into a rat!"* and collapsed into Bee's arms.

CHAPTER 7

HEADING SOUTH
ODARAPHRIM & TARTHANABELLE

"This way!" Tarthanabelle barked as he stomped off toward the Eastern Foothills.

Odaraphrim wondered if Tarth could feel his gaze. Probably not. Tarth didn't have time for such trivialities.

Ever since the group had reassembled near the southerly end of Ransome Ravine, most of Tarth's underlings had gathered around him, hoping to win back his favor. Not Phrim. He'd kept his distance, plodding along a dozen paces behind, keenly aware of how unwelcome he was. The only good thing about the situation was that it gave him time to reflect on recent events and what the future held for him.

He couldn't deny the allure of Tarth's ideas regarding liberating the Spire from Aarghathlain's spell. Yet, somewhere along the way, he must have followed the wrong root because his plan had been an unmitigated disaster. Aargh had escaped, the Wizarding Oath remained in place, and Tarth had reprimanded him in front of everyone. So much for demonstrating his leadership ability!

"What secret does Aarghathlain hold over you?" Phrim asked the back of Tarth's head as they trudged south. "Why did you refuse to move against him? Was it his magic? No, it couldn't be. If you were worried about Aargh retaliating, it would have happened already. Not only did Aargh not cast any spells on us, but he'd taken the cowardly way out and run away…twice!"

What had begun as a seed of doubt had grown into a full-on crisis of conscience. Phrim needed to reevaluate the path he was on, starting with his allegiance to Tarth. Where had this blind devotion come from anyway?

"And why does Tarth's opinion mean so much to me? He's not even my mentor. He's nothing more than a disgruntled wizard–as if there aren't plenty of those to choose from at the Spire!"

The promise of performing elemental magic had excited Phrim, that much he had to acknowledge. But that didn't scratch the surface of why he'd agreed to join Tarth's cohort. He'd wanted to be part of something big and important, and this had felt big…very big…at first.

How many nights had Phrim and the others sat uncomfortably in a disused greenhouse, listening to Tarth ramble about Aargh? Too many. Now, he wondered if Tarth's protestations about Aargh were nothing more than the disgruntled words of a pouty wizard who hadn't discovered magic himself.

As Phrim reflected on the wizard's speeches, he concluded that they resembled gripe sessions rather than concrete plans to restore the Spire to its former glory. The more Phrim considered this, the more he realized it wasn't Tarth's message that had persuaded him. The wizard had a gift. He could tap into a person's deepest desires, making them believe he shared their concerns. Tarth did this on such a fundamental level that a wizard didn't notice their needs were gradually changing to suit the wizard's goals.

Phrim didn't know where he'd gotten lost along the way, but he didn't recognize himself anymore. He'd been prepared to sacrifice Aargh and Holly-Mine's lives to impress his master!

A wizard coughed in a way that meant, *hey, pay attention,* and Phrim skipped a step. It was Flinghower, and he was glaring at Phrim for walking too close.

Odaraphrim knew Fling blamed him for Renfir's injuries, but that made no sense. He hadn't started the fight. He didn't even join in, not that Dilly would have been much help. Geckos weren't exactly known for their fighting ability. Maybe that was why Fling was upset. Who knew? But Phrim had no intention of asking.

Unlike Tarth, Odaraphrim *did* feel the weight of Fling's gaze, and he decided to hang back a while longer until things cooled off.

• • •

Tarthanabelle seethed as he blazed a trail through the wilderness toward the Once-Great Wall. Furious at being run off by Aargh's pathetic minions, he stamped through the brambles, not noticing that many chose to hitch a ride on his robes.

"The level of ignorance!" he hissed to himself. "How can they not see what's staring them right in the face?"

Equally frustrating were the crestfallen wizards dragging their feet as they walked beside him. What had possessed them to act so rashly? Burning Aargh's home with him and Holly-Mine still in it? Incredible!

Tarth stopped short, yelling, *"Fusarium circinatum!"*

Shocked by his outburst, the not-so-merry band of wizards fanned out to avoid running into him.

"Am I going to give elemental magic to these fools?" he muttered. "They don't deserve it after what they did. Wait a minute. That sounds like something Aarghathlain would say!"

Tarth shook his head as if to cast off any last vestiges of Aargh clinging to his eyebrows and reached up to re-tie his ponytail.

No one had the right to decide who had access to elemental magic–certainly not Aargh...or him, either. Yes, he'd give them elemental magic. He'd give it to them and anyone else who wanted it. What came after didn't concern him.

Pleased at the thought of reaching such an intelligent conclusion, Tarth continued walking, free to turn his attention to their current predicament. There had to be another explanation beyond insanity for what had happened at the clearing. Maybe Phrim and the others hadn't listened closely to what he'd said or only heard what they'd wanted to hear. That would explain why they'd misinterpreted his intentions and acted so irresponsibly.

Whatever the reason, he'd grown tired of their sulking. He didn't need a bunch of guilt-ridden hangers-on weighing him down. New plans needed to be devised, and courses of action prepared. Thankfully, it appeared Paladand and his cronies were in the dark. That was some consolation. Not enough, but it would have to do.

When the group reached the edge of the Once-Great Wall, Tarth passed right by, continuing to head south. The wizards had expected to turn right toward the Congregational House tunnel. They whispered anxiously to each other, which turned out to be the proverbial straw that broke the camel's back.

"Cut it out!" Tarth said, not stopping. "Even if we went back to the Spire, what then? Do you honestly think we'd be welcomed with open arms? Our path leads away from the school, not toward it."

His admonition made the whispers more urgent, and he whirled on the group a second time.

"Enough! All right? Enough! Continue with me and liberate magic from Aarghathlain's iron grip, or go back and beg for mercy. If you want to be bound by the Wizarding Oath forever, it's no skin off my nose. Of course, you'll be lucky if they let you continue to be wizards at all. I couldn't care less either way, but if you turn your back on me now, I'll never forget, and one day, you'll feel my wrath! Make no mistake about that. There will come a time when I control the magic in Ardilakk Valley, and I'll remember who stood with me and who stood against me."

"Mentor," Flinghower risked. "I don't think you understand. We aren't going anywhere. Some of us made a mistake–a terrible mistake–and we're sorry for that, but we have no intention of leaving."

Many sheepish faces agreed.

"We're confused, tired, and Renfir's hurt," he continued. "I need to tend his wounds. Would it be too much to ask to take a break for a few minutes?"

Tarth reveled in his mentee's penitence, even though he knew Fling had nothing to do with their current troubles. Odaraphrim had been the one who'd made a mess of his plans. If Flinghower hadn't overheard Phrim in the greenhouse, the night might have been an even greater disaster. Fling always kept him apprised of the whispers lurking in the shadows, and Tarth would reward his loyalty with magic.

Not waiting for a response, Fling continued, "We understand that you have a plan. No one doubts that, but could you clue us in?"

The anger on Tarth's face changed into a sinister grin. *Crack!* Tarth snapped his fingers with such force that several of the wizards jumped. The rest held their breath, anticipating the worst.

In a low growl, he said, "I wonder what the good folk of Gemini City will say when the Norters have a Wizards' Tower, too. That'll keep them awake at night!"

CHAPTER 8

OF TWO MINDS
AARGHATHLAIN & DRAMWITCH

After a lifetime of navigating trees' many branches of knowledge, wizards were generally adept at carrying on more than one conversation at once. It was one of the reasons Geminians viewed them as strange, which wasn't surprising. Watching a person talk to three people at the same time–with everyone looking in different directions–would give anybody pause. It was the main reason why Geminians used derogatory terms to describe wizards, calling them con artists, charlatans, or, worst of all, fortune tellers. If people didn't understand something, they tended to invent a nasty name for it, and members of the Spire had more than their fair share.

Unfortunately, sharing one's voice with a rat didn't remind Aargh of navigating a tangle of roots in the slightest, and his dream of holding simultaneous conversations in the Underoof (with Holly-Mine's help) and the forest (with Mnoonge's help) ended almost as soon as it began. The problem wasn't necessarily that he'd given Mnoonge his voice. That had worked nicely when they were in the tunnels together. The trouble started once they were separated.

In order to participate in the forest conversation, he had to open his mind to Mnoonge's senses, and he was instantly overwhelmed, marveling at how a tiny animal could be filled with…well…everything! The small rat's senses of smell and hearing were mind-boggling, and her sense of touch gave

Aargh the worst case of pins and needles he'd ever felt. He understood why she needed such acute perception, but his mind simply couldn't process that much sensory input—let alone carry on two conversations at once. No way. Impossible.

"There's always a catch to casting elemental magic, isn't there?" Aargh asked himself, struggling to dampen the intensity of his connection to Mnoonge. It took so much effort that, with increasing regularity, he couldn't form a coherent sentence.

At one point, the rat declared, "Absintent the areful knewing flobb!"

Aargh didn't even know what he was trying to say!

He soon realized that if he intended to communicate through Mnoonge, he'd have to experience the world as she did. How he'd manage that, he didn't know—and he might need to adjust his expectations for the rat, considering how poorly things were going at the moment.

Unable to figure out a solution, Aargh ran his shaking hands through his hair, and both Holly-Mine and Mnoonge yelled, "This is tearing me apart!"

• • •

The whole rat-speaking-with-Aargh's-voice thing threw Dramwitch, and he found himself as flummoxed as his mentor.

"Let me get this straight," Bee said, laughing and pointing at the rats. "You honestly believe Tarthanabelle is parading around as a rat to lure you away from me for some dastardly reason? Use that impressive brain of yours, Dram. Aargh is the only wizard in Ardilakk Valley who'd do something like this. Full stop. End of discussion."

Even though Dram found it hard to argue with Bee's logic, he insisted on asking a string of questions only his mentor could answer.

Aargh lost it when he asked, "Remember when I felt homesick? I told you about the marsh serpent. The one that used to slither under the trash?"

"Dramwitch, Wizard of the Third Circle, Mentee to the Wizard Aarghathlain, and former Assistant to the Head Wizard!" Mnoonge bellowed. "That is enough!"

Much to Bee's surprise, Dram didn't get upset at being scolded.

"It *is* you!" he said, clapping his hands. "That's such a relief."

With that, Dram said goodbye to Bee (whom Aargh had already asked to return to the Spire) and followed Mnoonge, Buck, and Wrulde into the Underoof. Unfortunately, the trip didn't go well.

First, he pinched his hand on the pipe's grate covering. Then, he learned why stairs were referred to as flights when he slipped the last tread and soared through the air. It did give him a chance to admire the construction of the ceiling after finding himself lying flat on his back on the cold stone. To top it all off, he stubbed his toe on a broken paver and wound up limping the rest of the way to The Meeting Place, where he arrived more than a little worse for wear. However, not even the pain of his trials could stifle his joy at seeing Aargh and his daughter.

"Mentor! It really is you! And Holly-Mine, too!" he exclaimed, hobbling over to give her a hug.

Holly-Mine laughed and hugged him back.

When he finished making sure they were okay, Dram remembered the pain in his hand, foot, and back and sat on the low stone shelf. He'd spent the entire trip explaining what had happened, but Aargh had missed most of it, trying to deal with his connection to Mnoonge.

Dram did his best to go through it all again, but the combination of the previous night's events, his arduous journey, and ping-ponging his eyes back and forth between Mnoonge and Aargh proved to be too much. So, when Aargh went off on one of his tangents, Dram's mind wandered, focusing on nice things such as floating peacefully on Lake Hîrdehn-dūl in the school's rowboat.

"Are you listening to what I'm saying?" Aargh asked with the small rat's help.

Mnoonge harrumphed. What else could she do? She was only the voice.

"I'm sorry. It's been one of those days–" Dram started to say, catching himself. *"Ceratonia siliqua!* I meant no disrespect. What happened to you and Holly-Mine was much, much worse."

"Don't worry about it," Mnoonge assured the young wizard, speaking Aargh's words. "I understand, but you need to listen to me."

"Actually, I heard what you said, but it doesn't make sense. Why would we let Tarth back into the Spire? He burned your house with you in it! And Holly-Mine, too. No way! Tarth can never be allowed to set one dinky toe on the Spire grounds ever again."

"If what you say happened is true, I understand how you feel, though it does seem out of character for Tarth," Aargh said through Mnoonge. "We've had our differences, but I've always regarded him as levelheaded, as far as wizards go. I would never have imagined he'd snap, for lack of a better term, but everyone has a breaking point, I guess." Aargh paused to consider this for a while before saying, "Come over here and sit with me."

As resolutely as he could manage, Dram limped across the tunnel to sit beside Aargh, still mumbling about fires and bad people.

Mnoonge had to scurry onto Aargh's leg to avoid having her tail smooshed.

"Do you remember taking the new Wizarding Oath?" Mnoonge said, speaking for Aargh.

"Yes, of course. I think the oath might be what Tarth is upset about."

"Exactly. Tarth wants to tap into elemental magic. Do you think that's a good idea?"

"Arbor, no! But tonight at your cottage, I did wish that I could speak to water the way you can. Maybe I could have saved your home."

"I appreciate the sentiment, Dram, but I'm afraid that wouldn't have been possible. The point is, you wished you could have used elemental magic. It's about the temptation."

"Yes, but wishing and doing are two completely different things. I wouldn't have done it."

"That may or may not be true," Mnoonge said for Aargh, "but even if you wouldn't have, do you believe the other wizards would have demonstrated the same restraint? What about Tarth?"

Dram couldn't argue with Aargh's logic.

"The honest truth is, the temptation is too great. And if that's the case, it leaves us with only one option: prevent its use altogether."

"You remind me of Bee," Dram remarked. "He thinks things through, too."

Mnoonge chuckled. Dram found it strange to see Aargh laugh but hear the sound come from the small rat sitting on his lap, but he went with it.

"It might be more accurate to say Bartlebee and I remind you of a certain wise wizard," Mnoonge said for Aargh. "You could do worse than to make time to listen to his stories."

Dram didn't need to be told whom Aargh was talking about: *Brindlewise, Spire Elder.* Everyone knew Aargh and Bee enjoyed spending time with the wizard with the long, gray beard and bushy eyebrows. One could say Brindlewise fit the general public's assumption of what a wizard looked like to a T.

Getting the conversation back on track, Dram said, "I'm not trying to contradict you, Head Wizard, but I think you made my point, too. That's why Tarth can't go back. What if he figures out how to use elemental magic? He's too dangerous to be let near the school."

"If Tarth has gone rogue, I shudder to think what he might be capable of, but there's more to it. Much more. You've been an excellent mentee, assistant, and student. You've never given me any reason to doubt your loyalty to the school or me. Therefore, I'm going to share a secret with you. You can never tell anyone, including those who are helping us. Do you understand?"

Even in his current state—emotionally drained, in pain, and thoroughly confused—Dram would never willingly break a promise he made to Aargh. "You have my word! Anything you say, Head Wizard."

"Enough of that, now. I'm not Head Wizard anymore."

"You'll always be Head Wizard to me."

Moved by his former apprentice's sincerity, Aargh touched Dram's hand.

Before being admitted to the Gemini City School of Wizarding, Dram's life had been hard—too hard for someone so young. Aargh had hoped to give the boy a chance at a better life, but that had proved to be a pipe dream. It turned out he couldn't spare his mentee, or anyone, from a lifetime of challenges. Living simply didn't work that way.

Dramwitch hailed from a tribe called Lowlanders, although the true meaning of that designation had been lost generations before. It was purely coincidental that they'd settled on what Geminians called the Lowlands: the marshes that ran along the western squares. The people who lived there had thick accents and beautiful red hair, which made them stand out from the other inhabitants of Ardilakk Valley.

Once a proud people from a far-off land rich with history, they were forced to eke out a living managing the city's dumping grounds. Their heritage hadn't disappeared quickly, of course. It had happened gradually, over time, swallowed by Gemini City's trash, the same way the wetlands had been.

In ancient times, the Lowlands were a pristine watershed covered with tall saltgrass and filled with fish spawning in its complex intertwined creeks. Herons and egrets frequented the shallows, and seals relaxed in its sun-warmed waterways.

At first, the city's dumping ground was limited to the marsh's northernmost tip, where Ardilakk's foothills met the Once-Great Wall. But, over the generations, it had grown until it completely covered the tidal lands and had even started tumbling into the River Wide. Lowlanders were the only inhabitants of the valley who ventured into the desolation of the Wastes.

The closest Geminians came to visiting the area was to watch automated trucks called rumblebugs scoop up the city's refuse and deliver it to the dumping grounds. These machines trundled along the streets and sidestreets, day and night, making a terrific racket. If their steam whistle didn't rattle a person's nerves, their clicking, ticking, and scraping certainly did. Many a Geminian nightmare featured a rumblebug's long metal arms, which were similar to a lobster's legs, with countless joints and grasping pincers on the ends.

The rumblebugs had impressive clockish mechanisms on their sloping faces that clanked and chimed, announcing the truck's next destination. The clock itself had markings corresponding to the twelve blocks from the Port Pier District to the Congregational House. It also had a small window near the center displaying which of the 24 east/west blocks was next on their route. Every Mundsday, they began their journey at 0Blocks1-20 and moved uptown to 11Blocks1-24, crisscrossing the city as they made their rounds.

There was one square, however, that didn't let the rumblebugs terrorize their streets: Old Eastie Sowtown. The townies ran their own disposal, being far more conscientious about recycling than most Geminians and having no intention of contributing to the mass of refuse covering the Lowland Wastes.

Across the city, the bug-like trucks dutifully moved around their assigned blocks, sweeping and scooping. When their boxtanks were full, they rolled toward the end of a street. There, they blew a long, shrill whistle followed by three short blasts warning people to stay back. Then, they dumped the refuse onto the Wastes, sounded the all-clear, and headed to the next block along their route.

The Lowlanders spent long days sifting through the trash disposed of at the ends of the streets and sidestreets. Day in and day out, the custodians of the wastes carted and sorted the rubbish, preparing for the next day's dumpings. All the while, the threat of disappearing into a sinkhole or being inhumed by a towering pile of garbage remained ever-present in their minds.

Sadly, Dram lost his family when a trench they were excavating collapsed. Unable to stop it, he'd watched as a seemingly unending pile of trash tumbled into the gulley. Even though there was little hope of rescuing his mother and father, the tribe had worked feverishly throughout the night to unearth them.

After the loss of his parents, Dram spent weeks wandering the city's streets. Over time, he made his way uptown as far as the western 7Blocks, where he found himself welcomed into the school. Not every hopeful was admitted, but Aargh had a good feeling about the boy and advocated for his acceptance.

Their first meeting came while Aargh and Wrudge were out for an evening stroll on the Eastern Grazing Field. A commotion had erupted outside the Spire Wall, and they'd rushed out the 78th Street Exit to see if they could help. To their surprise, they found a steam carriage precariously perched on the sidewalk and its driver screaming at a boy lying in the street. Aargh had instantly recognized his mop of red hair and Lowland clothing, made of strong denim to protect against sharp objects hidden in the rubbish. Apparently, the boy had darted out in front of a carriage, forcing it off the road.

In an attempt to defuse the situation, Aargh slipped the driver a few coins for his trouble and sent him on his way.

When he returned to the boy, who was still lying in the road, he asked, "What is your name, young man?"

"My name is Dramwitch, kind sir, and if I may, I'll be going."

Aargh smiled at the boy's Lowland accent. It had a singsongy musicality to it that he liked. "Before you go, would you explain why you ran into the street?"

Dram uncurled, revealing a tiny bird lying on the ground. "If I hadn't. He'd have run over her."

"I understand," Aargh said, helping Dram to his feet. "Why don't you come inside."

"Can I bring her?"

"Of course. Your friend is welcome, too. We have lots of animals at the school."

"I've named her Cheep," the boy said, proud of his cleverness.

"How accurate," Aargh laughed. "Dramwitch of the Lowlands and friend Cheep, let me be the first to welcome you to the Gemini City School of Wizarding."

Over the years, their relationship had continued to grow, culminating with Aargh's approval of Dram as his mentee. That's why he decided to trust Dram with the true nature of the oath.

"You see, Dram, it isn't about the words of the oath at all. If someone has been granted access to magic, willingly stepping onto the Spire grounds is all it takes to enact the spell," Mnoonge said, speaking Aargh's words. "The goal was to have every wizard make a direct connection to the Earth Mother, nothing more."

"But what happens if a wizard leaves the school? Can I cast elemental magic now if I wanted to?" Dram asked.

"No, I'm afraid not. Once the spell takes effect, it channels any build-up of elemental magic back into the earth no matter where the wizard goes. I call it *grounding*. This is why Tarth mustn't be allowed to teach students anywhere other than at a wizarding school. They wouldn't be bound by the spell. Hindsight being 20/20, I should have considered that possibility, but at the time, I was focused on controlling magic at the school."

Dram leaped off the bench, babbling as he stumbled around The Meeting Place on his sore toe. "What were we thinking, banishing Tarth and the other wizards from the school grounds? I guess we didn't know, but that's beside the point. Mentor, we must find them and return them to the Spire. I must tell the others!"

"No, you mustn't!" Aargh's voice burst out of the small rat and off the room's stone walls. "Sorry, Dram. I didn't mean for that to come out so loudly. I'm still getting the hang of this sharing my voice thing."

"You aren't the only one," Dram said, collecting himself. "I understand that it's a secret, but the others must be told. How else will I get them to allow Tarth back onto the grounds?"

"You'll have to figure that out on your own, but you can't tell anyone about the spell."

"Don't you trust them?"

"Absolutely. It's not about trust," Aargh explained with Mnoonge's help. "Spire wizards have always been entrusted with guarding the practice of magic."

"Yes, but what does that mean? I've never understood. Why can I do magic, but someone else can't?"

"You breathe the air around you, right? You can't see it, but you know it's there. Magic is like that. It's everywhere. It always has been, but most people don't notice it. However, once a wizard invites magic in, they can communicate with it. Do you remember when you visited Mother Tree, and she gave you an acorn?"

"Of course. How could I forget? I feel badly that new students can no longer visit her. Getting an acorn from your mentor is wonderful, but it's not the same."

"No, it isn't," Aargh agreed, with a wistful tone in his voice. He'd loved Mother Tree and missed visiting her.

"You were saying?" Dram asked.

"Yes, well, from that day forward, you began speaking with trees, right? But not everyone who collects acorns can speak to trees. Why?"

"Is it because it's not about the acorn? Because I always thought it was."

"You're not wrong, but that's not the whole story. First off, there's a difference between taking something from a tree and the tree giving it to you. And although Mother Tree may have opened the door by sharing her magic, you still needed help from someone who already had access to guide you through."

Dram thought about this for a moment before saying, "Thank you for giving magic to me. It's been a wonderful gift."

"I'm not sure thanks are in order, all things considered," Mnoonge said for Aargh, "but I'm glad you came to the school. You're the kind of wizard Ardilakk Valley needs. And that's the point I'm trying to make. Deciding who can learn magic in Gemini City is an intellectual ideal. One might say it's a civilized fantasy lasting as long as magic chooses to play along. We hold no intrinsic sway over elemental magic. It doesn't pay attention to our traditions or polite rules. It's a cornered animal waiting for the chance to strike, and we can't allow that wild animal to escape. That's why I grounded wizards here and at every wizarding school on the River Wide, only allowing them to call on magic through complex spells that restrict its use. Not that the other schools pose the same threat that the Spire does, but I'm more of a belt and suspenders kind of person if you take my meaning."

"I do," Dram remarked absently, not liking the sound of what Aargh was telling him. "I must say, it kind of sounds like clipping a bird's wings."

"In a way, I guess it is, but I've never thought about it that way."

"Head Master!"

"Please, Dram. Give me a chance to explain."

"But—"

"Before I continue," Mnoonge said for Aargh, "Please, say your *C's.*"

"This isn't a time for time for school lessons, Mentor."

"Humor me, and then you can decide if I made the right decision for yourself."

Dram grudgingly closed his eyes and recited, *"Calm Your Heart; Clear Your Mind;* and above all else, *Concentration is Key."*

"I never gave the words themselves much consideration," Aargh said thoughtfully. "They were simply the mantra we recited to center ourselves before casting the One True Spell, but I'm not so sure anymore. There might be more to it. Instructions, possibly? A message or a hidden meaning, perhaps? *Clear Your Mind* makes perfect sense. That's about the most wizardly thing any of us do. *Calm Your Heart* is an interesting one, though. I always thought it complimented *Clear Your Mind,* but does it? After the breaking of Ardilakk, when Holly-Mine taught me how to speak with fire, she opened my heart to magic—allowing my emotions to speak for me instead of my mind. So, if you take them separately, one might argue that having a clear mind relates to incantations or casting spells, and having a calm heart relates to performing elemental magic. The thing is, drawing on my emotions to communicate with the elements has been both easier and harder to master than I ever imagined. Have your emotions ever run away with you? Of course, they have. In a way, that's exactly what happens when you let the magic in, and if it accumulates too much, it bursts out the same way a temper tantrum does."

"That's terrifying!" Dram said breathlessly. "I'm thankful you can control it."

"That's just it. I can't. I learned that lesson aboard the *Prosperity*. Truthfully, I'm scared of what they…I'm…capable of doing. It's why I talk to the elements. I read stories from my diary and cast my spells, more for my own benefit than anything else. They're my way of keeping control of my emotions. I mean, we know the wind has been listening to our thoughts forever. That's how the forest became wise. So, I doubt she needs my silly words to understand my feelings, but I do it anyway. And I'm going to keep doing it because it's the only way I can think of to control the magic within me."

"But what does that have to do with grounding everyone?" Dram asked.

"Because the oath siphons off wizards' excess magical energy and returns it to the Earth Mother."

"When you say magical energy, you mean emotions, don't you?"

"In a manner of speaking, yes."

"You're controlling our emotions!" Dram yelled.

"Oh no! I'd never dream of violating someone that way. Hold on a minute. I'm not doing a good job of explaining this. Let me start again. What does love feel like?"

"I don't know. Warm. Comforting. Exciting."

"I agree. It's all of those things and many more. And what does it feel like when something bad happens to someone you love?"

"Worry. Sadness. Pain…unimaginable pain."

"Exactly. And love is only one emotion of many. Feelings like that are collectors of magic, and that can be dangerous for wizards. That's why I installed a sort of pressure valve in case that happens, similar to the whistle on a steam carriage.

When the magic builds to the point where it could be dangerous, the valve opens, and it flows back into the earth."

"So, you're trying to keep wizards calm so that no one… um…explodes?" Dram reasoned.

"You certainly have a knack for stating a point rather succinctly. That's a rare gift for a wizard," Mnoonge said, chuckling again as Aargh smiled. "You can decide for yourself whether I did the right thing or not, but either way, it's our responsibility to keep control of the use of elemental magic or who knows what unspeakable horrors could befall Gemini City."

"I need some time to consider what you've said, but don't worry. I won't tell anyone. I wouldn't dream of it! Besides, where would I start?"

"I honestly have no idea, but I'll have to deal with that one day. Of that, I'm certain."

Dram sat back down again and stroked Mnoonge's silky fur. She moved closer to make it easier for him.

"Head Wizard?" Dram asked. "How will you manage?"

"I'm afraid we're in this together, my friend."

"No, I mean not having your voice."

"Sharing my voice with Mnoonge is the least of my worries," the small rat said, pointing to herself.

"Can't you ask her to give it back?"

"Unfortunately, no. We don't use magic to take what isn't already ours."

"But it is yours," Dram insisted.

"Listen to yourself. Forbidden or not, I wouldn't do it. What kind of world would it be if wizards went around taking other people's voices? Or worse! Who cares whether it was mine, to begin with? The only way I can have my voice back is if Mnoonge casts the spell."

The way Dram's face fell spoke volumes. The idea of a rat casting a spell to restore Aargh's voice was so preposterous that the best he could do was offer his sympathies. "I feel useless. I wish there were some way I could help, Head Wizard."

"I appreciate the offer. You're a wonderful person, but please stop calling me that."

"Yes, Mentor."

"Come to think of it, I guess I'm not your mentor anymore, either. It's been more than a year since I left the Spire."

"One year, twenty-six weeks," Dram corrected. "And you aren't entirely correct. I never applied to have another mentor. Besides, I've learned more visiting you than I ever learned at the Spire."

"Somehow, I doubt that," Mnoonge said for Aargh, "but I do know that you need to move on. Finish your studies and graduate. You've worked hard, and you deserve the honor. In fact, if you'd taken a new mentor, you'd be a Spire Wizard by now."

"I'm not so sure. I think I'm on the thirteen-year plan," Dram said with a wry smile. "Truthfully, graduating doesn't mean as much to me as it once did."

Aargh grasped the young wizard's leg. "This won't last forever, and when it's over, the Spire is going to need wizards who can lead rationally and act accordingly."

Dram placed his hand on top of Aargh's. "I still don't know how to address you."

"How about we start over," Mnoonge said as Aargh carefully placed her on the shelf. Then, he stood and reached out his arm. "Hello. My name is Aarghathlain. My friends call me Aargh. It's nice to meet you, Dramwitch, Wizard of the Third Circle. I am honored to call you friend."

Dram also stood, favoring his sore toe. "It is I who am honored to name you friend, Head...um, I mean...Aarghathlain," he said, gripping Aargh's arm but making sure not to tweak his hurt hand. Then, Dram slapped himself on the head with his good hand as if he'd remembered something important. "I forgot to ask. Did you read my note?"

Late Morning: The Light Hours

CHAPTER 9

THEY'RE BACK!
THE WIZARDS' UNDERGROUND

Fizzbain's pronouncement from the roof of the Spire woke the entire school, making everyone scramble from their beds. This was most certainly not something wizards usually did, even when they were late for class. However, with no way of knowing what had happened, they all did what any self-respecting wizard would do: indulged in hearsay, supposition, conjecture, and wild allegations…lots and lots of wild allegations. Fizz had unwittingly jumpstarted a rumor mill unlike anything the school had seen in generations!

High above Gemini City, the Observation Lounge's gas lamps were extinguished to make seeing out of the room's glass walls easier. Luckily, the fog had dissipated–coming and going as it pleased–so everyone had a clear view. Of what, they had no idea, but it was clear, nevertheless.

Not being small enough to weasel their way through the forest of wizard legs, as the postulants had done, or old enough to command a place along the eastern-facing windows, the novices found themselves pushed back toward the center of the room. It was apparent that they wouldn't be able to see anything from the lounge, so they headed to the ground level. At least there, they could be bossed around by the self-important Wizards of the Third Circle. Sometimes, anything was better than nothing.

A flash of light on the other side of the city caught everyone's attention, and Ovatapier, an excitable wizard who wore vivid neon green robes, yelled, "Watch out, Aargh!"

The room instantly erupted with questions about what he'd seen.

"Sorry. The explosion surprised me. A tree must have fallen. I hope everyone got out of the way. Falling trees are pretty dangerous…" he said, backing away from the window.

His explanation did nothing to assuage the room's frayed nerves. They'd been watching for hours, and people had lost patience with the situation and each other.

"Get your elbow out of my side!"

"If you'd stop pushing against me, you wouldn't keep banging into my elbow!"

"Hey, watch it! That's my foot you're stepping on."

"What's it doing where I'm standing?"

"Stop fogging up the glass!"

"Does anyone have a posy I could borrow?"

A chorus of "Put that out!" came from the entire room when a Spire Elder lit a lamp to make it easier to read the oversized words of his favorite book: *Twinkle, Twinkle Little Star, and Other Simple Spells.*

"What's happening?" the old wizard asked. "There are a lot of people in the Observation Lounge for this time of the morning."

The situation was no better down below, on the Spire grounds. Candles in the school's classrooms had been lit to dispel the charcoal twilight, but Aargh or Holly-Mine hadn't been found. Students with lanterns prowled the greenhouses and stables while faculty members ventured into Wizardwood or walked the long shoreline of Lake Hîrdehn-dûl. Everyone hoped for a sign of their safe return; well, most of them did, as not all of Tarth's retinue had followed Phrim into the forest.

As the first rays of the morning sun caught the top of the Spire, a novice yelled, "Wizard Bartlebee is back!" as she frantically pointed over her shoulder and ran toward the school.

People immediately converged on the Congregational Footpath, emerging from Wizardwood and pouring out of the administration building. Its real name was Building #1, but no one called it that. Bee, the one and only Spire Wizard who typically had his indexing finger on the pulse of things, called it *The Complaint Department* because most conversations in that wing of the school began with something like, "I don't mean to tell you how to do your job, but–"

There was so much pushing and shoving that the onslaught more resembled a crowd of fanatics trying to get to their seats in the hippodrome than a bevy of dignified wizards.

"Some help here, FizzBit!" Bartlebee yelled, trying to avoid being crushed by the throng of would-be-wizards and their teachers.

Near the back of the pack, Fizz smiled. He felt much better, having left his queasy stomach back at the clearing. Along the way, Bee had begun calling him and his familiar FizzBit, which they both liked. All wizards and familiars were a team, but Fizz considered his bond with Bit to be unique. He'd never heard of anyone being able to speak with a toad's voice before!

Fizz cracked his knuckles and stretched his neck in preparation to fulfill Bee's request, but when he opened his mouth, no words came out. Instead, he voiced a long, high-pitched trill.

"Oh, excuse me," he said, growing red in the cheeks. "Bit, we talked about this. There are times when we get to use your

voice and times when I need to use my voice. We can sit by
the lake later and sing until your heart's content, okay?"

Bit croaked.

"Later. I promise."

Bit looked pleased with his wizard's assurance that they'd
get to visit the lake.

Starting over, Fizz yelled, "Quiet!"

"Uh, Fizz?" Pud asked, pointing to the crowd. "They're already quiet."

Fizzbain glanced around, and his cheeks grew even redder
as hundreds of startled eyes stared unblinkingly at him.

Bee broke the tension by complimenting his friend. "I can't
speak for anyone else, but I think you're on to something."

Bit chirped in response.

"Thanks, Bee. The floor is yours," Fizzbain said, stepping
aside.

As the morning sun crept down the Spire, it burned off the
last vestiges of fog, and the heavy night air dissipated into a
beautiful, crisp fall day. Unfortunately, this made it easier to
see the long line of wizards stretching to the school. Bee knew
how many people lived and worked under the Spire's shadow,
but having them queued this way was overwhelming.

"I recognize that you want to hear what happened at
Aarghathlain's cottage," he began, "but you'll have to be patient. Alantus is our first concern. He's been hurt."

Everyone started talking at once, and FizzBit bellowed,
"Let the wizard speak!"

Bee shook his head, amused by FizzBit's ability to be extraordinarily loud. "Please move off the path if you can. I know
there isn't much room as the trees march right up to the path,
but you need to find a way to let the healers through. Good.
Take Lan to the infirmary and tend to his wounds as quickly
as possible."

Paladand moved to go with Alantus, but Bee stopped him. "I need you here, with us."

The young wizard didn't want to leave Lan but did as he was asked.

"Now for the hard part," Bee said, turning to the gathering crowd. "Aarghathlain and Holly-Mine are safe. Yes, it's a relief, but that's the extent of what I'm prepared to share. The rest will have to wait. We should head inside."

Sighs of relief morphed into disgruntled whispers. How much longer were they going to be kept in the dark? But no matter what anybody said, Bee's lips were sealed, which was no small feat for the typically loquacious wizard.

Once the crowd dispersed, a single wizard remained between him and the school: Brindlewise.

"Many terrible things happen in the world, friend Bartlebee. Yes, it's true. But one of the most difficult to deal with is the betrayal of a trust. That hurts us deeply. Yes, quite deeply," the sage old wizard said.

Bee knew Brindlewise would get to the point in the fullness of time, so he waited quietly for his mentor to continue.

Brindlewise sighed and said, "Come. Walk with me."

The others followed a few paces behind.

"It's bad, Brindlewise. Much worse than I imagined," Bee explained, keeping his voice low as if he didn't want anyone to overhear their conversation.

"It could have been worse," Brindlewise said in his usual calm tone. "Yes, much worse. Aargh and Holly-Mine are safe. For that, we can be thankful."

"But that's just it. There's no way to know if they're safe or not. We lost track of Tarth when he ran into the forest. Then a rat appeared, speaking with Aargh's voice."

"That does sound like Aargh," Brindlewise agreed.

"That was my assumption, too."

"What did it say?"

"It…she…Mnoonge, I mean Aargh…whatever…said the rats would take Dram to where he was. I asked to go, too, but Aargh wanted me to ensure everyone got safely back to the Spire first, especially Lan."

"That makes sense. I hope Dram is with them now. I certainly do," the old wizard added to himself.

"There is one thing I can tell you with absolute certainty. Tarth is dangerous—that and the fact he's not alone. You should have seen the look in their eyes. It was terrifying, but Paladand stood up to him. You would have been impressed. Nerah, too. They did Aargh proud."

"Let's not forget poor Alantus," Brindlewise said, lifting one eyebrow. "He did his part, too, it seems. Possibly more than his part."

"There's no question about it! Lan was the best of the bunch," Bee agreed. "Strangely, he's been afraid of pretty much everything since we were boys. I remember one time he ran away screaming when an earthworm slithered out of a pile of dirt he was holding. But there, in the woods, he stood right between Renfir and the wolf's escape. I think there's more to Lan than any of us knew."

"That might be said of all of us. No one truly knows who they are or what they're capable of until they face a difficult trial. I imagine Lan gained a level of understanding about himself, too."

"I guess, but I'm fairly confident no one expected to have to endure a lesson like that! This isn't what wizarding was supposed to be. I wish we could go back to sipping wine and deciding where to hang people's favorite paintings. Those were the good old days," Bee reminisced.

"Were they?" Brindlewise asked. "Good old days for whom? Do you mean when twelve families controlled the city's money and politics? I imagine the Master Prefect preferred it that way, too, but whether he intended to or not, his alliance with the Wizard of the Council led to the lords' demise. Or are you talking about when the school prevented girls from studying wizarding? Is that the world you want to return to, hmm?"

"No, of course not!" Bee exclaimed. "That's not what I meant. I'm thrilled with the changes in the city and at the Spire."

"Of course you are, but words matter, Bee, and you should be careful how you use them. I understand wishing for the good things, but I'd rather not be hung upside down in the square again, thank you very much. Would you?"

"Definitely not!" Bee answered emphatically. "Out with the old and in with the new. That's what I always say!"

"Oh, you do, do you?" Brindlewise asked with a twinkle in his eye.

Bee smiled.

"I'm afraid this discussion is academic anyway," Brindlewise continued. "There's no way to bring back the good or the bad."

"No question. Not after tonight!"

Stopping short, the old wizard said, "Ah, my young friend, tonight has nothing to do with it. There's never any way to relive the past. We're forced to move forward and do the best we can. You, of all people, should understand that."

Yes, Bee understood loss. "It's hard. I miss him every single day. Fuzzball was a great familiar."

"I miss my Bruue, too," Brindlewise said, patting him on the back and gesturing for them to continue along the path. "Often, moving forward can be difficult. Yes, quite difficult. The unknown is always more challenging than the known, especially for wizards who were once able to divine the future. Now, we're the same as everyone else, taking each day as it comes and hoping for the best."

"Mentor?"

"Yes?"

"How did you get so wise?" Bee asked.

"By making mistakes, my friend. Lots and lots of mistakes."

CHAPTER 10

BRING YOUR OWN ROPE
TARTHANABELLE & ODARAPHRIM

Concerned that the rising sun would reveal their location to whoever might be looking for them, Tarth led his wayward companions off the path and deeper into the forest. He doubted Paladand and his group of cronies were tracking them, but why take the chance? His plans had already been disrupted enough for one day.

It didn't take long to find a suitable place to make camp, which was a good thing, too, because it meant not having to spend another minute listening to the other wizards dragging their feet through the dry leaves that carpeted the forest floor. However, before he let his companions rest–and to make sure he had time alone–Tarth assigned everyone a task. Most of the wizards were sent to fetch things like fresh water and dry wood, but not Odaraphrim. Tarth had a special job for him that involved sneaking into the nearest sidestreet to procure food and supplies.

Once everyone left to take care of their errands, Tarth breathed a sigh of relief. Like most wizards, he preferred doing his thinking without interruption, and this particular morning, he had a lot to think about.

• • •

It didn't escape Phrim's notice that Tarth had assigned him a dangerous job. By now, word of what had happened north of the Once-Great Wall had probably spread like wildfire throughout the city. And even if it hadn't, the footman could still be ringing his bell for their group. Hopefully, Big G had his hands full with other concerns—such as chasing street urchins or tracking down a vendor who'd pulled the old bait-and-switch trick on one of their patrons. How could he have known about the advertisement posted on the sheriff's door?

> *Does your current job have you down in the dumps?*
> *Do you think you're meant for something more?*
> *Apply to be the next Gemini City Footman!*
> *Good Pay.*
> *Flexible Hours.*
> *Start Immediately.*
> *BYOR**

The fine print at the bottom of the page read:

> **Bring Your Own Rope*
> *(Knot lessons available upon request.)*

After Big G recovered from his stint in City Cell #1, sleeping off the mother of all hangovers, he realized the job wasn't as rewarding anymore. There were many reasons for this, but one, in particular, topped the list: the wizard and the little girl had slipped through his fingers not once but twice.

This shook Big G's confidence so badly that he stopped singing the walking song he'd written to pass the time. For years, he'd chanted it, stamping along Middling Street. Now, it sounded silly to him.

Grab 'em, drag 'em, tie 'n' hoist 'em.
Crack the whip and find the next one.

Big G had tried to stick it out—really, he did—but there was no way around it. Being City Footman didn't hold the same allure it once had. This led to his wizard-hoisting numbers plummeting, along with his self-esteem.

Day after day and night after night, Big G found himself aimlessly wandering the streets until his frustration finally boiled over. Stopping smack dab in the middle of the Double "U," he'd thrown his whip to the ground, did an about-face, and marched himself down to the port piers.

Should he have given the rope back first? Absolutely, but he figured it might be useful where he was headed. Mariners never passed on a length of sturdy rope, and since Big G boasted expert knot-tying skills, it wasn't long before he found himself repairing nets on the banks of the river.

Of course, Phrim didn't know any of this, and it wouldn't have mattered anyway. City Footman or no City Footman, he had no intention of hanging around…or going back to Tarth, for that matter.

That's why, as he stepped onto 910th Sidestreet, Phrim pulled the hood of his black cloak over his head and never looked back.

• • •

Tarth sat under a large stone outcropping, assessing their situation. He had many pressing issues on which to ruminate. The most important involved a surreptitious return to the Spire and the best way to move around the campus unnoticed if they managed to make it that far.

A twig snapped nearby, and he paused.

When no one appeared, he grabbed a stick, ready to defend himself. "Who's there? Show yourself!"

For a minute or two, he listened.

"I can hear you breathing," he said with a laugh.

Anyone panting that hard had to be more afraid of him than he was of them, not that he was scared, mind you. The stick was more of a precaution.

"Do as you wish. I have more pressing concerns to attend to," he announced, tossing the branch away.

A young boy emerged from behind an *Acer pseudoplantanus.* Tarth had taken note of the tree because of its unusually apt name: sycamore maple. Its flaky bark definitely made it look sick. The boy didn't appear much healthier than the tree with his threadbare pants, dirty, loose-fitting shirt, and a complete lack of foot coverings. What a mess!

"What's this?" Tarth asked. "What are you doing sneaking around?"

The boy responded so quietly that Tarth almost couldn't hear him over the rustling leaves. "I was looking for–"

"At least move your mouth so I can read your lips. What's your name?"

"Ralph."

"Good. We're getting somewhere. And why are you lurking about the woods?"

"I have a friend. She walks here sometimes. I've been trying to find her."

"Oh, a girl, is it? I'm sorry, young man. I can't help you. I haven't crossed paths with any girls meandering through the trees today."

The boy didn't move. He just stood there, awkwardly staring at his feet. It was rather disconcerting.

Losing patience, Tarth decided to break the silence, but the boy spoke first.

"You're a wizard, right?"

"Why, yes. I am, but I have no idea how that would be of help to you. I don't have any spare shoes."

Ralph wiggled his bare toes. "I don't need any shoes, thank you."

There was more awkward silence.

"Listen, young man. You need to move along. I'm quite busy and need to get back to work."

"What if you asked the trees? They might have seen her," the boy suggested. "You might even know her."

Tarth sighed. People always assumed wizards knew each other. Didn't they realize how big the school was? It didn't matter that their robes were different colors, had distinct faces, and came in many shapes and sizes. Wizards were wizards as far as most people were concerned.

"I'm sorry, lad, but trees aren't what they used to be. Most wizards can't decipher anything intelligible from them anymore. Besides, there are lots of girls at the school. They're constantly underfoot."

"But this girl is special," Ralph persisted. "Her name is Holly-Mine."

Instantly, Tarth's demeanor changed.

"Holly-Mine, you say? You're absolutely right. I do know Holly-Mine. Such a sweet thing with those big brown eyes and fancy amulet."

"That's her!" Ralph exclaimed.

"I saw her last night, as a matter of fact. Isn't that a coincidence? What are the chances?"

Ralph took a step closer. "Do you know where she is?"

"How about this? If you come with me, I'll take you to her. Does that sound like a good idea?"

"Yes, please," Ralph said, beaming with delight. He'd do anything if it meant seeing Holly-Mine again. Anything.

Tarth motioned for the boy to sit next to him on a fallen log. "Come over here. The others will be back soon. We'll make a fire and have a bite to eat. Then, we'll go find your friend."

The boy stiffened at the mention of others.

"Oh, you thought I was alone," Tarth chuckled. "I can understand that. It's not unusual to cross paths with a wizard walking in the forest. Not this time, though. I have many traveling companions."

This made Ralph even more anxious.

"Don't you worry. They're wizards, too. I sent them to fetch water and dry wood for the fire. I doubt we'll have to wait long."

Tarth didn't know that Ralph had struggled with many things over the course of his short life, but waiting wasn't one of them. It was as familiar to him as breathing or going hungry.

"I have a question for you, young Ralph. What's your opinion about magic?"

"It's wonderful," the boy answered breathlessly as if he'd been running. "Holly-Mine showed me her necklace once. I'm pretty sure it does magic."

"Yes, I've heard that…" Tarth said, his voice trailing off. "Do you want to learn a little? I'd be happy to teach you. What do you say to that?"

"Yes, please. That would be amazing."

Tarth reached into his pocket and produced an acorn. "Here," he said, offering it to the boy.

Ralph liked acorns a lot. He had a whole stash of them in a secret spot he'd found on the lower blocks behind a brick he wiggled out of a wall. But even though he wanted it, he hesitated, unsure what to do.

"It's not a trick," Tarth said, laughing. "It's a gift. Here." He took the boy's hand and placed it on his palm.

A shudder ran through Ralph's body, causing him to drop the nut. Tarth picked it up and placed it back into Ralph's hand, making sure to curl the boy's fingers around it.

The wizard continued talking, but Ralph didn't hear what he said. He was too smitten with the beautiful acorn. He didn't know why, but there was something different about it that fascinated him. Ralph was so far away when Renfir stepped out of the underbrush that he didn't notice the wolf, but Renfir definitely noticed him.

Growl!

Surprised and caught between a paralyzing fear and wanting to run for his life, Ralph yelped.

Tarth grabbed the boy's arm. "You're rather excitable, aren't you? There's no need to be afraid. Renfir is our friend. He won't hurt you."

Flinghower's long nose followed Renfir out of the forest as he struggled with the weight of several large waterskins... which he almost dropped at the sight of Ralph sitting beside Tarth.

"Ah, here's friend Flinghower. Renfir is his familiar. Do you know what a familiar is, Ralph? Mine is called Griff. He's flying overhead."

Ralph was too scared to answer. He sat there glued to the log and staring at the wolf.

"Renfir's a good boy, aren't you?" Tarth asked.

The wolf decided that neither Ralph nor Tarth was worth his time, so he padded over to a bed of leaves that had collected at the base of the rockface. He circled it a few times before retiring to lick his wounds.

"Fling, this is Ralph," Tarth continued. "He's a close friend of Holly-Mine's, but don't worry. Ralph isn't dangerous, are you, my boy? You haven't taken any oaths, right?"

Ralph didn't understand what Tarth was getting at, but he got the impression that the wizard wasn't partial to oaths, so he shook his head.

Flinghower's face changed from surprise and alarm to a devious grin as he figured out Tarth's plan.

"Wonderful," Fling agreed, sitting next to the boy and offering him a drink of water.

"Ralph is going to accompany us on our journey for a while," Tarth explained. "I've promised that we'll take him to Holly-Mine. I might teach him a little magic, too. What do you think of that?"

"It's an excellent idea and quite an honor, young Ralph," Fling said, setting the waterskins on the ground beside them. "Wizard Tarthanabelle is my mentor, too, and as far as I'm concerned, he's the greatest wizard in Ardilakk Valley."

CHAPTER 11

A PUFF OF AIR

AARGHATHLAIN

Dram ranted as he paced along the tunnel. "You haven't read my letter? Head Wiz–, Ment–, I mean…Aarghathlain, you need to read it. It's important. You have a family. You're the heir to the 13th Lord of Marble House."

"Impossible. I grew up in the forest," Mnoonge replied for Aargh with her hands on her hips. Her expression equaled how ridiculous Aargh thought Dramwitch sounded.

"I wish you'd listen to me," Dram said, still adjusting to hearing his mentor's voice coming from the small rat. "Sometimes, I think you ignore what I'm saying."

Aargh jumped as if he'd been stung by a bee. Dram was right, but it still hurt. He knew he had a bad habit of not paying close enough attention to his former apprentice. It was something he needed to work on, especially considering how valuable Dram's instincts often turned out to be. Case in point: Aargh's return to the Spire. Dram had read the situation much better than he had. Even so, leaving the past in the past didn't come easily to Aargh.

Dramwitch had a well-earned reputation for telling fantastic stories about trolls in the Western Foothills or serpents winding through the intricate waterways under the city's vast dumping grounds. One story about a siren enticing sailors toward rocky shores upset a Spire Elder so much that he'd called for the boy's expulsion. Wizards usually loved to hear a tall tale, especially if it involved fancy parties with elegant hosts, but those weren't the kind of stories in Dram's repertoire.

Interestingly, he never told the one story people wanted to hear, the one about the *Ghost Riders of the Wastes*. Everyone in Gemini City believed the dumping grounds were haunted, but Dram waved people off, saying that was ridiculous. He'd never seen a ghost. Not once. But if you wanted to hear about rats so big they could swallow you whole, he'd be happy to tell you about them.

When he first came to the school, most of his teachers wrote Dram off as a dreamer with no qualitative potential for success. Not Aargh, though. He'd always believed his mentee to be an astute pupil with an oversized imagination. Dram's stories were his way of dealing with the challenges he'd faced. Aargh assumed he'd grow out of it someday, but hopefully not too much. The world needed more out-of-the-box thinkers.

Dram had never given Aargh any reason to doubt him. He'd been a trusted student, assistant, and colleague, and it was time for Aargh to give him the respect he deserved.

"You're right. I'm sorry for not listening. I'm more than a bit on edge. Mnoonge will be quiet, and I'll pay attention to what you have to say," the small rat said.

Dram accepted Aargh's apology and continued. "Before you and your father moved to the forest—"

"Are you honestly saying I lived in Marble House?" Mnoonge blurted out. "Oh, sorry. I hadn't intended to say that out loud. I'll listen. I promise. Mnoonge's lips are sealed."

Aargh put his hands on his lap, trying to give the appearance of a model listener.

After a moment, Dram decided it was safe to proceed. "All I'm asking is for you to read my letter."

Aargh hesitantly reached into his robes. The leather-bound book he carried felt soft and warm when he touched it. And there, poking out from between its pages, was the note. Dram had slipped the envelope into his hand the day he'd returned from his time aboard the *Prosperity,* but he'd never opened it. Holly-Mine had begged him to read what it said, but he'd put it away, not wanting any more adventures. So there it had sat, tucked between the blank pages of his new journal–the one he called *Holly-Mine's Diary* with the image of Mother Tree on the front–safely forgotten.

Now, it appeared he wouldn't be able to put off reading it any longer. When Aargh lifted the book, it fell open, right to the page with the letter. Of course, it did.

The small package announced:

for Aarghathlain the Returned

He tentatively pulled it from between the book's pages. It felt heavier than it should have, and he looked at his mentee questioningly. Dram nodded, and Aargh continued.

As he removed the note from the envelope, a locket attached to a delicate chain fell into his hand. Engraved on its soft gold face was the letter *A.* Curious.

Sticking his thumb between the folded pages, he opened the accompanying letter.

Dear Head Wizard,
I must begin this letter with an apology. I would never have opened the locket had I known what it contained. We

couldn't find you, so I visited Marble House to search for clues. That's where I came across the contents of this envelope. The locket was carefully wrapped in cloth and placed in a small box. I'm sorry, but the box fell apart when I opened it, aged as it was, and not well-crafted.

It contains a message from your mother. I never meant to intrude, but I had to listen to it. I deeply regret that decision and understand if you're angry with me. I sincerely hope you can forgive me.

Your Devoted Mentee,
Dramwitch

"What do you mean, listen to it?" Mnoonge asked, cocking an eyebrow.

Dram had Aargh's attention.

"You'd better find out for yourself," he said, taking Holly-Mine's hand and leading her around the corner to give Aargh privacy.

Also wanting to give Aargh some space, Mnoonge followed Dram, but at a distance. The wizard was still limping, and she didn't want to risk being trodden on.

Aargh rubbed a finger over the *A*. Could it be true? Did this charm contain a message from his mother? It was possible. He'd imbued items with magical properties, but, as far as he knew, only two people besides himself had discovered magic: the Wizard of the Council and possibly his mentor, Aldenthwaine…but why not more? What if the ability to cast elemental magic had always existed in Ardilakk Valley? He didn't know.

Also, with enough time and practice, even the Spire Wizards could concoct a spell to record a message and save it in an item. Though, the challenges of such a task would probably have discouraged them from trying. Only healers had created spells of that complexity, and that was because they pooled their resources.

Most incantations automated simple tasks that could just as easily have been performed with common tools such as an abacus or a little extra practice or time. Then again, why practice if you could say a few words and let magic do it for you? It wasn't hard to comprehend the logic in that.

Aargh turned his attention back to the locket. "It might be a trick," he thought, but that was a thinly veiled attempt to avoid opening it.

The truth was, he wanted to see inside. In fact, he was desperate to find out what Dram had discovered. But another part of him wanted to cast it into the water and watch it get swept away to the river and ocean beyond.

"If Holly-Mine were here, she'd tell me to stop worrying about it and open it. She'd be right, too," he thought.

"Don't be afraid, Papa," a gentle voice spoke in his ears.

"I'll try not to be, Sweet Girl."

Aargh pressed his fingernail against the locket's clasp. There was a soft click, and the two halves parted.

Nothing.

If he could have hmphed, he would have. Instead, he settled for glaring disapprovingly. Dram must have been imagining things again. Dignified Wizards of the Third Circle shouldn't lie about this kind of thing. Other things, maybe, but not this. He'd have to talk to his ex-mentee about it.

As Aargh moved to put the locket back into the envelope, it fell open the rest of the way. A pen drawing of a man dressed in upper lord's robes stared at him from the left side, and on the right, a beautiful woman smiled at him.

A puff of air tickled his nose, and a strained voice spoke...

My son, I wish I could be there for you, but alas, it is not to be. I would have held you in my arms, kissed your bruises when you fell, and helped you understand it isn't so bad when the light grows dim. Never forget that the light will shine again, even in your darkest moments. I promise.

Your father is going to take you away. Although Marble House is all you have ever known, you must leave now and never return. There are dangers here that threaten our world. May you both find a way to put this behind you. Be happy, my beautiful boy. I love you.

• • •

Outside the Meeting Place, Holly-Mine waited patiently for her father, twiddling her thumbs and tying (and re-tying) her shoes.

Dramwitch, on the other hand, was as nervous as a long-tailed cat in a room full of rocking chairs! No matter how many times Holly-Mine told him to sit, seconds later, he was on his feet again, pacing back and forth.

Then there was Mnoonge. Holly-Mine watched her closely. The spell Aargh had cast on the rat troubled her. It wasn't that she didn't trust Mnoonge, but she didn't believe her father fully understood the magnitude of his request.

"Hmph," Mnoonge said aloud, knitting her eyebrows.

"Excuse me?" Holly-Mine asked in her mind.

"Oh, nothing," Mnoonge responded using her rat voice.

But Holly-Mine knew it wasn't nothing. In fact, it was definitely something.

As if on cue, Mnoonge confirmed Holly-Mine's suspicions when she called out, "Wait! Please, don't go!" and immediately cupped her hands over her mouth.

She'd let the cat out of the bag this time, as people say. No rat ever said that, as cats were not something rats enjoyed contemplating as a general rule.

Holly-Mine had the corroboration she needed. If Mnoonge heard and spoke Aargh's inner thoughts without his direction, her father had given the rat more than his voice. She'd have to think about this more when she had the time.

• • •

"Wait! Don't go!" Aargh yelled in his mind, but his mother didn't answer. "I need you. Please, come back."

Frantically, he opened the locket again, desperately hoping for her to say more, but the message remained the same. He was so fixated on it that he didn't hear Holly-Mine join him.

"I know it's hard, Papa, but it's time to go. You've found her, and that's special. No one can take that away from you."

Aargh used his sleeve to wipe away the sweat on his face and followed Holly-Mine back to the others.

• • •

Mnoonge sensed Aargh's love for Holly-Mine and his need to learn more about his family, but her connection didn't stop there. Aargh carried worries filled with regrets, concerns, and guilt greater than anyone realized.

"Holly-Mine probably knows," Mnoonge reflected, "but if she does, she isn't letting on."

It felt unfair to be saddled with his troubles. Shouldering Aargh's conscience hadn't been part of the bargain. Mnoonge wondered if Wrudge had felt this way, too. If he did, he'd never mentioned it.

Was she being selfish? No. She had a right to feel however she pleased, but there was no denying the importance of keeping elemental magic from falling into the wrong hands. Ultimately, she decided the most appropriate course of action was to do her part. "Who knows, maybe I'll be able to sort out this mess."

To relax, she intoned the affirmation her mother had taught her. "No one should judge me by my size. I may be small, but I am mighty!"

• • •

As Holly-Mine and Aargh rounded the corner, a familiar voice greeted them.

"Hello, Aarghathlain. It's nice to see you again. I don't believe we've been formally introduced. My name is Gerald, former Head Butler of Marble House. Pleased to meet you."

Holly-Mine gasped and ran to the outlandishly dressed man.

"I hoped you'd come!" she said excitedly.

"I would never have found you without this clever rat's assistance. Do you know him?"

"Of course," Holly-Mine said, addressing the neatly coiffed rat. "Hello, Parsifal. Thank you for helping Uncle Gerald, as I asked."

"It was my pleasure," Parsifal responded, bowing low.

Holly-Mine curtsied, the way the ladies used to do at fancy dress parties in the high houses, and giggled.

"I must be going. I have things to attend to," the rat said, bowing again, but Mnoonge caught his eye. "Mnoonge, how may I be of service?"

"Will you be passing into the forest?" she responded with a much higher-pitched squeak than usual.

"I wasn't planning to, but I will if I must," he responded, keeping his voice low.

"No, no. I don't want to trouble you," she said, looking away.

"Don't worry," Parsifal said, touching her hand. "I'm sure he's safe. Last I heard, Buck was standing watch. I'll send word if I hear anything."

"Thank you."

Parsifal saluted and scurried off.

Mnoonge's embarrassment didn't go unnoticed, so they did their best to keep the conversation going.

Holly-Mine was quickest off the mark. "You've changed your clothes, Uncle Gerald. They're wonderful!"

The butler's austere black suit had been replaced with the most flamboyant combination of colors any of them had ever seen. But no matter how ridiculous his clothes appeared, he still carried an undeniable air of authority wherever he went.

"I'm glad they meet with your approval," the slender man said, lifting her up to hug her properly. "My, you've grown! You're almost as tall as your father, but I guess that's what girls do. They don't stay little for long."

Holly-Mine beamed as she squeezed harder.

"Not too hard. I'm liable to break," Gerald said with a strained voice.

She laughed in that particular way that fills hearts with joy. "No, you won't, Uncle Gerald! Don't be silly."

Silly? No one had ever accused him of being that before, but if it made Holly-Mine happy, he'd do his best to add it to his repertoire.

Aargh hadn't seen TTM since the flood of Geminians washed him away the night of the Great Fire, but it was as if they'd never been apart. The former head butler had risked everything for Holly-Mine, and for that, Aargh would be for-ever grateful.

"Dramwitch told me about Marble House," the ex-butler explained. "I'm sure you'll want to examine the ruins your-self, and, with your permission, I'll accompany you. I may be of service, having lived there for many years."

"Me too...I mean, thank you, Gerald. That would be most helpful," Aargh's voice wafted up from the tunnel's stone floor.

Gerald's eyebrow raised a little, and he asked, "And who is this speaking with your voice? You're not the rat who used to accompany Aarghathlain on his journeys."

"This is Mnoonge, and as you have already figured out, I've lent her my voice."

Gerald could tell by Aargh's reaction that Wrudge was no longer with him, and he apologized.

Aargh raised a hand.

Mnoonge raised her hand, too. This didn't escape both Holly-Mine's and Gerald's notice.

"Dearest Wrudge used his magic to help save me and the forest from the Great Fire. Without his sacrifice, the valley would have been lost. We're sad but also grateful to have had him in our lives."

Gerald felt a pang of remorse for the contempt he'd ex-pressed at the rat when they'd met on the steps of Marble House. At the time, he didn't understand the greatness of the Underoof Collective, but that had changed at the *Battle for Middling Street,* as he called it. There, the magical world of rats had been revealed to him, and Aargh had defeated the Wizard of the Council. It was one of his favorite stories to tell. Children loved the part when the rats glowed!

"Pleased to meet you, Mnoonge," he said, bending over and taking her hand gently between his thumb and indexing finger. "And what did you mean by *me too*, Aarghathlain?"

"Nothing gets by you, does it?" Mnoonge observed, speaking for the wizard.

"I do my best. It was advice my father gave me long ago. A trifle, really, but I keep his words close. *If you learn nothing else from me, learn this,* he said. *To be the best you can be, you must pay attention to every detail.*"

"Wise words from a wise man," Mnoonge said. "And I can attest to your achievements. Marble House was Gemini City's *pièce de résistance*. There can be no doubt about that. Not even Diamond Hall was better cared for. I speak from experience, having visited many of Upper Middling Street's halls in their heyday."

The small rat was the one speaking, but she'd have to take Aargh's word for it. She'd never visited the former high homes herself. Those homes were risky places for rats, and she preferred the lower blocks.

"That's kind of you to say, Aarghathlain. I can't say my time there was happy. My life is much better now if one can say such a thing after everything that has happened."

"No one will begrudge you that, I promise," Mnoonge said. "At least no one here. We understand."

Holly-Mine took Gerald's hand and put it around her shoulder.

"To answer your question," Mnoonge continued. "It seems I was born in Marble House to the 13th lord."

"Good grief," Gerald blurted, showing more emotion than Aargh had ever seen from the man. "You mean to say you're Bardelthlain's baby? I used to watch you sleep at night and bring you warm bottles of milk from the kitchen." He paused before continuing. "Wait a minute. Does that mean the professor's maps were of your new home in the forest? Astonishing."

"Gerald, are you saying you knew my father?" Mnoonge asked, getting as excited as Aargh.

"Absolutely. He was a great man. The staff was sorry when he left. If I may be so bold, I'd say he was the last great lord of Gemini City."

Aargh pulled out the locket, fumbling it in his excitement.

Holly-Mine held her father's hands to keep them from shaking. When that didn't work, she took the locket from him. "I'll show Uncle Gerald for you."

When she opened it, they all listened in amazement.

"Yes, that's your mother's voice," Gerald confirmed, "and the pictures are of your mother and father."

Unable to contain himself, Aargh asked a string of questions with Mnoonge's help, but Gerald stopped him.

"We have much to talk about. I hope it's not too forward of me to say, but I can tell you are tired. Why don't we find a seat, and I'll answer your questions as best I can? But please remember, it happened many years ago."

They moved into The Meeting Place and sat on the long stone bench that circled the centermost area of the space. It was too low for Gerald, but he made do.

"When we're done, we'll visit the ruins of Marble House and try to find more answers there," he suggested. "Until then, what would you like to know?"

CHAPTER 12

CALM BEFORE THE STORM
THE WIZARDS' UNDERGROUND

"Why don't we sit awhile," Brindlewise suggested.

"I love that idea," Bee said, jumping at the chance to delay their arrival at the school.

Looking ahead, he saw the complex's grand entrance and sculpture gardens framed by the rows of pine trees that grew along both sides of the Congregational Footpath. To Bee, it seemed silly to call it a path. It was perfectly straight, and the forty-five-degree diagonal line it cut through the trees would have joined the square's non-adjacent vertices if the school wasn't in the way.[4]

Of course, the footpath's name and angle were purely symbolic, as two blocks were situated between the school and the city's seat of governance. Speaking in practical terms, the Congregational Footpath's purpose was to provide a grand promenade for representatives invited to school functions. Many a Master Prefect had been led down that path on their way to the Wizards' Feast.

It had always looked odd to Bee, dividing Wizardwood the way it did, but he understood why it had been built. Politics

---

[4] Most wizards have no idea what non-adjacent vertices are. They only describe the Congregational Footpath in this way to sound knowledgeable. Engineering students, however, understand exactly what that means, having studied the road as a practical application of the calculations they work on in class. In layperson's terms, the path and the northeastern block's corner point directly toward the Congregational House like an arrow. Hence its name.

were as much a part of life in Gemini City as stonecutting and metallurgy. And paying homage to the lords of old fell under the column labeled *necessity* more than any actual sign of respect.

Garthelwaite and the others hung back as long as possible before finding a place to sit. They didn't want to intrude on Bee and Brindlewise's discussion and weren't particularly interested in rehashing the previous night's events.

"This is the calm before the storm," Pud said under his breath, trying to distract himself by watching puffy white clouds creep across the sky.

Tassior, known to most people as *The Gentle Wizard*, heard Pud and said, "It's okay. Don't worry. We'll get through this." His kind expression, coupled with the relaxing pale blue robes he wore, generally helped soothe people's nerves, but this type of thing didn't have an effect on Pud.

"We'll see," Pud muttered, pulling his auburn robes tighter around him. He wasn't sure anything would be okay after what Tarth had done to Aargh's house.

Paladand remained too focused on Lan's injury to pay attention to what his companions were doing. Legs were tricky to heal. Even when they showed no sign of malady, blood clots might lurk deep in their veins, caused by the trauma or by keeping them still for too long.

Afynn occupied his racing mind by scribbling furiously in the gravel, calculating the combustion rate of pulverized coal. He often worked on equations comparing different types of fuels as part of a consortium of concerned wizards and citizens trying to demonstrate the value of using more sustainable energy sources. Much to their frustration, the Norters' arrival had thrown a major kink in their plans.

The *Clean Air and Water Consortium* had just announced a public demonstration of how Geminians could harness the power of the Underground Falls when the interlopers had swooped in and built a blockade around it.

Now, they had no choice but to seek other options. Wind and the River Wide topped the list. Neither were as dependable as the Underground River, but beggars couldn't be choosers—not that the saying made much sense to Afynn's logical engineering mind. Everyone had the right to choose.

Several paces away, Illbrahss gave his golden retriever, Goldie, a snuggle before setting his viola case on the ground next to them. He never went anywhere without Ginny—a generous gift from his late mentor. Her case was a simple affair, consisting of a wooden box covered in thick burlap. Most people wouldn't have given it a second glance, never realizing it concealed a treasure beyond compare.

Generations before, the viola had been crafted by the famed luthiers of Caron-em, where it's said the oldest groves of spruce, willow, and maple trees grow on the River Wide. The instruments fashioned from that wood were revered as works of art, second to none, and Ginny was no exception.

Illbrahss undid the ties holding the burlap to the case, respectfully moving it aside. One after another, he pushed a series of buttons, each releasing spring-loaded gears that whirred as they slid delicate brass latches out of their clasps. Inside the case, a dark blue satin and velvet blanket covered the instrument.

He lifted it and grinned. "Hello, Ginny. Would you like to come out to play?"

As if in answer to his question, the wind caught the instrument's strings, resonating in perfect intervals.

The interior of the case's felt-lined lid held two bows. After flipping a small clip, he slid the lower one out of its holder,

giving its screw a few turns. When the bow's tension felt
right, Illbrahss drew it along a small sticky block. The horse
hair wouldn't grip the strings without the rosin, so he took
this job seriously.

When everything was ready, he played.

The wizards listened as Ginny's rich tones weaved between
the tall pine trees surrounding them. Its melancholic sound
evoked a deep sadness that touched their hearts, and Goldie
sat up to howl along.

"Illbrahss!" Onaveris shouted, interrupting the mournful
tune. "Haven't we had enough sadness for one day? Play
something happier!"

"I see what you mean," the musician said, lowering his instrument. "It's just that viola has such a warm sound. It's perfect for playing pretty melodies."

"Pretty might be a stretch," Pud grumbled. "Depressing
would be more appropriate."

"What's that song called, anyway?" O asked.

"Melody. Songs are sung," Illbrahss corrected.

"Whatever! What's the name of that mel-o-dy you were
playing?"

"*The Death of the Maiden,* by–"

A chorus of groans cut Illbrahss off, and the explanation
died on his lips.

Bee heard the commotion and did his best to defuse the
situation before anyone's feelings got hurt. "That's enough
music for now, Ill. How about you play us a tune after dinner."

"I'd be happy to. What about something more upbeat?
Um…*Haul Away My Lads, My Lads* is a good one! It's an old
sea chantey about the wreck of the *Favorite.*"

"Oh yeah, that sounds awesome," O said, kicking a stone
across the path.

"It's very dramatic!" Illbrahss explained. "It's the dead of winter, and there's a terrible storm. The schooner crashes into the rocks, and, in the morning, the frozen crew is found washed ashore, lashed to pieces of the ship."

Several people complained at once, and the musician decided to quit while he was ahead.

"There are plenty of other melodies to choose from," he said, wiping Ginny's strings and returning her to the case.

After a long pause in the conversation, Bee got up. "I'm feeling a little better. I guess it's time to face whatever awaits us at the school."

"If you're sure?" Brindlewise asked, "Then let's continue the journey home."

The Spire's famous sculpture gardens were directly between the wizards and the school. Although Bee couldn't see them in their entirety, he knew they stretched to the corners of Building #1. They served two purposes: to immortalize the head wizards who'd led the school throughout the ages and impress visiting dignitaries. They succeeded on both counts.

As Bee drifted between the statues towering over the garden, he wondered if his friend would be included there someday. He tried to imagine a statue of Aargh nestled among the Spire's former head wizards, holding his diary with Wrudge and Holly-Mine by his side. Oh, and he couldn't forget Guildebrande.

Although he couldn't answer whether or not Aargh would be included in the memorial, Bee knew one thing for certain: his friend's statue would be much shorter than the others. This tickled the wizard, and he chuckled.

"Something funny?" Brindlewise asked.

"No, not really. I'm a bit punchy."

"It's been a difficult day for everyone. Yes, it has."

"Actually, I was wondering if Aargh might be remembered here, in the garden. He was head wizard, after all."

"Not any time soon, I'm afraid, and not in the current climate," Brindlewise said.

They stopped in front of an imposing statue of former Head Wizard Aldenthwaine. It stood about halfway through the garden, quite near the Footpath. Aldenthwaine had one hand raised, and the other held a spellbook.

"We could use his help," Bee mumbled.

"Possibly," Brindlewise said, scrutinizing the statue. "He was a great wizard. I've never heard anyone dispute that, but I've always wondered…" In an uncharacteristically dramatic change, he continued, "I must warn you: don't expect a hero's welcome."

"I never expected that, but what are you implying?" Bee asked, caught off guard by the sudden shift in the conversation.

"Do you think it went unnoticed who was missing from the Spire? You're forgetting that Aargh has been absent from the school for a long time, and Tarth has many supporters here. Rumors have been flying about what happened, and once a rumor has been repeated enough times, it often becomes *fact* whether it's true or not. You may find it hard to sway those who have already made up their minds."

Hearing this, Garthelwaite protested, dropping the pretense that he wasn't listening to Bee and Brindlewise's conversation. "But they have no idea what happened. They weren't there!"

"When has knowing the truth ever gotten in the way of people believing whatever they want? You're smarter than that, Garth. You all are," Brindlewise said, turning around. "Besides, facts can be twisted. If a person has a mind to, they can fabricate all manner of scenarios to support their position."

Incensed, Paladand chimed in. "Once we tell them what happened, they won't be able to ignore the truth. Tarth nearly killed Aargh and Holly-Mine!"

"Shh," Brindlewise admonished. "Absolutely not. That's the last thing any of you will do. If you know what's good for you and the Spire, you'll keep your mouths shut. The school is already divided. Mark my words: Tarth will turn out to be the one who was wronged."

"You've got to be kidding," Bee said. "That's ridiculous!"

But Brindlewise wasn't known for kidding, and he'd never been ridiculous a day in his life. Bartlebee knew this, but he still couldn't help himself. Bee tended to wear his emotions on his sleeve more than most wizards.

"Trust an old wizard," his mentor said. "Situations are rarely as simple as they appear or people pretend. It's in our best interest not to tell anyone Tarth was involved. There's time for that later."

Bee fumed. He looked to his friends for support, but they stared blankly back at him. No one could fault Brindlewise's logic.

Pud shrugged his shoulders and walked toward the school, and the rest followed suit. The group didn't make it far before Chartlehill, *Steward to the Wizards Regent*, stopped them.

"Wizard Bartlebee, you are summoned to the Observation Lounge, where you will meet with the Board," he announced.

He was an unassuming wizard who wore thoroughly nondescript beige-ish robes (Bee honestly couldn't tell what color they were), but the haughty air Chartlehill carried with him grated on Bee's nerves.

"Wait. The regents want to meet with me? We just got back. How did they get here so quickly?"

The steward stared down his nose at such a ridiculous insinuation. "They had already convened on other business, of course. The matter of the school's head wizard, to be precise. The timing of your return is merely a coincidence."

Onaveris, who'd been not-so-quietly contemplating the exchange, said, "What do they need to meet about that for? It's no secret who they want to be head wizard."

Chartlehill shot a sideways glance in his direction, and Pud elbowed him in the side. O took the hint and stepped behind Illbrahss, out of the line of fire.

Bee didn't care why the regents were meeting. They'd have an audience for their story, which was all that mattered. Even if they couldn't tell anyone about Tarth, they had plenty of other news to relate. "This is fantastic. Come on. Let's go!" he said.

Steward Chartlehill raised his palm, stopping Bee in his tracks. "The invitation is for you, Bartlebee. The rest of you are to wait in the dormitory."

Bee protested, but Brindlewise calmly said, "Do as instructed. I'll accompany you in the uplifter if that's acceptable to you, Steward?"

"You may," Chartlehill said, inclining his head.

Brindlewise motioned for the others to wait in their rooms, saying, "Not a word to anyone."

"I don't suppose we have time to grab a snack on the way?" Bartlebee asked, but Chartlehill kept walking toward the school. "Of course not. I'll try to keep my stomach from protesting too much."

School hallways are funny things. They appear to go on forever—the exit at the end looking like it's moving away from you as you walk toward it. Teachers try to soften the corridors' severe institutional look by decorating their doors, but it never helps. Dark or light, painted white or colorful colors, it's easy to get lost in the maze of sameness. If a person returns later in life, they might experience a pang of nostalgia, regret, or even anxiety, but those vague emotions never rise to the level of the stress brought on by adulthood.

That being said, one sensation associated with school hallways never changes: the feeling of loneliness when they're empty. There's no place more full of life when school is in session, but when school's out, hallways become desolate places devoid of any semblance of humanity.

Bartlebee felt isolated and alone as they walked through The Complaint Department toward the rotunda. Other than Brindlewise and Chartlehill standing by his side, the stone-walled hallway was lifeless. Abandoned. Dead.

In more carefree times, postulants ran from class to class, annoying the heck out of the stoic Spire Elders. But those faded images were a far cry from what the school looked like these days. Rarely did anyone crack a smile. Students spent their free time whispering in corners and giving anyone who passed furtive glances. It was as if every conversation contained a secret only to be shared with trusted confidants. Bee wanted to be out of that hallway so badly that Brindlewise had to stop him from running ahead.

Once they reached the rotunda, he nervously waited for the uplifter to arrive. Bee clenched his fists as he stepped back, letting Chartlehill and Brindlewise enter first. He was happy to do this for his mentor, but he resented having to show deference to the steward. They'd never been friends, but after Chartlehill turned him in for helping classmates with their homework back when they were novices, their relationship had taken a decidedly downward turn. It wasn't as if Bee had cheated. His friends simply needed help with their lessons. That's all.

The three wizards stood silently as they were ferried skyward toward the Observation Lounge. It didn't take more than a few minutes, but the ride felt interminable to Bartlebee. When they emerged into the room, he saw several tables placed in a semicircle surrounding a single metal chair.

The uplifter's door opened with a resonant clang.

"Thank you for accompanying us, Brindlewise, Elder of the Spire. You may go," Chartlehill said, stepping into the room. "Wizard Bartlebee, if you would please follow me."

Brindlewise made eye contact with Bee and whispered, "Remember what I told you. Not a word."

Bee opened his mouth to protest but shut it again. Instead, he nodded, turned, and dragged his feet over to the lonely chair that had been set out for him. Before sitting down, he grabbed it and swung it around.

Caged by the uplifter, Brindlewise slipped below the floor, leaving Bee alone with the venerable Wizards Regent.

CHAPTER 13

THERE MAY NOT BE ONE TRUE ROOT
RATS & AARGHATHLAIN

Wrulde sat on the stone ring that ran around The Meeting Place in total disbelief. He'd done it. He'd returned to the Underoof before Buck! No one else would have considered that much of an accomplishment, but Wrulde did. Why? Because it was the first time he'd beaten Buck at anything. He'd even given Wizard Aarghathlain his report first, meaning he'd won twice in a single day! If anyone had told him this day would come, he'd have laughed out loud.

This called for a celebration.

First, he craned his head to make sure no one was watching. Then, he raised his hands, swished his waist, and did a little dance, finishing with a twirl and a bow.

"I could get used to this," he said, tamping down imaginary cheers with his hands.

Though rats of the Underoof Collective usually viewed themselves as equals–especially where cleverness was concerned–it didn't mean they were the same. Individual rats had strengths and weaknesses, the same as people. And where strengths were concerned, Wrulde was not well-endowed.

Gnawing?

No contest. Buck won every time.

Digging?

Let's say Buck never came in second.

Running?

Possibly, if Wrulde could stop coughing, and his legs didn't hurt so much.

Squeezing?

Wrulde did have Buck on size, but it didn't matter. Buck always managed to squish himself into and out of tight situations with far greater agility.

It wasn't a problem, though. Buck never held this against him. Instead, the bigger rat would bump Wrulde and say, "Better luck next time, old chum!" and they'd sniff out a quick snack before dinner.

Therefore, Wrulde's excitement wasn't surprising, but Buck wasn't far behind.

Back at the tunnel entrance, Buck hadn't seen hide nor hair of Tarth, but he'd refused to leave his post until relief arrived. One concept he thoroughly understood was protocol. He called it running a tight ship, but really, it meant no rat under his command shirked their duties…not ever, including himself. This had delayed his return, which left room for Wrulde's tiny triumph, but his friend's celebration was short-lived.

Upon arriving in The Meeting Place, Wrulde grabbed Buck by the hand and led him to an out-of-the-way corner. Buck protested, but Wrulde shushed him. No one had ever shushed him before, but after seeing Aarghathlain shuffle in, followed by Mnoonge, Holly-Mine, Dram, and Gerald, he was struck dumb anyway, so he let it slide.

The rats watched as Aargh milled around the space, mumbling to himself. They couldn't hear what he said, but the conversation must have been weighty because his shoulders were hunched over, and he had deep, dark circles under his eyes.

• • •

Aargh was tired. Not the *it's been a long day, and it's time to settle in for a good night's sleep* kind of tired, but the bone-weary exhaustion brought on by a maelstrom of events swirling out of control. Each new revelation pulled him farther into the abyss until he lost hope of clawing his way out again. Wrulde's report about Lan's safe return to the Spire had briefly made him feel better, but Aargh had plenty of other worries to take up the slack.

The worst part was that no one could convince him to take a rest. He was the closest he'd ever come to learning the truth about his past, and he steadfastly refused to stop. Aargh had spent years roaming Gemini City's streets, sidestreets, dark alleyways, and the waterfront, fulfilling his duties as *Spire Historian* and *Keeper of the General Generations*, but in all that time, he'd never heard the slightest whisper about his family— not one word. It was as if a spell had been cast over Ardilakk Valley to hide the past from him.

"Papa?" Holly-Mine asked. "Please take a rest. Not long. Just for a little while."

"I can't," Mnoonge answered for him. "Dram and Gerald have done what I couldn't: they found my family. When I remembered my father and the farm, that was a big break-through. I thought I was finally getting close, but…"

Dram took a breath as if to say something, but Mnoonge beat him to it, and Aargh sounded different. Almost angry.

"There's much more to my story, and I must find the truth. Don't you understand? For whatever reason, my past was hidden from me."

"Of course, Papa," Holly-Mine said with her usual kindness, "but you're tired. If you don't rest, you'll make yourself sick. I promise this will still be here tomorrow."

To everyone's surprise, Aargh launched himself off the bench he'd sat down on with such force that the air moved. "Tomorrow? Isn't a lifetime of waiting long enough? Why must I wait another day?"

The sound of Aargh's voice reverberated through the tunnels, and the ever-constant motion of the Underoof ceased. Rats aren't known for being still, so the halting of their movement made everyone's stomach lurch.

Mnoonge also sprang to her feet, shocking Wrulde and Buck. They watched as she scrambled onto a ledge to be closer to Aargh.

Once on top, she animatedly gestured with her hands, pacing with the wizard, saying, "Can you tell me what dangers my mother is warning me about, Holly-Mine? No? Of course not! No one knows! How could you?"

The image of Aargh and Mnoonge mimicking each other's movements was surreal—his emotions pouring out like the River Underground, bursting from the highland cliffs after the winter thaw.

"What about you, Gerald?" Mnoonge bellowed, speaking for the wizard. "Why did my father renounce his lordship and whisk me away to the forest? What were we supposedly putting behind us? And why did he leave everything he'd worked so hard to achieve, living in a high house as one of the city's upper lords? It doesn't make sense!"

"I'm sorry, Aarghathlain. I was only a boy, and besides, that was above my—" Gerald started to say, but Aargh had already begun interrogating Dram.

"How about the fact that my mother performed magic, Dram? In any of your conversations with trees, did you ever hear about women performing magic in Gemini City? Have you? Anyone?" He wheeled around, and Mnoonge yelled, "Can anyone explain what happened to my mother?"

Aargh slammed his hand against the wall, and a wave of energy traveled out in every direction. It warped the stone walls as it raced down the Underoof's many passageways, and the rats of the Mischief scurried away to safety. Dram, Gerald, and Holly-Mine stood there, shocked into silence by Aargh's outburst.

Buck, who'd never been scared a day in his life, inched closer to Wrulde, exchanging a glance as if to say, *We're out of our depth, old friend, aren't we?*

To their dismay, Aargh hadn't finished.

"I'm waiting? Can any of you tell me what's going on?" Mnoonge howled. "My own history has abandoned me. Me, *Aarghathlain the Not-So-Great! Wizard of the Blah, Blah, Blah. Historian and Keeper of Nothing*, and *ROOT READER...Root Reader...root reader...*"

As quickly as it had come, Aargh's rage spilled out of him like water through a downspout, splashing onto the river stones placed below it to prevent the garden path from eroding.

Mnoonge put a hand out to steady herself.

"I've got you, wee Mnoonge," Buck said, scuttling over to her. He took the rat's tiny hand and guided her to the floor.

"Thank you, Buck," she squeaked. "I believe I got a little overwhelmed."

"With good reason. You've got quite a wizard there."

A small part of Mnoonge wondered what she'd gotten herself into, but she pushed the thought away. She'd sworn to do her duty, and she would...later...after a short rest.

"I'll stay with you," Buck whispered, stroking her fur.

"Mmm," the small rat said, closing her eyes. "That's nice."

Embarrassed at losing control of his magic, Aargh hung his head. He risked a peek at his companions and immediately wished he hadn't. He'd given Dram the perfect demonstration of how tenuous his control over the magic he wielded was, and his apprentice was trembling uncontrollably from head to toe. Next to him, Gerald's mouth opened and closed as he tried to speak, but no sound came out. Then, there was Holly-Mine.

She deserved better. Fathers weren't supposed to act that way toward their daughters. He knew this, but he hadn't been able to stop. Elemental magic has a mind of its own, and, similar to emotions, it longs to be in control. It was Aargh's responsibility never to let that happen, and he'd failed miserably.

"Papa, we were only trying to help," she explained, bursting into tears and running down one of the many tunnels that fanned out from The Meeting Place.

The arcing stone amplified her sobs, and Aargh cringed. He ran after her, but Holly-Mine was much quicker than him, and he was forced to watch her disappear into the gloom. Hopelessly lost in every way, he leaned against the wall, slowly letting himself slide down until he reached the ledge. He wondered if the makers of the tunnels had put the shelf there for this purpose: for dejected fathers who'd yelled at their daughters.

"Pull yourself together, Aargh," he thought. "You need to put this right."

In an effort to calm himself, he focused on the trickling runoff flowing by his feet. When it slapped the stones, it reminded him of the *Prosperity*. He'd often listened to the river play against the hull on calm nights. It relaxed him, and his heart gradually stopped thumping in his chest.

Screwing up his courage, he reached out to Holly-Mine with his mind. "Sweet Girl?"

She didn't respond, but Aargh sensed her presence. Holly-Mine had tucked herself under a staircase. This wasn't the first time she'd run away and hidden this way, as there were few safe havens for people living on the streets, but Aargh could tell she was heartbroken that it had happened again.

"I'm sorry. It was wrong of me to yell. Can you forgive me? I don't know what came over me."

But that wasn't strictly true. He knew what had happened. He'd lost control. Why hadn't he listened to her and taken a quick nap to regain his strength? Blinded by an uncontrollable desire to learn about the past, he'd foolishly ignored the warning signs of his exhaustion. By doing so, he'd put them at risk, which was utterly unacceptable. *Aarghathlain, Steward of the Elements*, had been trusted by the Earth Mother to watch over the world's magic. It was his responsibility never to forget that. Not ever. Not even for an instant.

More importantly, he shouldered the mantle of parenthood, which brought with it greater responsibilities one should never ignore.

"You're right. I need to rest," Aargh thought, knowing Holly-Mine could hear him. "It wouldn't be wise to go out during the day anyway. If you don't mind, I'll speak with Gerald for a short while and then take a nap."

When Holly-Mine didn't respond, Aargh realized she needed space.

They'd moved lower in the tunnel system, so he settled into a more comfortable position and unsheathed Guildebrande to dispel the darkness. He also pulled out *Holly-Mine's Diary*. The golden image embossed on the cover shimmered in Guildebrande's light. It made Mother Tree's leaves appear to move as if they were blowing in the wind, and there, at her trunk, was trusty Wrudge.

"I'm sorry, my old friend," Aargh apologized to the image of his former familiar. "I never told you how much you meant to me. I've been trying to do better, but I fear I've slipped off the branch this time…possibly right out of the tree! I should have seen this coming. You would have. That was your specialty, wasn't it–sizing things up and figuring out what to do? Many a situation would have turned out differently if you hadn't been there to help me. If only you were here now…"

Aargh closed his eyes and sat quietly, listening to the water.

"I miss you. You were always supposed to be by my side. I mean, that's the way of things, right? Wizards and their familiars traveling the world of magic together? The possibility of losing you never crossed my mind. Ardilakk Valley is a much more complicated place than we thought. Well, you probably knew, but I was in the dark. I still am. It's like I'm trying to peer over the edge to see what's inside, but I'm not tall enough to reach."

Aargh had often experienced not being tall enough to reach. He wasn't the loftiest wizard at the Spire, not by a long shot–more like the shortest.

As he sat there, troubled by recent events, he did something unexpected: He smiled.

"Wrudge, do you remember the day we snuck into the kitchen to steal a taste of the pudding they were preparing for the Wizards' Feast? Oh, the look on old Fussybudget's face when she caught you tiptoeing across the counter. Priceless! You almost made it off before she grabbed that broom and started flailing every which way. What a ruckus! She kept missing you and hitting the pots and pans instead. I'm sure people heard it from the Eastern Grazing Fields to the stables.

I've never laughed that hard in my life, except for the time when Holly-Mine..."

As Aargh's thoughts returned to his daughter, the smile faded.

"You've made a right mess this time, haven't you, Aarghathlain? A right mess."

The weary wizard ran his fingers over the journal's cover, tracing the golden image pressed into the leather. Holly-Mine had given him this book when they'd returned home from their travels aboard the *Prosperity*. Somehow, she'd known he wouldn't be able to write in his old diary anymore... *Wrudge's Diary*. However, aside from recounting his first days aboard the ship, he hadn't written much in this one either.

He removed the short pencil strapped to the book's binding and reached into another pocket to retrieve a sharpener. He paused. The pencil's point was still sharp. Of course, it was. He hadn't used it. So he left the sharpener where it was and thought about what he should write.

TO7, 3-333

Dear Diary,
  They're coming for us. I must get Holly-Mine to safety.

After he'd written these few words, Holly-Mine appeared, staring at him with a remarkably stern expression on her face. It was the face of wisdom...the face of knowledge.

Aargh couldn't fathom what knowledge she possessed, but he was humbled by it, so he paid close attention to what she said.

"Papa, I need you to promise me something."

Aargh nodded.

"Promise that you'll listen to me."

Aargh nodded again as if to say *I always listen to you,* but she cut him off mid-nod.

"Don't patronize me."

Shocked, Aargh vigorously shook his head. He'd never do that! Not ever!

"You're my Papa, and I love you, but sometimes you follow the wrong root."

Aargh took a breath to speak—not that he could or needed to since she could hear his thoughts—but then decided to continue listening instead.

Holly-Mine approved of this decision. "Problems don't necessarily have a simple solution. You make your lists and examine your roots, searching for the right path forward, believing *the One True Root will never lead you astray,* but I'm telling you that isn't always the case. There will be times when there's more than one *True Root* and others when there's no correct way forward, only the path that lies before us. In those times, it doesn't matter what feels right. You simply have to carry on. What I'm trying to say is that you won't always be able to come up with the right answer. We have to understand that sometimes things are the way they are, and there may be nothing we can do about it."

Holly-Mine's words sounded familiar to Aargh. He'd once heard Doros tell his son, Bram, something similar aboard the *Prosperity.* Now, he knew how Bram felt that day as he struggled to put it all together in his mind.

Aargh had devoted nearly his entire life to finding the One True Root. Was it possible that it didn't exist? Was the future not as predetermined as he believed? That was too much to process at the moment, sitting in the Underoof as they hid from the wizards who'd burned their home, so he looked to his daughter for guidance.

Her familiar chocolatey brown eyes sparkled in Guilde-brande's light, but other things about her had changed. Her hair had darkened; it was now more of a rich honey color, and her skin wasn't as pale as it once was. It almost looked like she'd been spending time under the summer sun. Aargh wondered if girls' skin changed as they got older. He honestly didn't know.

Holly-Mine's face relaxed, and she became the girl Aargh saved from the clutches of the Gemini City Footman once again. Her father was genuinely trying to understand, and that was enough for her. "Papa?" she asked.

"Yes, Sweet Girl?" Aargh answered in her mind.

"Hold me."

And Aargh reached out his arms to the child.

Evening

CHAPTER 14

JUSTICE IS NEVER BLIND
THE WIZARDS' UNDERGROUND

Bee leapt out of his chair, convinced that any chance of getting through to the Gemini City School of Wizarding's Board of Regents about the previous night's events had faded like the sun behind the western foothills. "Is it me, or are you being intentionally obtuse?"

"Hold your tongue, Wizard Bartlebee, or we'll have you removed. Unwizardly behavior will not be tolerated during these proceedings. I suggest you take your seat immediately!" the chair regent commanded.

Bee grabbed his chair, slammed it onto the floor, and plopped down, resting his head on his arms. To say it had been a trying day would have been a great disservice to how dismal Bee felt.

First, Lan and O interrupted his bedtime tea with stories of mysterious wizards plotting in the greenhouses. Then, Fizz saw that Aargh and Holly-Mine's house was on fire–started by Tarth, no less! Then, as if that wasn't enough to deal with, his buddy Lan had been severely hurt in an attack by a familiar of all things!

By this point, there weren't many leaves left on Bee's tree. All he wanted to do was pour the aromatic cup of tea with lemon and honey he'd promised himself and crawl into bed. But no. Instead, he had to sit here being cross-examined for hours on end by the Wizards Regent.

After Tarth was named Interim Head Wizard, he'd institut-ed a spate of changes in a so-called attempt to preserve the old ways, which was ridiculous because prior to that, he'd spent years trying to prevent changes at the Spire using the same argument! His hypocrisy wasn't lost on Bee or any of The Wizards' Underground, but what could they do about it?

The worst change was having the school overseen by a board of wizards from other cities. This irked Bee to no end. Spire Wizards were perfectly capable of running the school without outside interference—especially from the self-impor-tant know-it-alls sitting across the table from him. In Bee's mind, there was one undeniable fact where wizarding was concerned: Gemini City was the epicenter of all things magi-cal. Everyone knew that. What could people from other cities tell the Spire about wizarding? Nothing. That's what.

It was true that wizards didn't have quantifiable evidence that magic came directly from Ardilakk, but it was pretty clear to anyone paying attention. Nowhere else on the River Wide boasted a Spire or wizarding school at the level of Gem-ini City, and it was well-known that if you needed a wizard to look into the future, Ardilakk Valley was the place to come. Not only had the Northern Forest always been filled with the most knowledgeable trees, but the farther you got from the valley, the less chance you had of finding one willing to talk.

Adding insult to injury, Bee wasn't permitted to see his in-quisitor's faces as they blathered on about things they didn't understand. This was because they were wearing regent masks. Tarth had insisted the coverings were necessary, saying justice had to be blind to be unbiased.

"Blind to whom?" Bee wondered as he attempted to catch a glimpse of what lay beyond the veil.

The masks were made of a translucent material designed to distort the wizards' facial features. He saw their eyes, but that didn't help much. Combined with their black cloaks, black boots, and long black gloves, the complete image they projected was unsettling. He assumed that was the point.

"Dear Wizards Regent," he said as politely as possible under the circumstances. "If you have me removed, how will you make any decisions, as I'm the only wizard in the room who witnessed the events."

The members of the council turned to each other and laughed out loud. Bee was stunned by their reaction.

"And this makes you an expert, Wizard Bartlebee?" the chair regent asked, thoroughly nonplussed. "I want to make sure I understand you correctly. Before you, sit the highest minds of our Order. Yet, you presume to suggest you are more capable of ruling on this matter than we are? Correct me if I am misunderstanding, but is this due to the fact that you were present at the events? The audacity of your argument is only superseded by the impertinence of the suggestion!" The chair regent then gestured to the other wizards, who nodded their heads in deference to each other.

Flabbergasted by the chair's dismissal of his question, Bee's mouth worked feverishly, trying to formulate a response. The notion that someone who hadn't been party to the events knew more than he did was so preposterous that he couldn't make a sound.

The board took advantage of Bee's silence–a rare occurrence where Bartlebee was concerned–and fired a series of questions at him in quick succession.

"You're saying there was a small fire in the woods, correct?"

"Yes, but I wouldn't call it small–"

"Answer the question," a masked regent instructed.

"Yes," Bee responded curtly.

"Did anyone get hurt?"

"Yes! Haven't you been listening? Poor Lan is in the infirmary right now because Renfir mauled him!"

"So you've said," a masked regent droned.

"It's true. Paladand had to heal him."

"Let me get this straight," a masked regent said condescendingly. "You're implying a Wizard of the Third Circle had the strength to heal Alantus' so-called serious wounds without losing control of the magic…on his own?"

"He did! I watched him do it. He saved Lan's–"

"That sounds a bit far-fetched, don't you think?" a masked regent interrupted, dismissively waving his hand. "Possibly an exaggeration to impress us?"

Many masked chuckles followed the regent's remarks. That sound got under Bee's skin, but another regent chimed in before he could react.

"Let me check my notes. Yes, it says here: *Wizard Bartlebee didn't see the attack happen.* Therefore, it might have been any wild animal."

"True. The forest is full of dangerous beasts," a weaselly-sounding regent added.

"It wasn't a wild animal," Bee attempted to correct. "It was Flinghower's familiar, Renfir."

"Why do you keep insisting on accusing Renfir of acting in such a dreadful manner?" the last regent on the right asked. "I've met Renfir. He's a good wolf."

"Yes, I have, too," another regent added, his low voice rumbling around the room.

What did these regents mean? How could they have met Renfir? They shouldn't know Fling, let alone his familiar. The board was supposed to be comprised of wizards from other cities, having had no contact with the Spire. That was Tarth's justification for convening the board in the first place!

"What's going on here?" Bee asked, but a flurry of questions cut him off.

"These hooded figures, did you identify any of them as Spire Wizards?

"I'm not supposed to–"

"How many were there?"

"I'm not sure, exactly. At least–"

"And you mentioned Aargh escaped, right?"

"Yes, but that's not the point."

"You've neglected to say if there was a leader to this fantastic band of rogue wizards. Was there?"

"If you'd give me the chance to respond, I'd–"

"It seems strange that there wasn't a leader."

"I'm trying to explain to you–"

Without warning, the regents stood, and the chair regent proclaimed, "There is no reason for further discussion on this matter."

"What?" Bee asked, also getting to his feet.

"Aargh is no longer a member of the Spire," the chair continued. "What happens at his home is not the school's concern. He can file a complaint at the Congregational House. It's their responsibility to oversee the running of the city, although, considering the alleged confrontation took place in the Northern Forest, I imagine it's beyond their jurisdiction, as well. As there is no further business, this meeting of the venerable Gemini City School of Wizarding's Board of Regents is–"

"Wait!" Bartlebee screamed. "I haven't told you about–"

"Excuse me," a regent interjected before the chair could gavel the meeting adjourned. "Please forgive the interruption, but I was wondering if I may request clarification?"

The chair regent nodded and said, "By all means. I yield the floor to Wizard Regent."

"Thank you. Wizard Bartlebee, we need to speak with Interim Head Wizard Tarthanabelle, yet we are told he is not on the grounds. Do you know where we might find him?"

What happened next was a blur because as Bee spoke, he simultaneously imagined his mother standing over him wearing her favorite apron–the flowery (floury!) one his father had helped him buy for her birthday–and wagging her indexing finger at him. *Don't you say things like that, young man,* she said in his mind. *I can't tell you what to think, but if it's impolite, stop it at the nose!* If only he'd listened to her advice.

"I'll leave it to you to put two and two together," he said. "You were the ones asking if the group had a leader."

Before the words finished coming out of his mouth, Bee knew he'd made a terrible mistake. Instantly, the board erupted in an uproar of condemnations. Regents reprimanded him for making baseless accusations, called for his censure, and even suggested throwing him out of the Order. The chair regent added to the commotion by repeatedly banging his gavel and calling for order. Amid the unwizardly uproar, Bartlebee couldn't make out most of the suggested punishments, but he wasn't trying very hard, either.

When order was restored and everyone sat down, the chair addressed Bee sternly. "You're lucky, Wizard Bartlebee. We could expel you for such scandalous remarks. You've had an emotional experience. Whether it was real or imagined is irrelevant. I'll give you the benefit of the doubt this time, but don't press your luck!"

"Wait, what? I was trying to–"

"Refined wizards don't accuse the most exceptional examples of the Order of being unwizardly! Are you unaware of the great advances Interim Head Wizard Tarthanabelle has championed for this school and Gemini City? Your staggering lack of decorum shocks us. Your lack of evidence to support your outrageous accusations appalls us. And your presumptuous insolence toward your superiors is galling. As no Spire wizard would ever act this way of their own free will, I must assume you have fallen victim to your emotions. You'd do well to reflect on your responsibility as a representative of the Gemini City School of Wizarding and practice your *C's.*"

"But there's something I need to–"

"You noted yourself: *It was dark, and the culprits were cloaked.* In all likelihood, they were hoodlums from the lowest squares or scalawags staying at one of those disgusting shelters. With each passing year, those places seem to move farther and farther uptown. What is Middling Street coming to these days?"

The Wizards Regent shook their heads in disbelief at the current state of things.

"Aarghathlain has a habit of frequenting those less-than-savory places," the chair regent continued. "I have no idea why he'd want to do such a thing, but he probably upset the wrong hooligan or some such nonsense."

Another regent added, "Let's not forget that he sailed aboard the *Prosperity.* Very unseemly for any Spire Wizard, let alone one of his standing. Very unbecoming, indeed!"

"Yes, thank you, Wizard Regent," the chair said, acknowledging his peer's remarks.

"I wonder how else he's been corrupted," the low-voiced regent added. "What acquaintances–if that isn't too civilized a term–has he made in the lower blocks? It's no place for a wizard."

"Here, here!" the other regents shouted, banging their hands on the table.

Bee fought to keep his mouth shut. He'd already made a mess of things, but how could they say that about Aargh? His friend was many things, but corrupt was not one of them. And why were they talking about the shelters that way? They sounded closer to the old lords than wizards. Was that it? What if they weren't wizards at all? What if they were–

The chair must have recognized that Bee had figured something out and, more importantly, that he was about to speak it aloud because he started talking very fast. "Listen to me, young man. You are confined to your room until further notice. You will not teach classes or have any contact with other wizards or students. When the time is right, you will receive word regarding what action will be taken against you for making baseless accusations about your esteemed colleague. You have embarrassed yourself, Wizard Bartlebee, and we will not subject ourselves to any more of your contrivances. Meeting adjourned!"

The chair regent slammed the gavel down, and the board members turned around.

Bartlebee stared at their black-cloaked backs in disbelief. He noticed Ermy's face sticking out of his robes and whispered, "That didn't go well."

Ermy looked at him as if to say *sorry* and crawled back into his pocket, where she'd been hiding from the commotion of the meeting.

"If you would come with me," Steward Chartlehill said, making Bee flinch. "I'll accompany you to your room."

Bee had forgotten that Chartlehill was standing in a corner of the Observation Lounge. That is, if round rooms can have corners.

"I remember where it is," Bee said irritably before realizing Chartlehill's offer wasn't a request.

The Steward gestured toward the uplifter's cage. "After you."

Bee wished Brindlewise had stayed, too. Chartlehill was lousy company, and it was a long way to the ground floor—not that there were any stops along the way. The uplifter had two buttons: a coral one labeled *Rotunda* and a mauve one labeled *Observation Lounge*. Bee wished there were others, such as a lavender button labeled *Cafeteria*. That would have been nice, as it had been a long day, and his stomach was making itself known.

CHAPTER 15

A SPARK OF TRUTH
TARTHANABELLE

Ralph kicked the dry leaves covering the ground. He was familiar with this part of the valley because he'd often come here to collect pinecones. Most of the forest's pine trees grew at the foot of Mount Ardilakk, but a long pinetum separated the city's northeastern corner from the Eastern Foothills. Some of the pinecones grew so large and heavy that he could only carry two at a time!

The wizards surrounding him also appeared comfortable making their way through the foothills, but why wouldn't they? Wizards spoke to trees. It made sense that they'd be used to walking in the woods. They might even enjoy it, but he couldn't tell. They looked brooding and mysterious to him, hiking through the forest in their dark, hooded cloaks.

As Ralph skipped along, he imagined seeing Holly-Mine again. First, he planned to say *hello* and give her a big hug. That would be great. Then, if he'd figured out how to do magic by then, he'd perform some for her. She'd be so impressed!

Thinking about these things gave him an idea. Maybe, if he asked nicely, Tarthanabelle would teach him a simple spell to practice along the way. Then he'd be ready when they got there. The possibility made him very excited! He was about to ask when–

CRACK!

Electricity arced from Ralph's hands to the ground at his feet, starting a small fire that he quickly stamped out.

Its concussive force made the wizards around him stumble, and Renfir growled at the boy. Every hair on the wolf's body stood on end as if he'd received an electric shock.

"Well done!" Tarth said, coming over to help put out the fire. "I knew you had it in you."

"What…happened?" Ralph stammered, his fingers rigid with fear.

"Don't be afraid. It didn't hurt you, did it?"

"No, sir. It scared me. I was thinking about Holly-Mine, and then…bang! What was it?"

"Magic, my dear Ralph. Magic," Tarth said, tousling his hair.

"But how? You haven't taught me anything yet."

"Oh, but I have. Though a better way to describe it might be to say I made casting magic possible for you, but that's neither here nor there. The only thing that matters is that Mother Tree has blessed you through my gift. Now you're a wizard, like us. It's a great honor. Cherish it."

Ralph didn't understand. What gift? The acorn?

Tarth motioned for the other wizards to gather around.

"I was like you once: a boy eager to learn the ways of magic. I made my way to the school, and they saw promise in me. During my first semester, I went with my class to visit the Heart of the Forest. That was when Mother Tree gave me an acorn, which I have now given to you."

Ralph pulled it out of his pocket and studied it by turning it over and over. He half-expected it to glow or vibrate, but it was just an acorn. In a way, that was disappointing.

Tarth saw the look on his face and knew what it meant. "You can't see magic, but it's in there," he said, pointing to Ralph's head. "In fact, magic is all around us."

"Then why can't everyone do magic?"

"Because there are rules. Technically, they're called the *Sacred Rules of the Wizarding Guild of the Ancient Art,* though most people refer to them as the *Wizarding Oath* or *Wizard's Creed.* The ninth rule states: *No wizard may perform magic whom the Mother Tree has not blessed.* Though, that one is less a rule and more the natural order of things. No one knows why, but magic is hidden from those who haven't visited her."

"But I never visited her. I don't even know where she is!"

"Unfortunately, you couldn't, even if you wanted to. She's gone now, but that doesn't matter. I visited her and have passed her gift on to you."

"Thank you," Ralph said, awed by the knowledge. "Since I already made magic happen, does that mean I don't have to have lessons and stuff?"

"Oh, I think lessons would be a good idea," Tarth said with a smirk. "However, you aren't bound like most wizards, forced to practice clumsy incantations and work for months figuring out the most rudimentary skills. You have access to a unique type of magic–elemental magic. This kind of magic doesn't need spells in the common sense of the word. All you need are emotions to make it work. Do you have emotions, Ralph?"

"Yes," he answered. "I have lots of them."

"That's a good boy."

"Mr. Tarth, sir?"

"Mentor will do," Tarthanabelle corrected.

"Mentor, I don't want to do any more magic right now if that's okay."

"Not to worry, Ralph. You can try again when you're ready. You've had a big day, and many people will be interested in hearing about your accomplishments. Very interested, indeed. Come. We're almost there."

A short time later, Tarth and his band of wizards emerged from the Eastern Foothills onto what used to be known as the Highland Grasslands. That was before the Norters had landed their airships and transformed it into the towering Metal City on the cliffs.

"Impressive, isn't it?" Tarth asked.

Flinghower and the others stared at the intimidating metal walls, flinching as the fortress' chimneys belched smoke and flame into the evening sky. Even the metal looked like it was on fire as the golden setting sun struck it from the side. None of them had ever been this close to the camp before (or wanted to be).

"It's even bigger in person," Kaltofenns said, tilting his head back. Kal was a stocky wizard, not typically bothered by anything, let alone walls, but this structure was on a different order of magnitude.

"Yes, it is," Tarth agreed. "I suggest we introduce ourselves."

"Shouldn't we wait for Phrim?" a voice from the back asked.

"Odaraphrim isn't coming with us," Tarth snapped. "He would have returned long ago if he was. He's made his choice, and choices have consequences. Let's go."

As they approached what appeared to be an entrance, the wizards crowded closer together.

"I heard the Norters don't let anyone in," Flinghower said, instantly regretting questioning Tarth's plan.

Much to Fling's surprise, Tarth laughed. "Then it's good that I'm not just anyone. Leave it to me."

He whistled, and two enormous metal plates parted.

"That's strange," Kaltofenns muttered. "It's almost as if they knew we were coming."

The edges of Tarth's lips curled into an evil grin.

Wendingsday of the 8th week
Nearing the End of the Day

CHAPTER 16

THE ONCE-GREAT MARBLE HOUSE
AARGHATHLAIN

Aargh woke from a fitful sleep, more tired than when he'd laid down. Covered in sweat-soaked robes, he stretched his stiff arms and legs. If any other wizard had found themselves in a runoff tunnel under the city, they'd have been beside themselves, but not Aargh. He wasn't any other wizard. Not only had he spent time in the tunnels before (thanks to Wrudge), but being damp and cold was pretty much a way of life aboard the *Prosperity*.

Alone in the schooner's brig, he'd often lay in the dark trying to decipher the sounds above him on the weather deck. Now, he did the same thing, except topside meant the meticulously organized grid-like streets of Gemini City.

Aargh tilted his head to one side, listening to a rumblebug roll overhead. It stopped, made a series of screeching and scratching sounds, and continued on its way.

"I wish our lives were that mundane," he thought, propping himself on an elbow. "Having an adventure isn't all it's cracked up to be."

Streams of lamplight crept into the tunnel from storm drains stretching into the distance. They let in enough light for him to make out the lines between the skillfully cut stones. The arcing rocks of the tunnel's roof abutted each other so tightly that they didn't need mortar to stay in place.

Aargh appreciated the skill it took to build without the aid of modern technologies.

After his outburst, Aargh had lost some of the urgency to continue the search for his past. This benefited his companions, as they needed to recuperate from their travels and process the stress of the situation.

Aargh shivered, but it wasn't because he was wet and cold. The terror of the nightmare that had disturbed his sleep was still with him...

"No, Papa! You mustn't go in there!" he screamed as his father ran into the barn to save the pony.

Flames exploded from the window he'd just climbed through, showering him with glass. When he looked up, his mother was standing next to him. Had she been there the entire time?

Surrounded by fire, she cast spells that reminded Aargh of the Wizard of the Council. He begged for help, but she didn't notice him lying on the ground. She was very tall, and the higher he reached, the farther away she appeared until it wasn't his mother any longer.

"Mother Tree is on fire!" he yelled.

"Hurry, Aarghathlain! There isn't much time!" a voice echoed in his mind.

He spun around, searching for whoever was calling to him, but saw no one.

Aldenthwaine began appearing in different places around the farm. Sometimes, he beckoned to Aargh. Other times, he laughed as Mother Tree, the farm, and the forest burned.

Unable to shake off the disturbing images–especially Aldenthwaine laughing–he told himself, "It doesn't mean anything," but he didn't believe that. Maybe moving around would help him feel better.

Being careful not to disturb Holly-Mine and the others, he navigated through the cramped space, trying to avoid an accidental bump or nudge. He was glad they were getting some rest, even if he couldn't.

Then, with nothing better to do, he paced the Underoof. The lack of rats in the tunnels didn't escape his notice. They probably wondered if the wizard they'd invited into their home could be trusted. At least Mnoonge hadn't left. He heard her dutifully scurrying along behind him. Aargh knew the special bond he'd shared with Wrudge would never be duplicated, but Mnoonge was exceptional in her own way, and he was thankful for her help.

Much to his surprise, he stumbled across a cistern used to collect rainwater but not from storm drains. This space was fed by openings in the ceiling designed to gather unsullied water falling from the sky, not the grimy runoff from Gemini City's dirty streets.

It was marvelous, with an arched stone ceiling descending at regular intervals to pillars that stretched on as far as he could see. In between the stanchions, there were several raised stone surfaces directly below the collectors. Even the reflection of the pale moon's light was enough to illuminate the entire space, aided by the still, mirror-like surface of the reservoir. Mesmerized by its calmness–a sensation that had eluded him of late–Aargh sat and waited. For what, he didn't know, but he sensed there was something extraordinary about this place.

A faint scratching caught his attention.

Mnoonge stopped moving. Clearing her throat to use her rat voice, she said, "My apologies for disturbing you, Wizard Aarghathlain. I noticed this…" she explained, pointed to a dusty canvas tarp, "and wanted to see what it was hiding." Being a rat from the lower blocks, she'd never visited this place before and was curious.

This didn't upset Aargh in the least. He knew rats were inquisitive creatures at heart, and he got up to take a look.

"It's a boat," Mnoonge said for him, removing its protective covering.

It was in surprisingly good shape, considering its age and apparent lack of use. It had a flat bottom, which Aargh assumed was designed to navigate the shallow water of the cistern, and a long pole to push it along. After his experience on the *Prosperity*, Aargh wasn't as averse to boating as he once was (excluding fancy dinners on palatial yachts, of course), and he decided to give it a try.

"Fancy a trip?" Mnoonge asked herself.

She looked doubtfully at the boat but climbed aboard.

The ropes holding it in place fell apart in his hands as he uncleated them, but the boat didn't move because it wasn't in the water. Instead, it had been placed on a series of stone rollers, presumably to keep it from rotting.

"Well, here we go," Mnoonge said as Aargh took hold of a lever on the other side of the starboard gunwale and pushed it down.

Behind them, a heavy weight attached to a chain lowered, driving a series of gears. Then, the boat rolled toward the water and slid off the dock into the cistern. Sitting in the stern of the boat, Aargh used the pole to slowly push them around pillars.

Mnoonge pointed toward a leather pouch that had been left on one of the stone circles.

"I see it," she told herself.

Using the pole to pull it closer, Aargh picked up the bag and put it in the boat. Mnoonge climbed onto his leg to peer inside. Then, he loosened the drawstring, holding it closed.

"Hmm."

Reaching in, Aargh removed a tiny whistle and a folded piece of thick parchment paper, yellowed with age.

Mnoonge wanted to tell him to put the whistle back, but Aargh used her voice first. "This looks like the kind of thing dog trainers use."

He blew on it, and Mnoonge grabbed her ears.

"Oh, sorry," she heard herself say. "How could I forget that you have exceptional hearing."

"How indeed," she thought but didn't say anything. It was still a little confusing speaking for herself and the wizard.

The piece of parchment turned out to be far more interesting.

When Aargh unfolded it, he realized it was a map of Ardilakk Valley, but not the way he knew it because it showed all four cities of the Ancient Quadropolis!

"This is fascinating," Mnoonge said as Aargh pored over the document. "Here you can see Eastie and Westie Nort. Look, they go right up to Falling Rocks. Wow, the forest was so much smaller back then. I guess that makes sense. And here's the Congregational House, and the piers are smaller, too. This must have been before the River Wide Shipping Consortium took over the Port Pier District. And what's this? I can barely see it."

The map was so faded that many of the details had been lost, but along the river west of the city, there appeared to be a cave drawn into the Western Foothills.

"I wonder what that is…"

Aargh lifted the paper to get a better look, and it fell apart in his hands.

"Oh no! I should have been more careful. I'm sure Holly-Mine would have liked to see this."

He did his best to sweep the pieces back into the bag and, after pulling the drawstring to close it, placed it back on the stone circle.

Although Aargh was sad at the loss of the map, he felt better than he had of late and decided to see if everyone was up yet. The last hurdle before returning was getting the boat onto the dock. It was tricky, but he managed to reset the launching mechanism, and they headed into the tunnels.

To his surprise, everyone was up and getting ready to go. Even the rats had returned. Unsurprisingly, he sensed they were wary of him in a way they hadn't been before. No surprise there. He would be, too.

"How are you, Sweet Girl?" Mnoonge asked for Aargh as his daughter threw the rucksack she carried over her shoulder.

"Fine, Papa, but I'd like to go with you next time you go searching for maps."

"But I wasn't looking for a map. We found it by mistake," he said in her mind apologetically, and she giggled. She was just having fun with him.

"What map is this?" Gerald asked.

"I think it was of the Ancient Quadropolis," Mnoonge said, answering for Aargh.

"I would like to see that. Did you bring it with you?"

"Sadly, no. It fell apart when I touched it."

Gerald looked crestfallen. "Maybe you could describe it to me sometime. I enjoy maps quite a lot."

"I'd be happy to."

Using her rat voice, Mnoonge asked, "Wizard Aarghath-lain? May I have a moment?"

"Of course," she told herself, and she scurried off to speak with Buck.

Aargh watched as she gently touched the bigger rat's hand.

"Nice," Aargh thought. "She deserves to have a life surrounded by Mnoongelings and Bucklings if that's what she wants…yes…she hopes to have a family. She'll make a great grandmamamama one day."

But would she? His thoughts were still fringed by darkness, and he wondered if she'd be given the chance.

"I wish the future wasn't hidden. Suffering through the difficult times ahead might be easier if we knew how things were going to turn out." He paused to consider this and wound up changing his mind. "Ah, well. I guess it's best if the future stays hidden. That way, we can hold out hope, whether our paths lead us to where we want to go or not."

Holly-Mine's cheerful voice broke into his reverie. "Did you sleep well, Uncle Gerald?"

"As well as can be expected, I guess. I find the sound of running water rather soothing. That was unexpected."

"Intolerable," Dram mumbled as he brushed off his robes.

Holly-Mine giggled as he wriggled and twisted to reach the last dirty spots.

"Such a rag-tag bunch," Aargh thought, observing his companions. "A deposed wizard, a homeless storyteller, an apprentice, a street urchin, and a rat."

"We're a sight, aren't we?" Holly-Mine said, winking at him before skipping ahead to strut alongside Gerald.

"That we are," Aargh agreed, thankful for Holly-Mine's ability to forgive, if not forget, as she never forgot anything.

The group didn't talk much as they made their way out of the tunnels and toward Marble House. Aargh, Holly-Mine, and Gerald had witnessed The Wizard of the Council's treachery firsthand, and Dramwitch, like all wizards, still had nightmares about the trees screaming.

Halfway along the stone staircase that led streetside, Mnoonge remarked, "There's no going back, is there?" and everyone stopped.

Aargh wasn't sure if he'd meant to say those words aloud, but he seized the opportunity to apologize.

"I haven't been myself lately. Who, exactly, I don't know, but definitely not me," Mnoonge said as Aargh stood uncomfortably, wringing his hands. "I want to tell you all how sorry I am. I appreciate your help. Really, I do. I couldn't face any of this without you."

"We understand," Dram said.

"Let's go, Papa," Holly-Mine encouraged, slipping her arm in his. "It's time to find some answers."

When Aargh climbed out of the streethole, the crisp night air cooled his sweaty brow, and he breathed in the comforting smell of autumn floating on the wind.

Gerald, who was looking the other way, found no such comfort. There it was: Marble House.

The noblest of the old lord's halls lay in ruins–its shattered remains standing out against the beautifully restored buildings of Upper Middling Street. Unlike the other high homes, it hadn't been rebuilt. Instead, it was left as a reminder of the destruction wrought by the Wizard of the Council.

On the ground in front of them, there was a large piece of burned-out trunk with a bright brass plaque nailed to it.

It read:

Here lies a piece of the oak tree that once stood
in the courtyard of Marble House.

Gerald knelt, placing his hand on the log. "Hello, dear friend. I'm sorry I couldn't help you."

"Don't be sad. She's at peace," Holly-Mine comforted, kneeling beside him.

"It's not right that they've left her here, lying on the sidewalk. She deserves better."

Holly-Mine smiled and put her hand on his knee. "That's not your friend, Uncle Gerald. That's an old, broken tree trunk. She's returned to the Earth Mother where she belongs."

It was Gerald's turn to smile. Even at the worst of times, Holly-Mine had a way of making him feel better. "Nothing could have prepared me for how hard it would be to return to this place again," he said.

"Me, too," she agreed.

"None of us were prepared," Mnoonge added as Aargh studied the remains of the house's famous marble balls.

The two spherical sculptures that used to flank the house's formidable entryway lay in pieces, shattered by the Wizard of the Council's spell.

Holly-Mine encouraged Gerald to come with her, saying, "I know how much you miss her, but let's go inside and see what we can find."

"Miss who?" Dram asked.

"The oak tree of Marble House," Holly-Mine explained. "She was Uncle Gerald's friend."

"Friend?" Mnoonge asked vacantly as Aargh tried to remember the house's facade.

He could picture the day well enough, walking uptown with Wrudge from their second-floor apartment in the lower blocks. As he wrote in his diary, his familiar explored the food carts and stalls they passed along the way. People and vendors had tried to get his attention, but he was too busy to stop. No wizard ever wanted to keep the lord of a high house waiting, and Aargh was no exception. It seemed ludicrous now. Who cared which wall their grandmamamama's portrait hung on?

"Gerald and the tree used to speak," Holly-Mine said brightly. "She was his teacher."

Finally, what his daughter was explaining to Dram got through, and Mnoonge asked, "Gerald speaks to trees?"

"Tree. To be precise. I've never tried to speak to another," the ex-head butler explained. "She was wise, and she knew a lot about the city. We talked nearly every day."

"And she never mentioned me?" Aargh asked through Mnoonge, wondering how his presence at Marble House had been so thoroughly forgotten.

"I'm afraid not."

The small rat cocked an eyebrow. "Strange. Anyway, It appears we have more in common than I realized."

"Yes. We've both lost a great deal but also gained much," Gerald said, looking at Holly-Mine. "I wouldn't dream of changing a single thing if it meant never meeting you."

She hugged him around the waist. "You're such a softy."

He blushed a deep shade of red that complimented his colorful clothing.

"I suppose we should keep moving," Dram suggested.

"Yes. Thank you for keeping us on task," Mnoonge said, but Aargh didn't move. He was thinking about how everyone only looked at him when Mnoonge spoke, which, in a way, was good because it meant they'd grown more accustomed to her speaking for him. But in another way, it was bad. Mnoonge wasn't only his voice. She deserved to be noticed, too.

Admittedly, being clothed head-to-toe in elegant hand-crafted blue robes with delicate gold embroidery made him a focal point, but he didn't wear the same oversized robes he once did. Now, they were close-fitting and midi-length, stopping above his ankles. No more tripping on the hem for him! And around his waist, he wore a leather belt and scabbard to hold Guildebrande. His attire was strange for a Gemini City wizard (member-in-good-standing at the Spire or not), but he'd grown accustomed to it.

Maybe he'd sew a pocket into his robes near the shoulder. That way, people could watch them both when he spoke. Unfortunately, he didn't have his sewing kit with him because now that his robes didn't reach the ground, he didn't need it as frequently anymore. He tended to leave it at home on the mantle above the fireplace…

The fireplace.

He didn't have a fireplace anymore…or his little sewing kit…or the bower he'd grown for Holly-Mine. They'd all been destroyed by the fire with everything else.

"The night is waning, and we don't want to draw attention to what we're doing," Gerald said.

"Yes, you're right. Sorry. I'm a bit distracted," Mnoonge explained as Aargh adjusted his robes. "Dram, you've been here before. Can you show us the safest way in, please?"

"Yes. It's over here. They've cleared a path for tours."

"Tours," Mnoonge hissed, reflecting how Aargh felt.

In front of them was a sign illuminated by a street lamp:

Take it in!
The splendor of yesteryear laid waste
by the Wizard of the Council.

Here lies the
ONCE-GREAT MARBLE HOUSE

Presented by the
Lord and Lady Preservation Society
of Gemini City, Inc.

"That sounds more like an advertisement for an attraction at the Middling Street Fair than a memorial," Holly-Mine said indignantly.

"Consider who's running it. I doubt they know the difference or care," Gerald pointed out.

She turned her back to it, stamping her foot and crossing her arms. "I can't imagine wanting to relive that day for any reason."

"Nor can I," he agreed.

"Over here," Dram said, pointing to another sign that read: *Enter for Viewing.* "We're lucky to have such a bright moon tonight. That will help. There's a place near the courtyard where we can start our search. It's used for lectures and to recount the events of the Great Fire."

"Have you taken the tour?" Gerald asked.

"Quite often," Dram admitted. "At first, it was so I could learn the layout and safely navigate the space, but later, I kept coming back. I guess I enjoy correcting the tour guides."

"Why would you need to do that?" Holly-Mine asked.

"They like to embellish the story. You know. Make it more sensational."

"How? What's there to embellish? He almost destroyed the city!"

"I suspect they're trying to get a rise out of the attendees," Dram said, stepping onto the path. "Be careful. There's a good bit of broken glass and jagged rocks, but it's manageable."

"Wasn't what happened terrible enough?" Holly-Mine mumbled, stepping around a mangled mass of twisted metal.

"It certainly was," Gerald said, following Dram into the ruins.

Holly-Mine stopped moving because she realized her father was still standing on the sidewalk. "Papa, are you coming?"

Aargh didn't move.

"Dram, would you wait a minute?" she asked.

"Of course."

He and Gerald watched as Holly-Mine retrieved her father. "Is there something wrong, Papa?"

Aargh shook his head, *no*. Then, he nodded, *yes*. "It's all wrong, isn't it? I still don't understand why the Wizard of the Council did what he did."

"Come, Papa. Let's worry about that later. Right now, Dram is leading us to a safe place to start our search."

"Okay," Mnoonge agreed, and Aargh let himself be guided onto the path.

CHAPTER 17

A MYSTERIOUS VISIT
THE WIZARDS' UNDERGROUND

TAP. Tap, tap.

After hours of work, Paladand placed his favorite mechanical pencil on the desk and leaned back to stretch his cramped back. The desk was a prized possession–one he'd saved for months to purchase–made from mottled quartzite quarried from far up the River Wide. He especially liked how the stone sparkled and shimmered in the soft glow of his oil lamp. Additionally, he'd commissioned a local artist to create fine metalwork legs to support the quartzite. Altogether, it was a workspace worthy of the Spire Wizard he hoped to become when he graduated.

"A place for everything, and everything in its place," he said, ensuring the pencil was situated parallel to the paper. "Is that you, Bartlebee?" he asked, not surprised to have someone knocking on his door late at night. Wizards kept odd hours.

TAP! Tap, tap!

The young wizard pushed himself back from the desk, stood, and peered out of the door's small peephole. A giant nose filled the viewer, magnified by its strong convex lens.

"Would you mind stepping back, please?"

Brindlewise's bearded face came into focus. "I'm an old wizard, Paladand. Are you going to make me stand out here in this drafty hallway all night?"

Paladand quickly unbolted the door and let the Spire Elder in.

"My apologies. I'd hoped you were Bartlebee. Do you know if he's been released yet? Last I heard, he was still locked in his room."

"I do. Yes, I do," Brindlewise said, sitting at Paladand's desk, which happened to be the only chair in the room.

Paladand had to force himself not to say, *and?* He knew Brindlewise had a habit of doing things in his own time, so he waited for the old wizard to continue.

"Sit, please," Brindlewise instructed, pointing at the bed.

Paladand thought it was strange being offered a place to sit in his own room, but he did as he was told—though he was careful not to disturb the bed covers too much. He took great care in keeping them neat and tidy, just as his father had taught him to do as a boy. Besides, as Dram liked to say, cleanliness was next to wizardliness, and Paladand tended to agree.

The young wizard hadn't kept much beyond fastidiousness from his life before entering the Spire, though he did continue to wear a crescent sun necklace. It was highly unusual for a wizard to wear jewelry, so he kept it hidden because he didn't want to offend anyone from their order. That didn't mean he was trying to hide it. It simply meant that he didn't make a big show of wearing it.

Besides, the front of his maroon robes depicted the sun's path from sunrise to sunset in earthy yellow-toned embroidery—an unmistakable image representing the Church of the Crescent Sun. Paladand was proud of his heritage, even if he didn't subscribe to his father's beliefs.

"Comfortable," Brindlewise said, assessing the young wizard's chambers. "I remember my old room. It was similar to this one."

"Every room shares the same layout," Paladand said, rubbing his repaired half-moon glasses with a fine silk cloth.

It wasn't the only time they'd been broken, but the circumstances in which it happened was certainly a first! He still had nightmares about Griff's sharp claws tearing them from his face.

"I suppose you're right," Brindlewise agreed, "but you do have a nice view."

Paladand couldn't argue there. His room overlooked the southernmost raised beds, which were filled with luscious vegetables in the summer and displayed an array of colorful flowers in the spring and fall.

Putting his glasses back on, he said, "I'm thankful for your visit, Brindlewise, but I'm pretty confident you didn't come to talk to me about my view."

"No, indeed. I didn't. I came to tell you that Bartlebee is still confined to his room. He isn't allowed to speak to anyone, so naturally, I dropped by to check on him."

"I'm glad you did, but this whole thing is outrageous. Can they do that? It's been over a week."

"Whether or not they can, they certainly have."

It wasn't technically an answer to the question, but it was true; therefore, Paladand took the matter as closed. "What about everyone else? Are we allowed to resume teaching yet? I have class tomorrow and need to check on several potions brewing in one of the healers' labs. I assume none of them have exploded or gone off, as I would have heard about that, but I need to check on their progress nevertheless."

"I'm afraid classes are the least of our worries," Brindlewise said without any additional explanation.

That sounded ominous to Paladand, but he held his tongue. The old wizard would eventually meander around to his point. While he waited, he turned down the corner of his duvet.

"Chartlehill will be visiting you soon," Brindlewise finally continued. "He'll direct you not to speak to anyone about the events in the forest. As long as you abide by that rule, you'll be free to return to your duties."

"Finally."

"After he stops by, I would like to ask that you join me in the sculpture garden."

It was an odd request, but Paladand assumed Brindlewise had his reasons.

The old wizard pushed himself out of the chair and stepped over to the room's solitary window. The moon's pale light had drained the grounds of their color, and the glass greenhouses appeared to be covered in phantasmagorical mirrors. The surreal image was still...too still, but for how long?

The pause in the conversation was long enough to be uncomfortable, and Paladand said, "Brindlewise, I have the feeling you aren't telling me everything."

"Likely because I'm not. Check on your potions, and come to the front of the school. Will you do that for me?"

"Of course."

"Then, I'll be off."

After he saw the old wizard out, Paladand sat back down on the end of his bed to wait for Chartlehill to arrive.

CHAPTER 18

A WHITE BELL OF EATHĒSIUM
HOLLY-MINE, DRAMWITCH & AARGHATHLAIN

When Aargh and his companions reached what was left of Marble House's courtyard, they briefly discussed the layout of the ruins and spread out to cover more ground.

Gerald and Holly-Mine headed to the rear of the house. It was the one place that still had tall walls, and Gerald wanted to see if any parts of the attik had survived the blast. Much to his surprise, some of it had, including the stone stairs to his old room. This revelation was particularly hard to reconcile on a night already filled with unexpected challenges. On one level, Gerald had hoped it had been demolished with everything else–that way, he could almost pretend it had never existed–but on another level, one that had been hidden away since the Great Fire, he was comforted by the sight of it.

"I suppose this corner of the house was shielded from the Wizard of the Council's magic," Gerald remarked, not knowing what else to say.

He was conflicted about how to proceed. That room had been his private space…his refuge…and it felt strange sharing it with anyone, even Holly-Mine.

"I'll stay here if you want me to," she offered.

Relieved by her insightfulness, he said, "That might be best. Are you sure you don't mind?"

"Of course not. I'll tidy these stones. Aren't they pretty? Even through the dust, they sparkle in the moonlight."

"That's because they're gemstones: rubies, emeralds, sapphires, and many others. Whenever I found bric-a-brac lying around, I put it in an old chest for safekeeping. To us, things like that are treasures beyond our wildest imaginations, but to the former lord of this house, they were worthless trinkets. Just think, if a jeweler set one of those stones, it might be worth enough to buy a house downtown or book passage on a streamliner to Ondlingstad."

Holly-Mine rubbed one on her cloak and held it up to get a better look at it.

"The chest must have gotten knocked over," Gerald explained. "I'm a little surprised no one found them before now. I guess scavengers mistook them for pieces of rubble like everything else. Anyway, like I said, the 15th Lord of Marble House's passion wasn't stones; it was exotic plants. They were quite beautiful, too, but I doubt any of them survived."

"Some things can't be replaced, can they?" Holly-Mine asked.

"No, Little One, they can't. Do you know what they used to call me when I lived here?" he asked, changing the subject.

"The Thin Man," Holly-Mine answered, picking a round-cut ruby out of a divot in the floor, not unlike the rubies in her amulet. "It's not a very nice name, is it?"

"I probably deserved it. I wasn't a nice person back then."

"Stop that, Uncle Gerald. You were sad. Everyone gets sad from time to time."

Gerald smiled. He appreciated how Holly-Mine looked at the world but couldn't forgive himself that easily.

"I had a nickname, too," she said offhandedly.

"You have many nicknames. I call you Little One. And I believe Aarghathlain calls you Sweet Girl."

Holly-Mine giggled. She loved those nicknames. "I mean, when people didn't know what to call me, they called me Brown Eyes."

Gerald liked that name. "That's much nicer than TTM."

"Yes, but it wasn't my name," Holly-Mine said matter-of-factly as she searched for more gemstones.

"That's true. Here," he said, handing her a stubby candle and a tinderbox he'd found. "I used to have lots of these. There were no windows in the attik, so I collected discarded bits of candles and stashed them away."

"Thanks," she said, putting the candles in her bag. "I'm okay for now. The moon is bright tonight."

Gerald nodded and headed for the stairs.

The first couple of steps were easy enough, but as he moved higher, a flood of memories returned, making him pause. He'd climbed those steps many times, and the more he thought about it, the more he realized how much he hated his old room. This place didn't represent refuge anymore. It was a prison where he'd locked his feelings away so no one would see the misery consuming him.

When he reached the top, he contemplated the door before opening it. He'd often wondered why the attik's doors were made of wood when everything else in the house was constructed from stone or metal. There must have been a reason, but he'd never asked the old oak about it.

He pushed on the door, and it crashed inward. "I'm all right," he called to Holly-Mine.

"I know," she said, not turning around. "Be careful."

"Always," he said, stepping over the broken door.

Like the rest of the house, the roof was gone, and the room was in an intolerable state, so he set about tidying the space. He understood the need to clean his room was irrational–especially amid such destruction–but he did it anyway.

Surprisingly, his bed remained more or less intact. He carefully turned back what was left of the covers, revealing a clean spot that looked entirely out of place. Before sitting down, he picked up two small books lying on the floor. When he blew on them, a cloud of dust filled the room, and he coughed.

Holly-Mine's voice wafted from the attik below. "You said you'd be careful."

"I am. It's only dust," he explained, watching a light autumn breeze carry it out of the room.

The first book was his *Tome of Triumphs,* or *T of T's* as he used to call it. Its contents consisted entirely of how he'd made other people feel inferior. This embarrassed him so much that he couldn't bring himself to open the cover.

"Was my life so bad that I only derived joy from other people's sorrow? I'll never write anything in you ever again," he said, putting it down. "And you. How are you today, *BoB?* Still gloating over my mistakes? Well, I've changed. I've learned that a mess-up here and there is to be expected from life. If you don't make any mistakes, you probably aren't doing much living, so here's to you, *Book of Blunders.* You don't upset me anymore. And you know what? You're right where you belong."

With that, Gerald placed the journal on top of the *T of T's* and strode out of the room, leaving his books and his old life behind forever.

As he descended the stairs, Holly-Mine smiled to herself.

Turning toward him, she said, "Uncle Gerald, come look at what I've found!"

• • •

Dramwitch sat on the edge of a depression he'd discovered on one of his previous trips to the ruin. It stood to reason that if anything had survived the explosion, it would be below ground, but he didn't relish the idea of climbing under the rubble, especially without a light of some kind. So he sat there, contemplating his next move.

He'd never visited any of the high homes in their heyday, being that he hadn't finished his Third Circle studies yet, but he'd heard stories about their opulence–tall mirrors that reached the ceiling, polished stone hallways, and decadent parties with even more decadent dessert platters that covered long tables in elegant dining rooms. Dram loved fancy dessert tables, not that he'd ever seen one, but it was fun to dream.

Sweets weren't a thing in the Wastes, especially if they needed to be chilled or frozen. Most people were lucky to scrounge enough scraps to call something a meal, so the sumptuous dinner parties held by the lords and ladies of Gemini City held a particular fascination for Lowlanders like him.

Of course, Dram was treated to all manner of delicacies at the Spire, such as saloop (a hot drink made from orchid roots or sassafras with milk and sugar), jellied eels, mincemeat pies, and treacle. But he'd have to wait to experience the annual Wizards' Feast until after he graduated. That was where the truly extravagant confections made an appearance. When that finally happened, he planned on grabbing the largest spoon he could find and sampling every trifle!

• • •

Aargh and Mnoonge chose to start their search in the study, or, more accurately, what remained of it.

"How are we going to find anything in this?" Mnoonge asked, speaking Aargh's thoughts aloud. "I'm sure scavengers have thoroughly picked through the wreckage."

Like most wizards, Aargh had always talked to himself. However, hearing the thoughts rattling around in his mind spoken aloud was unnerving, and he needed to be careful—like when Mnoonge commented on Gerald's new clothing. He'd been thinking about the stories he'd heard of a wandering storyteller in colorful garb but didn't mean to say, "They really are outlandish!" Thankfully, Gerald had taken it in stride, saying children were less afraid of colorful clothing than the black he used to wear.

It didn't take much effort to imagine how awkward it might be if his inner thoughts were revealed at an inopportune moment. He probably should have considered the possibility before giving his voice to Mnoonge, but he couldn't do anything about that now. He'd have to learn to deal with the consequences of a slip-up now and then.

That being said, enticing Dramwitch to join them in the Underoof had been a reasonably successful trial run of his and Mnoonge's connection. It hadn't been without difficulty, but everything had worked out in the end. Of course, the real test of their connection was yet to come, and time would tell if he'd made the right decision or not.

Aargh's body stiffened.

Clearing her throat, Mnoonge used her rat voice to ask, "What's wrong, Wizard Aarghathlain?"

"I'm not entirely sure," she said, returning to using Aargh's voice. "If I'm not mistaken, something here wants to be found."

Aargh knew it couldn't be a memory because he'd left the house as a baby, but what then? Did his mother share a thought with him that he was supposed to remember? Was that possible? He'd shared his voice with Mnoonge, so why not? The real question was, why had he been drawn to this spot?

The more Aargh focused on the sensation, the more conflicted he became. Whatever wished to be found also wanted to remain hidden at the same time.

"How peculiar," Mnoonge observed.

Aargh agreed, even though he'd been the one to say it. He could get used to having conversations with himself through Mnoonge. In a way, it was kind of fun.

Slowly, they picked their way across the room to where the lord's desk used to sit. Its mangled remnants were crumpled on the floor against what remained of the study's northern wall. There was a time when the desk had been elegant–a thin piece of polished marble sitting atop finely crafted metal lacework–but that time had passed.

"There's nothing here but rubbish," Mnoonge said, climbing onto a stone and shaking her head with Aargh's disappointment. "I was so sure, too."

The rock they were sitting on had a fissure running through it, but the slab wasn't split in two. Aargh supposed a weak vein had given way during the explosion–a hidden flaw revealing itself when pressure was exerted on it. He wondered if, when push came to shove, any weak veins would reveal themselves in him, too. He hoped not. Maybe they already had.

As they sat in silence, he absently doodled on the dusty floor, drawing the outline of Thelbaldus Harnock's constellation. Its story was one of Holly-Mine's favorites, probably because his stars were easy to find in the night sky. That and the fact he was known in the lower blocks as *Tharnock the First*. It was a funny contraction of his name that made her giggle.

• • •

In the far corner of Marble House, Holly-Mine studied the sky. "Uncle Gerald?"

"Yes?" he answered, putting down a damaged chalice.

"Tell me about Tharnock."

"The explorer Thelbaldus Harnock? The constellation, um, right there with the bright star at the bottom, right?" he asked.

"Yes, that's the one. Please tell it to me," Holly-Mine said with her best puppy-dog eyes.

How could he say *no* to that? Searching would have to wait.

"Tharnock, as you call him, is beginning to rise in the sky as autumn wanes and the solstice nears. It's said that he was the only person to have ever traveled the entire length of the River Wide–his voyage beginning and ending right here in Ardilakk Valley. Tharnock had many adventures along the way. He defeated mountain trolls, battled the famed Knights of Brauld, and was put to sleep by the Queen of the Night Faeries. But those trials paled in comparison to facing the dreaded Dragon Noir of Cairnoth Nor. It was there where he freed the young maiden Ilyaana, taking the dragon's power for his own."

Holly-Mine leaned on Gerald's leg, propping herself up on an elbow as she listened.

"After defeating the dragon, Tharnock lamented. He'd achieved his goal of conquering the river, and no other adventure captured his attention except one–to be a father. That's why he adopted Ilyaana, vowing to protect her from the evils that threatened the world. But as the tales of his accomplishments grew, so did his arrogance. Some say he believed he was invincible."

"Was he?" Holly-Mine asked as if she didn't already know the answer. It was all part of hearing the story, as far as she was concerned.

"Invincible? No. There's no question that he was powerful, but achieving something against all odds is not the same as being invincible. When they returned to Ardilakk Valley, he built a palace on the Highland Grasslands. They say it was a grand stone building with gold filigree and billowing banners that told the story of his adventures."

"It's not there now."

"No. It's long gone. Now the Norters live there in the Metal City. Anyway, from high atop his home, he often surveyed the river he'd conquered."

"Is it true that if you keep going on the River Wide, you end where you began?" she asked.

"That's what the stories say, but I've never made the trip myself. Though, I've often thought about how fascinating it would be to meet all the peoples of the river and to see the wondrous cities of the West. Maybe someday. Are you ready for me to continue?"

"Yes, please."

"One day, as Tharnock strolled along the high pass, he noticed a beautiful flower growing on the path. He'd only ever seen that particular flower once before, in Cairnoth Nor, at the mouth of the Dragon Noir's cave. He was sure Ilyaana would love to have it, so he plucked it from the ground to give it to his daughter. As Ilyaana returned from the farmers market on the outskirts of town, she saw what Tharnock had done and tried to stop him, but it was too late. When he breathed in its intoxicatingly sweet fragrance, he collapsed dead on the fields. This is why, when you trace Tharnock's outline in the sky, the brightest star of his constellation is the flower at his feet–the *White Bell of Eathēsium*, known collo-quially as *Tharnock's Bain*."

"That's terrible!" Holly-Mine exclaimed. It didn't matter how often she heard the story; it always upset her. "Have you ever seen one?"

"Eathēsium? Why, no. There aren't any dragons in the world, at least, not that I've heard of."

"What does that have to do with it?"

"It only grows near living dragons, feeding on the animal's power and warning travelers of the evil nearby. It doesn't mat-ter if dragons try to burn the plants with their fiery breath, crush them with their great taloned claws, or use magic to destroy them. As long as a dragon is near, Eathēsium grows, but the serpent must be careful. If they breathe in the flower's fragrant scent, it takes every last drop of their power at once, and they die just as Tharnock did."

"Why would it do that?" Holly-Mine asked.

"Maybe the Earth Mother grows them to protect people from dragons. Or, I guess, it could be the other way around. I haven't thought about it."

Holly-Mine wrinkled her nose. "Seems a little extreme to me."

"You might feel differently if you were in the presence of a wyvern, with its giant leathery wings…or a thunderous druk crashing down from the mountains…or worst of all, the ghastly hydra with its nine heads!" Gerald said, making his hands into claws and roaring.

"There you go again, being silly!" she said, laughing. "Dragons aren't always scary. I've read that some had colorful feathers and were as small as chickens. It's in my book, *Mythological Creatures, and Their Peculiar Habits.*"

"Yes, that's what they say," Gerald agreed.

"But you haven't finished the story. Continue, please."

"As you wish." Gerald put away his claws and said, "Ilyaana mourned the loss of her father–burying him near the base of the Eastern Foothills as far away from the Highland Cliffs as possible. The mound where his body lays is known as Widow's Peak."

"But why Widow's Peak, Uncle Gerald? Ilyaana was his daughter, not his wife."

"I think it's a metaphor for being left alone. Many husbands or wives, sons or daughters have been *widowed* by greed or lust for power."

"That's strange. There must be more to the story, don't you think?" Holly-Mine asked.

"Possibly. I am but a simple storyteller...a weaver of dreams. I am conversant in the proper way to greet captains and queens and can float unseen through a room, whispering sweet nothings in people's ears. How do I know they hear me? By the slight upturn of the corner of their lips. That's the extent of what I need, my fair lady, to achieve a life of happiness."

Holly-Mine laughed again.

Gerald bowed and said, "And that, Little One, is the most beautiful sound in the world."

She knew there was far more to Gerald than sweet nothings, as keenly as she knew there was more–far more–to Tharnock's story, but exactly what eluded her.

"Papa?" she said, reaching out to her father in her mind. "When we get back, will you tell me the story of the *Trial of Arkorar?* The one where Tharnock offers to sacrifice himself to save his daughter?"

• • •

"Yes, my Sweet Girl," Mnoonge said.

Aargh didn't add anything else or explain, so the small rat didn't ask. She assumed it was a private conversation between Aargh and Holly-Mine, and she was right.

"What's this?"

Aargh's shoe caught on a long, flat piece of iron, and he nudged it. It fell perfectly into a depression in the stone. He wouldn't have noticed it if the explosion hadn't dislodged the metal from its resting place.

"Curious," Mnoonge remarked for him.

Aargh got on his hands and knees to inspect it, and Mnoonge climbed down to join him for a sniff. When he brushed away the dirt, she sneezed.

"Sorry," she said.

"Ahem. No problem," she added in her rat voice. "It's a handle, isn't it?"

"Yes," Mnoonge answered herself again, trying not to lose track of who was speaking.

Aargh grabbed the metal and pulled. A thin, obsidian box slid out of the floor. It was a couple of inches wide, and since it was open on one side, it resembled a drawer more than a box. Inside, there was a small leather-bound book, not unlike Aargh's diary.

"That's strange," Mnoonge whispered as Aargh lifted the book out of the container.

Fascination became disappointment when Aargh realized there was no writing inside. As he flipped through the book's empty pages, a small envelope slipped out and fell onto the ground.

He stooped to retrieve it but paused. On the front was written:

for Aarghathlain

A letter addressed to him? But how? And why was it hidden in this book?

The note's bright white paper, crisp edges, and unfaded ink belied the desolation that had hidden it from view. It wasn't the mottled brown of modern recycled paper. This was the expensive white paper used by upper lords before the moratorium on cutting Northern Forest trees had been enacted. These days, unrecycled paper had to be imported, and few people spent money on something so frivolous as stationery. That is, except for the Lord and Lady Preservation Society. They used it by the ream.

Aargh turned the letter over in his hands. Taking the red wax between his thumbs, he broke the seal holding the flap closed but not before noting the mark of the Lord of Marble House stamped in it. Every lord wore a ring used to make their mark on letters such as this one. People said Opal Hall Museum contained a superb display of upper and lower lord's rings. Aargh didn't know if the collection was impressive, and he didn't care either. He'd be happy if he never crossed paths with anyone from the old high society ever again after what the Master Prefect did.

The truth was, learning about his connection to a lordship weighed on him. He'd have to come to terms with that one day, but for now, he tried to ignore the nagging knot in his stomach and focused on the task at hand.

With a deep breath, he carefully opened the flap, revealing several small sheets of paper inside. Each was folded neatly in half. As he opened the pages, he noticed the faint scent of ink and paper mingling together. A sense of nostalgia overwhelmed him like a memory was trying to surface, but it remained out of reach.

His mind and heart raced as he read the inscription at the top of the page.

Bardelthlain
Lord of Marble House

Aargh,

If you are reading this letter, my worst fears have come true. I couldn't keep the book away from you, and I am no longer part of your life.

I'm sorry, my son. I hope you have found happiness in the world without me and that you remember our time together fondly. You must never forget how much your mother and I loved you.

Tomorrow, we will set out for a cottage and farm I've prepared in the Northern Forest. I hope to leave the evils plaguing Gemini City far behind, but my heart tells me we'll be pursued wherever we go.

Magic will find you, of that I'm certain, and I have no doubt you will be drawn to the book. That is why I have left you this letter.

Aargh stopped reading and slumped onto a large, flat piece of marble.

Holly-Mine sensed the apprehension gripping her father, but she didn't go to him. This discovery was for him alone, and she didn't want to interfere. Instead, she directed Gerald to another area of the attik to continue their search.

When he was ready, Aargh continued reading.

I imagine you are wondering why I hid an empty book from you. The pages aren't blank. They're filled with the most dangerous spells ever created. Magic has always exist-ed, but few have learned to harness its power as he has.

Your mother has the gift. She's a great healer, but being bound by the rules of magic, she can't heal herself. Her last act was to conceal the contents of this book from prying eyes. I miss her. I have to get out of this house. There are too many memories here.

Aarghathlain, listen to me: DO NOT READ THIS BOOK!

If it were within my power to destroy it, I would rid the world of its evil forever, but I am no wizard, and it proba-bly wouldn't matter if I were. This magic is beyond anyone who yet lives.

If you read it, you'll be tempted to do things no person should do. No matter how painful it may be, let those who are gone rest and leave the future to those who have not yet come. The Great Cycle must be broken!

"My mother was a wizard," Aargh thought. "I wonder if Aldenthwaine was her mentor, too. And what does Papa mean? I thought the Great Cycle meant that everything had to return to the Earth Mother. You know, ashes to ashes, dust to dust."

The following line caught his eye before he could think more about it.

There's no way to tell if safety awaits us beyond the Once-Great Wall, but at least, if we're found, we won't have the book with us. That's why I'm leaving it behind. I can't imagine what it would take to reveal it to you—probably the destruction of Marble House. If that has happened, elemen-tal magic has likely returned to Gemini City. I doubt any-thing else could break your mother's spell.

There is magic in you. Powerful magic.
He wants it.
He will come for you.

Papa

Aargh was at a loss. What spells were so terrible that his father and mother chose to hide the pages on which they were written? Elemental magic was dangerous, true, but it wasn't good or evil. It was simply accessed differently than the intellectual magic of the Spire.

And if his parents were adamant about him not finding it, who or what had drawn him here? More importantly, who was this mysterious wizard? The Wizard of the Council? That didn't make sense. The imposter hadn't appeared to recognize him.

Aargh's hand drifted over the book's cover as it lay on his lap. It was warm and comforting. He imagined a mother's embrace might feel that way.

"This is her magic," Mnoonge said, lost in the wizard's thoughts.

Aargh knew it with every fiber of his being, and he longed to learn more, so he reached out to it, searching for her. Was she still there? Had she left her mark on the book when she'd enchanted it? Maybe if he–

"No, Papa! Stop! Don't speak to the book!"

Holly-Mine's voice was so sharp that it startled everyone.

"What? Who? Holly-Mine, what's wrong?" Mnoonge asked.

"You mustn't bring it back!" Holly-Mine yelled, picking her way toward him as quickly as possible, but the damage had already been done.

A searing pain shot through Aargh's hand, and he dropped the book.

Without realizing what he'd been doing, he'd released the tome's magic–ancient magic, neither his mother's nor his own–and now it was free.

CHAPTER 19

TOGETHER, WE STAND
THE WIZARDS' UNDERGROUND

The members of the The Wizards' Underground sat uncomfortably beneath the effigies of their forefathers, waiting for Brindlewise to speak. Eerie didn't even come close to describing the moonlit figures looming over them. Making matters worse, their familiars had also been immortalized in stone. One eagle was so masterfully crafted that its eyes stared in your direction, no matter where you sat. Fizzbain put his back to that one, but its stony gaze still weighed on his shoulders.

Everyone wondered why Brindlewise had called a meeting in the sculpture garden. It was a lousy place to gather in secret. Building #1's two stories of windows overlooked the area, and there were plenty of shadows for anyone lurking about to hide. Moreover, they'd been sitting quietly in the dark for nearly an hour. If Dram were there, he'd have gotten the meeting going. Organizing was his specialty.

Finally, Brindlewise cleared his throat as if he had something to say. Illbrhass, who'd been silently practicing a tune by moving his hand along Ginny's fingerboard, put the viola back in her case, and Paladand called to Pud and Tassior because they'd wandered to another part of the garden to chat.

"Our numbers are reduced this evening," Brindlewise began. "If the report Bee relayed is accurate–and I have no reason to doubt him–Aarghathlain, Holly-Mine, and

Dramwitch are safely hidden beneath the city. Let's hope they stay there."

"Never gonna happen," Garth muttered under his breath.

"What's that?" Brindlewise asked

"I said: I doubt Aargh will just sit around waiting. He's more of a get-up-and-go kind of person. Always has been."

"True, true," Brindlewise agreed, pausing before continuing his report.

"Any other news?" Paladand asked, prodding the old wizard.

"Yes, of course. Quite right. Alantus is making his recovery in the infirmary. I visited him before coming here. He's in high spirits, rambling on about saving an *Agalinis acuta.* I believe he'd like to transplant it to one of the greenhouses in the hopes of expanding its numbers. We're all grateful to you, Paladand, for helping him in the forest."

The wizards clicked their fingers in agreement–their version of clapping.

When the snapping subsided, Brindlewise continued. "Unfortunately, our friend Bee is still locked in his room–"

"It's not right," Onaveris blurted.

"No, O, it isn't, but the situation here at the Spire is far more precarious than even I foresaw."

After a lifetime of speaking with trees, Brindlewise had a bond with the future the others hadn't cultivated yet, and the way he addressed them was unsettling.

"I've brought you here this evening…Paladand, Garthelwaite, Pud, Fizzbain, Onaveris, Tassior, Illbrahss, and Afynn…to give you one last chance to leave our pact."

"Uh…what?" Afynn asked, shocked at the mere suggestion of such a thing.

"Let me finish. No one is telling you what to do, and I'm not pressuring anyone into staying or going. A lot has happened in the past week. Members of the Order have attacked Aargh, Bartlebee has been silenced by the highest authority at the school, and Alantus nearly lost his life to a familiar. In all my wizarding years, I've never heard of that happening in Ardilakk Valley. It's almost more than I can bear."

Tassior took Brindlewise's arm, helping the old wizard sit on a bench near him.

"Thank you, Tass. When we made our pledge that day in the Observation Lounge, I doubt any of us saw this coming. How could we? These events are unprecedented in the school's history. Therefore, it's important to understand that you may go if you wish. I promise, no one here will hold it against you."

The night seemed to stand still as they contemplated what Brindlewise had said.

Unsurprisingly, Paladand spoke first. "I can't unsee the burning of Aargh's home. It's brought back memories I thought I'd come to terms with. Memories that I now know will forever haunt me."

The distressed wizards fidgeted uncomfortably. No amount of time would silence the trees screaming in the corners of their minds. The postulants had no idea how blessed they were, having come to the school after the time of the fire–free from the torment of hearing every tree in Ardilakk Valley burn.

Paladand continued, resolved in his intentions. "I will not allow Tarth to represent the future of wizarding here, in the valley, or anywhere along the River Wide. I'm staying."

Garthelwaite stood next, removing Bertie from his pocket. "I've been friends with Aargh since we were kids. He used to feed Bertie worms from the flowering beds. And there was this time when I took a fishing line…do you remember that Fizz? That was a lark!"

Onaveris cleared his throat.

"Oh, yes. Sorry. I digress," Garth continued. "What I mean to say is, Aargh and I have had our share of laughs. I guess it's time for us to cry together, too. No matter what the future holds, I stand with you, my friends, and I stand with Aarghathlain."

One by one, the other wizards stood, each pledging their allegiance to the group, Aargh, and preserving the sanctity of wizarding in Ardilakk Valley. Having made their decision, The Wizards' Underground was about to adjourn when the earth shuddered under their feet. Overwhelmed by dizziness, they collapsed onto the garden's broad flagstones as the air filled with a cacophony of shouting voices.

Dazed and confused, Paladand pulled himself over to a bench. "Be quiet!" he yelled. "Please, I can't hear myself think!" but his companions weren't the ones speaking.

Atop their stone pedestals, the sculptures had come to life, pontificating on a wide variety of topics. One pair of statues were locked in a heated argument about the best way to bow to a tree before following its roots. Others expounded on magical principles as if teaching a class. A particularly upset statue banged his hand on a stone lectern, telling his students to settle themselves; there would be a test next Frittersday. And a short, sad-faced wizard mournfully called for his missing familiar in a vertex of the triangular space.

Terrified, Paladand crawled over Afynn, who was curled into a ball with his hands covering his ears. Only one wizard was on his feet, the most unlikely of their group, Brindlewise.

"What's going on?" Paladand asked, but the old wizard only lifted his arm and pointed across the garden.

There, standing near the Footpath, was Aldenthwaine's statue...the only one in the entire space not speaking.

"I'm afraid to ask what that means!" the young wizard yelled above the din.

Brindlewise slowly shook his head.

Then, as mysteriously as it had started, the statues ceased their gesticulations, and silence fell over the grand entryway to the school. The members of The Wizards' Underground helped each other to their feet, once again waiting for Brindlewise to speak.

"I realize you want to understand what just happened, but I don't have an answer. All I can tell you is this: something has been awakened in Ardilakk Valley that should have remained asleep. I feel it in my bones."

CHAPTER 20

A RIVER OF MAGIC
AARGHATHLAIN

Aargh vibrated with magical energy. He could practically see it hovering around him, the way hot surfaces shimmer on summer days. And there, lying on the dusty floor at his feet, was the book.

The one thing he desired more than anything else, to feel his mother's presence, was gone, and it was his fault. Somehow, he'd broken her spell, and he despaired.

"Mother, I've failed you," Mnoonge wailed.

His body tingled, and he instinctively tried to brush the sensation away. The tiny hairs on his arm crackled under his hand. His mother's magic might be gone, but something remained. Something older. Darker.

Not yet willing to touch it again, he kicked the book, and it flipped over.

Fine gold letters on the cover announced:

The One True Book of Spells
by
Aldenthwaine the Incipient

"No!" Mnoonge cried, holding her head between her hands. "It can't be. Aldenthwaine saved me from the fire. He brought me to the school. He practically raised me. This can't be. My father must be wrong!"

Holly-Mine yelled, "Uncle Gerald, the book!"

Snatching it off the floor, Gerald pulled off his belt and wrapped it tightly around the magical tome. He could feel the power emanating from its pages and wanted to make sure it stayed closed.

"Hey, what's going on up here? Did a wall collapse? You need to see what I've found," Dram called to the others as he climbed out of a deep clearing in the rubble. "Wait. Is Head Master...I mean...Aargh? Are you okay?"

"Stay there, Dram," Holly-Mine called to him. "We'll come to you. Gerald, please help Papa. Mnoonge, are you feeling okay?"

Holly-Mine let the rat crawl onto her hand and gingerly placed Mnoonge in the outer pocket of her rucksack. Once her father's companion was safe and sound, they made their way through the maze of destruction–both the ruin of Marble House and the world Aargh thought he knew.

The main path, used to give guided tours, was relatively free of debris, bringing them close to where Dram was impatiently waiting.

Mnoonge poked her head out of the pocket and said, "I'm feeling a bit better. If you don't mind, I'd like to carry it," speaking for Aargh.

No one moved.

"Gerald?" Mnoonge asked, holding out her hand the same way Aargh was.

"I don't think it's the best idea either," Holly-Mine said in Gerald's mind, "but it might be safer with him than anywhere else."

Gerald looked at her, and she nodded. Then, he handed the book to Aargh.

"I can feel it, too," she told him.

The ex-head butler of Marble House smiled weakly.

Aargh slipped the book into his robes as they zigzagged between the broken rocks toward the depression.

"You don't look well. Are you sure you're okay?" Dram asked his former mentor.

"I'll manage," Mnoonge answered for him. "I had a shock, but I'm better now. Show us what you've found."

"There's a tunnel under the ruins. I moved these stones and felt air coming out of this hole. Is there a river under us? I can smell water."

Aargh was puzzled.

"Everyone knows about the River Underground, but I've never heard tell of it flowing beneath the city. Mnoonge, does the Collective know about a river in this area?" the rat asked herself.

Clearing her throat, she answered in her rat voice, "No, Wizard Aarghathlain. As far as I know, none of the Underoof tunnels connect with a river."

"And what about you, Gerald? Have you heard about this?"

"No, but no one has ever seen the River Underground, except where it exits the cliffs. Therefore, considering its route has never been mapped, I suppose it's possible."

"Let's find out. Dram, lead the way," Mnoonge directed from the pocket in Holly-Mine's bag.

But they only made it a few steps before a gravelly voice commanded, "Halt! Who goes there?"

Unsteady from his fright, Aargh slipped, landing face-to-face with the halter's bearded visage.

Without missing a beat, Dramwitch inserted himself into the situation. "Hold on, Mr. Whoever-you-are. Show some respect! You're speaking to the greatest wizard of the age!"

"Great veins of ore, we've got a live one here, don't we?" the bearded face chuckled.

"Dram, let's find out what's going on before jumping to conclusions," Mnoonge said.

"But he–" Dram began before being cut off.

"Hold it right there, Sonny! You obviously can't tell your axe from your pick if you take my meaning. I'm supposing you've never met a dwarf before. Not many of your kind have, so I'll not be coming down too hard on you. But I'd thank you for not making any assumptions. Our language isn't as crude as yours with he's and she's and such. If you must call me anything other than my rightful name, I'd prefer they, if you please."

Dram stood there dumbfounded. A dwarf? Impossible! No one actually lived under the mountain, mining priceless riches to fill their underground hoards. Those were stories to entertain children at bedtime. Weren't they?

Far more in control of her faculties than anyone else, Holly-Mine extended her hand and said, "Nice to meet you! May I ask your name?"

"Of course. I'm Stump!" the dwarf said cheerfully, slapping their legs. "And a mighty appropriate name it is, indeed. And what's yours, young lady?"

"Holly-Mine."

"What an excellent name! As green as a summer's day and as red as berries against winter's blanket. It's a pleasure to make your acquaintance."

Holly-Mine took the edges of her green cloak in her hands and curtsied.

"By your leave, young Holly-Mine," they continued. "Unless I'm much mistaken, there's a wizard I need to meet."

"Greetings, Stump. My name is Aarghathlain, Son of Lord Bardelthlain. Though, I have only recently discovered my connection to Marble House," Mnoonge explained as Aargh reached out his arm to the dwarf.

"By Gîrdlūm's beard. You don't say! You're little Aarghath-lain! You must be. You've got your mother's eyes!" Stump said, skipping Aargh's arm altogether and pinching his cheek. "How's your father? And by the way, I realize I'm not well-versed in the latest fashions, but is it customary for Gemini-ans to carry around talking rats these days? It's not the most efficient mode of communication if you don't mind my saying."

The laughing dwarf reminded Aargh of Grunt. So much so that when he squinted his eyes and held his tongue just so, he thought he could see a resemblance. Not wanting to offend the dwarf if he was mistaken, Aargh didn't say anything. It might be that he hadn't met many dwarves.

"I'm sorry, but my father passed away years ago," Mnoonge said as Aargh lifted the rat out of his daughter's bag.

Stump immediately stopped laughing and climbed out of the hole. They were right out of a fairytale, from their worn leather clothing to the stout axe slung across their back. Add to that their deep brindled beard carefully woven into two long plaits and the shining gemstone hanging around their neck, and yup, Stump was a dwarf! No doubt about it.

Although Stump didn't stand as tall as Aargh, the wizard wouldn't have called them short. Compact, possibly. Stump looked as if they could carry the entire world on their broad shoulders without breaking a sweat!

"You have my deepest sympathies, Aarghathlain, Son of Bardelthlain," the dwarf said, bowing low. "I had hoped to see him again. I have many fond memories of strolling with your father and mother along the banks of the river. He never failed to stop and buy her a bouquet of purple phlox. The ones that bloom at night. They smell sweet...like almonds and honey."

Aargh was having difficulty processing what was happening, so Gerald stepped in to continue the introductions. "This is Dramwitch, Wizard of the Third Circle and former assistant to Aarghathlain."

"You've got spirit, young man!" Stump said, bowing low.

"Thank...you," Dram stuttered, still unable to believe he was in the presence of a dwarf.

"You've already met Holly-Mine," Gerald continued. "Aarghathlain's daughter."

"Ah, yes," Stump said with a wink. "You've got the sparkle about you, little princess. No gem will ever shine brighter."

"And I am Gerald, former Head Butler of Marble House. I must say, I'm curious. I never saw any dwarves roaming the hallways."

"No surprise there. We dwarves, haven't set foot in Gemini City since before the burning of the North Towns. It was Bardelthlain who discovered this here tunnel. He was the only Geminian to visit the chasm city in an age of the world. Of course, he never saw it during its heyday, but the North-rim are back, and it's thriving again! It's a good thing, too. There isn't much left for us dwarves under the mount. Most of our halls and mines were destroyed when Ardilakk cracked."

"It was you I saw in the ravine!" Mnoonge managed, overwhelmed by Aargh's emotions. "And there's a city at the bottom?"

"Absolutely! Though it probably wasn't me who you saw. I've spent most of the last thirty-three years–and many before–guarding the tunnel, but it was definitely the Brethren."

"The Brethren?" Mnoonge asked.

"Dwarven kind."

"Oh."

"This here's the only way to get there from Gemini City, thanks to your father reopening it. And, if you're so inclined, I'll take you to it. Though, we might have to do something about your outfit first. Dwarves don't take kindly to wizards," Stump explained.

"Why is that?" Holly-Mine asked, but she didn't get an answer.

Aargh had pulled Aldenthwaine's book out of his robes because it was poking him in the side, and the dwarf's reaction was immediate.

Stump went pale, at least as pale as a dwarf could go, and said, "You have the book! Oh no! He said it would call to you. You haven't read it, have you? Quick, Son of Bardelthlain, you must tell me!"

"No. No, I haven't," Mnoonge answered the dwarf. "But why? What's the big deal? Aldenthwaine discovered magic. So have I."

"The wizard who wrote that book didn't discover magic. Come with me. There's much you need to hear, and this is not a conversation to have out in the open."

The entire group moved toward the tunnel, but Stump raised their hands, blocking them from entering. "I'm sorry, but this is for Aarghathlain alone."

"But I can't leave my daughter," Mnoonge said for Aargh.

The small rat from the lower blocks felt how worried he was and involuntarily took a step toward Holly-Mine.

"Go ahead, Papa. I'll be fine. Uncle Gerald is here, and we can find Ralph. I promised I'd visit him. Besides, I can't imagine Ralph hasn't heard about our house. He might be worried about me."

"I don't know," Aargh said in her mind. "I promised myself I wouldn't leave you again."

"Papa, that's an impossible promise to keep. You can't always be with me. We'll go downtown, say hello to Ralph, and come right back." Then she turned to Gerald and said aloud, "We'll be careful. Right, Uncle Gerald?"

"Absolutely," the slender man agreed. "You have my word."

Aargh kissed his daughter on the forehead and backed away, pointing at the amulet.

"Dram," Mnoonge said. "We can safely assume Tarth will want to return to the Spire. Make sure he does, but also figure out how he got out without anyone noticing in the first place. We want him on the grounds, but not without us knowing."

"Aarghathlain," Dram said, still uncomfortable using his mentor's name. "It would be easier if I knew what we were looking for. Are you sure you can't think of anything? I mean, no one knows the school and city better than you."

"It's becoming painfully obvious that I'm in the dark about a great many things–things to do with my past, the city, and especially the Spire," Mnoonge explained. "I've never heard of a secret way off the school grounds. If I did, it would have made my exploits with Bee much easier, I can tell you."

Dram had a funny expression on his face. "I have trouble imagining you sneaking out. Weren't you worried about being caught? Or worse, expelled?"

"Can't say it crossed my mind. We were only having a bit of fun. Most of the time, when I left the grounds, I visited Mother Tree. When Bee came with me, we often climbed False Hope Bluff to watch the ships on the river."

"I once took the rowboat out after curfew," Dram offered.

"Did you now? You surprise me. I guess there's a little larceny in there after all," Mnoonge said, waggling her indexing finger at the young wizard.

"I was going to try and catch a fish, but I dropped my stick overboard and decided to watch the stars from the island instead."

Aargh and Mnoonge both looked at Dram. "Wait! Are you saying that you went to the island in the middle of Lake Hîrdehn-dūl? Alone? At night? You're made of sterner stuff than I thought!"

"It was no big deal. I didn't explore the ruins or anything."

"Too bad. If I wanted to hide a tunnel, I'd do it there. An ancient ruin on a haunted island sounds ideal for that kind of thing."

"It's not haunted," Dram said, a note of concern creeping into his voice. "Honestly, I can't imagine a tunnel being kept secret. It must be hidden. Maybe by magic."

"It's not impossible," Mnoonge said, stroking her chin the way Aargh was doing, though she didn't sport a goatee like he did.

"If we could see magic—like when healers cast their spell—we'd know for sure if Tarth was hiding something," Dram suggested.

Aargh considered this. Casting a spell on a single object was one thing, but enchanting the Spire grounds, city, or possibly all of Ardilakk Valley to reveal Tarth's subterfuge was an entirely different story. Though, to be fair, he wasn't above trying.

Dram waited for Aargh to come to a decision. His mentor often approached problems…opportunities (he was working on seeing the positive side of every situation)…from a different perspective, and he gave Aargh space to think.

"Guildebrande?" Mnoonge asked. "Would you be willing to assist me? I have an idea."

"It would be my honor, Wizard Aarghathlain," the blade replied.

After drawing the sword from its scabbard, Aargh lifted Guildebrande over his head, illuminating what remained of Marble House.

Mnoonge raised her arms and swayed as Aargh's magic flowed through her. "Great Earth Mother, please reveal what magic lives in Ardilakk Valley. We seek to understand what drives our brother to forsake our creed and persecute those who wish to preserve your generous gift."

A deep rumble shook the ground under their feet. Gulls along the shoreline took flight, mewing as they soared into the air, and the forest creaked and swayed. *She's coming!*

"WIZARD AARGHATHLAIN, STEWARD OF THE ELEMENTS, AND KEEPER OF THE PRECIOUS CHILD," the Earth Mother's voice echoed in the core of Aargh's mind and body, "YOU KNOW NOT OF WHAT YOU SPEAK."

"Help me to understand, Earth Mother. What is it that I'm missing?" Aargh asked through Mnoonge.

Although Gerald couldn't understand what the Earth Mother was saying, he sensed her presence and bowed.

Awe filled Dram's heart. His mentor was truly great! He'd always known it, but watching him speak to the Earth Mother was almost more than he could comprehend. "Are you seeing this? That's my mentor! Can you believe it? He's speaking to the Earth Mother!"

Holly-Mine took Dram by the hand and leaned her head on his shoulder. "Someday, you will, too."

Feats of that nature were far beyond the scope of Dram's wildest dreams, and he threw his other hand in the air and laughed.

Mnoonge continued, "I am here. I am listening."

The Earth Mother responded. "MUCH HAS BEEN GIVEN FREELY, BUT MORE HAS BEEN TAKEN BY FORCE. PROTECT

THE GIFT, BUT HURRY. YOU MUST CLOSE THE GATE BEFORE OTHERS TAKE WHAT IS NOT RIGHTFULLY THEIRS!"

Her answer took Aargh by surprise. The message sounded similar to the voice of the mount, but what were they trying to tell him?

Mnoonge heard the Earth Mother's response, too, through Aargh. Terrified by her awesome vastness, she scrambled to the top of a nearby pillar, trying to get as far away from the ground as possible.

"I don't understand. What do you—"

Aargh didn't have a chance to finish his question before a purple light appeared between the Mounts of Ardilakk. High above the Congregational House, magic burst forth, cascading into the valley. It reminded him of the Underground Falls in springtime, gushing out of the rock face below the Highland Grasslands.

Aargh, Guildebrande, and Holly-Mine glowed brightly, as did Mnoonge, Gerald, and Dram, to a lesser extent. Magic was everywhere, and it flowed from Ardilakk! Wizards had always said the mountain was the root of the valley's magic, but seeing it was indescribable as it poured out in great waves. There were eddies, rapids, and undulating pools rippling with magical energy.

Aargh's smile faded when he caught sight of the school. The magic didn't appear to be flowing to the Spire; instead, it was being gathered by it. Alarmed, he climbed to higher ground by scaling a pile of rubble.

"Papa, wait. It's too dangerous," Holly-Mine called after him, but he was already on top.

Even from four blocks away, he could feel it pulling on him. How strange. He'd never noticed it before. How was that possible? Maybe he'd become accustomed to it. This must be what the Earth Mother meant. Ardilakk had given magic freely to the world, but the school was taking more than its fair share by force.

"Dram, look at the Spire," Mnoonge directed.

"Yes, Mentor. I see it. I don't believe it, but I see it."

Aargh shifted his weight, and the stone beneath his foot gave way. Instead of falling to the ground, he found himself in Stump's arms.

"Thank you, Stump," Mnoonge said. "You saved me from a nasty fall."

"Wizards aren't known for their climbing ability, are they?" the dwarf asked rhetorically. "Can't you tell this pile of stones is unstable?"

"I must admit, that didn't cross my mind. Can you help me off of here?"

"Already am, and might I say, that is a fine weapon you carry, worthy of a wizard."

Guildebrande glowed even brighter.

When they reached the stone floor, Holly-Mine inspected her father's ankle. "You promised you'd listen to me, Papa, remember?"

"I'm sorry. It's just that I'm afraid there's more to Tarth's plan than any of us imagined. What if he knows what's drawing Ardilakk's magic to the Spire?"

"Whatever it is, it must be powerful," Dram suggested.

"You're right, and you'll have to be the one to warn the others. I fear something terrible is on the verge of happening," Mnoonge said, shaking with fright.

With his magical energy spent, Aargh dropped Guildebrande and fell into Holly-Mine's waiting arms.

"Papa, are you hurt?"

"I'm not so bad," he said in her mind. "I hope we aren't too late."

"Don't worry. The magic hasn't stopped flowing. That means Tarth hasn't done anything yet. There's still time."

"But how much?" he wondered.

Slowly, the river of magic faded, and the stars became visible again. Tharnock reappeared in all of his glory, as did the White Bell of Eathēsium.

Aargh looked up, thinking, "I hope we haven't already breathed too deeply the enticing fragrance of Tharnock's Bain."

CHAPTER 21

DAWN OF A NEW DAY

GEMINI CITY & TARTHANABELLE

Landingsday of the 8th week

Wide, sleepless eyes peered out of windows across Gemini City as the sun rose over the Eastern Foothills. No one had words for what they'd seen during the night or the terror it inspired. The purple river of magic they'd witnessed flowing around, over, and through everything proved what they'd been dreading ever since the defeat of the Wizard of the Council: magic in Ardilakk Valley was untethered and free to do as it pleased.

Compounding the situation, the Norters hadn't made contact yet. This resulted in countless sleepless nights as images of airships flying overhead or a black-clad army invading from the highlands plagued everyone's dreams. And the more time that passed, the greater their suspicions grew.

If that was all Geminians had to worry about, they might have been able to keep their fear in check, but the strange sounds and eerie golden glow emanating from under the streets made them feel like they were being assaulted from every direction. To say they were on edge would have been akin to calling a Giant Sequoia the perfect houseplant. Things were spiraling out of control, and the city's representatives knew it. So, without delay, they headed to the Congregational House to try and prevent a catastrophe.

Topping the list of things to discuss was how to deal with the Norters. There was no question that they had also witnessed the magic, but nobody knew how they would react. That's why it was essential to make it abundantly clear that if magic belonged to anyone in Ardilakk Valley, it was Gemini City, and they had no intention of letting the interlopers take it from them.

As the Grand Rotunda filled with representatives, the discussion centered on determining what preemptive steps they could take to contain the Norter threat. Gemini City was done waiting to see what the people in the highland camps were planning. If conflict was coming, it would be on their terms!

• • •

Tarth stood on a flat rooftop surrounded by a haphazard collection of metal buildings, which wasn't unusual because he was looking down on the Northrim's Metal City. The fact that he'd glowed from head to toe, however, was unusual, to say the least.

"So, Aargh, you figured it out," he thought, examining his hands. "At least you've figured out part of it. But are you prepared for what you'll find hidden under the Spire? I wonder." Tarth rounded on his companions, making them flinch. "It's time to forge a new path."

"But Tarth," Flinghower stammered. "We were…glowing!"

"So what? I told you I'd find a way to cast elemental magic, and I will. Ralph, here, proves that. Feel free to stand there gawking at Aargh's little trick if you want to, but I have work to do." Turning to the west, he continued, "This is where I say goodbye to you, Gemini City. The next time we meet, you'll wish I'd never left."

With that, he walked to the edge of the building, where he was met by triumphant cheers from the crowd assembled on the streets below.

"Magic!" he hollered. "For too long, the people of the north have been forced to float above the world, deprived of a place to call home. For too long, generations of your ancestors have drifted wizardless through time. And for far too long, the Sowtowns have prevented the Northrim from reaching their full potential. Follow me and reclaim your ancestral homelands!"

Cheers echoed between the city's metal walls.

"What do you think, young Ralph?" Tarth asked, pointing to the sky. "Would you like to learn how to make magic like that? I imagine your friend, Holly-Mine, would be impressed. No?"

"Can I?" the boy asked, wide-eyed and eager to learn.

"Oh, yes. You will," Tarth said, tousling the boy's scraggly hair. "And it will be spectacular. A new day is dawning in Ardilakk Valley."

Sattersday of the 8th week

CHAPTER 22

OIL AND WATER

AARGHATHLAIN

Aargh sat motionless in the tunnel beneath Marble House, sensing the air moving around him as it flowed back toward the city. It had an earthy scent to it with a touch of dampness. Not a moldy, rotten stench but the fresh, wholesome smell of running water.

It couldn't have been more than a few days since he and Mnoonge had parted ways with Holly-Mine, Gerald, and Dram, but the oppressive darkness wore on him. At least some light filtered into the Underoof through storm drains and stormhole covers. Here, it didn't matter if his eyes were open or closed. It all looked the same: black.

Stump, for his part, didn't appear to be affected, often chatting away as if they were taking a stroll in the park on a beautiful autumn day–not that the pair had spent much time walking. The exhaustion of having to grope his way along the stone passage, coupled with the stress of recent events, had taken a heavy toll on Aargh, and they often stopped to rest. He couldn't sleep, though, so mostly, they spent the time talking or munching on jerky and dried fruit.

Aargh marveled at how comfortable Stump was below ground. It wasn't that the dwarf could see in the dark, per se–more that they had an innate understanding of their surroundings. Aargh didn't know if this was a dwarven trait or simply that Stump had spent so much time in this tunnel.

Either way, Aargh wished he possessed the dwarf's skill at navigating in the dark.

Mnoonge, who was sitting close to Aargh (but not too close as she didn't want to get squished by mistake), asked, "Stump. How long is this tunnel?"

"4.855 miles."

"Wait. What?" Mnoonge blurted, not only adept at speaking for Aargh but also capturing the exact tone he was going for. "Are you saying we could have been there in a few hours?"

"No, Son of Bardelthlain, that is not what I am saying."

"But–"

"If we were walking on city streets, possibly, but have you been paying attention? We haven't exactly been walking in a straight line. Dwarves don't just blast through anything they want. Well, sometimes we do, but only when the terrain is too unstable to burrow safely. We are following the natural flow of the bedrock. There'll be plenty of twists and turns, ups and downs, before we get there. How are you at climbing?"

Aargh didn't like the sound of that.

Sensing the wizard's displeasure, Stump said, "Don't worry. I'll get you there in one piece, but the next part will be tricky. We'll set here for a spell and have dinner first."

Aargh raised an eyebrow at Stump's pun but didn't acknowledge it. It was true. Since entering the tunnel, he hadn't felt a single seam, crack, or divot beyond the natural state of the stone except for the bricked-up doorways they'd passed at the start of their journey. Intrigued by their presence in the otherwise pristine tunnel, Mnoonge asked about them for Aargh.

"Observant, aren't you, Son Aarghathlain? You're right. In ye olden days, this tunnel connected the twelve high houses.

There was even an entrance to the Congregational House, but they were sealed long before you were born. They'd have stayed shut, too, if your father hadn't excavated the one from Marble House. Lord Bardelthlain was different from other Middling Street lords. He didn't have a problem getting his hands dirty...in a good way, I mean! No need to worry yourself about that."

Aargh pictured his father humming a happy tune as he mucked out the stall or weeded the garden. He didn't know if the images were memory or a flight of fancy, but he savored them nonetheless.

"How about a piece of root gum?" Stump asked.

Aargh didn't respond. His mind was still back on the farm, helping his father gather vegetables.

"Good for calming the nerves," Stump tried again.

This time, the dwarf got through, and Aargh made a face. "No thanks. I can't abide the stuff," Mnoonge said.

"Does that mean you, too?" they asked, addressing Aargh's companion.

Mnoonge didn't want to be rude, so she cleared her throat and responded using human speech for the first time of her own accord. "No, thank you, Stump, but I appreciate the offer."

It was Mnoonge's turn to make a face. She was used to speaking for Aargh, but she'd never used the common speech to express her thoughts. Rat speech was far more practical, comprised of vocalizations that didn't require your tongue to do funny things in your mouth.

"Suit yourself," the dwarf said, popping the unappetizing grey mass into their mouth, unfazed by the talking rat.

Aargh, however, was definitely fazed!

"How did you do that?" he asked Mnoonge in her mind. "I didn't realize you could speak our language."

"Neither did I," she responded in kind. "It came out on its own."

"Fascinating. You are full of surprises," Aargh complimented.

"Thank you. I'm doing my best."

"You certainly are," Aargh thought, focusing his attention on the dwarf.

It was so quiet in the tunnel that Aargh heard Stump chewing the gum. They'd made it to the pull-your-teeth-out-of-their-sockets part. Later, they'd get to the tasty bit, but, as far as Aargh was concerned, it wasn't worth the effort because after that came having to spit it out before the spicy mass burned a hole in your cheek. Yuck![5]

"I've got a can or two of hash in here somewhere if that's more to your liking," Stump offered. "It's about time we had a hot meal. Even dwarves get tired of dried berries and jerky."

"You've had hash this whole time?" Aargh thought. Then he quickly added, "Don't say that out loud, please, Mnoonge."

It was good that he did, too, because she'd already taken a breath.

Tired of conversing in the dark, Aargh asked Guildebrande to provide some light. The sword agreed, and Aargh removed the blade from his scabbard. It didn't feel right asking him to perform such a menial task, but the sword didn't appear to mind. Even so, Aargh kept the lantern trick to a minimum.

---

[5] Spitlicking is a game where a group of people attempt to keep a piece of root gum in their mouth the longest. It's popular throughout Gemini City, from school playgrounds to bars where winners' names are listed on betting boards (as well as any injuries they incurred by keeping it in their mouth too long). The name comes from what people do after they give up: lots of spitting and licking their lips.

As Stump rifled through their pockets, Aargh and Mnoonge caught glimpses of a wide variety of bits and bobs. They saw a tiny engraved box, a piece of cheese wrapped in cloth, a handful of metal spheres (Aargh didn't know their purpose and assumed they must be part of a dwarvish game), a flask, a waterskin, bandages, a bundle of string, a surprisingly large chunk of charcoal, a few candles, gloves, a length of chain, a small mirror, a worn whetstone, a bone smoking pipe, a vial of oil, and a funny Y-shaped stick with a stretchy band across its widest part.

Of the other various items, one caught Aargh's attention more than the rest—a writing journal about half the size of his diaries with a small pencil strapped to its binding for safekeeping.

"I can't figure out where they put everything. It's as if their pockets are bigger on the inside than they look on the outside," Mnoonge said in Aargh's mind.

"What, oh, yes," she heard herself say. "Their pockets go on forever."

Finally, Stump produced a can opener and a battered metal tin. "Why don't you conjure us a fire? This stuff is pretty disgusting cold, with the fat congealed on top. Nothing worse than slimy hash."

"Well, I…" Mnoonge started to say but trailed off.

She almost asked if Aargh meant to say more but didn't because of the strange expression on his face.

The Earth Mother's vastness shook Aargh to the core; that was true. She spoke with an ancient voice, incomprehensibly old and wise but also kind. Even if no one around him understood his troubles, the Earth Mother surely did, which comforted him.

Then there were the mighty Sisters Wind and Water. Aargh couldn't deny their capriciousness, but they also had a tender side. Wind forever lulled him to sleep as he sat under a shady tree, and Water glistened in the summer sun, filling him with peace.

Fire, on the other hand, was a different story entirely. It might pretend to be gentle, but even a solitary candle flame could burn your fingers, and Aargh hesitated.

Underneath their copious eyebrows, Stump's eye twitched. Although dwarves are content spending long hours, if not days or years, in solitude, they're demonstrative when they gather. Therefore, the uncomfortable quiet that settled over their conversation bothered Stump. They stood there holding the can and opener in one hand and a bundle of kindling in the other, desperately hoping Aargh would say or do something.

Thankfully, after an agonizingly long time, Aargh agreed. He was steward of every element, after all, not just the ones he liked. Besides, ignoring fire was probably a bad idea. He wouldn't be surprised if he needed it one day.

"Won't people notice the smoke floating out of the tunnel?" Mnoonge asked as Aargh arranged the sticks into a pile for the third time. He was trying to put images of their cottage burning out of his mind, but it didn't work.

"It won't smoke much. It's dry. Besides, a wisp or two of smoke doesn't hurt. Helps keep people thinking the house is still burning."

Aargh looked up, and Mnoonge asked, "How do you know that's what they think?"

"I may be underground, but I'm not deaf! I can recite the tour guide's speech by heart," Stump said, changing his voice to simulate a Geminian accent. *"Watch your step, please. We* are entering the courtyard where the evil Wizard of the Council began his reign of terror. Those people with good eyes will be able to see faint wisps of smoke rising from the rubble."

"Is that really what they say?" Mnoonge asked.

"Every hour on the hour."

"Disgusting."

Stump laughed. "I'm not complaining. It keeps most folks away, which is good. Now and then, kids wander in at night. That's when I get to do my famous ghost imitation. Oh, it's a lark to watch them run away screaming!"

Stump realized Aargh was struggling with the fire, so they kept talking.

"For a while after the explosion, it was tricky keeping people out. I had to block the tunnel. But, when things got quiet again, I reopened it in case your father returned. That didn't go over well with the Directorate, but I'm glad I did, or we wouldn't be sitting here together."

Aargh nodded as if he was listening, but he hadn't heard a single word. He was entirely consumed by how fire danced to its own crackling tune and how it often looked like glowing worms slithering under the bark of burning embers.

"Are you ready to try?" Mnoonge asked in his mind.

Aargh jumped. "Yes. Okay." With the rat's help, he asked the wood to burn...but not too much...just a little...but enough to warm their dinner...if you please...and if it isn't too much of a bother.

It wasn't the most elegant spell he'd ever cast, but it worked. Instantly, small flames leapt from the sticks. He could hear the fire eating its way through the wood. The size of the fire didn't matter. Its ravenous hunger triggered something in him.

Stump saw the concern in Aargh's eyes and placed a heavy hand on his shoulder. With a congenial look in his eyes, almost entirely hidden beneath their plaited beard and bushy eyebrows, they said, "Don't worry, Son Aarghathlain. We need fire. Without it, our food would be raw and our beds cold, and no one wants cold tootsies in winter! Come, let's eat. We'll talk more after."

Aargh returned Guildebrande to its sheath, and as he did, the sword said, "I await your next command, Wizard Aarghathlain."

Throughout the simple but pleasant meal, Aargh watched the dancing fire glisten in the dwarf's eyes. If the stories of their metal-working skills were true, he imagined dwarves had a special connection to the element. When they reached the ravine, maybe he'd visit a foundry or a blacksmith's shop. That would be fun.

Even though taming metal through smelting ingots, forging, and casting was as much a part of Gemini City's rich history as stonework, he'd never visited the businesses where they did such things. Most wizards considered those places below their station, but not Aargh. The possibility of watching metal being transformed from lumps of ore poured into molds or hammered into a beautiful sword fascinated him.

Aargh loved the concept of transformation, from wearing a disguise to teaching students. He enjoyed watching the craftspeople lining Lower Middling Street ply their trade or the excitement of seeing seeds he'd planted grow into fruiting plants. The concept of starting at one point and ending at another was no different to him than following roots to the future.

Then, a thought occurred to him. "Wait!" Mnoonge said. "Smoke every night? You must be able to make fire yourself."

"Of course I can! I wouldn't be much of a dwarf if I couldn't. I wanted to see more of that fancy wizarding of yours up close and personal. I've never had dinner with a wizard before, except your mother, but she didn't do that kind of magic."

Mnoonge stood there irritably tapping her toe, arms crossed, with Aargh's emotions written all over her face. He'd been tricked into performing magic for the dwarf! Didn't Stump know that it wasn't a show? Magic was serious business, especially when it involved fire. Getting up, Aargh stormed off into the dark beyond the firelight.

Clear.
Calm.
Concentrate.

With swan-like grace, Aargh unsheathed Guildebrande again, lifting the sword before him. The blade shimmered with anticipation.

Together, they practiced three sets of nine forms representing wind, water, and earth. As they assumed the first form, Aargh focused on his connection to the elements. He stepped forward, bent his front leg, and lowered his body toward the ground.

"Rigid branches break in a strong wind," his familiar instructed.

The sword-wielding wizard did his best to heed Guildebrande's advice, making his movements as fluid as possible. He slowly extended his free hand, palm out, feeling the air pass around it. With his other arm, he held the sword parallel to the ground and moved it back until the tip of the blade nearly brushed the edge of his ear. He heard Guildebrande humming with contentment. Aargh brought the sword around until his hands met in front of him. The instant they touched, the form was complete, and his magic joined with Guildebrande's.

Moving in silent contemplation, they practiced form after form. In his mind, Aargh was far away, standing under the bright summer sun in a clearing with Holly-Mine by his side.

"I'm not sure that will help you much in a fight," Stump said, leaning against the wall.

Aargh flinched. He was crouching near the floor with his right leg over his left knee, holding Guildebrande across his body with both hands.

"It's not supposed to, really," Mnoonge explained. "It's more to keep me centered and calm."

"Hmm. Where did you learn it?" the dwarf asked.

"It's a combination of my fencing lessons, the way Holly-Mine dances with the trees, and Guildebrande's magic. We call this form, *Sapling bends in a light breeze.*

"Is that so? I'm going to stick with *heavy axe cleaves in two* if it's all the same to you," Stump said, laughing as they walked back to the fire.

"Thank you, Guildebrande," Aargh thought as he sheathed the sword.

"We should review *Crane stands on one leg.* I believe we could achieve a more stable center. If you'd lift—"

"Later," Mnoonge said, cutting off the blade. "I need to ask Stump a question."

"As you wish," the sword replied.

Aargh had successfully let go of his anger, but that left room for other things. That's why the next thing Mnoonge asked wasn't about the fire or Stump's remarks but if the dwarf would be willing to tell him about his mother.

The sincerity of the request was inescapable, but Stump didn't immediately answer. They were confined in a tight space, and the dwarf had heard stories about the *Prosperity.*

Aarghathlain's magical outburst was legendary, so Stump hoped the wizard's relaxation session had worked.

"Your mother was a right gem," they said. "Deep as an emerald but sparkling like a diamond."

Stump continued like this for quite a while, comparing Aargh's mother to all things bright and beautiful, as dwarves are wont to do. And although Aargh appreciated the compliments and flowery language, he wasn't interested in hearing about vegetation or stones.

Unable to wait any longer, Mnoonge interrupted, "But Stump. What about her magic? Tell me about that, please."

The dwarf pivoted mid-sentence. "Ah yes, magic and dwarves, not a good combination. Nope. Not good. Oil and water, really."

"Why is that? Don't dwarves have wizards, too? And why do dwarves hide themselves from Geminians? It's such a mystery to me. No one knows that you're there, at the bottom of the ravine. The trees didn't even mention it to me."

Stump seized on the last thing Aargh said. Anything to avoid speaking about his mother's magic. "It wasn't always that way if the stories are to be believed."

"Personally," Mnoonge said, "I'm coming around to the idea that there's a fair amount of truth in the old tales."

"Might be. Dwarves love a story, and ever since I was a dwarfling, I've been told to keep my distance from wizards."

"Then why are you helping me? And why did you help my mother and father?"

Stump kept a firm hand on the tiller, steering the conversation away from Aargh's family. "If someone else jumped off Ardilakk, would you jump, too?" they laughed. "At some point, a dwarf needs to decide for themselves. It was my choice to investigate what the fuss was about, and I'm glad I did. Besides, it's not as if I climbed out of the tunnel and helped your parents straight away. They had to earn my trust first, which I'm happy to say they did. Of course, that's just me. I'm sure you can imagine the first time Lord Bardelthlain poked his head into the chasm, folks were none too pleased! But he had a way about him that put people at ease."

"It's been decades since my father left the city. Why didn't you return to the ravine?" Mnoonge asked.

"You have a lot to learn, Son Aarghathlain! Never known a dwarf to crumble that easily."

"But weren't you lonely?" Aargh understood being lonely, having been locked in the brig aboard the *Prosperity*.

"Oh, no. Dwarves are pretty solitary much of the time. Besides, I've got ways to pass the time, and I visit the ravine. Anyway, getting back to wizards, are you familiar with the year of the Quivering Quake?"

Mnoonge nodded along with Aargh, even though she'd never heard of the Quivering Quake. It was amusing to her. She enjoyed sharing Aargh's thoughts, and she was proud to be able to help the wizard.

Aargh smiled. Mnoonge's amusement made him happy. Their magical connection was growing, but it wasn't the same as with Guildebrande or Wrudge. Apparently, sharing speech created a unique bond. Aargh assumed this was because communicating required much more than words. He hadn't expected to make such an intimate connection with the small rat, but he was glad he did.

Mnoonge prepared to recite the age-old nursery rhyme people-mothers sang to their babies. She'd never heard it before, but that was no matter. They were Aargh's words.

Long, long ago, the earth did shake,
it was the year of the Quivering Quake.
The ground opened wide to the stars above,
and Ardilakk rose like a mourning dove.
High above the ocean, high above the sea,
its peak points north, and its feet are 'neath me.
So look upon Ardilakk standing far above,
and remember small things grow with a mother's love.

"Well done, Mnoonge!" Stump said, clapping their hands. "That's the one. Ever wondered what it means?"

Aargh had a sneaking suspicion that he was about to get schooled.

CHAPTER 23

THE POWER OF SILENCE
DRAMWITCH & BARTLEBEE

"I don't believe this. No, I do not believe this," Dram said as he paced outside Bartlebee's room in the wizard's wing of the Spire dormitory. "Have they lost their minds? When did the school start locking wizards in their rooms?"

"No offense, Dram, but I've traveled this road, and it doesn't lead anywhere," Bee grumbled.

Dram put his ear against the door to hear better, not that it helped. "This is an injustice! An outrage! I'm going to march right over to the Interim Head Wizard's office and give him a piece of my mind!"

"Shh! Keep your voice down! Besides, Tarth is the current Interim Head. Sooooo, either the office will be empty, or it won't be, but either way, it wouldn't be a good idea."

"Yeah, right. I almost forgot," Dram said, slumping against the door. "What can I do?"

"You'll figure something out. You're far better than most wizards at getting things done…and done well, I might add. Aargh has often told me how impressed he's been with your work."

"That's kind of you to say, Bee, but I'm afraid I'm a much better doer than a thinker. Got a plan? I'm your man!" he said half-jokingly.

"I guess you'll have to be daring this time and make something happen on your own."

"That's what I'm trying to do," Dram whined. "The Head– I mean, Aarghathlain–gave me the who, what, and why, but I have to figure out the how, when, and where. And speaking of *hows*, how can I do that with you locked in there and me out here? I need your help."

"Wait a second. Did you say Aargh told you what to do?" Bee's quizzical voice threaded through the keyhole in the metal door.

"Yes, well, no. Sort of. This is Aargh we're talking about. He told me what needs to be done but didn't give me any details on how to do it."

"I must say, I'm not used to you being so indecisive."

"I've never been asked to–" Dram stopped mid-sentence. He'd been raising his voice again. He anxiously checked the hallway to make sure no one was listening. All clear. Continuing with a quieter voice, he said, "It began when the river of magic appeared."

"What do you mean?" Bee said, exasperated. "I hate being locked in this room. Nothing ever happens in here. Especially not rivers of magic."

"It happened a few nights ago," Dram explained.

"I must have slept through it."

"That's too bad. It's not every day you get to glow!"

"What? You glowed?"

"Everyone did."

"Why didn't anyone mention that to me!" Bee said, springing up from his bed. "You can't drop that into the middle of a conversation and move on. I need details. Wait a minute. I have an idea. The door to your left is a broom closet. Go in there and wait for my signal."

"You're kidding, right?" Dram asked. "I'm trying to figure out how to save the Spire, and you're telling me to hide in the broom cupboard? I'm not that inept!"

"Of course, you aren't. Just do it. I promise you won't have to wait long. Trust me."

"Whatever," Dram mumbled as he opened the door to the closet. "Here we are, crazed wizards on the loose, Bee locked in his room, and me going to have a confab with a broom. Perfect. Aarghathlain would be so proud of my achievements under his tutelage. Ew. What's that smell?"

Carefully moving a filthy mop to the side with his foot, Dram planted himself on an overturned bucket and waited for Bee.

It was dark.

It was damp.

It was smelly.

"I've had enough!" he announced to the bottles of cleaning fluid stacked haphazardly on the metal shelf above him.

He was about to leave when a scratching sound grated against his ear. Hopefully, another rat had come to give him a message, so he leaned over to investigate. Much to his surprise, he saw a finger sticking through the wall.

"State your purpose," he said to the finger.

"Dram, can you hear me?" Bee's muffled voice asked.

"I'd be able to hear you better if you pulled your finger out of the hole."

"Oh yeah, right. Hold on. It's wedged in there pretty good."

Dram watched as Bartlebee wriggled his finger, trying to pull it out.

"Funny how fingers like to stick into things but don't always want to come back out again," Bee's muffled voice said as he pulled and twisted harder.

"Should I push from this side?"

"No! Wait a second. I'll get it. There. Ow! Remind me not to do that again."

"Don't do that again."

"Ha, ha. Very funny." Bee's complaining was much clearer now, as was his recitation of a rather impressive list of tree names. "Make yourself useful and find a broom handle to make it bigger."

Dramwitch didn't understand why Bee sounded so upset with him. He hadn't been the one foolish enough to stick his finger through the wall.

"I could get expelled for this," Dram said as he jammed the mop handle into the hole. "I can see the headlines now: *Read all about it, Assistant to the Head of Wizarding School Expelled for Attacking Spire Wall with Broom Handle.*"

"What are you going on about in there?" Bee asked. "Hurry up!"

"Give me a second!" Dram hissed, balancing on one leg and leaning over a pail of dirty water.

THUMP!

A piece of the wall popped out.

"Excellent!" Bee exclaimed, sticking his hand through the enlarged hole and giving Dram a thumbs up. "Now, what's this river of magic and glowing thing you were talking about?"

Dram did his best to explain what had happened. Well, most of it. He didn't know how to broach the subject of bringing Tarth back, so he put that off as long as possible.

"Wait. You're saying Aargh's mom was a wizard, too?" Bee asked. "That is so cool! And here we were, proud of being progressive by letting girls into the school. That's rather ironic when you think about it. But you still haven't told me about the river of magic. Did it flow from Ardilakk? It must have. Where else would it have come from?"

Dram paused. "Uh, Bee?"

"Yeah?"

"That's not the only thing I haven't told you about."

"There's more? Tarth tried to burn down my buddy's house with him and his daughter inside; the most revered teacher to ever lead the school might be a bad guy; Aargh is heir to Marble House; Dwarves exist and are living in Ransome Ravine, and you're telling me there's more?"

"It has to do with Tarth," Dram said sheepishly.

"Not much to discuss there. I haven't been locked in here that long. I was there, remember? We need to keep that traitorous snake charmer and his cronies as far from the Spire as possible. I'd rather hear about this river of magic. That sounds fascinating."

"That's just it. It's…um…the opposite," Dram said, bracing for Bee's reaction.

"I'm sorry. I must not have heard you correctly. The opposite of what?"

Unable to contain himself any longer, Dram blurted, "Aargh wants us to find a way to bring Tarth back to the Spire."

"WHAT?" Bee roared so loudly that his metal door couldn't prevent his voice from echoing down the long stone hallway.

"Quiet! People are trying to read," a muffled voice called from a room across the hall.

"And sleep, if you please!" another wizard added.

There was always someone telling people to be quiet in the wizard's wings. It made the upper dorms pretty much the last place Wizards of the Third Circle wanted to be, except for Paladand. He fit right in with the older generation.

As Dram sat quietly in the broom cupboard, he realized something: he wasn't as keen on having an adventure as he once had been. Telling fantastic stories about impossible feats or terrible beasts was one thing. Being part of the story was completely different! Paladand might have it right: quiet, solitary study. That's what he could use. However, the healer was changing, too. He and Nerah had proved that beyond a shadow of a doubt when they'd stood up to Tarthanabelle and fended off Renfir and Griff.

"We're all changing," Dram muttered as he listened to Bee rant about Tarth, familiars, fire, elemental magic, and anything else the wizard could find to be upset about.

"Is Aargh out of his mind? If Tarth comes back to the–" Bee stopped mid-sentence.

There was a strange silence, and Dram almost asked if he was still there.

Then Bee's voice drifted through the opening again. "There's more you aren't telling me, isn't there? Aargh wouldn't want us to bring Tarth back without good reason."

Dram panicked. "No, Bee, really. That's it. So, do you want to hear about the river of magic now? It was beautiful. Aargh cast this spell, and oh, you should have seen it! Guildebrande shone with the light of the sun and spoke to Aargh. Can you imagine? A sword as his familiar!"

"Yes, I've heard about Guildebrande. It's pretty impressive, but don't try to change the subject. You aren't going to get away with not telling me Aargh's secret. There will be time for rivers and swords later. Let's go. Out with it."

"Come on, Bee. Give me a break. I can't. I promised."

"You can't possibly tell me that you believe Aargh would keep something so important from his best friend in the whole world. Can you?" Bee asked.

"But he told me I wasn't supposed to tell anyone. There weren't any exceptions."

"Oh, so that's what I'm reduced to…an exception? How lovely. I've always dreamed of being an exception–a footnote on the page of history: *While his best friend Aargh, former*

Head Wizard of the Spire, and Dramwitch, trusted sidekick, saved the world, Bartlebee, lowly Wizard of the Spire, sat in his dorm room with no knowledge of the events unfolding in the outside world."

"That's not what I meant!" Dram said, stumbling over the words as he tried to explain himself.

"I guess the time I pulled Aargh out of the prickly bush because he'd climbed in so far he couldn't get back out again doesn't count for anything, does it? When it comes down to it, I'm just another run-of-the-mill puller-outer to you," Bee pressed Aargh's former mentee.

"Well, I—"

"I mean, the world wouldn't have missed him if he'd stayed stuck there forever, right? It's not like he's done anything special."

"Now, wait a minute—"

"I completely understand, Dram. You're far more important than I am. You're the big man in town, Assistant to the Head, apprenticed to the Great Aarghathlain. I'll just sit here and keep my mouth shut. I'm the wizard who got sent to his room."

"You're making this hard for me. Don't you understand? I'm trying to do what's right. Aargh gave me specific instructions not to say why Tarth had to be kept on the grounds."

"Hmm. It's not that he needs to be in the school; he needs to be on the grounds." Bee didn't miss a trick.

"I didn't say that—"

"Yes, you did. You said *Tarth had to be kept on the grounds.* That's exactly what you said. You tell me you need my help but won't tell me why. Aargh took you into his confidence. I understand that, but if you don't explain what's going on, I can't be of any assistance. Friends trust each other, don't they,

Dram? I guess I was laboring under the delusion that we were friends. Boy, was I wrong."

"That isn't fair! You're family. I used to call you Uncle Bee when I first came to the Spire. Funny, I hadn't thought about that for quite some time. Anyway, your opinion matters to me."

Dram was met with silence.

Unsure of what to do, he asked, "Bee?"

Bee didn't answer.

"Can you hear me? Did the hole get blocked again?"

More silence.

Dram fidgeted. "Hellooooo? Are you there?

Nothing.

"Please, answer me, Bee. I'm at a loss here."

The tension got to be too much, and Dram broke. "Okay, okay! I'll tell you. The spell Aargh cast on the Spire isn't the oath we take; it's on the place. Anyone who sets foot on the grounds is prevented from using elemental magic. He says it's too dangerous, and we must keep Tarth from training students outside of the school because the spell wouldn't bind them, and Aargh is afraid of what might happen."

Bee whistled a long falling whistle. "That was a mouthful. People are going to be pretty upset when that juicy tidbit gets out."

"It's not going to get out! I told you. It's a secret, and I can't tell anybody."

"I guess we saw how well that worked out. By tomorrow, the whole school will be arguing about it," Bee chuckled.

"That's not fair! I said I wasn't supposed to tell you. You made me."

"Sorry about that, but I did warn you. You're in the ring with the champ!"

It was Dramwitch's turn to give the silent treatment.

"I promise I won't tell anyone," Bee assured him.

Silence.

Unperturbed, Bee continued. "Why doesn't he expand the spell to cover the valley?"

"He doesn't want to cast a spell on top of another spell because there's always a catch, and he doesn't want to risk hurting anyone. Though, we didn't discuss that much. On my way here, I tried to figure out a way to do it but haven't come up with anything yet," Dram answered, unable to stay quiet.

"We'll have to defer to him on that one. If there's a way, he'll figure it out."

"Agreed."

"I think our first responsibility is determining how Tarth got off the grounds," Bee continued. "We don't want him sneaking back without us knowing. By the way, do you know what Tarth meant when he said he had business at the Spire?"

"No, but Aargh's worried about that, too."

"Great minds and all."

"*Prunus serotina!* This is a mess," Dram hissed. "What are we going to do? Aargh's pretty sure the river of magic is connected to Tarth, too. Is it me, or does it feel like Tarth is way ahead of us?"

"We do seem to be bringing up the rear," Bee agreed.

It wasn't in Dram's nature to sit around when there was work to be done, and the inactivity got the better of him. He leapt to his feet without paying attention to his surroundings and unceremoniously banged his head on a shelf. "Ouch!"

"You all right in there?"

"I hit my head."

"Did it knock some sense into you?"

Dram had no trouble imagining the smile on Bee's face. "Actually, it might have. Hold on a minute. Yes, that might work. I've got a plan to get you out of there. Leave it to me!" Then, he cracked the door to see if the coast was clear. Satisfied that he was alone, Dram snuck out of the broom closet and headed for the washroom.

• • •

"There he goes," Bee said, flopping onto his unmade bed, "and here I stay."

He leaned forward to unpin a small tapestry that he used to cover the hole he'd made in the wall. The hole would never be big enough to escape, but scratching at it gave him something to do.

"I hope this doesn't take too long. I'm missing all of the fun."

Just for the heck of it, he crumpled a piece of paper and tossed it into the recycling bin. The metal container chirped, and Ermy poked her head over the edge.

"What are you doing in there? Come over here, you silly thing."

The stoat slithered out of the basket, scampered across the floor, and scrabbled onto the bed beside him.

"Did I ever tell you about Fuzzball? No, I don't believe I have," Bee said as he stroked Ermy's soft brown and white coat. "He was my familiar before I met you. Actually, it's not common for wizards to have more than one familiar. It has to do with the magic. Even butterflies that typically live only weeks in the wild last a lifetime when they're bonded with a wizard. And if a familiar does pass away, wizards often don't take another. They become known as forestwalkers–wizards who walk the woodland paths alone, without a familiar by their side. The truth is, it's hard to bond a second time. I'm sure that's why Aargh took Guildebrande as his companion.

Or, I should say, made the sword his companion. He couldn't face replacing dear old Wrudge. Can you blame him? Wrudge was a good rat."

Ermy squirmed onto Bee's lap, burrowing between his robed legs. When she was comfortably situated, he continued.

"Anyway, Fuzzball was a great familiar, too. He was an Angora rabbit. Do you know what that is? They're pretty popular. They have soft fur. My mom made that scarf over there out of Fuzzball's coat."

Alarmed, Ermy sat back on her hind legs.

"No, don't worry. That isn't why I lost him. I brushed him each night before bed until I had enough of his hair to spin a ball of yarn."

Ermy laid back down, relieved, but she stared at him intently from her nest in his yellow robes. Even among wizards, Bee's clothing made a statement.

"Honestly, I don't know how it happened. I may not want to either."

Ermy kept watching him.

"No. I don't want to talk about it right now."

The stoat didn't budge.

"Oh, I see. You're using my own tactics against me. Well, I'm telling you, it won't work. I'm not that easily swayed."

She stuck her neck out toward him and stared unblinkingly into his eyes.

"All right! I'll tell you. You're a stubborn little thing, aren't you? Give me a minute."

Bee lifted Ermy off his lap and placed her on the bed.

Wistfully gazing out his window, he said, "I used to read under the oak tree on the Eastern Grazing Field. I can't bring myself to do that anymore. You see, one day, Fuzzball was hopping around, nibbling on new shoots, and I lost sight of him. I didn't notice that he'd gone around to the other side of the tree. Not that I would have. He often hopped off to find fresh grass to munch. Have you ever watched a rabbit eat? It's hilarious. They topple a long stalk and suck in it, jiggling and wiggling as it disappears into their mouth. So silly. Anyway, it was late in the day, and I nodded off. I had a terrible nightmare where Fuzzball was squealing in pain. When I woke, it was actually happening. I leapt to my feet and raced around the tree, but he was already gone. It could have been a person, a wild animal, or, trees forbid, another familiar, for all I know, but as I stood there, I felt his magic leave me. After that, I took time off from teaching and gave away most of my books. This is the only one I kept," he explained, moving over to the empty bookshelf and picking up *101 Magical Things You Can Make With Angora Wool.*

Bee held the book closely before placing it back on the shelf.

"That's why I was scared when we got separated in the woods. Don't do that again, okay?" he asked, sitting beside her. "But you know about losing loved ones, don't you? I'm sorry about your family. If I had anything to say about it, no one would be allowed to trap in Ardilakk Valley ever again."

Ermy scurried over his leg, settling comfortably into his pocket.

"Hey! That tickles!" Bee said, comforted by the knowledge they had each other.

CHAPTER 24

HISTORY IS WRITTEN BY THE VICTORS
AARGHATHLAIN

Dwarves could talk! Aargh and Mnoonge sat for hours by the fire, listening to Stump meander their way through dwarvish lore. Even Aargh couldn't keep everything straight with so many begats, heroic feats, and more precious stones than there were trees in the Northern Forest–none of which answered any of his questions. That is, until Stump said, "…the Quivering Quake happened because of the dwarves."

"Finally, we're getting somewhere!" Aargh thought.

Mnoonge barely stopped herself from blurting out Aargh's reaction. It wasn't easy, but she hid the words with a well-placed cough.

Blissfully unaware of Aargh and Mnoonge's impatience, Stump stroked the end of their beard as they spoke. "Way back, dwarves lived side by side with magic in the valley. They had little choice, with things like faeries hiding in the trees. Tricksy creatures, faeries. Can't say I'm not glad they aren't hanging about anymore."

"Faeries?" Aargh thought.

Mnoonge's face scrunched into something between *What did they say?* and *That explains a lot!*

"Over time," Stump continued, "dwarves grew weary of the fleeting glimmer of pixie magic floating in the evening sky and constructing ephemeral homes out of wood. They wanted to work with materials strong enough to stand the test of time and adorn themselves with precious gems forged deep underground by the Earth Mother. So, they pleaded for help, and one day, the Dark Wizard appeared."

"Like the nursery rhyme?" Mnoonge asked for Aargh. "And you're positive it was one wizard and not two because the poem does say, *Two dark wizards, facing as they stood?*"

"Yes, I'm sure, Son Aarghathlain. It's a story."

"But why was he called the Dark Wizard? Did he wear dark-colored robes?

Stump sighed. "You and your people are so literal! It had nothing to do with what he wore or how he looked. It was because he hid his intentions. Imagine peering into a hole. You're confident there's treasure at the bottom, but you can't see it because there isn't any light. Understand?"

"I guess, but–"

"Nope! You and your small friend are going to sit and listen to this story. You can ask questions when I'm finished. Got it?"

Aargh twisted two fingers in front of his mouth as if to lock his lips shut–not that he could have said anything even if he wanted to.

Mnoonge didn't make any promises. She knew that she didn't have control over whether she spoke or not. That was up to her wizard, and she was sure he wouldn't be able to keep her mouth shut.

"Where was I?" Stump asked no one in particular. "Oh, yes…the Dark Wizard. The Brethren rejoiced because their prayers had been answered. At least, that's what they thought at the time. He made Ahrdylakkun-thūl rise above the valley and used Dūnhyldun-thîr to bore a hole from the foot of the mountain to the great river. But soon it became apparent that the Dark Wizard wasn't a gift from the Earth Mother–"

"Where did he come from?" the rat interrupted. "If magic comes from the Earth, and he was a wizard, it stands to reason the Earth Mother had granted their wish."

Even Mnoonge found herself frustrated with Aargh's inability to stay quiet. Wrudge had often told the Underoof Collective how, for hours on end, Aargh listened attentively to people and trees. It was his job, after all, but that hadn't been her experience. This Aargh was so filled with desperation that he never kept his mouth shut.

"Let me finish!" Stump said, becoming annoyed. "You do know it's rude to interrupt a dwarf when they're telling a story, don't you?"

"Yes, of course," Mnoonge apologized for Aargh. "I'm doing my best. Sorry."

"Right then. You'll keep your mouth shut?"

"Her lips are sealed," Mnoonge mumbled, shooting Aargh a glance that spoke volumes.

"If you can control yourself, we're getting to the good part."

Aargh sat up straight and folded his hands, the model of a good listener.

Stump had their doubts but forged ahead anyway. "A new governing body was created, called the Directorate, comprised of representatives from the different clans. To no one's surprise, they spent most of their time arguing. However, even the most skeptical dwarves couldn't ignore the benefits of having the Dark Wizard's help, nor could they discount the signs that he'd hidden his true intentions from them. Caught between a rock and a hard place, you might say, they decided to stay the course. Down they went, burrowing under the feet of the tallest mountain on the river, discovering riches beyond their wildest imaginations. The deeper they dug, the more interested the Dark Wizard became with their work. It was almost as if he expected dwarves to find something he knew was there.

"The time had come for the Directorate to take action. You see, the Dark Wizard wanted to enslave the dwarves. That way, he could harness their strength and skill to do his bidding. But dwarves have always been crafty and wise, and they devised their own plan. Deep under the mountain, they discovered a magical chamber encrusted with diamonds, but that's another story. I imagine there will be many dwarves inspired to tell you about it when they lay their eyes on you."

This statement struck Aargh as odd, but Mnoonge put her hand on his leg and glared as if to say, *You can ask about that later.*

"The dwarves kept the chamber a secret in case the wizard betrayed them. When that day finally came, as they knew it would, they were ready. The Brethren tricked the Dark Wizard, entombing him under Ahrdylakkun-thūl forever—doomed to have his magic reflected back upon himself a hundred-fold for eternity."

Mnoonge couldn't hold back the river of questions flowing out of Aargh any longer. "Did he escape? Was it the Wizard of the Council? Is that why he had the power to burn the Northern Forest and the ancient northern cities? It must have been him!"

"No, Son Aarghathlain. The Wizard of the Council didn't possess the power to raise mountains."

"But he did!" Mnoonge insisted as Aargh paced, jabbing his right hand with his left indexing finger. "He broke Ardilakk in two! I saw it with my own eyes! Right there, behind the Congregational House, I watched it crack in half."

"There's a big difference between breaking a thing and creating it, Son Aarghathlain. Besides, if what people say is true, the Wizard of the Council stole his magic. The Dark Wizard didn't need to steal magic. He was magic."

This idea silenced Mnoonge. What did Stump mean?

Stump took advantage of the silence and attempted to finish the story. "Those were bountiful times when the people of the river and dwarves lived and worked together, but it didn't last. Eventually, the Brethren left the valley to live under the mountain, and a rift opened between the Northrim and the Souters."

"*Souters.* Interesting. I've never heard Geminians referred to that way before," Mnoonge said.

"They weren't Geminians back then. The Souters–those who lived in Eastie and Westie Sowt–were part of the great Quadropolis. Unfortunately for the North, the South imposed heavy cartage taxes, pier taxes, and taxes on trade itself, which they could do because they controlled the port. You get the picture. That's how the Souters grew wealthy and hired dwarves to build their cities of stone."

"Wait, what? Which cities?" Mnoonge interjected.

"Here we go again," Stump said, rolling their eyes. "I just told you! The ancient dwarves called them Dahr Thahlehn-fîr, the stone towns in the valley. You call them Gemini...the twins, if you will."

"That can't be right. People built the city, not dwarves," Mnoonge said, sticking out her head toward the wayward dwarf.

"Hmm," Stump said, adjusting their plaited beard. "It appears folks have forgotten from whence they came. Ever wondered why the old buildings don't have any mortar, but new buildings do?"

"No, not really. I assumed the craft of building had evolved over the centuries."

"Made cheaper, you mean, and with less skill," Stump said, obviously offended. "And what's your explanation for the Once-Great Wall collapsing? People built it, of course! No dwarf wall has ever decayed. Not one!"

This revelation upended everything Aargh believed about the city. Geminians prided themselves on being the river's greatest stonemasons, but it turned out the exquisite stonework of the city hadn't been built by them!

Aargh realized the dwarf had stopped talking, and Mnoonge apologized again. "I'm sorry, Stump. I meant no offense. As Spire Historian, I studied Gemini City's history for years, but it appears I wasn't told the truth."

"Not a problem, Son Aarghathlain. We dwarves are quick to get offended, but we're just as good at forgiving. You'll see when we arrive."

Aargh didn't want to appear more ill-informed than he was (though that might not be possible the way things were going), but he needed to ask about something that had intrigued him—a mystery that had fascinated him since boyhood.

Mnoonge wore an expression that looked a lot like, *are you sure about this?*

"Yes," he responded in the rat's mind. "What if the stories are true?"

"As you wish," she squeaked, clearing her throat and speaking in her rat voice. Then, in an effort to make clear she wasn't the one asking the question, Mnoonge used the common speech to say, "Wizard Aarghathlain asks: Will we get to see the Marauders' hoard in the ravine?"

Stump made a strange sound like they were trying to stifle a sneeze and then guffawed so loudly that the sound ricocheted off the stone walls, echoing into the distance in both directions.

Aargh had anticipated being wrong, but it was still disappointing.

"That's a good one." Stump said. "I'd forgotten the tales of the Marauders' Hoard. First off, they're called Nahmanians, or Nahms for short. There's no need for name-calling. And the great city of the ravine is called Dahr Kahlahd-dîm. It's a dwarf city! Oh, Son Aarghathlain, you have much to learn."

Deflated like the Norters' great balloons after their ships landed on the highlands, Aargh finally decided to stop opening Mnoonge's mouth and listen. He was deeply saddened by the possibility that everything he'd learned from Sowtownie trees was a lie.

Stump worried that they might have shared too much. Aargh had grown quiet, which was disconcerting considering how talkative the wizard had been, but the dwarf didn't want to risk interrupting his ruminations.

When they couldn't take it any longer, Stump suggested, "Why don't you rest, Son Aarghathlain? You'll feel better in the morning."

"I don't understand how you do that," Mnoonge said, yawning with Aargh.

"Do what?"

"How can you tell when it's night or day, morning or evening? It's pitch black in here."

"A dwarf knows," Stump said, touching the side of their nose.

Aargh shook his head. It seemed dwarves would have to remain a mystery. Hopefully, the fog in his mind would clear when they got to the ravine.

Stump pushed themself up with a grunt and walked away from the fire. "I'm going to see a merchant about a garble. When I get back, we'll settle in for the night."

Mnoonge mumbled a response, but even she didn't know what she'd said. Aargh seemed to be even more preoccupied than usual. The small rat chalked it up to anxiety about their impending arrival at the ravine, but it was more than that.

Aargh tried to distract himself by tidying his robes, but he felt off. His stomach hurt when he tightened the sash, so he loosened it again, but that didn't help. The sensation grew into a throbbing, and he felt the urge to get to his feet.

Mnoonge perked up. She knew that feeling. "Stump?" she called to the dwarf. "I think–"

"Danger, Wizard Aarghathlain!" Guildebrande shouted, but the warning came too late.

The earth shifted under his feet, and he stumbled.

"Get down!" Stump yelled.

"Wait. I'm coming to you," Mnoonge replied.

"Do as I say, you foolish wizard!"

But before Aargh reached the ground, the tunnel lurched. He hit the ceiling, and darkness took him.

CHAPTER 25

LIGHT AT THE END OF THE TUNNEL
AARGHATHLAIN

Aargh's head pounded, and his ears rang like the Crescent Sun's bells on Sundsday morning.

"What happened?" he tried to ask, but no sound came out.

He tried to take a breath, but the thick, dust-clogged air got caught in his throat, and he coughed into his sleeve.

"Is anyone there?" Silence. That's right. He couldn't speak out loud because he'd given his voice away!

Aargh moved to sit up, but even in the darkness, the world spun around him when he raised his head.

"Mnoonge, I can't find you!" he called to her using his mind.

He frantically searched his pockets. Not there.

"No sudden movements, Aargh. You don't know what happened."

Unable to sit up, he propped himself against the wall. He couldn't see and, without being able to speak,–

"Oh no! I can't ask Sister Wind for help! What a fool I was to give my voice away."

In his delirium, a mixture of reality, memories, and fantasy assaulted his throbbing head in the pitch-black tunnel.

Bram clinging to the bowsprit of the Prosperity...

"Don't watch Sweet Girl."

...the footman chasing them down Middling Street...

"Run! We have to get to the alleyway!"

...the Wizard of the Council appearing out of Marble House...

"Wrudge, I'm lost. Glow so I can find you!"

To Aargh's surprise, his familiar responded, but it wasn't Wrudge.

"Although you're not entirely wrong, Wizard Aarghathlain, I am not Wrudge. I am your faithful servant, the Sword Guildebrande," the blade said, slicing through his confusion.

"Of course, Guildebrande," he answered in his mind. "We're in the tunnel. Right. I'm sorry."

"Would it be appropriate for me to glow at this time?" the weapon asked.

"Yes, please."

Aargh unsheathed the sword, but the dense air reflected the blade's bright light. Coming to his senses, Aargh realized Guildebrande had said something he didn't understand. "What did you mean when you said I wasn't entirely wrong?"

"You enchanted me using Wrudge's magic," Guildebrande answered as if this was common knowledge.

Aargh struggled to his feet, his knees wobbling beneath him.

"Steady Wizard Aarghathlain."

"That's impossible," Aargh thought, ignoring the sword's warning.

"That's a curious thing to say, seeing as you enchanted me."

"But I didn't know I was enchanting you at the time!"

"That may be, but you did, nonetheless," Guildebrande said as if nothing could be more obvious.

"Wrudge used his magic to save me from the trees. I couldn't have used it to enchant you."

Guildebrande responded flatly, "No, he didn't."

"What?"

"Wrudge didn't save you from the wailing of the forest. He gave you his glow, and you used it to cast a spell."

"Don't say that, Guildebrande! I can't bear the thought! He did it. He gave me the strength I needed. It wasn't me. I didn't take it from him. I didn't steal his glow!"

"Why do you speak that way, Wizard Aarghathlain? Wrudge gave it to you freely, and now it resides within both of us."

"No, absolutely not! I won't allow it! I want my friend back. Please, tell me what I have to do. Wrudge has to have his glow!"

The sword sagged in Aargh's hands. Guildebrande had done this once before when they'd first met, but what had he done wrong this time?

"I'm sorry, Wizard Aarghathlain," the sword explained. "Wrudge is gone. I cannot give back his glow. We must both come to terms with that."

Aargh's mind screamed, "Wrudge! Are you in there?"

"Of course he is," Guildebrande answered. "Wrudge lives in me the same way he lives in you, Holly-Mine, and the Underoof Collective. Wrudge's memory lives in all of us, as does his magic, and you must use it now."

"But how?"

"Wizard Aarghathlain, I am more than a sword."

Aargh didn't understand what Guildebrande meant. "I know that."

"I don't believe you do. You don't trust me."

"Trust you? Of course, I trust you! You're my familiar. I trust you with my life!"

"No, you don't. You call to Wrudge in your hour of need, and when I offer my magic to you, you don't take it. You don't rely on me the same way as Wrudge or Mnoonge. I can do this, Wizard Aarghathlain. We can do this together."

Aargh swooned again, leaning his head against the wall.

"Are you hurt?" the sword asked.

"I am, but not in the way you're thinking." He realized this was a funny thing to say, considering they were communicating through his thoughts, but the sword understood what he meant. "Guildebrande, I'm sorry from the bottom of my heart. I guess I couldn't see past the fact that you're a sword— something entirely inconsequential in the grand scheme of things, no more important than me being a person. We are what we are; that's undeniable, but that should not have clouded my judgment as it has no bearing on our relationship. I was wrong. Can you forgive me?"

"Always, Wizard Aarghathlain. I exist to serve you."

"No. That ends today. You are not my servant. You are my partner and companion. My confidant. My friend and, more than anything, my equal."

Aargh's thoughts forged new bonds with the sword, and the blade glowed brighter.

"Teach me, Guildebrande. Teach me how to let Wrudge's glow guide us!"

"Yes, Wizard Aarghathlain. I will. Let us save our friends!"

Wrudge's glow moved through the sword's hilt and into Aargh's hands. As the magic made its way along his arms, he felt its warmth fill his heart with joy. A vision of Wrudge appeared in Aargh's mind. The rat looked over his shoulder at his wizard and winked.

Wrudge's glow burst forth from Aargh and Guildebrande, dispelling the cloud of dust in the tunnel and lighting the space as brightly as the midday sun. Then, Guildebrande left the wizard's hand and floated into the air. Aargh stood there, shocked at the destruction wrought upon the dwarven tunnel. The roof had collapsed, and there was no sign of Stump or Mnoonge.

"Wizard Aarghathlain," Guildebrande said. "We must begin our search."

Aargh immediately got to work, sifting through the wreckage. One of the sharp rocks cut his finger, and he pulled his hand back. He was about to check it to make sure it wasn't too badly damaged when a slight movement caught his attention. It was Mnoonge! Her unfocused eyes stared into oblivion, and her body quivered as she took quick, shallow breaths.

"She's hurt! And I don't know what to do."

"Do not be defeated!" Guildebrande bellowed. "We never abandon our friends while we still draw breath."

"But I'm not a healer."

"No, you're not," the sword's steely voice boomed. "You are the great *Wizard Aarghathlain: Wielder of the Sword Guildebrande, Keeper of the Precious Child, and Protector of the Mighty Rat, Mnoonge.* You will find a way to save her. You must!"

"I will," Aargh promised, remembering how he'd helped Grunt. He didn't need to heal her. He needed to share his strength with her. That way, she could heal herself. Aargh closed his eyes and focused on the small rat.

"Mnoonge, we're connected," he thought. "Guildebrande and I freely offer ourselves to you. Use the spell I cast. Take whatever power you need to heal yourself. Do not resist."

Mnoonge's weak voice responded in his mind. "But you've already given me so much. If it's my time, I am ready. There will be others who can answer Wizard Aarghathlain's call. I can ask no more of you."

"Too often have I asked others to do my bidding. It's my turn to answer another's call. *Mnoonge of the Underoof Collective*, it is I, Aarghathlain..."

"And I, Guildebrande!" the sword added.

"...and we are here for you."

Mnoonge's foot twitched.

"Yes! That's it! More. Take more!" Aargh thought. "Did you see that Guildebrande? Did Mnoonge glow?"

"Yes, she did," the sword agreed.

The small rat's glow pulsed again...and again. It grew brighter, and Aargh slapped his knee in delight.

"She's doing it!"

Mnoonge gasped, and her glow faltered.

"Hurry, Guildebrande! We need to give her more magic!" Aargh pleaded.

"Wait," the sword directed. "And watch."

Mnoonge took a deep breath and stretched her arms.

Aargh moved to help her, but Guildebrande stopped him. "She needs to do this on her own. She needs to understand how strong she is."

"But—" Aargh protested.

"Trust me," Guildebrande insisted.

Mnoonge rolled over. Aargh could see the strain on her face, but she made it to her feet.

"You are an amazing rat!" he thought. "Wrudge would have been so proud of you!"

Mnoonge tried to answer Aargh, but something was wrong. She tried again, barely managing a raspy cough.

"Your voice!" Aargh thought. "Mnoonge, you can't speak?

The rat shook her head.

"Oh no! What will we do?"

"I can speak for you," the sword offered.

"Thank you, Guildebrande, but speaking my words and speaking with my voice are not the same thing. I can't address the Earth Mother without Mnoonge. Holly-Mine warned me this would happen, and I didn't listen!" Aargh frantically searched for a solution. "Roots! I need roots," he thought.

Neither of them understood what he meant, but Aarghathlain looked rejuvenated.

"Guildebrande?" he asked.

"Yes, Wizard Aarghathlain."

"I'm going to ask a great deal of you."

The sword girded himself for what was to come and yelled, "Do as you will! I am ready!"

In one swift motion, Aargh grabbed the sword out of the air, held it upside down, and thrust it deep into the ground with both hands–making a direct connection between himself and the Earth Mother. Wrudge's glow became the color of the trees, the water, and the wind...the glow of life itself!

Aargh screamed in his mind, caught between the agony and ecstasy of being in direct contact with the Earth Mother. He struggled to hold onto Guildebrande's grip as flashes of the past, present, and future appeared in his mind.

Dramwitch and Garthelwaite standing on the island in the center of Lake Hîrdehn-dūl, helplessly watching as the boat floated away...

Holly-Mine and Gerald passing along the Eastern Foothills...

His father placing Aldenthwaine's book in the secret drawer in the floor...

Aargh's head filled with images the way a deep pool collects water cascading off the side of a mountain.

"Focus…Wizard Aarghathlain. You must…ask…her quickly," the sword stuttered, struggling against the powerful magic threatening to shatter him into jagged shards of steel. "It's now…or…never."

With Guildebrande's, Mnoonge's, and the glow of Wrudge's help, *Aarghathlain the Great* gathered his thoughts and asked the Earth Mother to return the tunnel to the way the dwarves had made it.

"DO NOT ASK THIS OF ME," her voice thundered in his heart and mind. "LET THE PAST REMAIN THE PAST, THE PRESENT UNFOLD AS IT MAY, AND LEAVE THE FUTURE YET TO BE DISCOVERED."

Once again, Aargh had not fully considered the ramifications of his words when speaking to the elements, and he struggled to rephrase his request. Words mattered, and he knew this. The script of a spell had to be spoken precisely as it had been written for the incantation to take effect. The things he said to his daughter had weight he never understood before becoming a parent. And the words he used to call on the elements, no matter how carefully chosen and well-meaning, always carried consequences he didn't anticipate.

Realizing that time was growing short, he risked asking again, "Earth Mother, giver of life, please clear the way so that we may rejoin our lost companion."

The ground rumbled under their feet.

"Protect…Mnoonge!" Guildebrande yelled.

Holding onto the sword with one hand, Aargh kneeled. He reached down and touched the small rat. She grabbed his hand, and the three of them watched as the broken stones strewn about them sank into the earth, leaving an open space where the cave-in had been. When the trembling stopped, Aargh wrenched the sword out of the ground.

Guildebrande's glow faded, and a thin voice spoke in Aargh's mind, saying, "Until next time, friend Aarghathlain."

A sound reminiscent of fingernails on a chalkboard grated against his ears, and a torch blazed forth in the darkness. Aargh saw Stump standing many paces away, close to an opening in the tunnel. Stacked near the dwarf was a stash of torches and other provisions.

"That was some fancy wizarding!" Stump said, walking toward him. "Well done, Aarghathlain, Son of Bardelthlain. You are worthy of your father's name."

Delighted Stump was unhurt, Aargh tried to respond, but Mnoonge was already asleep, and Guildebrande was too exhausted to speak. Instead, he placed his hands together and bowed.

"You're welcome," the dwarf said.

Aargh lifted Mnoonge off the floor and placed her in his pocket.

"Will she survive?" Stump asked.

Aargh nodded.

"Good."

Then, the wizard motioned as if to write in the air.

The dwarf understood. "Ah. I have a piece of charcoal in here somewhere and a bit of cloth if you'd like something for that finger. Give me a minute."

Aargh nodded.

As the dwarf rummaged around in their pockets, they said, "I'm assuming I don't have to point out to you that dwarven tunnels don't collapse of their own accord, and before you say it—not that you can, but you know what I mean—no, that wasn't an earthquake."

Aargh curled in the indexing finger he'd raised and closed his silent mouth. It appeared Stump spoke finger, too. Was there anything the dwarf couldn't do?

"That was no quake," Stump said, still sifting through their pockets. "Trust me; if the Earth Mother wanted our attention, she wouldn't need to destroy a tunnel to get it. That was magic."

Aargh couldn't deny the presence he sensed around them... ancient magic.

"And you may have noticed where we ended up: you on the city side and me on the dwarven side. That was a message, plain and simple. No question about it. I'd say someone doesn't want you visiting the ravine. Ah, here we are. Charcoal and a bandage."

Aargh absently took the blackened lump but didn't write anything. Stump wasn't wrong. He'd felt this kind of magic once before, at Marble House, but it didn't feel confined this time. Something expansive had awoken in Ardilakk Valley. As he thought about this, his hand drifted to Aldenthwaine's spellbook, which was still tucked into his robes.

"Here, let me see that," Stump said, taking Aargh's hand and tying the cloth around the wizard's finger. "We should keep moving. I'd rather not get caught by anything like that again. Besides, we're almost there, but we need to fix your..." the dwarf gestured to Aargh's clothing. "We don't want to go traipsing into the ravine with you looking so wizardy. Hows about you sorcel something more dwarf-like."

Aargh smiled. *Wizardy* was kind of his thing, but he understood what Stump meant. Besides, he loved to disguise himself. It was a basic tenet of being a wizard. He even used to wear reversible robes to help him blend into the crowd. They'd come in handy more than once, visiting the lower block shelters and spending time on the piers, but he didn't wear those robes anymore. Even if he did, they wouldn't have helped in this instance. This is why, during their journey under the city and forest, Aargh had often contemplated another way to create a disguise, and getting to put his theory to the test sounded like fun. He'd worry about the cave-in later.

But how could he ask more of Mnoonge? She'd been through so much already. Then again, it might be a moot point if her voice hadn't returned. He was about to wake her when the small rat spoke in his mind.

"I'll try," she said, unable to hide her weariness.

"I'm sorry to ask this of you, but I'm afraid Stump's right. It's no longer safe for us to stay in the tunnels, and we want to fit in as much as possible with the good folk of the ravine."

"You don't have to explain," she answered. "I understand."

Mnoonge's movements felt labored and slow, and he waited patiently for her to appear. After a few minutes, her head poked out of the pocket.

"I can speak a little," she said in a hoarse whisper, "but I don't know how long it will last."

"It'll be enough," Aargh said in her mind. "Thank you."

Owing to the fact that people and clothing are comprised of earth, water, and air, it stood to reason that he should be able to rearrange them a little…or maybe a lot! Therefore, to get a better feel for what he wanted to do, Aargh reached out to the stone and darkness surrounding them–two things close to every dwarf's soul. Then, with Mnoonge's help, he called on the elements to transform him.

Truthfully, he was more than a little nervous. The first time he'd called on the wind, he'd landed in the river and been taken captive by pirates. When he'd given his voice to Mnoonge, it had come with consequences no one could have anticipated. Now, he'd asked to be transformed into a dwarf, and a terrifying thought popped into his head: what had he missed this time?

Panic overwhelmed him as he realized his feet had become one with the stone! He pulled with all his might but couldn't extricate himself from the ground. He watched in horror as his legs grew thick as tree stumps. And, as if that wasn't bad enough, he began to shrink! This was alarming, but since he didn't have far to go to be dwarf-height, the shrinking slowed, offering him some solace, but the respite didn't last long. Next came the most frightening part of the transformation. He reached up to scratch his ear and found that it was much larger and fleshier than it had been. He would have let out a rather unwizardly scream if it was within his power, but before Aargh knew it, there he was, a dwarf cloaked in a heavy fur mantle.

"Whew. I guess that wasn't as bad as it could have been," he thought, relieved that he hadn't turned into a rock or lump of ore.

Just to make sure, he patted himself all over. Yup. Everything was where it should be, at least as far as he could tell. Hopefully, there wasn't anything amiss on the inside. Since that was beyond his ability to check, he decided to relax and enjoy the transformation.

Stroking his long, plaited beard, he thought, "That's a nice touch!"

"Not bad!" Stump cheered. "Not bad at all. We're going to have some fun!"

Aargh wanted to thank Mnoonge, but she'd already crawled back into her pocket, and he decided to leave her alone. He'd thank her later.

Using the lump of charcoal, he scrawled on the wall: Language?

"Don't you worry. You won't be in the dark. Dwarves speak the common speech. It's good for trade. Of course, we have our own language, too, but I'll be there to help."

Stump clapped the disguised wizard on the back, and the trio continued on their way.

The remainder of their journey passed quickly as they squeezed, climbed, and crawled under the forest. The expertly crafted tunnel they'd entered connected to a vast underground cave system—a subterranean world utterly foreign to Aargh but not to his dwarven form. He carefully skirted dark pools of still water that looked like smooth black mirrors, marveled at tall stalagmites that gave the open spaces an otherworldly appearance, and weaved this way and that, avoiding dripping stalactites that pointed down at him from the ceiling. Stump insisted they wouldn't break off and fall on them, but Aargh didn't take any chances. Finally, Aargh saw a light and excitedly tapped Stump on the shoulder.

The dwarf laughed. "Yes, I see it, you silly wizard."

Aargh lifted his hands and shrugged his shoulders as if to ask, *What is it?*

"That, Son Aarghathlain, is the dwarven city of Dahr Kahlahd-dîm!"

CHAPTER 26

PAWNS ARE THE SOUL OF THE GAME
DRAMWITCH & BARTLEBEE, ABOARD THE
PROSPERITY, ODARAPHRIM & HOLLY-MINE
Sundsday of the 8th week

Bartlebee leaned out of his second-floor dormitory window and called to Dram on the grass below. "You woke me for this?"

Behind him sat a mountain of sheets blocking the door. They hadn't been delivered in Bee's typical laundry bag with the fat bumblebee embroidered on the side. Today, the wash had come via a wheeled canvas laundry truck, the kind more commonly used to collect dirty towels outside the kitchen and showers.

Poor Mizelthorn must have had quite a time rolling the heavy container to his room, but when Dramwitch instructed you to do something, you did it—even if you thought Ghyrig (who used to play mundsling before discovering his calling to become a wizard) would be a far better choice. Why? Because Thorn was so thin, it would have been accurate to describe him as stick-like. No matter how often people sat beside him in class or passed him in the halls, they did a doubletake, especially when struggling to push an enormous pile of sheets up the ramp to the second floor.

"Your plan is for me to shinny down a rope made from sheets tied together? Are you crazy?"

"Very possibly," Dramwitch muttered. "It wouldn't surprise me. I am a wizard."

"And in full view of everyone, too. Nice," Bee added in a hoarse whisper.

"There's no one here. Everyone's waiting in the cafeteria," Dram explained. "I announced an All-School Meeting."

"A meeting first thing in the morning? How unwizardly! Whatever it is must be pretty important. What's it for?" Bee questioned as he fumbled with the sheets, trying to find an end.

Dram stood on the grass with his arms tight to his sides, clenching and unclenching his hands nervously. "Not, *for what? With whom?* The Head Wizard, of course."

"They elected a new one already?" Bee asked, engulfed by sheet-rope. "Boy, I hate being stuck in here."

"No. I mean, I don't know. Possibly. I didn't ask. What does it matter? It's what I do, remember? Call meetings and stuff," Dram responded, growing increasingly uncomfortable standing amongst the raised beds.

"How clever of you. I bet Aargh would be proud of the way you're abusing the skills he taught you."

"Ooooo," Dramwitch fumed. "You really push my buttons! I don't see you devising any brilliant plans."

"Sorry, Buddy. You're an easy mark. Do these sheets have an end?"

"You'd better hurry, Bee. They won't stay confused forever, and the others are waiting for us."

"I'm trying! Besides, I don't think you have much to worry about. Wizards aren't known for being quick in their decision-making. I imagine they'll hang around for at least an hour trying to figure out why they're standing there. Pretty nice plan, come to think of it."

"Finally, some appreciation," Dram said, pacing in circles. "Toss me the rope so we can get out of here!"

"That's what I'm trying to–"

Cutting Bee off, Dram said, "Shh! Don't do anything yet. I need to check on something."

"Gimme a break!" Bee exclaimed, sounding much clearer, having extricated his head from the pile of sheets. Looking out his window, he watched Dramwitch tiptoe to the nearest greenhouse.

Dram listened.

Giggles.

A young voice said, "Here, try this one. It's the best."

"Doesn't anyone pay attention to instructions anymore?" Dram asked himself through gritted teeth.

"Mmm, that's delicious!" a high voice agreed, giggling again.

Dram threw open the door. "And what do we have here? Didn't you hear there's a mandatory meeting in the cafeteria?"

He must have sounded more convincing than he felt because a boy to his left started bawling, and a tiny wisp of a girl regurgitated the sweeties she'd been eating right into her lap.

Mortified that he'd scared them so badly, Dram softened, saying, "Please, help your friend to the infirmary and, afterward, head over to the meeting."

"Yes, sir," a boy with long hair said. "Let's go, Grettles. I'll help you."

"Thanks," Grettles muttered, wiping her mouth on her sleeve.

Earlier that morning, Dram had scolded himself for skipping breakfast. Now, he was thankful that he had, or he too might have needed a lie-down.

Once the postulants entered the school, he rushed back to Bee's open window.

"What was that about?" Bee asked.

"You don't want to know. I'll need to do a little cleanup in the greenhouse after you make it to the ground," Dram said. "I wish I had that mop and bucket."

Bee peered out the window, saw the sickening green color of Dram's face, and decided not to ask any more questions.

• • •

"Come!" Bram said.

"You called, Captain?" Grunt asked, sliding down the ladder.

The *Prosperity* wasn't the longest ship on the River Wide, but getting to the captain's quarters from the engine room quickly took effort. The fastest way involved climbing the aft ladder, passing between the port and starboard brigs, crossing the hold, climbing topside, and sliding down the captain's ladder. However, since Grunt's collection of wrenches was currently covering the aft ladder (he'd wanted to reorganize them for some time), he had to go the other direction. That meant using the fore ladder to enter the mess, climb into the pilot house, and cross the weather deck first.

"Ah, Grunt. Nice of you to join us," Bram said, motioning to a chair. "As you can see, Gracie and Sadie are already here."

"Sorry, sir. Ebba had a clinker," he explained, huffing and puffing.

"Not to worry, but now that you're here, we can begin. Please, take a look at this." As he spoke, Bram walked over to the sideboard and opened one of its many drawers. Then, he lifted out a small wooden box. "I received a message recently, and I'm interested in your opinion as to the meaning of its contents," he explained, returning to the desk.

"Someone sent you somethin' in a box?" Grunt asked. "It sounds alive. What's rattlin' around in there?"

"Aargh's stone."

"What?" Gracie asked.

Instead of answering her question, Bram showed them.

When he opened the box, the stone shot into the air. It spun so fast that the golden arrow on its surface appeared to stay in one place.

Gracie immediately reached for the sextant sitting on Bram's desk.

"No need for that," he said, lifting the box and covering the stone once more. "I've already checked. It's pointing directly at Ardilakk Valley."

Grunt sprang out of his seat. "Aargh needs us! We have to go!"

"Spill some wind, Grunt. I doubt it's Aargh."

"But that's his stone!" the engineer insisted.

"First off, Aargh said he'd call on the wind, not make the stone do whirlies. Secondly, this isn't very Aarghish. I don't know how to explain it, but I've used the stone enough to know his magic feels different, and this certainly isn't how it usually behaves. Aargh's magic is more subtle than this. This feels like someone is trying to make us believe Aargh is calling. Or maybe it's just reacting to something magical that's happened and has nothing to do with us or Aargh. That's why I've called you here."

"We should check it out!" Grunt said, folding his arms. "We cain't be ignorin' nothin' to do with Aargh."

Bram nodded. "Agreed." As he put the stone back in the sideboard, it plopped to the bottom of the box with a thunk. Bram slid the top back, tilting the container so the others could see inside. After placing it in the drawer, he said, "That's interesting. Gracie, what's your take? Should we answer the call of the stone and return to Ardilakk Valley?"

"Whatever the Captain wishes," she answered bluntly.

"I'm asking for your opinion."

"I do have a bit of unfinished business to attend to," Gracie said, flexing her mechanical arm.

"Sadie, the hold?" he asked, turning to the boatswain.

"Our cargo is cataloged, stowed, and ready for trade," she confirmed, double-checking her whiteboard.

"And Grunt, what about Ebba?"

"Purrin' like a kitten!" the engineer said confidently.

The others turned to look at him, and he grunted.

"Well...uh...more like a tiger with a head cold, but she's ready for duty."

"Then we're in agreement. Sadie, send word to the Queen of Arkorar. I won't be returning to the palace this evening for our usual game of *Tin Tan Taine*."

The engineer grunted again, and Bram shot him a glance.

"Quartermaster, ready the ship to make way," he commanded. "We leave for Ardilakk Valley immediately!"

• • •

A light mist fell, making the cobblestones glisten under the streetlamps' melancholy light.

"Pssssst!"

Odaraphrim pulled the hood farther over his head and kept walking.

"Hey, fella, can you give us a hand?" someone said, obviously trying to disguise their voice.

The wizard stopped. "Don't do it, Phrim," he told himself. "The last thing you need is to talk to shadows."

"He ain't gonna help us," another disguised voice said.

That didn't sound like a rapscallion wanting to rob him. "Come into the light," Phrim demanded.

"We can't do that," a third voice whispered.

"Very well, then I'll be on my way."

"Wait!" the first voice hissed.

Odaraphrim watched as several people stepped out of the shadows. They wore a variety of clothes that neither matched nor fit well.

"That's better," Phrim said, pulling back his hood.

"He's a wizard!" one of the women exclaimed. "Run!"

Phrim had never heard an accent like theirs before. The R's at the ends of words sounded like *ah*. So, instead of saying wizard, it sounded more like *wizahd*.

"Hold on a minute," Phrim said, raising his hands and signaling for them to wait. "What are you so afraid of?"

"Don't tell 'im Pawd," a tall, thin man said.

"What choice do we have, Lank? He knows about us. All we can do now is pleads for help."

Phrim was intrigued. "Help to do what? I have no money."

"We don't wants your money. We wanna talk to someone in charge. We's members of the Northrim," Pawd explained.

"Northrim? What's that?" Phrim asked. Then it dawned on him. "Your Norters!"

"Shh!" the wizahd lady said. "Are you tryin' to get us killed? We know what people in town thinks about us. It's just as bad in the camps. Geminians distrustful of Northrim–Northrim distrustful of Geminians. That's why we came. We want to stop the situation from gettin' outa hand. People gots to keep cool."

Odaraphrim understood this all too well, but what could he do? There was no going back to Tarth, and he certainly wouldn't be allowed to return to the Spire. As for the Congregational House, he couldn't imagine the Norters being welcomed with open arms. They'd probably wind up being hog-tied and thrown in the dungeon if such a thing existed. He didn't know for sure, having not spent much time at Gemini City's venerable seat of government, but he didn't care to find out either. One thing Phrim did know was that all of them—Tarth, the Spire Wizards, or the city's Representatives—would find a way to make their lives miserable, and no one deserved that fate.

Once he'd escaped into the city, Phrim had spent much of the intervening time pondering Tarth's defense of Aargh at the clearing, and it had started to make sense. Tarth appeared to have a plan (a bad one, in Odaraphrim's estimation, but a plan notwithstanding), and that had to be respected. Then again, respecting someone's choices and going along with them were two entirely different things. Hence, Phrim's decision not to go back. In the end, nothing had turned out the way he'd expected, so maybe that would be true of the Norters, too.

The more he thought about it, the more he realized one truth to be self-evident: neither Aargh nor Tarth were headed in the direction he wanted to go. Therefore, it was time to find a new way…Phrim's way.

"I can help you," he said, coming to a decision. "But we need to get off the streets. There's a shelter not far from here where we can talk. Follow me."

• • •

Holly-Mine rocked back and forth as she munched on a warm roll from her favorite cart, *Bwain's Bread Bakery and Butter Stand*. One of the chair's swivel glides had rusted off, making it tipsy like a drunken sailor. She enjoyed finding chairs like that. They were much more fun than having to sit upright and still.

Over the last few days, she'd worked up quite an appetite, walking around Gemini City searching for Ralph. So, once she and Gerald had gotten to the shelter, she'd kicked back to listen to him tell one of his stories like everyone else.

"Those were the good old days, weren't they?" Gerald asked the room.

Everyone agreed, whispering vague things they'd heard about the rise of the southern towns.

"In those days, no one was left out in the cold, people had a roof over their heads, and folks could afford a warm meal to fill their bellies. Some say it was our fair city's heyday, though it wasn't called Gemini City back then. No. In fact, at that time, there wasn't only one city in Ardilakk Valley; there were four. Together, they formed the Ancient Quadropolis. The one I'm going to tell you about today still exists. In fact, it's sitting directly over our heads. This part of Gemini City was once known as Westie Sowt.

"It's the lowest part of the city, built right on the marsh-lands, unlike the eastern side that rises toward the highlands. This makes it susceptible to flooding, but no one has ever seen the mighty River Wide rise as it did during the Fort-night Flood. It's hard to imagine, but the river swelled so high it reached second-story windows! The lower blocks were almost entirely submerged, and the piers were washed away, but not the buildings. They were built with such skill that not even the raging River Wide could hurt them. Don't be-lieve me? Go outside and study the walls of the 0Block build-ings. If you look closely, you'll see the high water marks etched into their corners. Let me tell you how it happened…"

After hoisting herself out of the chair, Holly-Mine handed the remainder of her roll to a thankful woman and drifted around the outskirts of the room. She could tell Ralph wasn't there but wanted to look anyway.

As Gerald talked, she sauntered over to the shelter's disused serving tables. They were covered with dusty metal plates and the odd spoon or mug here and there. It had been many years since city shelters had provided much more than a cold floor to sleep on or a place to come in from the rain.

Holly-Mine wrinkled her nose. Shelters were smelly places on rainy days. Unless she had no other choice, she'd waited out storms under a staircase or in an overturned trash can. Even they smelled better than the rooms packed with wet people and wetter animals.

These days, she enjoyed a good rainstorm. She loved to hear it pitter-patter on tree leaves or drip-drop on the river. But the best part was when it stopped, and she breathed in the earthy petrichor rising from the ground at her feet.

Holly-Mine's fingers brushed a spoon, and it fell to the floor. She bent over to retrieve it and remembered something from her days living on Gemini City's streets. With a twinkle in her eye, she ducked under the table, wondering if she'd see marks on the wall. Yes! They'd stopped at one of the old shelters.

Holly-Mine had spent many hours speculating about the scribbles etched into the walls behind shelter tables. Her favorite one was a tree with a person sleeping under it. It wasn't much more than a few scratches and a stick figure, but she understood what it meant. Even though she'd never met the people who'd left their epitaphs on the walls, they shared an unspoken bond.

Lying on the floor, she inched her way over to the farthest corner, looking for a particularly special mark. There it was: two curved lines with circles underneath. Eyes. Her eyes. It had been years since she'd scratched them into the cement, but there they remained.

Using the spoon, she added the outline of a rat and a shining star next to her eyes. She kissed her fingers and placed them on the image. "Holly-Mine, Wrudge, and Papa together."

When she was ready, she slid herself out from under the table and continued to survey the perimeter of the room, but not before returning the spoon. Hopefully, it would be needed again someday.

A few steps away, she found a group of rats dining on a stale piece of bread behind a pillar.

"Friend Holly-Mine. How are you?" a thin rat asked.

"As well as can be expected, Throod."

The rat seemed pleased that Holly-Mine remembered her name.

"We are sorry...

"...for the loss..."

"...of your home."

"That's very kind of you to say. We're thankful for the Underoof Collective's support. Have you seen Ralph by any chance?" Holly-Mine held her hand out to demonstrate his height. "He's about this tall and has stringy hair that hangs over his eyes."

The rats conferred and answered in turn.

"We know Ralph."

"He often leaves us treats,"

"but we haven't seen him since he left."

This puzzled Holly-Mine. "Left to go where?"

"The last time any of us heard,"

"he was headed south with a band of wizards,"
"toward the Metal City on the highlands."

"How strange. Was he with Dramwitch or Aarghathlain?"
"Neither."

"He was traveling with Tarthanabelle…
"…through the Eastern Foothills."

At the mention of the wizard's name, Holly-Mine went rigid. The change in her demeanor happened so suddenly that the rats stopped chewing. They sensed how upset she was, and they weren't the only ones. Reminiscent of a distant thunderstorm, Holly-Mine's emotions rumbled through everyone's bodies, and the shelter became still.

Gerald left off his storytelling mid-sentence. "Holly-Mine?" he asked in her mind.

"Uncle Gerald. I'm glad you realized you can speak to me this way."

"I wasn't sure I could until you responded. And…I think… there's something else," he said, trying to understand what he felt—emotions as strong as the roots of trees and as raw as a cold winter's night. He began shaking so much that his teeth chattered.

"Uncle Gerald, be calm. Everything will be fine," Holly-Mine said soothingly in his mind. "There will come a time when we can talk about it, but that time is not now."

"I'm sorry. I…" he said, trailing off, unable to put what he sensed into words. "Your secret is safe with me. I promise."

Holly-Mine looked kindly at the man who'd stood with her in defiance of the Wizard of the Council.

Regaining his composure, Gerald said, "Tell me what has happened. Why did you get upset?"

Holly-Mine's smile faded. "Tarth has Ralph."

Gerald immediately leapt into action. To say this was out of character for the ex-Head Butler of Marble House would have been a gross understatement, but he didn't have the time to worry about such things. Pleasantries would have to wait. A friend of Holly-Mine's was in trouble, and they had to go!

PART IV

THE WIZARDS' SPIRE

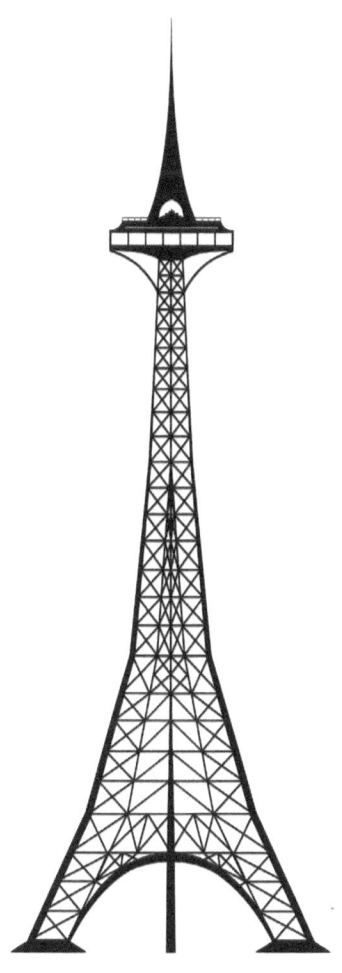

CHAPTER 1

THE OLIPHAUNT IN THE ROOM
AARGHATHLAIN

Dear Diary,

If the sun doesn't rise and set, has a day passed? I ask because I feel stuck in one long sleepless night, shrouded by the endless dark of this wretched tunnel. Here, there are no birds singing in the trees or ships floating on the river—only an infinite black void stretching ahead and behind. At least in the Underoof, light filtered in from storm drains and streethole covers. Down here, an obsidian murkiness waits impatiently to reclaim what little area we carve out with our meager meal-time fire.

Of course, I have Guildebrande, but asking him to light the way doesn't seem right. He's not a candle, after all, and I get the impression that asking him to perform such a menial task hurts his feelings...though he professes not to mind. Thankfully, after the cave-in, we made it to Stump's stash and have a torch now, but it isn't terribly bright. Don't get me wrong, I'm grateful for any light, as groping along the passageway wore on me, but I wish it were a tad brighter.

It's possible my confusion about what day it is might not be due to the darkness. I'm finally following the One True Root, but it hasn't made my path clearer. Quite the opposite! I've never been so lost. Before, I had my work as Spire Historian, but even that's been taken from me. Our home is gone, fantastic bedtime stories have been made real, and I've learned that lessons taught in the hallowed halls of the Gemini City School of Wizarding were nothing more than lies. Now, as I sit here on the eve of my next great adventure, I'm wondering what surprises Ransome Ravine has in store for me.

I've dreamed of this day—getting to explore the deepest place in the valley—though Stump has informed me that, once again, I have the wrong end of the stick. No surprise there. I keep thinking I'll run out of things to be incorrect about, but no. The world's never short of another revelation waiting to poke a hole in what I know…or thought I knew.

It has crossed my mind that there might be more to this hidden history thing than forgetful trees or me not asking the right questions. I mean, my job took me all over Gemini City and Ardilakk Valley. At least one tree should have heard there were no Marauders in the ravine or that my mother had magic, wouldn't you think? It seems I've been in the dark for much longer than the past few days—more like my entire life.

What I need to figure out is this: Did the trees hide the past from me because they didn't know? Were they trying to protect me from something? Or, worst of all, were they forced to keep me in the dark against their will? That's a chilling thought! Whatever the reason, I need to find out the answer.

The more I think about it, the more I wish my parents had been honest with me about magic and the world. Papa never mentioned it. Not once. If he had, I might have been more prepared. I respect that they were trying to protect me, but what if they made things worse by shielding the truth from me?

I'll have to put that thought aside for the time being. I have enough to worry about at the moment. Hopefully, everything will become clear after I visit the ravine.

On a different note, I'm fascinated that my mother was a healer. It certainly explains a lot, but not everything. If healers existed in the past, where'd they go? I considered expanding the school's curriculum beyond talking to trees my greatest achievement, but it turns out magic is no stranger to Ardilakk Valley. Yet another thing I had wrong. Maybe the Spire suffered the same fate as I have? How awful if that means generations of wizards have been frittering away their power instead of helping people. But no. There must be more to it. Nothing is ever that simple–not in my experience.

Anyway, I have more news to share if you can believe it. I recently learned that my father was the 13th Lord of Marble House. Shocked doesn't even begin to describe my surprise. I wonder how different my life might have been had I grown up on Upper Middling Street. Would I have gone to school to become a wizard? Probably, I guess, but it's interesting to think about.

Of everything that's happened, the hardest revelation I've had to endure relates to my lost familiar, Wrudge. It turns out he didn't save me from the wailing of the trees, at least not the way I thought. Apparently, he gave his glow to me, and I used his magic to silence the trees myself. Then, I inadvertently passed his glow on to Guildebrande. That makes me both sad and glad at the same time.

If it were possible to give Wrudge his glow back (or stop him from giving it to me in the first place), I wouldn't hesitate–not for one second. I miss him dearly. Of course, I'd never take it away from Guildebrande, either. Not only is it forbidden to use magic that way, but he's his own…um…person, I guess. Guildebrande's kind of singular, being the only living magical item in the world, at least that I know of. I guess there could be others, but I doubt it. Either way, he's unique, but I wish Wrudge were here, too…

Sorry, Diary. I got distracted there for a bit, but I'm back. The truth is, I'm avoiding talking about the oliphaunt in the room: Aldenthwaine's book, or, as he called it, The One True Book of

Spells. *It sits in my pocket like a lead weight, but I dare not look at it. Not yet, anyway. Even so, I'm drawn to it. I can tell it wants me to read it. It wants to share a secret with me, but I'm afraid of what that might be. Holly-Mine is, too, and if she's worried, it's best to be careful. So, I'll wait. I've spent a lifetime not knowing it existed. What's a while longer, I guess?*

Speaking of Holly-Mine, I hope she's okay. She and Gerald went to find Ralph, and I sent Dramwitch back to the Spire in the hopes of convincing the others to let Tarthanabelle back into the school. That way, he'll be prevented from teaching unbound students. Truthfully, I shudder to think what trouble Tarth and his followers might cause. Anyone willing to burn a house with its occupants still in it is capable of anything.

Ah, I see that Stump is ready to go. I hope we make it to the ravine today. A dwarven city! Amazing.

In a way, I'm disappointed to find out the Marauders…uh… Nahmanians didn't hide their treasure down there. That would have been something, but dwarves? That's even better!

It's been too long since we've spoken, Diary. I've missed writing in you, and I hope we chat again soon.

Oh yeah, there's one last thing. I can't help but think the clock is ticking. Toward what, I have no idea, but whatever it is, it's coming, and I don't think it will be good. At least, that's what my gut tells me, though that's a problem for future me, I guess. Today, it's time to visit Dahr Kahlahd-dîm, and unless I'm greatly mistaken, this will be a day to remember.

Aargh

CHAPTER 2

THE NIGHT BEFORE
HOLLY-MINE
Sundsday of the 8th week

Holly-Mine attempted to calm her racing mind by breathing in the cool night air. After several days of searching for Ralph, hearing that he'd been seen with Tarth had shaken her to the core. In general, she kept a cool head, but recent events had taken a toll. The loss of her home, her father's outburst in the Underoof, and the revelations at Marble House had left her nerves frayed and her mind flitting from one thought to another in quick succession. In a way, it was like the barrier between her memories had been broken, and they were all playing back at once.

Amongst the clutter, one thought kept rising to the surface: she couldn't imagine Ralph had willingly gone with the wizards unless he didn't recognize the danger. What's worse, if Tarth had somehow befriended Ralph, then he was unwittingly playing into the wizard's duplicitous hands because, make no mistake, Tarthanabelle was the very definition of danger.

Gerald called to her from somewhere beyond her thoughts…Geminians' thoughts…the forest's thoughts…everything's thoughts…swirling around her mind. She saw his outstretched hand pointing toward the stairwell they'd climbed out of, where boisterous voices echoed up from below the street.

Holly-Mine smiled. Laughter had that effect on her, but it wasn't the only sound that brought her joy. She listened–and heard–in a way no person other than the most adept Spire Elder could ever hope to understand. The sounds in her mind echoed into the distance, morphing into shapes…the Spire… the Mounts of Ardilakk…an acorn…the groaner. She focused on the old whistle buoy's mournful voice floating through the air like a ghost from beyond the grave. She remembered the day Bram had brought the *Prosperity* alongside the old channel marker…

Holly-Mine felt a tug.

Cutty was holding onto the back of her cloak to keep her from falling overboard, but she pulled away, leaning harder against the gunwale. She wanted to touch it. No, she needed to touch it.

The tips of her fingers brushed the buoy's weather-worn surface as it slid by, and she watched as it faded into the darkness, mesmerized by its benevolent hooting.

A resonant guffaw brought Holly-Mine's mind closer to the present. She thought about how Gerald had made quite a stir, stepping over people as they'd rushed out of the shelter, but stirs weren't all that unusual in those places. Truth be told, it wouldn't be a Gemini City shelter without one kerfuffle or another, and it didn't take long for everyone to move on.

People weren't the only ones in Ardilakk Valley who enjoyed hearing a good story. Trees did too, and so did Holly-Mine. And, when it came down to it, few places offered a better selection than Gemini City shelters. However, no matter how many tales were told, one stood out from the rest: *The Great Splishety-splash!*

It always began the same way, "Let me tell you about one humdinger of a brouhaha…"

Many years ago, the Gemini City Doublets lost the River Wide Mundsling Cup to the Ondlingstad Porters. Drunk with excitement (and more than their fair share of rum), the members of the Porters' team decided to have a little fun by crashing a lower-block shelter. That was their first mistake. The local boys wouldn't have been welcomed either, but being from Ondlingstad, Gemini City's chief rival on the river, the Porters never stood a chance.

If the out-of-towners had chosen to visit a hostel or a posh uptown hotel where most of their fans stayed (the kinds of places that had tiny bars of soap in their showers…or showers at all), the team's reception might have been different. However, that wasn't what they chose to do, and although shelters were usually considered welcoming places, even they had their limit.

Generally, the folks who frequented those lowly establishments didn't go in for mundsling and the hype that surrounded the competition for the cup. Why? Primarily because the team's logo—Gemini City's familiar black line flanked by two stars—was the same symbol that had been forcibly tattooed on most of their palms. That kind of indignity left a mark on much more than one's hands, and being reminded about it by a group of drunken fools from down the river proved to be the straw that broke the garble's back, so to speak…but the team's folly didn't end there.

Their second mistake was assuming they could take on an entire shelter's worth of hungry people. In short order, they found themselves running for their lives toward the port piers.

When the first player hit the water, the crowd laughed.
When the trophy followed them in, the crowd erupted with
cheers. Anyone who didn't know better would have thought
the Doublets had won the game.

Holly-Mine studied her palms. The memory of the tattoo-er's needle pricking her hands made her skin crawl, and although many years had passed since that day, the feeling of powerlessness remained. Ralph's hands bore the same marks. It was something they'd share forever, or so she thought.

The mist changed into a light rain, and Gerald touched her gently on the shoulder.

Holly-Mine blinked, fully returning to the present. "How long have we been standing here?"

"Not long," he reassured her, "but the night is chilly, and it's starting to rain. Let's go before we catch a cold."

Holly-Mine wanted to go, but her feet didn't move.

Gerald noticed her hesitation, and he tactfully suggested a more considered approach. "Why don't we enter the forest at the city's northeast corner? It's safe to assume that Tarth is doing his best not to call attention to himself after what he did to your home. It's even possible that he's been holing up, waiting to see if the coast is clear."

Holly-Mine looked unconvinced. "But what if he's already on his way to the highlands?"

"Well, I imagine if he's already begun the trek south, he's traveling slowly, sticking to the woods for cover. Therefore, it's unlikely he and his companions have made it to the river yet. If we start at the city's northeast corner, we're guaranteed not to miss them since he'll have to round the Once-Great Wall before heading south."

There was no doubt that Gerald's logic made sense because he was a master at going undetected. It was one of his favorite pastimes back when he held the position of *Head Butler of Marble House*. Now, the tall, lanky man stuck out like a sore thumb, covered in outlandishly colorful clothing, but that didn't mean he'd lost the knowledge of how to be stealthy.

Holly-Mine didn't like the idea of wasting time going in the wrong direction. She didn't know precisely where Tarth was headed, but several days had passed, and she had difficulty imagining Ralph wasn't already on the highlands, in the Norters' camp, or floating down the river on a ship. But Gerald's explanation of how important it was not to get ahead of Tarth on the trail persuaded her. Neither of them wanted the wizard sneaking up on them from behind. Besides, if Ralph had escaped, or the wizards had been waylaid for whatever reason, they might lose time, having to double back to search for them. If the trees had been more helpful or the frenetic wind had settled, she might have felt differently, but they were on their own for now, and in the end, she reluctantly agreed. Yet, neither of them moved, not wanting to face the long walk to the eastern corner of the 11Blocks.

Gemini City covered three miles of valley floor from the piers to the Congregational House and not more than twice that from side to side, but they weren't traveling in either of those directions. Their path led from corner to corner, which meant a zig-zaggy adventure through many squares.

Gerald looked around. They were a couple of blocks east of the Lowlands and about the same distance from the piers. That meant they were almost as far away from their destination as possible and still be in the city.

Something caught his attention, and he sniffed the air. "Do you smell that?"

"I smell many things," Holly-Mine responded. "Which one do you mean?"

The air in this part of town carried with it a plethora of scents—a mixture of pleasant and not-so-much, especially here, sandwiched between fishing boats offloading their catch and the dumping grounds of the Lowland Wastes. Then again, the rain had washed away many of those smells, if only for a short while. Even the oil left by steam carriages was currently snaking its way toward the river. What remained was...

"Licorice?" she asked.

Gerald took a deep breath. "Possibly. It might be star anise tea." He loved a good cup of tea and could use one right about now.

Holly-Mine struggled between having a warm cuppa or rushing off to save her friend from Tarth. "This must be how Papa felt back in the Underoof," she mumbled.

"Did you say you're not feeling well?" Gerald asked, pulling himself away from the enticing smell.

"On no, I'm fine. I'm just tired and hungry."

Holly-Mine opened her rucksack and removed the short, green cloak Dramwitch had given her as a birthday present. In truth, she'd never told him or anyone else which day she was born on because she didn't enjoy being reminded of the wand or what the Wizard of the Council did to Mother Tree. Therefore, Dram brought her a present every time he visited. That way, he figured he was bound to get it right sooner or later!

Pulling the cloak over her shoulders, she said, "If it's okay with you, I'd like to stop by the apartment."

"That sounds like a great idea," Gerald agreed. "Is it far?"

"It's on the corner of 45th and Middling above a café, but I'm sure it's closed."

He sighed both because it wasn't nearby and the café was closed.

"Don't worry," Holly-Mine said, seeing the disappointment on his face. "We can stop for a snack on the way. Something else must be open."

The thought of that raised both of their spirits, and they headed toward the center of town.

It wasn't long before Holly-Mine was sitting on the apartment's balcony, curled in her favorite traveling jammies–a giant onesie that covered her from head to toe. Aargh had bought it for her the previous season, on an especially cold night when they'd popped into town to watch the Midswinterfest tree lighting ceremony. The trip stuck out in her mind because it was one of the few times they'd visited the city after leaving the Spire.

The lack of frequency of their trips was also why she'd left her fuzzy jammies in the apartment. She'd made a point of telling her Papa that it gave them a reason to return, and she was glad she did, too. The autumn air had grown chilly, and its funny slipper feet kept her tootsies warm.

On their way from the lower blocks, she and Gerald were shocked to find that most of Middling Street's vendors had closed early. It was disquieting to see this part of the city empty, even in the middle of the night.

The tension behind everyone's eyes and the curt way the vendors addressed them made it clear people were on edge. Luckily, Holly-Mine's second favorite food stand, *Glenda's "The Gilded Gooseberry"* cart, was still open, and she'd procured a large slice of gooseberry pie.

Holly-Mine loved *Glenda's*, but *Bwain's Bread Bakery and Butter Stand* topped her list. "Bwain" made the best sweet rolls on Lower Middling Street, true enough, but his daughter, Tilda, was the main reason Holly-Mine held the stand in such high regard.

Tilda had taken over the business when her father retired, and she was one of the nicest people Holly-Mine had ever met. On those days when she hadn't been lucky enough to find a happy penny, Tilda still slipped her a warm roll from the back of the cart, winking and saying, "A treat for my little lady."

Holly-Mine missed seeing her friend. It had been a while since Tilda had sold the cart to focus on caring for her father full-time. The new owners, Murt and Bert, were friendly enough, but it wasn't the same. Even so, she still visited the cart whenever possible to buy a roll for herself and one for someone who needed it more than she did. Kindness didn't cost money, but rolls certainly did.

Gerald stretched his long, lanky body and yawned. "I'm tired. Are you ready to go to bed? Uh, Little One?"

Holly-Mine had already fallen asleep in her cozy onesie with the half-eaten piece of pie in her hand.

Careful not to wake her, Gerald carried her inside. Once through the door, he stood there, not knowing what to do. The apartment had a small galley kitchen, a smaller bathroom, a stone-topped desk, and a metal couch with cushions.

"Where do you sleep?" he asked, not expecting an answer.

One of Holly-Mine's fingers uncurled and pointed toward the ceiling.

Beyond the couch, a collection of metal boxes had been stacked along the wall, forming a makeshift staircase. It led to a sleeping loft above the kitchen and bath.

"No way. I'm not climbing those stairs with you in my arms. You'll have to be content with the couch tonight," he said, putting her on the sofa's soft cushions.

Then, he went to the kitchen to locate a rag to wash her gooseberry-stained hand and searched the stair-boxes for a blanket. He found an earthy-toned comforter with leaves embroidered on it that looked perfect and placed it over her, tucking in the edges.

Putting the seat cushion from the desk chair under his head, he fell fast asleep on the floor beside her.

Mundsday of the 9th week
Year Three Hundred and Thirty-Three
of the Modern Age
Dawn

CHAPTER 3

A WIZARDLY RETURN
AARGHATHLAIN

"Welcome to the ancient dwarven city of Dahr Kahlahd-dîm!" Stump announced as they emerged from the tunnel.[6]
D'Aargh hesitated.

That was what Aargh called himself now, having decided it would be appropriate to have a dwarfish name to match his appearance. Stump tried to tell him that *D'Aargh* sounded more like a place than a name, but he'd insisted on using it. He liked the way it rolled off his thick, dwarvish tongue.

He also liked that his wizardly limbs had been replaced by stocky dwarven legs. They felt stable–rooted, if you will–almost connected to the earth beneath him, and his thick-fingered hands bulged with muscles when he made a fist. He'd never had muscles like that before, and he enjoyed watching them move under the skin. They were the kind of hands that didn't need magic to move mountains.

The only part of the transformation that gave him pause was his face. He hadn't seen it yet, and judging by the feel of his nose and ears, it might take a substantial amount of getting used to!

---

[6] A literal translation of Dahr Kahlahd-dîm in the common speech would be *The Hidden City of Kahlahd.* (Dahr: *City* or *Town*) (Dîm: *in shadow* or *hidden*)
  *NOTE: the letter *R* is rolled (known as an *alveolar tap* or *alveolar flap).*

Unable to move, D'Aargh watched from the protection of the shadows.

As he stood there contemplating his next step, he held a conversation with himself about the emotions he'd struggled to hold in check throughout their journey under the city.

"I had no idea what events were being set in motion as I fell down the steps all those years ago."

"A tree might have told you."

"If I'd known what to ask."

"True, but it hasn't been all bad. Don't forget, Holly-Mine came into your life that day."

"How could I? It's the best thing that has ever happened to me."

"And Gerald, too."

"Yes, but I knew him as TTM back then, and we weren't friends yet. Then, the Wizard of the Council started the Great Fire, and elemental magic was revealed to me. Now, I never stop worrying about some kind of catastrophe happening at the school."

"But that's why you changed the Wizarding Oath—to protect everyone."

"I meant well, but I might have gone too far."

"At least it kept everyone from blowing themselves up."

"Hindsight being what it is, I probably should have bonded with another familiar right away. Maybe if I had, I'd still be the school's head wizard."

"I doubt Tarth would have stood for that, even if you had."

"Ah, I see your point."

"Now, you've enchanted Guildebrande, met a real-life dwarf, learned Marauders were Nahmanians, found out you lived in a high house, discovered your mother was a wizard, and Aldenthwaine was—"

"Stop!" D'Aargh yelled in his mind.

He wasn't ready to condemn Aldenthwaine yet. Perhaps his parents were wrong, and the book he carried under his robes contained miracles, not dangerous incantations. Aldenthwaine had been his lifeline after the death of his father. The least he could do was not jump to conclusions, right?

He felt utterly alone, and not just because he was a human about to enter the ancient dwarven city of Dahr Kahlahddîm…in Ardilakk Valley, Gemini City, and in his life, too. Even so, he sensed a newfound sense of control awakening within him. He might not know the whole story of what was going on, but he finally had the ability to choose whether or not to take the next step, right?

Clearing her throat to use her rat voice, Mnoonge said, "Nope."

Giving away his voice—one more mistake in a long line of miscalculations—had resulted in disastrous consequences. Why he'd been so arrogant as to believe he could exist in two places at once, he'd never figure out. Holly-Mine had warned him not to do it, and she'd been right as usual.

"I don't have a choice, do I?" he asked Mnoonge in her mind. "Too many people are counting on me to figure out what's happening and, hopefully, put a stop to it."

"Correct," the small rat from the lower blocks responded in kind.

He knew she was right, but he didn't move. His world had been flipped upside down, and the revelations just kept coming. What secrets would be revealed if he took that last step into the ravine? The thought struck fear in his heart, but—

"What are you waiting for?" Stump asked.

D'Aargh jumped. What, indeed? "Enough dithering, you silly wizard. If Holly-Mine were here, she'd say the same thing," he thought.

Therefore, without another second of hesitation, D'Aargh stepped out of the tunnel and into the light.

The earth shuddered from the mountains to the river when his foot touched the ground. A wizard had returned, the first since the Brethren had barred magic from the ravine, and the world was aware of his presence. D'Aargh felt it, too–an opening of sorts.

Stump laughed. "You certainly know how to make an entrance, but I'd keep that wizarding stuff to a minimum if I were you."

"I'm trying. I promise," Mnoonge responded for D'Aargh from the bottom of her pocket.

Stump shook their head. "I imagine asking a wizard not to do magic is akin to telling a dwarf to shave their beard. Never going to happen! Come on."

"How are you not affected by the light? It's so bright!" Mnoonge said as D'Aargh shaded his eyes.

It wasn't that bright, but compared to the long dark of the tunnel, it was positively blinding.

"Light, dark. Hot, cold. It makes no difference to me. I'm a dwarf, remember?"

"Must be nice to–"

D'Aargh's pocket stopped mid-sentence. There were dwarves everywhere!

Stump had to put a hand on the disguised wizard's chest to keep him from falling headlong into the busy thoroughfare. Awestruck, D'Aargh surveyed his surroundings until his eyes settled on the water rushing through the ravine.[7]

---

[7] The tunnel from Marble House enters Dahr Kahlahd-dîm near the ravine's southerly end, where the river leaves the underground city and burrows beneath the Eastern Foothills. A large crag in the rock face conceals it from view. However, crags in rock faces are most certainly a dwarf thing, and every dwarf in the city is aware of the tunnel's existence, not to mention where it leads.

Unable to control himself, Mnoonge's muffled voice exclaimed, "That's the River Underground!"

The presence of the river didn't surprise D'Aargh, but the overwhelming emotions he experienced laying eyes on it for the first time were completely unexpected. To the best of his knowledge, no living Geminian had ever gazed upon the mysterious River Underground as it made its enigmatic way to the River Wide. Now, he was standing so close that he could feel the coolness of the air emanating from it.[8]

When he lifted his gaze from the fast-flowing water, the full weight of how far beneath the forest floor they were landed on him. "So much stone!"

Aargh had sensed that the Marble House tunnel was traveling in a downward direction, but he hadn't fathomed the extent of their descent into the earth. A long, jagged line revealed the bright blue sky high above them, but it was only the slightest hint that a world existed beyond the ravine's rock walls. No wonder the river wasn't visible from above.

As he stood there staring at the distant sliver of blue sky, the weight of the stone around him triggered his anxiety. So

---

[8] Ever since the Dark Wizard brought forth Ardilakk, Gemini City's famed River Underground has sliced its way through Ransome Ravine. The one place people can see it is east of False Hope Bluff, where it bursts from the highland cliffs in a torrent of falling water—a perpetual source of fascination along the river and beyond. In springtime, the falls shoot out of the rock face like a douser's hose, shaking the earth under everyone's feet. In the winter, it freezes into sheets of cascading ice, dyed blue and pink, with the minerals the river carries from the mountains.

Much to many onlookers' annoyance, the Norters obstructed the view of the waterfall with their bridges and river blockade for most of the last couple of years. Any requests that had been made for permission to visit the valley's natural wonder were answered with silence.

The dwarves' name for the river is Dūnhyldun-thîr or River Door. If Geminians had remembered this critical piece of information, they might have found their way into the ravine. Instead, it remained a mystery for generations until D'Aargh stepped out of the tunnel that led from Marble House.

far down. Far from the world. Far from his Holly-Mine. Far from the city and the Spire.

"Remember your *C's*," he told himself.

Then, a thought occurred to him–a comforting thought. Here at the bottom of Ransome Ravine, he wasn't farther from the forest but rather closer to the Earth Mother.

Closing his eyes, he reached out to her. He sensed her presence, and she felt him, as did Sisters Wind and Water. *Aarghathlain, Steward of the Elements*, had nothing to fear. He was right where he belonged, amongst friends.

"Holly-Mine would love being this close to her," D'Aargh's pocket said.

"What's that?" Stump asked above the hubbub.

"Just talking with myself."

"Nope, I'll never get used to that. Not going to happen," Stump said, shaking their head and diving into the crowd. "Keep up if you know what's good for you!"

It took every ounce of D'Aargh's concentration to follow Stump along the path. He kept having to quickly step to the side or shift his shoulders to avoid bumping into oncoming dwarves. More than once, he came close to running into someone, but with Mnoonge's help–she called out directions when it looked like D'Aargh wasn't paying close enough attention–each crisis was averted.

It reminded him of the circus' glass maze, where a long line of people pushed into the door, forcing everyone to keep moving and think fast because if they didn't, they'd wind up running headlong into a transparent wall blocking the way. Here, the walls were stout dwarves, and they looked equally immovable to D'Aargh.

He was about to ask if they could take a break when Stump spun around and motioned toward the wall.

"It'd be best if you stay here while I take care of a few things. I won't be long," Stump explained. "Don't wander off. I'll be back in a jiffy."

D'Aargh attempted to tell Stump he wasn't planning on going anywhere, but the dwarf was already gone, having been swallowed by the crowd. Relieved to have the chance to collect his thoughts, D'Aargh studied the ravine city's occupants as they passed.

Covered in dust and dirt, many appeared to be coming home after a long day's work, and he wondered if they were reopening the mines under the foot of the mounts. D'Aargh recognized many of their tools, such as shovels or pickaxes, and noted countless lamp reflectors and welding shields that were similar to the ones workers in the Port Pier District used or could be seen up the river at shipyards in Essexborough. Some even resembled Grunt, dressed for a hard day's work beneath a steam engine.

What D'Aargh didn't see was anyone strolling around, dressed in the fashion of Upper Middling Street's highest society. Clearly, Ransome Ravine wasn't a lost stronghold of the Marauders–Nahms, D'Aargh corrected himself. It was a vibrant river city hidden deep below the forest floor.

High arching stone bridges connected two wide roads on either side of the River Underground. Some were narrow footpaths, while others were sturdy enough to hold small shops and vendors' wooden carts. Every last inch of both teemed with dwarves. Beyond the bridges, long staircases lead to several higher stories, possibly more, as each was set back farther than the one below. Each level was lined with rooms carved out of the ravine's walls.

D'Aargh's fascination with the chasm city and its colorful inhabitants knew no bounds. During his time as Spire Historian, he'd never heard about dwarves, Dahr Kahlahd-dîm, or the secret way into the ravine through the River Underground. The whole thing rivaled the fantastic stories contained in the *Chronicles of Thelbaldus Harnock!*

Letting his eyes get swept downstream with the racing water, he looked at where the river exited the gorge. He was shocked when a large animal emerged from the shadows. Mnoonge almost shouted that a monster had breached the dwarves' defenses, but that was before D'Aargh realized the beast was harnessed–tethered to a long barge laden with goods and people.

Then it came to him. "That's a garble!" his pocket exclaimed. "That thing is an enormous garble!"

"'Course it is," a grumpy old dwarf said as they passed. "Might want to get your face out of your pint now and then."

But D'Aargh wasn't drunk, and his spirits weren't dampened, not in the least. He'd never seen a garble that size before. The ones back home sat on the counter or slept in a cupboard under the silverware drawer. This animal was the size of a steam carriage. Its hulking body and stumpy legs were covered with tough gray skin, and its long, thick face swayed from side to side as it moved.

"The Great Auntilees of the world would have a difficult time getting that thing to peel their rutabagas!" D'Aargh's pocket remarked. "Or maybe not. Auntilees tend to be pretty formidable, too."

Mnoonge chuckled, but she didn't understand what Aargh found amusing. Auntilees were broom-wielding, screaming terrors, and there was nothing funny about that!

As they watched, the garble trumpeted. Then, satisfied it had made its position known, the massive animal dipped its head to take a drink. Its water trough had been cleverly positioned so that when the garble stopped, the boat it had dragged upstream floated alongside a small pier. The ferry's hands tossed ropes to workers who wrapped them around cleats and immediately offloaded the passengers and cargo. The whole process took no more than a couple of minutes. Afterward, the beast was enticed to reverse direction to prepare for the return trip.

"Probably with a rutabaga," D'Aargh's pocket commented absently.

While the garble munched on its treat, its handler–a thickset dwarf wearing a long, leather coat–removed the harness from its head and slipped it over the animal's stumpy tail. D'Aargh wondered about the dwarf's attire. Their coat had metal studs on the shoulders, as did their belt and gloves, but why the garble's handler needed protection was a mystery since the animal was clearly domesticated.

As he watched, the dwarf scratched the animal under its chin. It obviously enjoyed that because it stretched its neck to allow the dwarf to reach its best spot, moaning with delight. D'Aargh couldn't help but smile, as did Mnoonge, though she was still deep in the pocket and couldn't see out.

Tearing his gaze away from the dwarf's beast of burden, D'Aargh studied the boat's passengers and did a double take. Were his eyes deceiving him? "It can't be. Norters!"

This time, Mnoonge scrambled out of the pocket to see for herself. Sure enough, the visitors were handing crates and barrels to gruff-looking dwarves, offloading the barge as if they did it daily.

"The Norters trade with the dwarves!" she said for D'Aargh.

Then, everything fell into place.

"Of course. The Underground Falls."

The Norters hadn't forgotten their past the way Geminians had. Not only had they returned to Ardilakk Valley, they'd flown right to the highlands, making camp above and below the falls. Nobody suspected anything because no one knew this was the way to the ravine, let alone that dwarves lived there.

"Smart. Very smart," Mnoonge said for D'Aargh before climbing back into her pocket.

After the newcomers completed their business, the Norters prepared to visit the city. They looked like anyone else except for their black clothes, tall boots, and goggles. Truthfully, if their attire had been less aeronautical, they'd have easily passed for Geminians.

D'Aargh didn't know why, but this realization concerned him. It was probably nothing. Then again, why had the Norters been adamant that there be no communication with Gemini City when they were working with the dwarves?

He didn't have time to consider what this meant for Ardilakk Valley because Stump reappeared, and once again, they rejoined the dwarven throng moving north.

The last thing D'Aargh saw was the garble's handler uncleat the boat and pat the animal on the rump. Then, it slowly made its way back into the tunnel toward the River Wide. Doubtlessly, the water ran too fast to risk riding on it untethered, so day in and day out, the garble ambled along the River Underground's banks, ferrying goods and people from the city to the Norters' camp and back again.

"Rather ingenious," D'Aargh's pocket commented as a second garble emerged from the gloom on their side of the river.

"Come with me," Stump said. "I bumped into someone you'll enjoy meeting. I'm sure he'll be happy to meet with you, too."

D'Aargh didn't miss that Stump referred to the person as *he* and not *they*.

"This should be interesting," D'Aargh's pocket remarked as they stepped between two dwarves who looked more like boulders than people.

CHAPTER 4

AN EARLY MORNING MEETING
THE WIZARDS' UNDERGROUND

As the sun began its daily trek down the Spire, the members of The Wizards' Underground sat in a greenhouse in the southeast corner of the school's grounds. It was the smallest of the hothouses, and they were crammed together like flowers overflowing a colorful spring window box. Their equally colorful language made it clear how upset they were at being called to a meeting at the crack of dawn…the second day in a row! The previous day, Dram and Bee hadn't shown when they were supposed to, so they'd had to reschedule.

After Bee made his big escape from the dormitory building by shinnying down the sheet-rope Mizelthorn had delivered, he and Dramwitch went to the same greenhouse where the postulants had attempted to skip the All-School Meeting. Bee tried to get Dram to explain what had happened as they tidied the space, but all the younger wizard would say was that he hoped Grettles felt better. Bee decided to let it go because his friend looked green around the gills, and he didn't want to clean up more than one mess. Besides, the only thing that mattered was that he wasn't locked in his room anymore.

Once they finished, Bee and Dram attempted to join the other members of The Wizards' Underground but got stuck when the All-School Meeting ended early. Of course, the head wizard had never shown up, which shouldn't have been a surprise to anyone considering the school didn't have one, and Interim Head Wizard Tarthanabelle was who-knows-where. Therefore, they'd adjourned to do more important things, like complain about the meeting that had never happened.

"Wow!" Dram said, pushing Bee inside the nearest greenhouse. "I thought it would take them longer to realize no one was coming."

"What do we do?" Bee asked, hiding under a raised planting bed.

Dram paced back and forth as he pondered their situation. "I'm not sure. Give me a minute. Who brings you food in the morning?"

"Thorn, but I'm never awake when he gets here. He usually leaves it in the hallway."

"Perfect. No one will realize you aren't in your room for a while."

"Really, Dram? A giant sheet-rope is hanging out of my dorm window. That definitely won't raise suspicion."

"*Picea glauca,* I forgot about that!" the younger wizard exclaimed.

Bee grabbed Dram by the sleeve and pulled him under the planting bed. "Shh, keep it down. Someone is coming."

The greenhouse door flung open, and a group of wizards rushed in.

"Why are we wasting our time looking for him? He'd be a fool to stay here," one of them said.

"Yeah, if I were him—which I'm not, of course—I would have run right out the Westie Street exit and never looked back," another wizard added.

Bee recognized their voices but didn't bother checking to see if he was right. Instead, he burrowed under a pile of burlap bags filled with peat. It didn't smell great but did an excellent job hiding his bright yellow robes. Dram did the same thing, though his brown robes fit right in.

Pinned down by the constant coming and going of people looking for Bee and exhausted from everything that had happened, they wound up falling asleep. When they woke that evening, Dram panicked because they'd missed the gathering of The Wizards' Underground.

After more than a few breathing exercises and multiple recitations of his *C's*, Bee finally calmed Dram down, though it took a while longer to convince him to set up a new meeting. By the time Dram returned the next morning, Bee was beyond grumpy and extremely hungry. Dram rooted around in his messenger bag and came up with a bag of trail mix, which did little to assuage Bee's grumpiness or hunger.

Now, they were stuffed into the smallest hothouse on the grounds, along with everyone else (and their familiars), and no one was happy.

Despite their best efforts, the members of The Wizards' Underground struggled to devise a strategy to search the school, Spire, and the surrounding area. Some of the wizards wanted to fan out, covering as much space as possible, but Lan and Tassior thought it would be a better idea to team up in case they met Tarth. Pud took it upon himself to disagree with every suggestion—a time-honored wizarding tradition that everyone both respected and was furious about at the same time.

"We don't need to waste energy searching over there. I'm telling you, there is no tunnel in that area. I run that way with Belk every morning!" O said, slapping his leg.

Belk perked up at the sound because that was how O called to him after he'd retrieved a stick. When the greyhound realized there was no stick, he went back to sleep.

"Keep your voice down," Garth said. "Do you want everyone to hear us?"

"Who's going to hear us?" Illbrahss asked, nervously fingering the notes of his favorite song on his arm. "No one in their right mind would go near this place."

"I think that speaks volumes about the assembled," Pud grumbled.

Few buildings on the grounds offered privacy during the day. Whether their succulent fruits or vegetables attracted snackers on the way to class or fragrant flowers enticed would-be studiers to distraction, greenhouses were busy places. However, a couple of less-frequented buildings sat disused near the Spire Wall. Those usually contained less desirable plants no one wanted to mess around with; hence, Alantus' reason for choosing *Glass House 3.1-2a* for their meeting.

This greenhouse was between plantings due to an unfortunate incident involving a rosary pea–a rather dangerous plant and pet project of Wizard Alpamdāzor, former Wizard of the Spire. He had been one of the school's more eccentric wizards, which was saying something. He wore a shock of white hair on top of his head and had a habit of touching his thumb to each of his fingers as he spoke. Lan repeatedly warned Dāz of the danger, but the wizard just patted him on the back and ushered him out the door.

Sadly, poor Alpamdāzor's story came to an untimely end when he mishandled a crop of the plant's seeds. After the white-haired wizard's passing, the greenhouse had been carefully cleaned, but people still kept their distance. That's why, as they talked, Bee sat in a corner, not moving a muscle. He didn't care how skillfully the vine and its many leaves, roots, and seeds had been extricated from the greenhouse. He didn't plan on touching anything.

Less concerned about the danger, Dramwitch got to business, pairing the wizards by scribbling names and locations into his journal. This worked out well because there were twelve of them. The thirteenth member of The Wizards' Underground was Aargh, but that was only an honorary position. It wasn't the safest plan, but what other option did they have?

Much to his delight, everyone let Dram do the work in peace, which played right into his hands because Aargh's ex-apprentice had a plan.

Brindlewise asked if anyone had an idea as to how they might alert each other if one of the search parties found Tarth's escape route. Tassior recommended ringing the old dinner bell.

On most days, it stood silently atop a pole outside the large animal barn. Other than students being dared to pull the rope (usually during graduation ceremonies), it hadn't been used for any meaningful purpose in ages.

Brindlewise clapped his hands together. "That's settled then. If anyone finds the tunnel, one wizard will ring the bell while the other remains to stand guard."

Brindlewise and Paladand reviewed Dram's work. Both agreed that the ex-assistant to the head wizard had done a superb job.

No one noticed that he'd put Lake Hîrdehn-dūl under his and Garthelwaite's names. They wouldn't have cared even if they had, but Dram did. The last time he'd spoken with his ex-mentor, Aargh had suggested the lake sounded like the perfect place to hide a secret tunnel. Dram agreed, and he wanted to be the one to find it.

He hadn't noticed any signs of it during his previous visits, but he hadn't been looking for it either. This time, he'd leave no stone unturned. And, to make absolutely sure he didn't miss anything, he'd bring his close friend Garthelwaite.

The meeting was about to adjourn when a shudder ran through the ground.

"Oh no," Fizzbain said, feeling ill. "What was that?"

Ever since their meeting in the sculpture garden, Fizz had been plagued by dreams of stone statues coming to life. The worst one involved a short wizard chasing after him, calling for his familiar.

"Calm yourself," Brindlewise said. "I don't believe you need to be concerned."

Paladand agreed. "That was different from the other night. It didn't feel…"

"Dangerous?" Pud asked.

"Evil," Paladand corrected.

They'd all experienced the strange magic when the statues had started speaking–not to mention Aldenthwaine's unwizardly silence–but no one had risked describing it. At Paladand's mention of the word evil, everyone became acutely aware of how close the air felt in the greenhouse, and beads of sweat glistened on their brows.

"I'm afraid Paladand might be right," Brindlewise said, breaking the silence.

Afynn disagreed. "I don't think so. I believe it was…uh… more hungry."

That was the final straw.

"I need air," Fizz said, limping out of the greenhouse and holding his hand over his mouth.

The other wizards weren't far behind, though Bee had to stay back until Dram brought him an old set of robes. Yellow wasn't the best color to wear when you didn't want to draw attention to yourself.

Before the group left, Brindlewise wished them the wisdom of the old forest, and they dispersed to search the grounds.

CHAPTER 5

DARK CORNERS AND WICKER BASKETS
ODARAPHRIM & RATS

Odaraphrim's Northrim companions–Lank, Pawd, Chpader, and Malba–shuffled closer to the prize waiting at the end of the line, albeit at an agonizingly slow pace. It had been a long night, and everyone hungered for something…anything…to stop their bellies from grumbling.

A kind-looking woman, wearing a white apron and a broad, toothy smile, stood at the bottom of the stone stairway that led into the shelter. The smell wafting from the wicker baskets she'd brought made everyone swoon.

The ragtag group of wanderers who'd cornered Phrim the previous evening practically fell over each other as they joined the queue to get one of her freshly baked rolls. Luckily, the mismatched clothing they'd stolen from washlines fit right in with the people seeking refuge beneath Gemini City's streets, and no one had any idea they were from the Metal City on the highlands.

Although Phrim assured them there was enough food for everyone, nothing could keep their mouths from watering and their stomachs from aching at the promise of something to eat. That's why, when they finally made it within arm's length of the basket, Chpader elbowed Odaraphrim out of the way and snatched a roll from the server's hand, exclaiming, "Thank the skies. Food!"

The server didn't look upset, though. She just smiled and handed Phrim a second roll. "Here. She looks like she could use another."

Much to everyone's relief, there was plenty to go around, and the group retired to a quiet corner to talk and eat.

At first, Phrim's companions' thick accent made it difficult for him to understand what they were saying, but he was getting used to it. He found it amusing when they said *wizahd* instead of *wizard*. It almost sounded as if they were cursing at him, which, in a way, made perfect sense.

"The Northrim's on the brink of falling apart," Pawd said, putting almost the entire roll in his mouth at once. He was a rough-and-tumble fellow with a chip on his shoulder and thick, calloused hands used to doing hard work. "There are those who wants to take to the skies again and others who wants to put down roots."

"Then there's that wizard. What's his name?" Chpader asked, already working on the second roll Phrim had passed to her. She also looked like someone who'd spent the better part of their life working under machines, and her attitude was as strong as her arms.

Lank answered her. "Tartenbell, I think."

At the sound of Tarth's name, Phrim perked up. Thoughts of what he'd done in that wizard's name weighed heavily on his mind, but more than that, he struggled to understand how easily he'd been manipulated into behaving in such an abominable way. After burning Aarghathlain's cottage–with him and his daughter still inside!–he'd begun to wonder what else he might be capable of doing.

That thought terrified Phrim because something in the back of his mind told him he'd have the pleasure of finding out sooner rather than later. Later would be preferable, but since wizards had lost the ability to follow trees' roots to the future, he'd have to wait and see what was going to happen like everyone else, and that road was slow…very slow.

"Tarthanabelle," Phrim corrected, handing the remainder of his bread to Malba, who also looked like she needed it. He'd never seen someone so tiny. Not only that, but she kept her hair pinned tightly to her head, which gave her the appearance of a child. That was, until you noticed the taught muscles under her skin and the intensity of her eyes. "How do you folks know about Tarth?"

"He's been visiting our camp ever since we arrived," Lank explained.

Pawd slammed his fist onto the cold stone floor. "Stirring things up, I say! He's going around saying he can gets us back our land."

"Is that so?" Phrim asked, studying their faces for any trace of deception. "I knew Tarth was up to no good, but I didn't think he'd gone that far."

The group exchanged concerned glances, and Phrim remembered they were just as wary of him as he was of them.

Doing his best to assuage their fears, he said, "Don't worry. I owe no allegiance to that wizard. Not anymore."

"Is that why you's is helping us?" Chpader asked after poking him in the side to get his attention.

"Let's just say I have a score to settle."

Lank shifted uneasily. "I don't like the sound of that."

"You don't have to because it doesn't involve you," Phrim snapped, speaking louder than he'd intended.

The group looked around to see if anyone noticed, but the usual chatter of the shelter never faltered.

"Look. We don't want to get mixed up in whatever's going on between you and Tartenbell. We're trying to calm things down, not make 'em worse," Lank explained.

It wasn't a question, but it was clear that Lank and his companions were waiting for an explanation from Phrim about why he'd gotten upset. Even though he knew this, Phrim didn't respond immediately, not wanting to misstep again. He'd been on edge lately, meaning more than usual, and he wanted to keep his emotions in check. He had enough trouble to deal with without drawing unwanted attention toward himself. So, as they sat there in silence, he took a little time to gather his thoughts before speaking.

When he was ready, he said, "There's nothing to get mixed up in. What I should have said was that I'm familiar with how Tarth operates. If I can get close, I might be able to distract him long enough for you to speak with your friends or, better yet, get him out of the city altogether. I overheard him and Flinghower–another wizard–talking about something he wants. I might be able to use that to our advantage."

The look on his companion's faces told Phrim he hadn't done a good job of convincing them he was on the up and up.

"You know what that sounds like to me?" Pawd asked. "Trouble."

Lank nodded. "Geminians are up in arms about the Northrim. The Northrim wants to take back what was once rightfully theirs. And wizards are in the thick of things, looking out for no one but themselves. This is a right mess!"

Phrim couldn't argue with that. "You're not wrong, but I wouldn't group all wizards together. I believe Tarth is forging his own path, and it doesn't lead back to the Spire."

"Well, that's obvious. He's in the Metal City right now," Pawd grumbled.

"Exactly, which is why I need to go there, too. Can you get me into the camp?"

Malba looked surprised at the suggestion. "Sure, but why? It was hard enough getting outa there. We don't wants to go back."

"I wondered if you spoke," Phrim said with a smirk.

"I do when I needs to," the smallest of their party said, folding her arms defiantly.

Phrim's smirk turned into a smile. He liked her spirit.

"I said I'd help, and I will," he continued. "But you must realize that no one will listen to you at the Congregational House. I'm pretty sure they'd be thrilled to get their hands on a few Norters. Uh, sorry. Northrim. And we can't go to the Spire either."

"Why not?" Chpader asked. "You just said Tartenbell isn't one of them no more."

"That's a very long story. Suffice to say, we'd be as welcome at the Spire as a rumblebug in your living room."

Chpader huffed. "I don't have a clue what that means. Why do you have to speaks funny? Can't you just speak plain-like so we can understand?"

It hadn't occurred to Phrim that he probably sounded as strange to them as their accent did to him. They may not look that different, but they came from vastly different places, and it would behoove him to remember that.

"It just means we can't go there," he explained. "That's all."

"So what do we do?" Lank asked.

Phrim leaned in, keeping his voice low. "That's the question, isn't it? The entire city is buzzing with news of cheering coming from the camp. I'd bet my last happenny Tarth's about to make his move, and I want to know what it's going to be."

"He's good at whipping people into a frenzy," Lank agreed.

Looking around, Phrim said, "I wonder if anyone else shares your views."

"You mean, wanting to calm things down?" Pawd asked. "Yeah. Loads of people don't want no trouble. That's why we left in the firstest place."

"Yeah. There's those who want to do stuff Tartenbell's way and others who want to make friends," Chpader explained. "I mean, we had no trouble with the ravine. Why not the city, too?"

Shocked, Phrim sat up straight. "Wait. You've entered Ransome Ravine?"

"Of course we have," she said offhandedly, as if visiting the ravine was as normal as rhubarb pie on Sundsday. "All you have to do is travel up the River Underground. It's a mighty fast river, though, so you've gots to be careful. Once you get in the tunnel, you don't wants to get spit back out again."

Phrim was taken aback. "It can't be that simple to get into the ravine. And what are you doing in there? Is that where you're planning to live?"

Pawd stopped Chpader from answering. "We ain't s'posed to talk about that."

"Hold on a sec'," Phrim protested. "You can't spring something like that on me and not tell me about it. Wizards have been trying to see into the ravine for generations. It's one of the biggest mysteries of the valley!"

"Some things are going to have to be left unspoken," Lank said. "I imagine you ain't tolds us everything neither, right? We all gots our secrets."

Phrim shifted uncomfortably. Yes, he had secrets. Too many, including a few he'd dearly love to forget.

A nagging feeling told him that whatever was happening in the ravine would complicate the already tenuous situation in Ardilakk Valley, but, for now, he'd let the matter lie. "I understand, but I can't figure out what Tarth is doing from out here. I need to get closer to him."

"Calm yourself," Malba said, placing her hand on Phrim's arm. "We'll figures this out."

He couldn't remember the last time another person–any person–had shown him kindness, and he reflexively pulled away. "Okay. You get us into the camp, and I'll deal with Tarth. Is it a deal?"

"How you gonna do that?" Chpader asked, obviously not liking the idea of challenging the wizard. "He's kinda scary."

"Yes, he is," Phrim answered, rubbing his arm. "He's very scary."

At that instant, the ground shuddered beneath their feet.

"What was that?" Pawd asked, brushing dust off his head.

"Powerful magic. Extremely powerful magic," Phrim said, standing up. "It's time for us to go."

• • •

Throod watched as the highland people talked to a wizard in a corner of the shelter. After Holly-Mine's reaction to hearing about her friend, Ralph, the Trust had instructed the entire Mischief to report suspicious activity…and wizards secretly meeting people in dark corners unquestionably qualified as suspicious.

The thin rat slipped out of a hole in the wall, climbed into a broken drainpipe, and scurried out of the shelter. Once she reached the street, she had a choice: duck into the nearest stormhole cover and follow the tunnels to The Meeting Place or travel above ground along the city's streets.

Feeling a might peckish, she opted for the latter as there was a better chance of finding a snack.

CHAPTER 6

WILLOW BRANCHES SWAY
HOLLY-MINE

A puff of air brushed Gerald's cheek, and he opened his eyes. Above him, rays of sunshine filtered through a noble oak's golden leaves, rustling in a light autumn breeze.

"Hello, sleepyhead," a kind voice said in his mind.

"Hello, Grandnanananny," Gerald replied. He didn't know why he called the old oak tree of Marble House that, but for whatever reason, it seemed to fit her kind manner and infinite wisdom.

"Did you have a nice rest?" the tree asked.

"I did. Would you tell me a story?"

"Later. It's time to find Ralph."

"Ralph!" Gerald sat bolt upright. What a strange dream.

The sun's early morning light streamed into the room, blinding his eyes and forcing him to peer between his fingers. To his surprise, he saw the silhouette of a tree swaying in the wind. "But Aargh doesn't have a tree in his apartment," he thought.

Slowly, his eyes adjusted. How foolish of him. It wasn't a tree. It was Holly-Mine standing in the morning sunlight, gracefully moving through a series of forms.

"What are you doing?" he asked. "It looks hard."

"Papa uses it to practice with Guildebrande. I think of it as dancing with the wind. If you were wondering, this form is called *willow branches sway in a light breeze*. It means: remember that it's important to be flexible because rigid things don't bend; they break."

Holly-Mine slowly brought her arms around as she spoke until they were stretched to either side. Then she lowered herself toward the ground. Gerald almost jumped off the floor to catch her. How did she not fall over?

Her left leg was bent so low that she almost touched the floor while her right arm and leg were held out to the other side. She brought the fingers of her left hand together like she was daintily holding the handle of a small bag.

"It's not that hard," Holly-Mine said. "I'll show you how if you want."

"I'm not sure that's for me," he said, struggling to understand the graceful moves. "Is there one called *stands straight as a pole?* That would be more in line with what I could handle."

Holly-Mine burst into laughter, lost her balance, and toppled over.

"Are you all right?" he asked.

"Of course," she said, popping back up, "but I'm starving. Let's get a—"

A deep rumble made the valley shudder.

"What was that?" Gerald asked. "An accident on the street, perhaps?"

Holly-Mine had a faraway look in her eyes. "Papa's entered the ravine."

Before Gerald realized what was happening, Holly-Mine had her rucksack over her shoulder and was out the door.

"Come on," she beckoned to him. "Let's go find Ralph!"

Gerald put the pillow he'd borrowed back on the desk chair and followed Holly-Mine out of the apartment. Before closing the door, he glanced longingly at the shower.

As they stepped onto Lower Middling Street, Gerald looked around. The crisp air had more than a hint of winter, but the sun warmed his face. Now that morning had arrived, the world looked more normal than the previous night. Vendors were lifting their canopies into place, preparing carts to sell their wares, and carefully organizing displays.

Even though he knew Tarth was outside the city, heading toward the Highland Grasslands, Gerald worried they might encounter some of his followers. Then again, if Holly-mine wasn't concerned, they probably didn't have much to worry about, but he kept a wary eye out for anything suspicious, ready to whisk her away to safety at the first sign of trouble.

"Uncle Gerald, look! Isn't this amazing?" she asked, grabbing his arm and hauling him over to a brightly colored stand.

Its fruity sign announced: *This Juice Is Worth The Squeeze!*

"One, please," Holly-Mine asked, handing over a happenny.

A rosy-cheeked lady in a colorful apron swiveled around and handed her a lemon. "Take ya peeeeek," she said in a thick lower-block accent, motioning to an assortment of fruit and vegetables stacked around the cart.

Holly-Mine tapped her chin as she contemplated the options. She settled on a beautiful red and yellow honeybeecrisp apple, placed it onto the elaborate squeezer, and pulled the lever with all her might. Gears spun and pistons mashed, ensuring every last drop of succulent juice dribbled into her cup.

After thanking the lady, she turned to Gerald and announced, "Now, I'm ready for the day!"

But that was only the first of many carts, stalls, and stands she needed to visit before they reached the Once-Great Wall.

Gerald watched her flit from vendor to vendor, greeting many by name. Most welcomed her with open arms and were happy to fill her rucksack with tasty treats.

When she finally tugged the string to close her bag, he asked, "Are you sure you're ready?"

Without answering, she skipped over to a flower stall, dropped a coin in the cup, grabbed a vibrant yellow cone-flower, and stuck it behind her ear. "Yes," she said confidently and marched off.

First, they headed north to 78th Street, which they followed to the easternmost square of the city. At that point, the traveling-in-a-straight-line portion of their trip ended. From there on, they walked one block north and one block east until they made it to the wall.

It was only about four miles, but they didn't reach their destination until late morning. There were too many exciting things to explore along the way, and it felt good not to be running from one emergency into another. Despite the looming threat of Tarth and worries about Ralph, they couldn't help but enjoy their time together.

Once they arrived at the Once Great Wall, Gerald prepared a small picnic area for an early lunch. While he did that, Holly-Mine sifted through her bag, trying to decide what to sample first. Whether it was the beautiful day, having a plan to find Ralph, or simply spending time together, it didn't matter. They were in high spirits, chatting away as they sat between the city and the trees.

"There's a promenade along the top," Holly-Mine said, pointing up.

Gerald leaned back to see past the archway above them. "Yes, I've been told it offers beautiful views. And, if I'm not mistaken, it leads directly into the Congregational House."

"That sounds wonderful. I'd like to see that."

"Me, too," Gerald agreed.

"Someday," she said wistfully. Holly-Mine breathed in the dry scent of late autumn. The forest's vibrant yellows and reds had already turned into more rustic colors, and the ground was littered with fallen leaves that crunched underfoot. Then, out of the blue, she added, "I know you saw the people in the shadows."

Gerald coughed. "I didn't want to bring it up. We were having such a nice time."

"Don't worry. They weren't wizards."

"I know. I think they were members of the City Guard, but I have no idea why they were lurking around corners and in alleyways."

"They think they're being helpful, keeping an eye on things."

"I wonder," Gerald said, looking at the two-story stone buildings on the city side of the wall.

As lovely as their respite was, thoughts of people watching from the shadows couldn't be ignored, and soon, they were walking again, following the path south through the Eastern Foothills.

Holly-Mine touched each sister-tree they passed. They all had unique personalities, and she loved every one of them. Some grew tall and straight, while others twisted this way and that. She especially enjoyed feeling the different bark types, whether smooth or feathery, rough or coarse.

Gerald, for his part, struggled to keep up, being larger than the girl and having much less experience with forests. There were no smooth marble hallways to follow or carefully organized rooms to navigate. It all seemed chaotic to Gerald, even with a path to follow.

He enjoyed looking at the forest, but traipsing through it was another matter entirely. Rocks hid under damp moss, making him stumble, and roots reached out of the ground to trip him. Then there were the brambles. His colorful pants proudly displayed a wide variety of prickly burs they'd collected as they walked.

"Do you mind if we take a break?" he asked.

Holly-Mine didn't want to, but when she saw the state of his legs, she said, "Oh, Uncle Gerald! That looks awful!"

He smiled weakly. "I believe the forest is trying to tell me something."

"Nonsense! I've told the trees about you, and they're grateful that you spent so much time with Sister Oak at Marble House. Without you, she would have been completely alone."

Gerald wished he could have saved the old tree, but the Wizard of the Council's magic was too powerful.

"Wait here. I'm going to fetch some old man's beard," Holly-Mine told him. "I'll be right back."

He watched as she skipped into the woods, absently plucking a particularly prickly burr off his pants.

"How's an old man's beard going to help? I've never liked an itchy chin, but it looks good on Aargh. Though a goatee isn't much of a beard. Now, Stump, on the other hand. That dwarf had a beard!"

Gerald went on talking to himself, trying to take his mind off his legs, but curiosity got the better of him. He gingerly lifted one of his pant legs and winced at the sight of the scratches. Then, he slid the pant leg back down, deciding he didn't need to inspect the damage after all.

Thankfully, Holly-Mine didn't take long. When she reappeared between the trees, her arms were overflowing with a yellowish, cottony mass. Gerald noticed its wispy strands trailing in the wind behind her as she pranced along the path.

"What's that?" he asked.

"I told you, old man's beard. It grows on the trees. I'm sure you've seen it before. It's everywhere in the forest."

"Fascinating. What does it do?"

"It'll keep your scratches from becoming infected."

Gerald decided that it would be a good idea to research herbal remedies. Apparently, that kind of knowledge came in handy in his post-Marble-House-life.

Holly-Mine placed the fibrous mass on his cuts and scrapes, pulled out a clean tunic from her pack, and ripped it into strips.

"Stop! What are you doing?" Gerald asked, horrified that she was tearing her clothing.

"Don't worry. I never go out without throwing in an extra one."

"But that's your shirt!"

"Oh, Uncle Gerald, you mustn't fuss. I can get another. Papa never stops buying me stuff. He shouldn't. I don't need much, but he doesn't like it when I say no."

Gerald tried not to care but decided he'd have to purchase her a new one when they returned to the city.

As she worked, Holly-Mine said, "No, you don't. There. All finished!"

He marveled at the girl. There was much more to Holly-Mine than met the eye. Of course, he'd suspected that ever since the day they'd met in the wine cellar, but after their conversation in the shelter, he knew there was more to her.

"There's more to you, too," she said, moving closer and leaning her head on his shoulder. "Much more."

Still not fully recovered from recent events, they dozed off.

"Do you mind turning off the alarm?" Gerald asked, sleepily rolling over.

"Uncle Gerald, wake up!"

"That's not a clock," he said, opening his eyes.

Perched high in the branches of a nearby tree, a cardinal was making a loud metallic chipping sound.

"No, that's not a clock. It's a warning," Holly-Mine explained, looking around. "How are your legs feeling? Can we keep going?"

"What are you talking about?" he asked with a mischievous grin. He was holding his walking stick as if waiting on her.

Holly-Mine burst out laughing. "I've never heard you make a joke before!"

He bowed low and said, "I'm glad I amuse you."

"Very much."

Stepping over to him, Holly-Mine took his hand, and they set off toward the Norters' camp together.

The quickest way would have been to head south until they reached the low pass and taken it east, but that would have left them walking out in the open. Instead, they chose to head farther into the Eastern Foothills and follow a meandering path she and her father had often traveled in search of juicy blackberries. It led directly to the foot of Widow's Peak, but even when they got there, they didn't leave the safety of the trees.

From the shadows, they counted the guards patrolling the city's tall metal walls. It quickly became apparent that there were too many sentries to escape detection. Since they couldn't breach the perimeter under the light of day, they sheltered in place for the time being.

In order to pass the time, Holly-Mine suggested they play a game called *Either/Or*. She and her father often played it while waiting for dinner to be ready, and it always made for a fun time.

Gerald wasn't sure he'd be very good at it but was willing to give it a try. "Do you like carrots or boulders?" he asked.

"Uncle Gerald!" Holly-Mine exclaimed, grabbing her stomach and laughing.

"What? That's a perfectly legitimate question. Farmers would probably say they like carrots because they can grow and sell them, but they wouldn't want to encounter a boulder in their field because it might break their hoe. And stone masons—"

Holly-Mine laughed harder and said, "Oh, stop. Please. I need to catch my breath!"

Gerald sat there waiting for her to calm down, not understanding what was so funny.

"You are hilarious!" she said, giving him a hug.

He wasn't sure if it was a compliment or not.

"Let me explain," she said. "You need to pick things that people might actually have to choose between. Understand? Like...um...cake or pie? Get it? No one goes around having to choose between carrots or boulders!"

"Yes, I see. I like cobbler. Can that be considered a pie? I especially like it with a dollop of vanilla ice cream on top."

"For you, Uncle Gerald, it counts," Holly-Mine said, giggling. "And I like cake."

"Any particular kind?"

"Well, I'm not sure I ever met a cake I didn't like...but... my favorite is one my father makes with two layers of yellow cake with brownie in the middle. Then he puts fudge icing over the top. It's yummy!"

Gerald imagined what it looked like. "Wow, that's a lot of cake!"

"Yes, that's it," Holly-Mine said, clapping her hands.

"Can I try again?" he asked. "I've got a better question this time. I promise."

"By all means."

"Do you like steam whistles or haddock?"

"You're doing that on purpose!" Holly-Mine cackled.

"Doing what?" he said with a sly smile.

Then, they burst out laughing together.

"Another one! Another one!" she insisted.

"Okay. Are you ready? This is a good one…"

Late Morning

CHAPTER 7

KNIGHTY KNIGHT
AARGHATHLAIN

"How are you doing in there?" Mnoonge asked herself.

"Perfectly well, Wizard Aarghathlain," D'Aargh's companion responded, using her rat voice. She wasn't the one who had to bob and weave their way through the oncoming rush of dwarves. If it were up to her, she'd scurry along the drainage ditch where few dwarven feet trod.

Completely forgetting about his disguise, D'Aargh beamed, loving every minute of their walk along the Dūnhyldun-thîr. A passing dwarf growled, and he remembered Stump's warning not to look like one of those tourists gawking at everything. Quicker than a longboat speeding across the River Wide, D'Aargh changed his expression from a smile to a grimace, and from then on, he kept his gawkage to a minimum.

The lowest level appeared to house the ravine's business center—a wide variety of trades that would never be allowed on Upper Middling Street. He saw armories and apothecaries, blacksmiths, bookshops, and pubs. A particularly interesting shop emitted a mysterious reddish-orange glow from a deep hole. The sign above the archway announced in the common speech:

Finegole's Hole In The Wall Foundry

Leaning against its opening was a funny-looking character leisurely blowing smoke rings into the air as he puffed on a long wooden pipe. At first, D'Aargh thought he was a child, but a second glance told him that wasn't the case.

The man wore a brown leather vest neatly buttoned over a white tunic and was very short—even shorter than the dwarves. The character caught him looking and winked. D'Aargh nodded and kept moving.

In contrast to most wizards, he felt right at home spending time amongst the working classes, though it had been a while since he and Holly-Mine had spent time in the lower squares. He missed the excitement of the port piers, vendors offering a variety of tasty treats, and popping into a shelter for a story or two. With any luck, Holly-Mine and Gerald had found Ralph, and they were doing those things right now.

The next level of the ravine city couldn't have been more different than the first, with businesses catering to everyday needs. There, the store owners had pulled out all the stops to entice would-be clients into their shops. Window boxes overflowed with the warm colors of autumn, and signs announced things like:

Buy one and get what you paid for
or buy two and get a mutton loin free!

and

Don't bother asking for water,
we only sell fermented drinks at the
Bang, Clang, and Sang!

Several eateries had outdoor seating areas where servers deftly moved through mazes of tables and chairs. Unlike the reflector-wearing miners below, these dwarves had quaffed hair tied back in long ponytails. No one likes to find a hair in their soup, not even the dwarves of Dahr Kahlahd-dîm!

Many of the storefronts had exquisite tile or stonework surrounding their entryways. One particularly ornate shop's mosaic was made from a bright reflective material that made D'Aargh have to shield his eyes when he looked at it. It didn't appear to bother the dwarves.

Above that level, there were no signs or gaudy displays—only simple potted plants outside plain metal doors.

"That must be where everyone lives," D'Aargh's pocket remarked. "I wonder what a dwarf's house is like?"

"You'll have to speak up," Stump called over his shoulder.

"Nothing. I was talking to myself again," D'Aargh's pocket said. Then, Mnoonge continued speaking in Aargh's mind. "My apologies, Wizard Aarghathlain. It can be hard to tell the difference between what I'm supposed to speak aloud and what you're thinking."

"No worries. I'm not always sure myself!" he thought, and they both laughed, though only Mnoonge made any sound.

Of everything D'Aargh saw, the jewelry shops piqued his interest the most. Back home, stores selling gemstones were restricted to the highest blocks, but even then, they were rare.

Everyone in Gemini City came out to watch when the big, black ships with rows of guns entered the port, forcing other boats to give way. Once docked, the hull would open like a drawbridge, and an armored steam carriage would emerge. He wondered how they drove the rolling fortresses with such tiny windows. And what if a pedestrian stepped onto the road? Maybe they didn't care.

Aargh had never been to a jewelry store before, as only the wealthiest inhabitants of Gemini City frequented those establishments. He wouldn't have been admitted anyway without displaying his family's seal, which, until recently, he didn't know he had.

D'Aargh felt Mnoonge moving around, and he noticed she'd nibbled a hole in the bottom of her pocket. This way, she could see the splendor of the ravine city for herself and not have to take his word for it. He sensed that the gemstones the dwarves wore were of particular interest to her.

Tapping the hilt of his sword, he thought, "I believe you fit right in, Guildebrande. It appears everyone in Dahr Kahlahddîm wears a sparkling gem or three."

"So it would seem, Wizard Aarghathlain. The shafts of light do catch the gem in my pommel quite nicely," the sword responded proudly.

"This way!" Stump said, pointing ahead. "But it's best we stop in here first. You're cleverly disguised, but without a little sparkle, no one will believe you're a dwarf."

Stump's hand came down on D'Aargh's shoulder, and he found himself dragged across the road and into:

Thrairn's Bedecked and Bejeweled
Shop of Bedazzlery

He couldn't decipher the dwarfish runes on the sign above the door, but the name was also scrawled on the wall in the common speech, presumably for the benefit of the visiting Norters. He appreciated the courtesy just the same.

D'Aargh blinked as he entered the shop. Bedecked was right! The store boasted a multiplicity of sparkling cut gems, fine jewelry, and hand-carved statuettes filling glass-covered display cases, covering long tables, and hanging from the walls. He'd never seen such an array of precious stones in his life. Not only that, but nothing was locked away behind bars. Everything was just lying about!

"Stump!" a deep, dwarvish voice called from the rear of the store. "I'll be there in a minute. You and your friend have a mosey around while I finish over here."

D'Aargh heard the shop owner chatting away with a customer in the back of the store as he stood gobsmacked by the display of finery.

"That's a wonderful piece," they said somewhere beyond the sparkles. "Let me look under your beard. Why yes! It matches your skin tone perfectly. Shall I wrap it, or will you be wearing it today? Excellent choice. Here, let me ring that up for you."

Stump whispered in D'Aargh's ear. Well, they spoke as discreetly as a dwarf can, as being quiet isn't a renowned dwarf trait. "Thrairn's proud of their inventory. Be a good wizard, and don't offend them."

"Okay," the disguised wizard said, more like a question than a statement.

Then it happened. Thrairn reappeared, grabbed D'Aargh by the shoulders, and knocked their heads together. He instantly saw stars, and Stump had to steady him from behind.

"Welcome to my humble shop! What can I do you for today, Stump and companion?" the jeweler said amiably. They wore a leather apron and a set of colored loupes clamped to a pair of glasses, much like what Grunt used, only far more delicate since they were for working on jewelry and not a giant reciprocating double piston return connecting rod marine steam engine like Ebba.

"Nice to see you, Thrairn. You'll have to excuse my friend. They're a tad under the weather. Too much coal dust, if you catch my meaning," Stump said, touching the side of their nose.

"Ah, gotcha. That's no matter. I'm sure we can find what you're looking for. Is there anything special you had in mind...hmm...an earring, perhaps?"

Seeing that D'Aargh still couldn't think straight enough to form words, let alone string a sentence together, Stump responded for him. "That's an excellent idea."

"Then, come right over here. I have a wide assortment for you to choose from. Peruse away! While you do that, I need to check on something."

After Thrairn glided away to knock heads with other customers, a gusher of unwizardly things spouted from D'Aargh's pocket, ending with, "*Pinus strobus!* What did they do that for?"

Stump chuckled so low it almost sounded like grumbling. "I may have forgotten to mention how dwarves greet each other."

D'Aargh rubbed his temples. So far, he'd managed to get down to two stars and hoped they, too, would go away soon.

"Are you positive this is necessary, Stump?" the disguised wizard's pocket asked. "I'm not used to wearing jewelry. What if someone tries to steal it?" D'Aargh instantly regretted opening Mnoonge's mouth.

"That may be how Geminians behave, Wizard Aarghathlain, but no dwarf would ever take what isn't theirs!" Stump harrumphed, turning their back on the wizard.

"I...But...Oh, Stump. I meant no offense. I'm still learning, remember?"

"How could I forget? You may look like a dwarf, Son Aarghathlain, but you're far from being one!"

"I promise I'll work on it," D'Aargh's pocket said sheepishly.

"Good! Now, which of these beauties interests you?"

Mnoonge poked her head out to take a look, saying, "I gave my money to Holly-Mine. How will I pay for it? Come to think of it, what kind of money do dwarves use?"

"Leave that to me," Stump said, clapping D'Aargh on the back. "It's the least I can do for Lord Bardelthlain's son."

D'Aargh protested but quieted down when Stump held their indexing finger in the air. To be fair, it was a rather convincing finger!

Regardless of who was planning to foot the bill, D'Aargh still had to pick something, and he had no idea where to start.

Wizards enjoy the finer things in life, true enough, and they wear beautifully embroidered robes but rarely wear jewelry. That extravagance remained the purview of the lords and ladies of Gemini City, or it used to. Now, anyone could wear what they wanted, but few could afford such luxuries.

Midway through suggesting he should pick a stone that complimented his eyes, Mnoonge cut Stump off, shrieking, "Aaaaargh!"

D'Aargh had caught sight of himself in the mirror.

A stern face covered with a thick, reddish beard stared back at him. It had a bulbous, fleshy nose and eyebrows so thick they almost hid his eyes. His eyes! He hadn't changed the color of his eyes! That was a crucial oversight, as dwarves appeared only to have brown or green eyes, not blue. Before he had the opportunity to ask Stump about it, Thrairn reappeared, and his eyes definitely hadn't escaped their notice.

"I'm assuming that strange sound you made means you found an agreeable gemstone. No? Let me help," the jeweler said. "With those eyes, you'll be wanting to go with something dark. Black opal or moonstone, possibly? Ooh, isn't this fabulous?"

As Thrairn spoke, they selected a stunning black opal earring. D'Aargh thought the stone shimmered like the moonlit ocean on a calm night, but it wasn't only silver and black. When Thrairn twirled it between their fingers, the gemstone caught the light of a carefully placed overhead lamp, revealing an infinite array of colors hidden beneath its polished surface.

"You don't have to say a word. It appeals to you. I can tell. It's written all over your face...and in those bewitching blue eyes of yours."

Was Thrairn standing very close to him? And was that their hand on his bottom?

Thankfully, Stump stepped in, putting some distance between the wizard and the jeweler, saying, "They'll take it."

"Excellent! I'll grab my gun," Thrairn said, rushing off.

"Gun?" D'Aargh's alarmed pocket asked.

"Don't worry. It doesn't hurt much. You probably won't even feel it." Stump explained, waving off the wizard's concern.

Mnoonge hid her head, muffling D'Aargh's voice. "What do you mean: it won't hurt much?"

When Thrairn returned, they immediately set to work by plopping D'Aargh into a swiveling chair, tilting his head back, and swathing his ear in alcohol. It wasn't the typical stuff, either. Whatever it was, he hoped they didn't drink it because it smelled awful.

"Hold steady. You don't want me shooting you someplace an earring shouldn't go," Thrairn said, making a gravelly sound D'Aargh took for a laugh.

He tried to stand, but Stump held him in place.

"They're squirmy, aren't they?" the jeweler asked, leaning on D'Aargh's head to prevent irreversible damage.

POP!

D'Aargh caught a whiff of sulfur when the gun went off and fainted. He came to when Stump threw a glass of water on his face.

"See, that wasn't so bad," Thrairn said, stroking D'Aargh's wiry dwarfish hair.

Coming to his senses, D'Aargh jumped out of the chair and made a break for the front door.

Stump stopped him, saying, "Don't be rude. Wait here while I pay."

In no time, D'Aargh found himself in possession of a new earring, a pierced ear, and a small vial of disinfectant...

"...to be put on once in the morning and once at night. When you do, spin the post. But clean your hands first, or it'll get infected. Now, doesn't that look nice!"

D'Aargh couldn't respond. He was too busy trying not to lose his breakfast.

As Stump ushered him out of the door, Thrairn called after them. "I close at ten. Feel free to stop by...and bring those fascinating blue eyes with you!"

The door shut behind them with a jingle.

Mnoonge curled in the bottom of the pocket, rubbing her ear. Her connection to Aargh had grown stronger with each passing day. Soon, she'd have to speak to him about it, but not right now. Her ear hurt too much, and her head spun like a top.

The earring felt strange. It pulled on the side of his head despite not weighing much. D'Aargh moved his hand toward it, but Stump made it there first.

"Didn't you hear Thrairn?" they asked. "Wash your hands before touching it."

"Oh yeah," Mnoonge said for Aargh.

The thought of the gold post sticking through D'Aargh's ear made the small rat feel queasy. After clearing her throat, she did her best to speak with her rat voice. "If you don't mind my asking, Wizard Aarghathlain, why do people think sticking something through themselves is a good idea?"

"Mnoonge," she heard herself respond. "I wish I could answer that question for you, but I don't know. It is pretty, though."

Mnoonge had to agree. It was a beautiful stone.

Distracted by his ear, D'Aargh collided with a burly dwarf with a black leather patch covering one eye. The dwarf wore a long black leather jacket with studs on the shoulders and had an unruly black beard decorated with a line of beads woven into it.

Mnoonge's muffled voice apologized, "Oh...uh...sorry. I didn't mean to—"

But she got cut off when the enraged dwarf asked, "What did you say, you progeny of a mountain troll? Come over here, and let me teach you a lesson!"

Without missing a beat, Stump came to the rescue yet again, yelling, "You're as brittle as sandstone, you gravel-headed lump of clay. Back off before I grind you into paving pebbles!"

The two dwarves stood face to face, grimacing. Stump went all out, making their eyes wide and sticking out their tongue. It worked. The burly dwarf backed down, and as quickly as the altercation had begun, it was over.

The one-eyed dwarf clapped Stump on the back and said, "You've got spirit! What did you say your lineage was?"

"I'm Thar Mordahk-dahl Tymlyn of the clan Tymlyn-m'Hahl, but you can call me Stump. My family mined the Ore of Ardilakk for generations, and now we walk the streets like common beggars!"

"And I am Tehk Dahrkyln-dahl Thorehdol of the clan Thorehdol-k'Hahl at your service. We, too, were forced from the roots of the mount when it cracked. That's a ferocious face you've got there!"

"Thank you," Stump said. "It's been in my family for generations. We're exceedingly proud of it."

"I can see why. Hmm," Tehk said, stroking the beads woven into a thin braid down the center of their beard. "The m'Hahl and k'Hahl clans are closely related. We might be cousins! This calls for a celebration. Come, celebrate with me, cousin Stump! Let me buy you a drink!"

Tehk grabbed his newly discovered cousin and knocked their heads together. D'Aargh winced sympathetically, and Mnoonge put both hands over her eyes.

"Some other time, cousin Tehk. I have to take my friend to the infirmary. They took a blow to their noggin," Stump said with a wink.

Tehk looked D'Aargh up and down. "Thought they looked a bit off. Another time, then!"

The dwarves knocked heads again and went their separate ways.

"I don't understand how you do that," D'Aargh's pocket said.

Stump shook their head. "You're kidding, right? We're dwarves. Can't think of a better way myself. And what exactly were you trying to do, anyway? Get us killed? You never apologize to a dwarf! You must be out of your mind."

"Sorry…I mean…it won't happen again," D'Aargh's pocket apologized.

"No matter. We're here!" Stump announced as if they'd arrived at their destination, which they had.

The sign above the door proclaimed:

Welcome to the
Knighty Knight Pub & Inn.
We guarantee you'll drink 'til you drop
and sleep like the dead!

In the middle of the faded arcing words was the image of a knight lying on the ground with a second knight standing over them, preparing to run them through.

"We're not going in there, are we?" Mnoonge asked for D'Aargh, her tiny hand reaching out of the hole and pointing at the door.

Images of being caught in a dwarvish bar fight filled D'Aargh and Mnoonge's shared minds.

"Of course we are! Don't you remember? Someone's waiting to meet you. Can't do that standing out here."

Stump gave D'Aargh a shove, and in they went.

CHAPTER 8

BACK BY LUNCH
THE WIZARDS' UNDERGROUND

"What's…the rush?" Garthelwaite stammered, huffing and puffing as he and Dram hurried toward Lake Hîrdehn-dūl.

Not willing to go any slower, Dram called back to him, "Aargh said he thought the island would be a great place to hide a tunnel, and I think he's right!"

"Glad I brought lanterns," Garth said, lagging behind and not at all interested in tunnels.

The Spire grounds weren't overly expansive, but with the school situated right in the middle, it wasn't possible to cross diagonally from corner to corner. That left wizards with three options: skirt the outside of the buildings, use the streets that cut through the center of the complex, or enter the school, pass through the rotunda, and travel through a second building before emerging on the other side.

Dram insisted they go the long way because there was less chance they'd run into people wondering why he'd called an All-School Meeting for no reason. Even the scandal of Bee escaping from his dorm room didn't overshadow what had been dubbed the *Where In The World Is The Head Wizard, Oh Yeah, We Don't Have One* meeting.

Their path took them along the bridleway, past Wellspring Pond, and between the barns. From there, they crossed West 78th Street, snuck through the western carriage park, and cut across the Northern Grazing field. The last leg of the trip, the

Path To The Pier, took them through Wizardwood and right to the shores of Lake Hîrdehn-dūl.

Garthelwaite was familiar with the lake, having walked that way many times with Bertie, so going there didn't concern him. Rowing out to the island in the school's rarely used skiff, however, did.

Even if he forced himself to overlook the thought of being surrounded by the lake's inky black water, he couldn't ignore the stories about the haunted island. How did he end up with this search area, anyway?

"Hopefully, we can tell from the shore," he suggested, almost catching up.

"You're joking, right? We're going to have to go to the island, Garth. I doubt there'll be a sign announcing: *Hey, you! Yes, you! There's a secret tunnel over here. Come, look!*"

"I wouldn't mind if that were the case," Garth said, looking like a child standing with a popped balloon at the end of a string dangling from their hand.

"Besides," Dram continued. "I've been there before. It's no big deal."

"Maybe for you, but I'd rather not be dragged into the earth by a dwarvish ghost. Not today!"

Garth continued to grumble about lakes and ghosts, but Dram kept going. He was on a mission. Aargh's mission.

Wasting no time, he jumped into the small rowboat he'd expertly tethered fore and aft, with a small fender in the middle to prevent it from banging against the pier. "Get a move on!" he said impatiently.

The boat was a simple affair with a pointed bow, square stern, and a flat bottom. The rower sat amidships with a place for passengers in the bow and stern. It was the perfect boat for floating on the lake if wizards enjoyed that kind of thing, which they didn't. If it weren't for Dram, it would have remained unused, wasting away until it sank.

As it was, he took care of it as if it were his own, sanding and varnishing the hull, replacing boards, and reefing out any rotted caulk (replacing it with new cotton and oakum). Part of the recaulking process involved letting the boat soak underwater until the wood swelled. That was always exciting because it represented the start of a new season.[9]

Most wizards preferred supping with the ship's captain rather than rowing around a forest-bound lake at the Spire. But considering Dram hailed from the Lowland Wastes (which still had waterways here and there), it wasn't surprising that he enjoyed spending time on it. Lake Hîrdehn-dūl—or more accurately, Lahk Hîrdehn-dūl, in the old tongue—was the closest thing to the marshes in the city, and it comforted him.

The lake stretched across the northwestern block and almost to the Congregational Footpath. When the wind blew from the right direction, Dram could float the entire way from one end to the other, watching clouds in the sky framed by the tall trees that grew along its banks. It was a nice place to hide from the busy city, which he still hadn't fully adjusted to after growing up on the sparsely populated dumping grounds. He occasionally threw in a line but never caught anything. Folks called it fishing, after all, not catching.

Not one for messing about in boats, Garthelwaite hesitated before sitting on the dock and sliding himself gingerly onto the aft thwart.[10]

---

[9] Oakum is hemp fiber soaked in pine tar.

[10] A thwart is a beam that runs laterally across an undecked boat. It provides structural rigidity for the hull and, in some vessels, a place to sit while rowing.

Dram chuckled. "You act as if you've never been on the water before. I know you visit here with your familiar."

"I don't need to take the boat out because Bertie sticks to the shoreline. At most, she swims over to a log to sun herself, but most of the time, she just paddles among the weeds. All I have to do is follow on the Lakewalk."

Dram locked the oars and pushed off. "Then, you're both in for a treat today! Maybe she'll meet a friend out here. There have to be other turtles in the lake."

"As long as it isn't the snapping turtle. That monster looks prehistoric! By the way, where's Cheep?"

"Oh, she's up there," Dram said, cocking his head to the side. "She spends most of her time in the trees. I hate the thought of locking her in a cage the way my family used to keep canaries. Of course, we had them nearby for a reason. Kind of an early warning system if you know about that kind of thing."[11]

Garth understood what he meant.

Everyone at the Spire knew where the Third Circle Wizard hailed from, but Garth was surprised Dram had mentioned it. Even though he'd lost his parents many years ago, Dram rarely spoke about them or anything related to the Lowland Wastes beyond the mythical creatures of his stories.

"I could get used to this. It's quite peaceful," Garth remarked, changing the subject.

"Really?" Dram asked, rocking the boat and bursting into laughter.

Garth grabbed the thwart so tightly that his fingers went white with the pressure.

---

[11] Lowlanders keep canaries nearby as they tunnel, sift, and sort through the Waste's vast dumping grounds. This helps protect them from exposure to dangerous gasses that build up in the rotting trash.

Dram reached over and patted his friend on the shoulder. "I don't think you're ready for a life on the water yet."

"You might be right," the older wizard agreed. "Don't do that again, okay."

"I won't. Sorry," Dram said, stifling a giggle.

He would never have pulled that kind of stunt with Aargh or Bee (not even Fizzbain). It wasn't that Dram respected Garth less than his contemporaries; their relationship was simply different–one that began when a much younger Dram had taken Garth's *Root-Reading for the Discerning Student Capable of Telling the Difference Between Tap, Lateral, Oblique, Sinker, and Fine Roots.*

They certainly weren't like-minded wizards or even had similar dispositions. Dram was a high-spirited, creative thinker who wore his emotions on his sleeve, while Garth found joy (and solace) in quiet contemplation of the taproot system of the ginkgo biloba tree. Even so, Garth was glad they'd become such close friends. Dram would make a fine addition to wizarding in the valley.

As they drifted across the pond, Garth listened to fish jump and birds sing.

When they landed, Dram grabbed a lantern and hopped onto the muddy shore. "Let's go. If we hurry, we can make it back by lunch."

Garth thought that sounded like a great idea because he didn't want to spend more time on the island than they had to. However, after carefully stepping out of the boat, he froze. The reality of what they were about to do hit him, and he stared at the ruins.

It looked giant up close! Garth knew it was only a folly, constructed as a place to escape the stresses of city life, but even though it had been weathered by the ages, it had a presence that he couldn't put into words.

Regaining his composure, Garth slowly made his way up the embankment toward the structure. "Are you sure this is safe?"

"Uh, no," Dram replied. "It's called a ruin, right? That generally implies it's falling apart, so watch your step."

"This is getting worse by the minute," Garth muttered, picking his way between the disfigured stairs.

Once inside the island's dilapidated gazebo, they searched the area, but it yielded no clues. Vines strangled its tall pillars, the roof had caved in, and its once-smooth steps stuck out at odd angles. The only interesting thing was that although most of the building had decayed, the floor was flat and sturdy.

"Solid as a rock," Garth said, stamping his foot. "Strange."

Dejected, Dram sat on the catawampus steps, burrowing his head into his hands.

Garth joined him. "Don't be disappointed," he said, patting Dram on the back. "We have plenty of other places to search."

"But I was positive we'd find it here," Dram said through his fingers.

"No surprise there. It's creepy!"

They sat there for a while, listening to the wind and the trees, before Garth made a suggestion. "I was thinking. It's pretty odd that the floor is in excellent condition, even though the rest is falling apart. Don't you think?"

"I guess."

"Maybe it's hiding something?"

Dram jumped to his feet. "That's it! You're a genius! We've been looking in the wrong place! Come on!" Not wasting another second, he ran to the other side of the ruins.

"You had to open your big mouth, didn't you?" Garth said, shaking his head.

"Garth, come here! You have to see this!"

Rushing after his young friend, Garth found Dram ripping at an old bush strategically placed to hide a set of metal doors.

"Nice work!" Garth exclaimed.

"Thanks. Help me open this. It's locked."

Using a heavy stick, they pried apart the doors. Dram flung them open, and they stared into the darkness. It definitely led below the ruins.

Dram made to go down the steps, but Garth stopped him. "It's time to tell the others."

"But we don't know if it's the tunnel yet."

That was true, but Garth didn't relish going in there without backup. He was sure there'd be spiders and other creepy-crawly things. Turning away, he looked longingly at the Observation Lounge, sitting safely atop the Spire. If he could think of some way to convince Dram to wait, they could gather the others and–

"Garth?" an echoey voice called to him.

"Oh, no! The ghost is coming for me!" he thought.

"This must be where the tunnel is hidden," the voice came again.

Realizing it wasn't a ghost, Garth called into the darkness, "Where are you? What are you doing?" but he knew the answer before the words came out of his mouth.

Dramwitch had descended the stone steps under the ruin while his back was turned.

"What are you waiting for? You need to get down here!" Dram insisted.

"I'm coming. Give me a minute to light my lamp."

Luckily, the steps were dry, and Garth had no trouble climbing down to the hidden room.

"Isn't it amazing?" Dram asked, slowly turning around in the center of the space.

Holding the lamp above his head, Garth inspected the chamber's curved wall. "This is old construction. See? No mortar. That's probably why this part didn't fall to pieces like the rest."

Dram wasn't paying attention, having disappeared into the shadows. "I think I've found what we're looking for!"

Behind the stairway, there was a tunnel that traveled in a northeasterly direction.

"Looks like it points right at the Congregational House," Garth observed. "I wonder if there used to be a direct connection between Gemini City's seat of government and the Spire."

Dram turned to head into the tunnel. "There's only one way to find out!"

"Oh no! This is where I draw the line," Garth said, grabbing Dram's arm before he could take another step. "You heard Brindlewise. One of us waits here, and the other rings the bell. And we don't go into the tunnel until they've arrived. Got it?"

"Fine," Dram said, scuffing his foot on the dusty floor.

"Don't worry. You'll get the opportunity to explore it soon enough, and I'll tell everyone that you were the one who found it."

Garth took hold of Dram's shoulders, turned him around, and marched him back up the stairs. Once outside, they closed the doors and re-covered the entrance with the bush.

Dram dragged his feet as they walked to the front of the gazebo. When they got there, he asked, "Uh, Garth? Where's the boat?"

"How should I know? I left it right there!" Garth said, pointing to where the bow had cut a groove into the island's muddy shore. "We aren't alone! The ghosts must have taken it!"

"Really, Garth? No one stole it, especially not ghosts. It's right over there. You didn't tie it up, did you?"

"Was I supposed to do that?"

"Yes. Boats float. It's what they're made to do. When you get out, you tie them up. That way, they don't float away. Oh, look! It's demonstrating that principal right now," Dram said facetiously.

Garth shrugged his shoulders. "I guess you learn something new every day. Sorry about that, Dram. What do we do now? Send smoke signals? Yell until someone hears us? It's a might cold to go swimming and that snapping turtle…" he said, nervously eyeing the lake's still black water.

Dram clapped Garth on the back. "Don't worry, my friend. We aren't going to do any of those things. Fire up that lamp of yours. We're going in!"

CHAPTER 9

A BRIEF DETOUR
ODARAPHRIM & RATS

Chpader's stomach grumbled so much that it jiggled her insides. The rolls she'd had for breakfast didn't make up for the meals she'd missed in recent days, and her mood deteriorated as the morning wore on. The enticing treats offered by the vendors they'd passed–the ones she couldn't afford–did nothing to improve the situation.

Malba tapped her on the shoulder. "Here."

"What's this?" Chpader asked, eyeing the dirty rag.

Malba opened the bundle, revealing the half-eaten roll Phrim had given to her. "Go on. Take it."

Chpader didn't have to be told twice. "Thanks."

Malba smiled as she put the rag back in her pocket.

By early afternoon, Odaraphrim and his Northrim companions had crossed into the Eastern Foothills, where they touched the city at 67th Sidestreet. This was far enough away from the low pass to avoid the near-constant activity that surrounded the northern edge of Old Eastie Sowtown. Sticking to the woods, they made their way to the grasslands.

"Hey, do you see that?" Pawd asked. "Over there by the mound where we hid our clothes."

Phrim tried to see what Pawd was pointing at. "What are you referring to? Widow's Peak?"

"That ain't no peak," Chpader said scornfully. "You should see the mountains where we come from. They's amazing to look at."

Phrim had almost forgotten that Chpader and the others were people of the sky. What wonders they must have seen, floating amongst the clouds. Movement caught his eye, and he leaned around the tree for a better look. "Pawd's onto something. People are snooping around the hill."

They'd kept off the path so as not to meet anyone, but it appeared they'd been outwitted at their own game.

"*Ceratocystis fimbriata!*" Phrim cursed. He'd always had a short fuse, but lately, it felt stubby and perpetually lit. "Do you think they're looking for you? Maybe someone saw you leave the camp."

"No way. We was fullacare," Lank whispered.

"What about sentries? Do guards patrol the perimeter?"

"Onliest from the wall," Pawd explained. "They never leave the city."

"Well, someone did today!" Phrim hissed. "There's a person as tall as you, Lank, poking around the Peak."

Lank stepped alongside Phrim, trying to get a better look. "If they find our clothes, we'll never get back in."

"Hey, where's Chpader?" Pawd asked, looking around.

Lank pointed to where he'd last seen her. "She was just here."

Phrim caught a glimpse of their companion making her way through the woods toward Widow's Peak. "What is she doing? She's going to blow the whole thing!"

"Do we go after her?" Pawd asked.

"No. That'll draw more attention to us," Phrim said, grabbing his arm. "I hope she keeps her mouth shut if they catch her."

Pawd wrenched his arm away from the wizard. "Don't be talking smack about her. We trusts her better than you!"

Phrim didn't respond. There wasn't any value in arguing unless they wanted to get captured, which, admittedly, had a certain level of appeal. At least they'd be inside.

Pawd gave the wizard a sideways glance as if to say, *I sees your wheels turning, but I don't has to like what yous is thinking.*

"Can anyone see her?" Lank asked, breaking the tension of the moment.

Phrim made to retrace their steps in the other direction. "I don't like this. It's too quiet. Let's get out of here."

There was no way the others would leave their friend behind, but before they had a chance to argue about it, Chpader stepped into the clearing. "They's is wearing our clothes!"

"Who is?" Pawd asked.

Chpader held her hands out, one high and the other low. "A girl and a tall, thin man."

"What are the chances anyone else would fit into Lank's clothing?" Phrim asked rhetorically.

"I woulda thought not good," Lank said, sitting on a fallen log.

Pawd was ready for action. "Let's jump 'em."

"Yeah, there aren't a hundred ways that could go wrong!" Phrim snapped. "There must be another way. What about the blockade?"

Chpader scoffed at the suggestion. "That's crazy. There ain't no trees on the water to hide behind."

"No, but your people take boats on the river. There might be a way for us to sneak in with them."

"I gots a cousin who fishes," Malba offered.

"That's good," Phrim said, feeling like they were getting somewhere. "What about the Bluffs? We can watch the boats go out tomorrow morning. Perhaps we'll see something useful."

"Let's stop at that farmy place on the way," Chpader suggested. "I hear they gots fig trees. I loves me some figs."

"I'm not sure where you mean. Old Eastie Sowtown?" Phrim asked.

"Whatever that place in the city with the trees and farms and stuffs near the bluff," she explained.

"Yeah, that's the one," he said.

It was the last place he wanted to go, having just steered them away from that square. Ever since its walls had come down, Old Eastie Sowtown had become one of the busiest places in the city. But the harder he argued against it, the more resolute his Northrim companions became. Ultimately, he gave in, and they headed to Gemini City's famed square with no straight roads.

• • •

Throod stopped chewing, astonished by the sight of the wizard and his strangely dressed companions walking right toward her. What were the chances? Nervous about being noticed, she took a step backward and–

SNAP!

"Eeeeek!" Throod screamed, scurrying madly this way and that, trying to escape the trap that had clamped onto her tail.

The pain got the better of her, and she flopped onto her side. Every rat had heard of this happening, and Throod was terrified of what she might have to do to escape.

A shadow passed over her, and she looked up. It was the short, quiet woman from the wizard's group.

The lady reached toward her, and Throod panicked again. But instead of grabbing her, the woman fiddled with the trap.

Throod tried to warn the lady that it was dangerous, but she didn't appear to understand.

Suddenly, her tail came free, and Throod sprinted to the nearest storm drain. Sharp pains shot through her body each time her damaged tail hit the ground, but she didn't stop. With one last push, she launched herself through the hole, turning to see if the lady was chasing her.

She wasn't. The woman remained on the other side of the street with a pleasant expression on her face. As Throod watched, she waved and then rejoined her group of friends.

Throod sat there considering this strange turn of events. As a general rule, people weren't friendly to rats, but maybe she'd jumped to conclusions at the shelter. Reporting to the Mischief would have to wait. Instead, she'd follow the wizard for a while longer to get a better picture of the situation. However, she needed to tend her tail first.

Using her tiny hands, Throod gingerly inspected the damage. The tail's jaunty angle and excruciating pain confirmed that it was broken. At least it wasn't bleeding. That was a close call.

Throod had plenty of practice working through difficult situations; therefore, she gathered her thoughts, did her best to put the pain out of her mind, and crawled out of the drain. Once back on the street, she followed her new friends, wondering if they had any more surprises for her.

Afternoon

CHAPTER 10

TWO CAN PLAY AT THAT GAME
HOLLY-MINE

Holly-Mine ducked behind Widow's Peak. "What's this?" She asked, noticing a pile of neatly folded clothing partially covered by the tall grass that grew in the area. "They're Norters' clothing."

"Who would leave their belongings lying around?" Gerald asked, admiring a finely crafted pair of leather boots.

"Let's find out," Holly-Mine said, striding over to a thin sapling growing near the forest's edge. "Hello, Sister Beech. I know you're preparing to sleep for the winter, but may I ask you a question?"

Gerald hadn't spoken to a tree since the night of the Great Fire, so he watched the conversation from afar.

When she returned, Holly-Mine had a strange expression on her face. "Norters have been sneaking into the city wearing clothes stolen from wash lines."

"How clever," Gerald said, examining the pile.

"That's what I thought at first, but now I'm not sure. What happens when people go out to bring in their undies and find they're missing? That isn't nice."

"No. It certainly isn't," he agreed.

"Why not just say 'Hi!' instead of sneaking around? Maybe people wouldn't be as scared of Norters if they introduced themselves."

If only it were that simple. Gerald knew they were beyond pleasant greetings and did his best to explain the situation without making it sound too dire. "It might be more complicated than that, Little One. I don't know why the Norters didn't introduce themselves when they first got here, but I do know this: from the first sound of an airship flying overhead, Geminians were primed to be scared, and that would have made any contact difficult. Besides, try to look on the bright side. Your discovery presents us with an opportunity."

"Are you suggesting what I think you're suggesting?" Holly-Mine asked with a wry smile because, of course, she knew exactly what he was thinking.

Gerald laughed as he slipped on one of the boots. "Why don't we see if we can make this clothing work for us."

The city changed in many ways after the Great Fire. Magic wasn't only for the wealthy elite, and once-smooth walls were now covered with intricate bas-reliefs of trees and leaves. The only thing that hadn't changed was Geminians' fashion sense–except for the gilded garments of the lords, that is. The old vestments had been retired and donated to the Upper Middling Street museums. Sapphire Hall, now called the Sapphire Lyceum, housed the most complete collection.

People who enjoyed that sort of thing paid a 'pentce or two to walk around statuesque metal and stone mannequins modeling replicas of the robes, cowl, and golden seal of the Master Prefect and other lords. And every ninth Frittersday, the Preservation Society sponsored the *Sapphire Soirée Reception at the Lyceum*. There, attendees pretended to be lords or ladies for the evening. The whole affair was immensely popular with the old families.

Modern Gemini City fashion had replaced the upper crusts' robes with tailcoats, white gloves, and a cane. However, their walking sticks rarely touched the ground as no self-respecting socialite ever allowed their handstaff to get dirty! These cane carriers were often accompanied by ladies wearing colorful fascinators and dresses with full backs and slim front silhouettes. More often than not, the dresses were covered with expensive lace imported from a Snowy Mountain enclave called Chantillytown, renowned for its fine needlework.

The working classes donned more practical clothing. Vendors clad themselves in shirts or tunics with leather vests and trousers. Day jobbers and factory workers wore allovers, and traveling folk (including wayfarers and deckhands) wore a variety of exotic outfits popular in other cities. The poorest members of society wore anything they could get their marked hands on—often too small or too large (and never warm enough in the colder weeks).

Norters, on the other hand, wore tight-fitting black shirts with leather pants and jackets outfitted with an array of gadgets. Apparently, flying in the air required special equipment unfamiliar to those tethered to the earth.

Whether or not they knew the items' purpose, Holly-Mine and Gerald had fun trying them on. Holly-Mine was especially fond of a brocade leather corset she laced over her shirt and a fancy pocket watch she found under the pile.

When she pushed a button at the top, it popped open, revealing a see-through face full of tiny gears and springs. A window displayed which of the nine days of the week it was, and four small hands told the time and date (one each for hours, minutes, and seconds and a longer arm pointing to the week of the year). Holly-Mine had never owned a watch before, and she loved it. She assumed it must be precious to its owner, too, so she planned to take good care of it and put it back when they returned.

Gerald was pleased to be able to put an entire ensemble together, replete with goggles, suspenders, and knee-high boots. "You wouldn't see anyone walking Gemini City's streets wearing this," he said, inspecting his new attire.

"Perfect! You look so smart," Holly-Mine announced, picking out a jacket for herself.

Gerald didn't feel smart. The boots and gloves were too tight, and although he was used to wearing black, the leather made strange sounds when he moved.

Once Holly-Mine was satisfied, she said, "Let's find out what's behind those walls."

"But we don't know how to get in. And I bet they have a password."

"That won't be a problem. It seems our disguised friends are visiting the city on the down-low. Sister Beech told me about a break in the wall about a quarter of a mile in that direction. We'll stick to the woods and make camp until we're ready to slip in," she explained.

"What if, in the meantime, the others come back and find we've taken their clothes?"

"Then they'll have quite a lot of explaining to do, I would think, but I doubt the guards are paid to listen. Besides, maybe having to take some of their own medicine will teach them not to steal people's clothing off their washlines and sneak around pretending to be someone they aren't."

Gerald didn't attempt to explain the complexities of the current sociopolitical situation to Holly-Mine. Why burden her with such trivialities? After years of serving as the head butler of Marble House, he was intimately familiar with how people chose to interact (or avoided interacting) with each other.

Things could have been different if the Norters had sent a delegation before arriving en masse. Even a polite message on fancy letterhead might have softened the blow. Now, he doubted any gesture of goodwill would be reciprocated, let alone civil; therefore, sneaking was probably the only option left open to them for the time being.

Instead of telling her this, he asked, "Isn't sneaking what we intend to do, too?"

Holly-Mine didn't miss the hint of a smile playing at the corner of his lips (or the explanation about the Norters he was attempting to formulate in his mind).

"Turnabout's fair play, don't you think?" she quipped.

"Touché. After you, my lady. Lead the– Get down!"

A group of guards had gathered on top of the wall and were pointing in their direction.

"Don't worry," Holly-Mine said. "They don't see us."

Gerald almost asked how she knew, but this was Holly-Mine. If she said the Norters didn't see them, they were safe.

"There's smoke coming from the foothills," she explained. "They're trying to figure out if they need to check it out, but none of them wants to leave the safety of the camp."

The guards appeared to decide it wasn't worth their time and dispersed. Once the coast was clear, she motioned for him to follow her up the side of Widow's Peak to get a better look at their surroundings.

"You really can't see much from here, can you?" Gerald remarked.

"Well, no," Holly-Mine giggled. "There's a giant wall in the way."

"You know what I mean. If the Norters' camp weren't blocking the way, we still wouldn't be able to see most of the River Wide. The hill is too low, and the cliff is too high, just like the story says."

"Hey, do you think Tharnock's under here?" Holly-Mine asked, knocking on the hill. "I could ask."

The blood drained from Gerald's face. "No, don't!"

"Are you telling me you're superstitious, Uncle Gerald?" she asked playfully.

"I'm not. Well, maybe a little, I guess, but it's not that. If he isn't there, it would make his story and constellation less somehow, and if he is there, yuck!"

"There you go, being silly again."

Gerald took that as a sign that he was making progress. Being silly didn't come naturally to him, and he wanted to cultivate it as much as possible.

Holly-Mine stuck her indexing finger into the dirt and said, "First of all, it's no big deal if he's under there. It may not be commonplace for Geminians to bury those who've come before us under the ground, but many cities do. Papa says there wouldn't be room in the valley for everyone if we did, and that's why we have ciners. Besides, don't you think using ashes to plant a new tree is beautiful?"

"I certainly do," Gerald agreed.

"And if Tharnock isn't there, it wouldn't make his story any less special to me. I'd still want to hear it."

"And I'd want to tell it to you," Gerald said, hugging her. "You never cease to amaze me, Little One."

Holly-Mine smiled. "I won't ask if he's under here if you don't want me to."

"That's a relief," Gerald said, relaxing. "I'd rather you didn't."

"Okay. I won't."

The pair slid back down the grassy hill after deciding not to move from behind the mound until after dark. Holly-Mine turned her rucksack over, dumping the rest of the treats onto the ground, and they whiled away the afternoon in pleasant conversation. Unbeknownst to them, they would be the last pleasant words they'd share for a very long time.

CHAPTER 11

THE MOTHER OF ALL DESSERTS
AARGHATHLAIN

D'Aargh opened the door, and the raucous sound of the pub hit him in the face like a fist. That and an actual fist hit him squarely in the nose–purely by accident, of course. The fist-throwing dwarf offered to buy him a drink, but Stump declined, saying they had more pressing business to attend to than errant knuckles.

Mnoonge thanked Stump for D'Aargh as he was otherwise engaged checking his nose. The fleshy knob felt strange, but as far as he could tell, it hadn't been knocked out of joint.

"Dwarven noses are quite resilient," he thought, making a mental note. He had no plans to test the theory further as wizards–even disguised dwarven ones–weren't generally cut out for fisticuffs.

The room was so full of beards and boots that D'Aargh had to squeeze himself through. All around him, tankards clanked, and rousing songs shook the dust from the rafters. Boisterous cheers assailed him as he passed a side room where dwarves played games. Most of the challenges appeared to require strength or skill at throwing things. Both D'Aargh and Mnoonge desperately hoped Stump didn't intend to go in there, as neither thought arm-wrestling a dwarf would end well. Luckily, Stump led them to the other side of the main room, where they sidled up to the bar. Then, they tapped a stocky character on the shoulder and–

Grunt!

"Hello there, Stump. And hello to you, too, Friend of Stump. Name's Grunt…and this here's my better half. Meet Level III Engineer Gwynynn. She's a looker!" he said with a hearty grunt. "You need to watch out for that one!"

Hearing his friend laugh was music to Aarghathlain's ears, and he had to restrain himself from wrapping the engineer in a bear hug and congratulating him on getting married. And Gwynynn had achieved Third Level, too! How wonderful!

"Whadaya havin', Friend?" he asked.

"Water," D'Aargh's pocket replied, and he quickly feigned a cough, realizing that he hadn't moved his mouth when the rat spoke.

Grunting, the engineer said, "'Round here, 'tis best you be having' somethin' a might stronger."

"He'll have what you're having," Stump chimed in.

"I guess he will! Another for my friend, Bahrkî!"

Stump slapped Grunt on the back, saying, "I'll leave you to it. I'm sure you have lots to talk about. Good to see you, Cousin."

"Pleasure 'twas all mine," Grunt responded, raising his bottle, as did everyone at the bar.

Mnoonge's mouth dropped open at D'Aargh's realization that he'd been right. There was a resemblance!

Grunt turned to his wife and asked if he and his new friend could have a private word.

"Of course," she said, bending over to kiss him on the forehead. Although much taller than the dwarves, Gwynynn appeared to fit right in, immediately joining in a rousing rendition of *Cut That Tree Down With The Axe I Gave Ye*.

"She's a keeper! That she is, and she can reach stuff on the top shelf, too. That ain't no small thing neither," Grunt said, hopping off the barstool. "Follow me. You can bring that talkin' pocket of yers, too. That way, we can have a proper chitchat."

D'Aargh noticed that Mnoonge had stuck her nose out of the hole to have a sniff, and he gently pushed her back in.

In a dark corner of the dining area, Grunt found a booth where they could conversate in private, as he put it.

Not one to beat around the bush, the engineer got right to the point. "I see the rat's got yer tongue, there, Aargh."

D'Aargh's cheeks blushed, not that anyone could have seen, considering most of his face was covered by a thick beard. "How did you know?"

"Did you really think you could fool ol' Grunt? Cain't pull the wool over my eyes. Oh, no, you cain't."

"Honestly, I'm surprised that no one else has noticed," D'Aargh's pocket replied, slightly embarrassed.

"I imagine folks have, but, as a general rule, dwarves don't go pokin' their noses into business that ain't theirs."

"But how did you recognize that it was me? There are lots of wizards in the valley," D'Aargh's pocket asked, more than a little deflated. He was rather proud of his disguise.

"Only one wizard *in par-tickler* would think of somethin' like that," he said, taking a long swig from their bottle. "The clincher was yer talkin' pocket there. No dwarf's ever let their pocket do their conversatin' for 'em. And only one wizard's got a thing for rats, as far as I know."

That was true.

Changing the subject, D'Aargh's pocket said, "I must say, I'm surprised to see you drinking. I thought you stayed away from alcohol."

"Whadaya my grandmamamama? First off, I'm on leave and can do whatever I please. Second, not that I'm needin' to explain myself to the likes of you, but there ain't no alcohol in this. They may call it beer, but it's only got ginger, water, and sugar with a bit of fizz. Try it. It's good with a twist o' lemon."

D'Aargh wasn't just thirsty. He needed a drink! So, he eagerly took a mouthful and instantly regretted it.

The second the fizzy concoction touched his tongue, he spit it back out again. A cheer rose from the crowd, and he pushed himself farther into the booth.

"Seems you've already figured out how to compliment the barkeep. You always were a fast learner!" Grunt said, taking another swig.

D'Aargh wiped his tongue on his sleeve, but it didn't help. "How do you drink that stuff?" Mnoonge asked, climbing out of her pocket and onto the table. "It burns!"

"That's the best part, you duffer! Don't drink so much next time. You'll get used to it."

"I doubt it," Mnoonge said, looking at the bottle.

D'Aargh lost track of time as Grunt regaled him with stories about everything that had happened since he'd re-boarded the *Prosperity*. Not much had changed: Gracie was tough as nails, Sadie kept things shipshape, and Bram was a right good captain.

"And Doros?" Mnoonge asked.

Grunt got a wistful look in his eye, and he raised his bottle—as did every dwarf in the establishment because if one raises a glass, they all do.

"To Doros," Grunt said.

"To Doros!" countless dwarves replied so loudly that more dust fell from the beams above their heads. Then, they drank, slammed their tankards on the table, and stamped their feet.

THUMP! Thump, thump!

D'Aargh stared in awe, thinking how apt the term Brethren was for dwarven society—not because they were similar to the Monks of Kartethusia who were said to exist on nothing but the drop of water from the petal of a lotus flower–but the close-knit members of a fratremity.[12]

"Poor Doros succumbed to his injuries not long after my return to the ship. That man's eyes twinkled at the very mention of his son," Grunt said, slowly rotating the bottle of ginger beer with his fingers.

"That had to be hard on Bram."

"Indeed."

"Did he have a service?"

"Of course! Bram had Doros wrapped in sailcloth, as sailors should, and we set him in the ocean off Ondlingstad. T'was a right good send-off, it was."

As D'Aargh listened, an image of Doros and Bram sparring surfaced in his mind. Many a night, he'd watched the pair through the interrupted view of the starboard brig's window. D'Aargh's hand strayed to Guildebrande's hilt. Thanks to Doros and his trusted familiar, he'd survived their perilous adventure on the high seas.

"He taught us much," Guildebrande said in D'Aargh's mind, feeling the wizard's reminiscence.

"And I'm grateful for it, too," D'Aargh replied in kind.

Seeing Mnoonge wanted to try the ginger beer, D'Aargh picked up a small bowl of nuts, dumped them onto the table, and poured the fizzy libation into the container.

"Try it at your own risk," Mnoonge said to herself.

Thinking about family, dwarves, and the *Prosperity* brought another thought to the front of D'Aargh's mind.

"Grunt? Forgive me for asking, but why is your name so different from your cousin's?"

---

12 Whereas a fraternity is generally associated with a brotherhood and sorority is associated with a sisterhood, *fratremity* is a neutral term referring to a sibling-like group where the members may not be related and of any identity.

Grunt took a swig of his drink and said, "That's a long story, there, Aargh, and a bit of a sore spot if I'm bein' honest. You see, my great-great-grandmamamama was one of yer kind—the tall valley folk. Well, you ain't so big yerself, but you take my meanin'."

"What does that have to do with your name?" Mnoonge asked for D'Aargh as she stuck her tongue out to sample the drink. It made the question come out more like *Utt oes at ahve oo oo ith or ame?* but Grunt got the gist.

"Dwarves are a proud folk in general, but more than anythin' else, they're proud of their lineage," he said. "Unless a person's only got dwarf blood, you cain't be a member of a clan."

Mnoonge cleared her throat and cried out, "That's terrible!" using the common speech—incensed by the thought of being separated from her clan. Mnoonge knew a lot about that kind of thing, being a rat.

D'Aargh became upset, too. Grunt, an outcast? Outrageous!

"Calm yerself there, Aargh. And you, too, small rat. It's all right."

"My name is Mnoonge, if you please. I am the thirteenth daughter of the seventh son of Clan Oon," she explained, bowing low.

"Wrudge had a clan?" Aargh asked in Mnoonge's mind.

"Wrudge was a proud member of Clan Aarghathlain. When he became your familiar, he renounced his familial clan and joined yours," she replied.

Aargh choked. "I swear, I never asked him to do that, Mnoonge. You have to believe me!"

"Don't worry," she said in his mind. "No one made him do it. It's how Wrudge showed his loyalty to you. His decision didn't offend the Mischief—quite the opposite. His actions honored the entire Underoof Collective. Pledging allegiance to a clan is about the most serious oath of loyalty a rat can take."

Aghast, Aargh struggled to reconcile what Mnoonge said with what he knew of his former familiar, or, to be more accurate, what he didn't know. Wrudge was definitely a loyal rat. He'd proven that, standing before the Great Fire and giving up his glow to save everyone. Yet, Aargh had much to learn about his former companion. If only he'd had more time. Unfortunately, he'd found out how precious time was the hard way...a lesson learned too late where Wrudge was concerned.

D'Aargh wiped a tear from his eye, and so did Mnoonge. She considered telling the wizard that their connection had grown so strong that their feelings were intermingling, but she held her tongue. She didn't want to interrupt his reunion with Grunt.

Although the engineer couldn't hear the exchange between the wizard and the rat, he could tell they were having a conversation. It wasn't hard to figure out what they were discussing, either.

"Seems we all have stories to tell," Grunt observed, raising his bottle. "To friends past, present, and future—the lifeblood of our lives!"

"Here, here!" the crowd cheered, banging their tankards and stamping their feet again.

"Listen, Aargh. I made peace with my past long ago. Don't mean it hurts no less, but I'm not ashamed of my heritage, no matter what folks say. Besides, I'll let you in on a secret. Just because my clan name ain't the same as theirs," he said, nodding at the dwarves seated nearby, "it don't mean I don't have one."

D'Aargh remembered the first time he met Grunt. *Name's Grover Theadorastall Palmerston, the Third, Chief (and only) Engineer of the Prosperity at yer service!* he'd said, gripping Aargh's arm so tightly the wizard thought he might pass out. The *Prosperity* and her crew were Grunt's clan. That made perfect sense.

After that, the conversation hit a lull, and they drank their ginger beer in silence for a while. Well, Grunt and Mnoonge drank. D'Aargh's new dwarf side wished for a stronger drink with less ginger (or, if ginger had to be involved, for it to be fermented). They called it beer, after all.

In an attempt to take his mind off his thirst, Mnoonge said, "I can understand word not getting out about Dahr Kahlahd-dîm from the Norters. They haven't made contact with Gemini City yet, but how has it stayed secret if the crew aboard the *Prosperity* knew about it, too? Surely, someone would have let it slip at one point or another. No one in Gemini City has any idea this is here."

The engineer slammed his hands on the table in delight. "And that's the way they like it," he said, grunting. "Fancy a stroll?"

Since Grunt clearly had no intention of answering his question, D'Aargh decided seeing more of the dwarven city was a good idea. He had plenty of time to press his friend on the details of why he and Gwynynn were in the ravine and, more importantly, how they'd gotten here.

Of course, it made sense that Grunt might be accepted, and possibly the few remaining Nahms, too, but Gwynynn? He must have missed something because she was a Porter.[13]

---

[13] A person who hails from the port city of Ondlingstad is called a Porter. This term originates from ancient times when the settlement that later became Ondlingstad was known as the First Port on the River Wide.

"Sounds good," Mnoonge said, taking one last sip.

She looked longingly at the drink as D'Aargh slipped her into his pocket. If she were bigger, she would have brought it with her.

D'Aargh had a funny feeling that he wanted to stick the bottle of ginger beer in his pocket along with Mnoonge, which seemed odd. He didn't like the stuff, so why did he want to bring it with him?

Shaking off the sensation, he followed Grunt out of the pub and onto the shadowed street. It was strange to see the bright sky above and yet be surrounded by darkness. As he studied the underground valley stretching out before him, a horn blew a long, solemn tone. The sound echoed off the walls, burrowing into D'Aargh's heart the way dwarves bored into the earth and filled him with sadness.

The inhabitants of Dahr Kahlahd-dîm stopped moving, and the chasm became eerily quiet. D'Aargh's pocket asked what was happening, but Grunt stopped him as every dwarf lifted a gemstone and sang. The low, somber tones echoed in the deep ravine trapped between its high stone walls.

Grunt translated:

The sun once shown upon our brow.
The earth above we tilled and ploughed.
But underground, our hearts did yearn,
for treasures hidden, our eyes did turn.

One fateful day, the earth did crack.
Our brethren trapped deep in the black.
Forced to walk once more above,
we sing to them, we sing to them,
forgotten not, our kith and kin.
…forgotten not, our kith and kin.

When the dwarves finished, they kissed their stones and returned to their business, more subdued than before.

"Do they do that every night?" D'Aargh's pocket asked.

"It's not night yet, but yes. When the shadow reaches the High Ledge, the Brethren remember those who were lost. They have since the cracking of the mounts."

D'Aargh pondered this as they walked along the Dūnhyl-dun-thîr (the great River Underground). How terrible! How many lives had been lost when the mountain crumbled? Their entire community had been forced from their homes—not unlike the Norters if the stories were to be believed. He wondered how any dwarf could be happy, considering what they'd lost. Then again, if he'd learned anything from recent experiences, it was that the people of the ravine were a sturdy breed, and he felt confident they'd persevere.

Grunt led D'Aargh and Mnoonge on a whirlwind tour of the once-lost city of Dahr Kahlahd-dîm. They stopped at carts and popped into shops and businesses. The engineer never stopped talking, and D'Aargh never stopped listening. He was on the job again, making discoveries and learning about a people who'd been forgotten by history, and that made him happy.

Since D'Aargh had missed lunch, he asked if they could have an early dinner. Not one to pass on a good meal, Grunt agreed, and boy, did he make a show of it. On the second level, Grunt brought the wizard to a restaurant called *The Missing Link*. The sign was a chainmail shirt with an arrow sticking through it. Underneath, words in the common speech read, *Make yourself at home so we can fill that hole!*

Inside, dwarves sat shoulder to shoulder, eating family-style as servers placed food at intervals along the tables. D'Aargh had no idea what anything was, but there was plenty of it, and it tasted delicious—well, everything except the cheeses. He didn't understand how dwarves ate food that smelled that strong, but they seemed to enjoy smearing it on grained breads or lifting hard chunks on the tips of their knives.

His hunger satiated, D'Aargh pushed back from the table, saying he couldn't possibly eat any more. Mnoonge felt the same way, which was unusual for a rat...but then the dessert appeared!

Not one but three servers emerged from the kitchen, carrying a broad silver platter with a dessert sculpted in the shape of Mount Ardilakk. The patrons chanted and stamped their feet as the servers glided toward their table. When they set it down, the restaurant exploded with cheers.

D'Aargh almost hurt himself trying to pronounce its name in Dwarfish. He'd never heard a word with so many consonants before! Grunt said it translated as *The Mother of All Deserts*, and he wasn't kidding, either.

Before they dug in, the restaurant quieted, and a dwarf lit a trough of alcohol that surrounded the confection, caramelizing its sugary icing. Then, a server sliced the mountain right down the middle, ceremoniously creating the Mounts of Ardilakk as they stood at the head of the valley. The dwarves bowed their heads briefly before getting to their feet. Apparently, tradition dictated that The Mother of All Deserts should be shared (as was pretty much everything else, too, D'Aargh noticed), representing that although dwarves may belong to different clans, they were all part of the Brethren.

One by one, dwarves scooped out large pieces with their broad spoons. D'Aargh didn't care. He loved every minute. Besides, there was plenty of the creamy, chocolatey, desserty goodness to go around!

When they finished, D'Aargh struggled to extricate himself from the chair. Barely able to move, he lumbered out of the restaurant in time to watch the Shadow Lighting Ceremony. One after another, torches flared, filling the chasm with glimmering orange light.

At first, he almost lost the dinner he'd just enjoyed when tendrils of fire wormed their way into his thoughts, reminding him of his and Holly-Mine's escape from their burning house. Fire had never been his friend, yet he relaxed as he watched the golden light reflected off the glistening river make gentle shadows dance on the stone walls. This wasn't scary. It was warm and homely, and he thought of Holly-Mine. He mentioned to Grunt that he longed to tell stories and roast apples with her in the forest high above.

"If it's stories you want, why don't we find some?" Grunt suggested.

"That's a wonderful idea," D'Aargh's pocket agreed.

That's when D'Aargh discovered he'd been wrong about yet another thing. The river wasn't the lowest level of the dwarven city. It went down farther than up. Of course, it did. D'Aargh chastised himself, feeling foolish for not considering the possibility.

The engineer grunted at D'Aargh's look of amazement as he led the disguised wizard to a flight of stone stairs deep under the Dūnhyldun-thîr.

CHAPTER 12

THE END OF THE ROAD
THE WIZARDS' UNDERGROUND

Brindlewise, Paladand, and Nerah prowled the deepest reaches of the school's basement, looking for Tarth's tunnel. They made quite a team, the oldest Spire Elder and the youngest Wizard of the Third Circle in more than a century.

Although everyone called it the basement (usually in a low voice), the underground levels weren't a basement at all. They were Ardilakk Valley's original center of wizarding, abandoned after the school moved above ground.

Lighting torches to stave off the darkness, the trio moved easily through the first-level corridors. Each hallway revealed more of the same–long-abandoned classrooms, offices, and workspaces. Most contained nothing more than rotting metal furniture, spiderwebs, and the odd rat on their way to someplace more hospitable. A few rooms were piled high with boxes, which was precisely what they'd expected to find as this area was used for storage–which basically meant, *the place where wizards put things they had no intention of using but couldn't bring themselves to part with yet.* In fact, many years before, Aargh had been pushed into one of these boxes on his first day of class.

Unsurprisingly, the stairwell leading to the next level of the underground school was barred as this was the farthest anyone had dared to go in years, as far as they knew. However, thanks to a heavy crowbar they found, Brindlewise and Paladand were able to continue their search.

As they spiraled toward the next level, Paladand marveled at the stonework. Each step fitted perfectly with the next without the need for mortar. There wasn't a single gap or buckle, which amazed him, considering how old they were. Whoever built the old school knew their stonework.

They saw no markings or identifiers on the archway they passed, so Paladand called this area Level II. Brindlewise agreed it was a sensible name.

This floor turned out to be more interesting to explore. It contained multiple rectangular labs filled with scientific equipment and had cupboards and shelves lined with vials, scales, and beakers. A few even displayed the remnants of abandoned experiments. On the tables, microscopes were placed at intervals, still peering at desiccated specimens situated below their lenses. In the back of one lab, they found an old hideout, presumably used by students in the distant past. Empty bottles littered the floor, and a rotting mattress lay collapsed in a corner of the room. Nerah didn't like the smell of that place, so they didn't linger.

The lower they went, the mustier the air became—heavy with the smell of mold and rotting things. Whereas the stone walls and floor had been dusty before, now they were damp and covered with a slimy black fungus. They did their best not to slip or touch it.

Room by room and level by level, they moved deeper into the earth but found no sign of a secret tunnel or other means of egress from the school's ground. After hours of investigating with no luck, they took a break in a lab that didn't smell too musty.

Paladand sat in silence, munching a handful of dried cranberries and nuts and poking at a few broken relics of the past.

They might have been interesting to study at a different time, but now they only served to remind him how unsuccessful their search had been.

The break didn't last long as neither wizard wanted to spend more time than they had to in the decaying underbelly of the school. Paladand wondered aloud how much deeper they would have to go but had his answer before he took another step. Right in front of them, the hallway came to an unceremonious end. The young wizard had hoped there'd be some indication that they'd reached the terminus of their search. A sign saying, *Good job! You made it to the bottom. Now, get out of here before you catch something unpleasant!* would have been nice.

"I was positive this was how Tarth did it," Paladand said, disappointed by their lack of success. "What better way to escape detection than a tunnel hidden under our noses?"

"True, Paladand, true," Brindlewise said thoughtfully, "but aside from this and the room across the hall, it looks like we've reached the end of the road. Yes, we have."

Nerah chuffed, and the wizards turned around. A smell had piqued her interest, and she stalked her prey. Her paws didn't make any sound as she crouched low and took a few careful steps. Even Paladand felt uneasy about how quiet she could be. The young wizard put his indexing finger to his lips and motioned for Brindlewise to stand aside.

Nerah stopped...listened...took a few additional steps... and sniffed the air. In this way, the trio crept forward.

Curiously, they passed the last doorway and continued to what appeared to be a dead end. As they approached the stone wall barricading the way, Nerah sniffed where it met the floor. Then she sniffed the left side, too, and they realized she'd found a secret door!

The wizards immediately set about trying to open it. Brindlewise pushed on every stone while Paladand heaved against one side. They even tried to lift it, but it was no use. It didn't budge.

Brindlewise slumped against the wall, sweat dripping from his face. "I'm afraid I'm not much help in the lifting department."

"It's not your fault. I don't think brute force will get us through," Paladand said, pointing to Nerah, who was pawing at a patch of moss.

Her sharp claws peeled the covering away, and she scratched at the stone underneath. Then, as she had with the door, she sniffed.

"Nerah, rest!" Paladand commanded, crossing his arms.

The panther lay on the floor, nonchalantly licking her paw.

"Impressive," Brindlewise complimented. "How long did it take you to teach her to do that?"

"Let's say it's a work in progress. Cats, big or small, have a mind of their own."

Brindlewise chuckled as he watched Paladand toss Nerah a treat from a pouch he carried around his waist for good measure. She deftly caught it in midair.

"Some things never change, do they?" the young wizard said to the panther. "Do you remember the day we met? I was tossing bits of this and that into the forest, and you leapt out of the underbrush. You were tiny back then."

Nerah paused, looked at the wizard, and returned to cleaning her paw.

The young wizard's smile left his face as he remembered that day. He'd been following his father on a pilgrimage into the deepest reaches of Largarin Forest when Nerah had leapt into his life.

Paladand bonded with his familiar long before learning the wizards of Ardilakk Valley talked to trees. The son of a missionary, he'd spent his earliest years traveling the River Wide with his father. That was where he learned to practice his C's, although that wasn't what he called them. Being mindful was one of the three pillars of The Church of the Crescent Sun, and Paladand took the responsibility seriously. But as close as some teachings were on the surface, his father's faith and wizarding couldn't have been farther apart. Instead of having faith in a divine purpose, wizards attempted to peer through the veil, which led to a rift between them.

His father tried to persuade him to stay, but Paladand had already made up his mind. Unable to comprehend his son's decision, the preacher became increasingly agitated–decrying the evil that was wizarding. Unfortunately, this only served to drive a wedge deeper between them. It got so bad that one day, Paladand left for the Gemini City School of Wizarding and never looked back. He often heard his father ringing a bell on Middling Street, but they hadn't spoken in years.

Although being forced to choose between his family and the Spire made him sad, he never regretted becoming a wizard. Paladand healed people, and he hoped his father could find it in himself to be proud of his son's achievements one day.

The young wizard touched the crescent sun charm he wore around a chain under his robes.

"Are you through reminiscing?" Brindlewise asked. "It's not like you to get distracted."

"I wouldn't call it distracted. More...mindful."

"Ah. How wizardly of you. If you'd be willing to be mindful over here for a minute or two, I believe Nerah has made another discovery," Brindlewise said, pointing at the floor.

The wizards studied the stone. Unskilled hands had chiseled it out and put it back in. This was what they'd been looking for.

"Well?" Brindlewise asked.

"It might be a trap."

"It's possible, but where is that youthful impetuousness? There must be a little leap-before-you-look in there somewhere. Take the initiative."

"You know perfectly well that I'm not like that, old man," Paladand shot back, smirking as he stepped on the stone.

Air blew into the corridor as rusty gears ground into motion, and the wall pivoted. Both wizards instinctively shielded their faces, but this air didn't smell rancid or musty. It smelled like...autumn leaves.

"How intriguing," Brindlewise commented, looking at the door. "Not what I expected. No. Not what I expected at all."

When Brindlewise's foot crossed the threshold, the corridor illuminated with a soft glow, making the walls and ceiling shimmer like air hovering above Gemini City's streets on hot days.

"I guess our journey continues," he said, heading deeper under the school.

CHAPTER 13

OLD EASTIE SOWTOWN
ODARAPHRIM & RATS

The southeasternmost corner of the city occupied only one square, but the inhabitants packed a lot into that space. They had to, having been walled off by the lords of old for their non-conformist ideologies—the Upper House's fancy way of saying the townies had refused to reject the use of wood in favor of metal and stone. After work on the Once-Great Wall was completed, splitting the Ancient Quadropolis in half and cutting off the North's access to the river, it was only a matter of time before Old Eastie Sowtown suffered the same fate.

However, tragedy has a way of bringing people together and that was precisely what had happened. After scaling the walls surrounding their square, townies had joined the fight to save Gemini City from the Great Fire. One by one, they'd helped pass buckets of water up the city's long streets from the river to the forest. After that, no one could ignore the disservice that had been done to both peoples by blocking off the townies, and although it took a while, the barrier was taken down.

By that time, the forest in the southeasternmost square had been magically renewed by Aargh's spell, and what Geminians discovered astounded them! Nestled in a basin between the city, the western cliffs of the Highland Grasslands, and False Hope Bluff was a forest oasis. Entirely self-sufficient, they'd learned to care for their small patch of trees in a sustainable way and farm the land that lined the eastern and southern sides of the square. It was a mystical place, worthy of the stories of old, and it immediately became a popular tourist destination. The once-hidden square of the city provided Geminians a way to reconnect with their roots before the stone cities had been built. It might be said that reunification was the one good thing that came out of the Great Fire.

To Phrim, it felt as if they'd stepped back in time, and that had nothing to do with the lack of straight roads. In point of fact, there weren't any roads at all, just footpaths and winding dirt passes barely wide enough to drive a horse and cart through. Above his head, walkways connected the trees, leading to open platforms and round treehouses with thatched roofs. Even the buildings on the ground were round, like a ball that had been cut in half.

It didn't take long for Chpader to find the figs, but when she reached for one, a gnarled older gentleman, as wrinkly as dried fruit himself, placed his walking stick between the woman and the tree.

"And who might you be?" he asked through a toothless grin. His words slurred together, and he had a slight lisp, but Phrim had no trouble understanding what he said.

Chpader hadn't noticed the man curled at the base of the tree, and she jumped back, startled when he spoke.

Phrim may have been rough around the edges (as much as a wizard can be rough), but he could turn the charm on like the best of them when he wanted to. He'd been educated at the premiere wizarding school on the River Wide, and after years of being condescended to by moldy teachers, something had to have rubbed off.

"This is Chpader, kind sir," he said, bowing low, "and I am Odaraphrim of the Spire."

"I know what you are, wizard, even if you aren't wearing the outlandish robes those folks usually wear," the wrinkly man said. "I don't believe I've seen your kind here before. Are you disguised? Hey, wait a minute. You're not here to cause trouble, are you?"

"No, sir," Lank interjected, stepping forward. "I's Lank, and this here's Pawd and Malba. We's passing through, and—"

"Don't play games with me! You know as well as I do Old Eastie Sowtown is the end of the line unless you're looking for a long drop off the high cliff. And if you can't see fit to be honest with me, I'll thank you for being on your way."

"Hold on a second," Pawd said, but Phrim stopped him.

"My apologies, sir. We've offended you. I assure you that was not our intention. On my honor as a Spire Wizard, I will do what I can to make it up to you."

"Hmm. You want figs, right?" the old man asked, scratching his stubbly chin. "This is a co-op. Are you familiar with the concept?"

"Yes. You share ownership of the land and work it together, also sharing what it provides," Phrim answered more curtly than he'd wanted to—a reaction to having been talked down to for so long and having to recite definitions and histories during class.

Politics and wizarding had always gone hand in hand in Ardilakk Valley. He knew that, having taken *The River's Economies And Societal Structures* with crotchety old Evelsorcerin. It was the driest class he'd ever had the pleasure of napping in.

The old man looked somewhat mollified. "Exactly. And have you done any work on that land today?"

"No, sir, we haven't," Phrim said, seeing where the conversation was headed. "With your permission, we'd be happy to work for a hot meal and a bag of figs."

"Hmm. Would you now?" the man said, pulling out a coin from his pocket. "Call it in the air."

Phrim watched the sun glint off its surface as it spun, and he jerked, shocked by an image of flames that popped into his mind. "Uh, heads!" he yelled, pushing the fiery image away.

"Heads it is. Seems luck's on your side today. Go talk to Elsie over there. She'll point you in the right direction, and we'll find out if those dainty wizard hands are capable of an honest day's work."

"Thank you, sir. May I ask your name?"

"Bud'll do."

"Thank you, Bud. I look forward to trying some of your delicious figs later."

"Hmm. We'll see," Bud said, going back to sleep under the tree.

Elsie turned out to have a streak running through her as tough as steel, but she had a hearty laugh that made Phrim smile despite himself. She was clad in a pair of heavy boots and worn allovers that spoke of many hours of labor under the hot sun.

Throughout the day, Phrim worked harder than he had in his entire life. It felt good to be working with his hands, that is, until he realized the Northrim were picking circles around him. He'd have to step up his game if he were to do his share.

The experience solidified what Phrim had already realized. Wizards were self-serving, entitled snobs who locked themselves away in their fancy Spire, letting the so-called commoners (who, it turned out, weren't common at all!) do their work for them. Sure, wizards grew fruit and vegetables and cared for their familiars, but most of that was for show. If a crop went bad or someone forgot to water the strawberries, they simply sent a carriage downtown to collect what they needed. These people relied on honest, hard work to survive. He decided wizards could learn a thing or two from Old Eastie Sowtown.

By the time they finished for the day, the ground was dotted with enormous bushels of radishes, turnips, beets, and carrots–and that was only from their field. Phrim hoped he'd have the opportunity to try the green beans. They were a particular favorite, especially sautéed with lemon and garlic.

When the dinner bell rang, Phrim enjoyed the best meal he'd had in ages–including a plate full of perfectly cooked green beans. The townies sang songs around a fire and played all manner of games. Quiet Malba was particularly good at something called *beanbag*–a game where two teams tossed a sack of dried beans into a hole about ten paces away. It reminded Phrim of a popular game from Krillia called *cornhole*, but you didn't get any points for landing on the board (only if your bag went in and was the last one to land on top). It wasn't as easy as it looked, and Malba had the knack.

Phrim didn't know where they found the energy after working all day. He could barely keep his eyes open, but even so, he couldn't remember a time that he'd felt so content or fulfilled. So much so that he was almost able to put the disaster at the little cottage in the woods out of his mind...almost.

Dilly crawled out of his pocket, stopped halfway up his sleeve, and hopped onto a nearby branch. Seconds later, she changed color to blend into her surroundings. This reminded Phrim of the reason he'd originally wanted to perform elemental magic. Interestingly, that didn't matter as much anymore.

The townies weren't flashy, but they changed the world with their bare hands by working together. True, their way was difficult, but that made the reward even sweeter. And, besides, pulling a carrot out of the ground was pretty magical in its own way.

Phrim felt a tap on the arm, and he turned around.

Smiling a toothless grin, Bud handed him a burlap bag with a long shoulder strap full of ripe figs.

"Thanks, Bud," Phrim said, accepting the satchel.

"Hmm. You earned it. You worked hard today for a wizard."

Phrim smiled at the old man's joke, took a fig, and handed the bag to Chpader, who looked like she might explode if she didn't get one immediately.

He and Bud talked for a while until Phrim needed to turn in.

"Early to bed, early to rise!" Bud said, winking at Phrim. "Elsie will sort you out for the night."

"If it's all the same to you, I'd like to sleep under the stars."

"Suit yourself. Nice night for it."

But Phrim didn't get to enjoy the night sky or witness the light show on the highlands that happened later that evening because he fell asleep before his head hit the soft pine needles beneath him.

• • •

Throod was confused. She'd watched the wizard work the entire day in the fields, and aside from seeing a wizard willingly get his hands dirty, there was nothing suspicious about that.

The smallest of their group, the woman who'd freed her from the trap, must have noticed her because she tossed a carrot in her direction. The thin rat cautiously sniffed it and took a bite. Delicious. When she looked up, the wizard was also looking at her and pointing at her tail. Throod almost ran, but since they didn't approach her, she returned to nibbling the carrot.

Why had she been concerned about the wizard and his motley crew of companions? The kind lady had saved her from a terrible fate, and the wizard had made many new friends. He'd even worked alongside farmers. That wasn't how bad people acted. To top it off, they were sitting together, eating dinner, laughing, and dancing. A wizard dancing? What was happening?

Throod decided it was time to return to The Meeting Place and tell her story to the Trust. They'd know what to do. It would be a slow trip because her tail was swollen and tender to the touch, but she could do it.

When she was a pup and playing with her siblings got out of hand, they'd say, *You're fine. Walk it off.* So, with the memory of many bumps and bruises, she gritted her teeth and did precisely that.

Evening

CHAPTER 14

WHEN ONE DOOR CLOSES
(Another Opens)
HOLLY-MINE

"Look," Gerald whispered, pointing at the boundary between the grasslands and the forest. "Lightening bugs."

Tiny flashes of light illuminated the rustic fall foliage as the insects danced between the trees.

"It's a strange name for such a gentle creature, don't you think?" Holly-Mine asked. "They deserve better."

Gerald raised an eyebrow. "If you say so." Technically speaking, making up names wasn't his strong suit, but he liked the concept in principle. "How about *flying bugs with glowing bottoms?*"

Holly-Mine laughed so hard that she had to clamp her hands over her mouth to avoid making too much noise.

"Shh!" Gerald said, looking around the Peak to see if the guards had heard. "We have to be careful!"

"Then stop making me laugh!"

The poor ex-butler of Marble House sat there thoroughly perplexed. It sounded like a perfectly logical name to him.

"Oh, Uncle Gerald, I'm sorry. You caught me by surprise with that one. Maybe we can come up with a prettier name. Can you imagine if people were called *animals that walk on two legs and have opposable thumbs?*"

She had a point.

"What do you suggest we call them?" he asked.

Tapping the side of her head as if that might trigger an idea, she said, "How about…twinkle-star beetles."

"That's a beautiful name. It's far better than lightning bug, which is more than a bit of a misnomer. I can't imagine anyone being shocked by one, and they certainly don't flash like lightning. More like twinkling stars, as you said."

"It's settled then. We'll call them twinkle-star beetles!" Holly-Mine exclaimed. "Now, let me take a look at those legs of yours."

Gerald's tummy felt queasy at the thought of seeing them again, so he tried not to look.

"You have nothing to worry about. They're healing nicely!" Holly-Mine announced. Satisfied with her work, she re-covered the cuts and scratches and said, "Okay. It's safe to look."

Not much bothered Gerald back at Marble House. Kitchen mishaps and Middling Street carriage accidents happened with surprising regularity, but this was different. These were his legs, and they were in a terrible state!

"I'm going to take a quick nap," he said, hoping his stomachache would go away. "Don't let me sleep long."

"I won't."

He smiled meekly and rolled over to get comfortable.

Holly-Mine couldn't rest. She was too busy wondering what they'd find when they entered the Norters' camp. Would it be busy like Lower Middling Street with vendors lining the streets? Or quiet like the forest? And what would the buildings look like? If they were anything like the ships that had flown overhead, it would be as if her bedtime stories had come to life.

She hadn't lost sight of why they were there, to find Ralph, and she certainly hadn't forgotten about Tarth, but she also couldn't deny how excited she felt at finally seeing beyond the

Metal City's walls. Being careful not to disturb Gerald, she crawled out from behind the mound to watch the sunset as she waited.

Its warm autumn glow covered the highlands like a comforting blanket. This was usually her favorite time of day because it reminded her of roasting strawberries and telling stories with her Papa. He called it golden hour—the time when the world took on a soft, yellowy-reddish hue. However, when the sun dipped to the horizon, everything grew long shadows, and Holly-Mine was reminded of their cottage burning. She instinctively pulled her legs in and wrapped her arms around them, deciding the twinkle-star beetles would be far more entertaining.

Looking back toward the forest, she watched the bugs flicker on and off as they danced in the waning light. Then, something miraculous happened. Slowly but surely, they synchronized their lights until the beetles were flashing at the same time. As quickly as it happened, it faded into randomness again, and she sighed with contentment.

Resting her chin on her crossed arms, she said, "Thank you, tiny friends. That was beautiful."

Soon, the light changed into the dusky blue of twilight, and Holly-Mine decided it was safe to look at the sky again. Although the earth was shrouded in shadow, the hidden sun continued to illuminate the sky, shining from beyond the horizon. Its rays caught the clouds floating above her in one last gasp of day. They transformed from gray into a variety of reds and oranges with purple fringed edges. No matter how difficult things got, sundown always reminded her that beauty existed in the world, however fleeting.

After the colors faded, the spectral gloaming of evening settled over the highlands. This was their cue to continue the search for Ralph, so she crawled around the mound.

"Time to see if we can find our way in," she whispered.

Gerald yawned and rubbed his eyes. "Yes. Right."

"What were you dreaming about?" she asked as if she didn't know.

"A beautiful summer's day. I was sitting with a group of children, telling them a story about the curved roads in Old Eastie Sowtown."

"That sounds wonderful. Would you tell that story to me sometime?"

"I'd be happy to."

Holly-Mine shivered in the cool evening air.

"You're chilled to the bone!" Gerald said, rubbing her arms to warm her up. "Where's that leather jacket you found?"

She pointed to the ground and stuck out her hands so he could put it on for her. The arms were far too long, but she didn't care. It felt soft and warm.

"Ready to go!" she announced, hopping up and grabbing her rucksack.

Gerald's clothes were also made of leather, and they creaked when he got to his feet. "Me, too. I think."

They moved from tree to tree, paying close attention to the top of the walls. In this way, they skirted the forest's edge, looking for the way in. Sister Beech had told Holly-Mine to look for a squiggly womp. Neither of them knew what this meant, so they searched for anything that might be considered squiggly or possibly wompy.

Gerald spotted it first: a wet marshy area. The dark mass formed a sinuous line stretching across the grasslands or, more accurately, what remained of them. It originated under the encampment's wall and smelled revolting.

Holly-Mine became incensed. "Why are they doing that? They can dump whatever they want somewhere else, but they shouldn't be messing up the grasslands! How will the sheep graze? Besides, the Lowland Marshes are already gone because of this kind of thing. What's next, the forest?"

Gerald did his best to calm her, but he felt the same way. Norters were supposed to be people of the land. In fact, it was said that the ancient people of Eastie and Westie Nort never used nails or other metals in any of their woodworking. He'd thought this meant they were against the industries of the southern districts, but that seemed at odds with present-day Norters. These people were undoubtedly masters of metalworking, and he wondered what had happened to affect such a dramatic change in their society.

"Figuring that out is a problem for the future," he told himself. "We need to focus on finding Ralph."

Holly-Mine agreed, but she still wanted to give the Norters a piece of her mind, and she would, too, if given the chance. Everything from the animals and trees of the forest, to the grasslands, to the flowing waters of the river were sacred to her. She had no intention of allowing further damage to the valley's natural beauty and resources. However, Gerald was right. Ralph came first.

Beyond the swamp, they located a gash concealed in the metal wall. It was so well-hidden that they'd have never found it without Sister Beech's help.

Once they were in position, they waited for the stars to come out. When it was dark enough, they stealthily crept to the hole, careful not to step on the sludge seeping out of the Norters' camp. Sister Beech had been right. It was definitely a squiggly womp.

With one last look at the trees she loved, Holly-Mine disappeared behind the encampment's metal walls.

Breaching the wall turned out to be easy enough–almost too easy–but once inside, they had no idea how to proceed. Gerald had expected to find streets bustling with people popping in and out of buildings shaped like grounded airships, but this wasn't the case at all. Instead, they found themselves stuck between high walls with no sign of windows or doors anywhere. Adding fuel to the fire, so to speak, the corridor was illuminated by flashes spurting out of tall chimneys high above them. The formidable structures felt imposing. Dangerous.

In contrast to the calm, lengthening shadows the sun made as it went to bed, the shadows cast by the fire bursts looked angry and foreboding, jumping from one place to another. Light cascaded down the walls, and Holly-Mine fell to the ground, cowering with her hands over her head.

"What's wrong?" Gerald asked, bending to help her. Seeing Holly-Mine this way reminded him that she was still a child, no matter how tall she'd grown or what secrets she held. "It's going to be okay," he said, lifting her to her feet.

"I'm sorry. I thought something was falling on me from the sky. Isn't that strange?"

"Not at all," he said, making sure they were safe. "This isn't a nice place, is it?"

"No. How do they live in here? It's…"

"Uninviting?" Gerald finished for her.

"Not quite as strong a word as I was going to use, but it'll do."

"Maybe we're between buildings," he suggested, "like an alleyway. There are lots of those in Gemini City. It may look different once we leave this corridor."

"I have my doubts," Holly-Mine said, kicking the dirt under her feet.

Once covered with lush grasses, the highlands were dusty and dead. Yet another thing that upset her.

"What now?" Gerald asked.

"Give me a minute," Holly-Mine said. Then, she stepped over to the wall, steeling herself against what she might find.

Gerald watched as she reached out a trembling hand, reflexively pulling it back the second her fingers made contact with the metal.

"What is it? Did it shock you?" he asked.

"No," she answered, rubbing her fingers. "It's cold. It surprised me."

To Holly-Mine, most metal felt lifeless. Not Guildebrande, of course, but that might have been because the sword was literally alive. The groaner hadn't felt that way either, as the old whistler buoy had taken on a life of its own, beckoning sailors home when the fog was so dense you couldn't see your hand in front of your face. Nor did the ore or minerals trapped inside rocks. Those were beautiful. Natural. Of the Earth Mother. But metal like this, metal that had been ripped from its birthplace and beaten into submission by people, felt dead, and she didn't like it.

Holly-Mine became aware of the smell of rust and grease permeating the air. She grimaced. It reminded her of the steam carriages that carried wealthy people through the crowds that lined Gemini City's grid-like streets. She'd seen those cabs nearly every day of her short life but never ridden in one. Holly-Mine supposed it might be fun, bumping and clattering along Middling Street with people watching as you passed. Be that as it may, she avoided the kind of person who indulged in such things. Her friends were of the street, as was she, and that's where her feet would stay.

Deep in thought, she lifted her hand again and ran her fingers along the wall's rough, textured surface. It was weathered and worn as if it had been forged generations ago. She noticed something else, too: quiet. Intrinsically connected to the world, Holly-Mine had never experienced silence before, not ever, until now.

She loved listening to the stories floating on the wind and speaking with her sisters in the forest. Every living thing Holly-Mine had ever touched talked to her, but not here. For the first time in her life, her mind wasn't filled with the sounds of the world around her–only silence–and she felt isolated and alone. The sound of nothingness unsettled her, and she struggled to keep calm.

Slowly and carefully, she traced a line on the wall with her fingers to focus her thoughts. It wasn't a solid piece of metal as she'd initially assumed. The wall was comprised of interlocking plates, not unlike an intricate jigsaw puzzle. She wondered if the parts could be separated and reconfigured into another shape. If so, the possibility of what the Norters could build would be endless. Why, then, had they created these walls? They seemed to serve no purpose.

"It's made of many pieces," she said, turning to Gerald. "One of these plates might be a door."

"Yes. I wondered about that. It seems strange to have a corridor with no openings."

"Let's go a little farther," she suggested. "Hopefully, it will open up around the corner, and we can see better."

Gerald followed, but an uncomfortable feeling nagged at him. When they reached the place where the corridor turned abruptly to the right, they peeked around the corner.

More of the same.

"I don't like this. It's almost as if…" Holly-Mine paused. "…it's leading us somewhere. We'd better go back."

Gerald agreed, but as soon as they stepped in the other direction, the air filled with metal screeching against metal, and the walls folded and stretched, splitting apart into countless sections.

There was a dreadful wailing, and BANG!, a new wall slammed onto the ground, blocking their escape.

"Run!" she yelled, heading deeper into the camp.

BANG! Bang, bang!

A new wall blocked their way.

SCREEEEECH!

Another wall pulled apart into several pieces, and a new path appeared. Holly-Mine pivoted to see how close the walls were getting, and Gerald reached out a hand to stop her.

"Don't!" he yelled, grabbing her in the nick of time.

A slab of metal sliced through the air, tearing her jacket. She slipped her arms out and watched as the coat flew into the air, caught on the corner of the plate.

They locked eyes as if to say, *that was too close!*

A wall swung open, revealing a new corridor to their left.

"Run!" Gerald yelled.

Grinding metal.

Whirring gears.

Walls slamming.

Dirt spewing.

Eyes burning.

Holly-Mine pulled her shirt over her mouth to filter out the dust. "Left!" she screamed. "No, right!"

They lost any sense of direction as they avoided being crushed or smashed by the reconfiguring walls.

Holly-Mine tripped and sprawled onto the ground. A metal plate swung overhead, and she threw her arms in front of her face. Gerald grabbed her arm and pulled. The wall hit the ground, crushing her rucksack mere inches from her shoulder.

"I'm stuck!" she yelled.

"Hold on," Gerald said, pulling a knife out of his pocket and cutting her free.

Engulfed by a cloud of dust, they huddled together, trying to catch their breath. There was an enormous whoosh of air and then silence.

"I think it's stopped," Holly-Mine sputtered, coughing into her arm.

"I believe you're right. Allow me to help you."

Holly-Mine let Gerald lift her to her feet and pat off the dirt. Her nerves were frayed, and her eyes were bloodshot from the dust clogging the air. They stood there, hunched over and wheezing, unsure what to do next. Gerald tried to ask if she was hurt, but he coughed instead.

"I'm okay," she replied, "but I'm–" She stopped mid-thought.

They were standing on the outskirts of a wide-open space. It was a courtyard of some kind, and Holly-Mine wondered if this was where Norters gathered or played games. In the center was a circular building surrounded by glass walls, and standing behind one of its wide panes was a young boy banging on the window. He wore a tight black shirt, black leather pants, and a long black leather jacket that reached the ground.

"Ralph?" Holly-Mine asked, unable to believe her eyes. "Gerald, hurry! Ralph is trapped in there!"

CHAPTER 15

AHÎKEHNN-DEHLN
AARGHATHLAIN

D'Aargh let his mind be swept away by the dark water racing past his feet. He sensed its strength and felt the coolness of the air it displaced as it flowed through the ravine. Taking one last opportunity to soak in what he could of the above-ground world, he turned and followed Grunt into the Ahîkehnn-dehln.

When he'd first arrived in the ravine, D'Aargh hadn't noticed the cleverly hidden entrances under the bridges crossing the Dûnhyldun-thîr. Even after being told they were there, he still didn't see one until he almost fell in. Thankfully, Grunt had grabbed his belt in time.

As they descended, Grunt chatted away, explaining there wasn't an equivalent word for Ahîkehnn-dehln in the common speech. "Undergroundcellarcity'll do," he said, grunting.

"It feels different down here, doesn't it?" Mnoonge asked Aargh in his mind.

He didn't need to answer. It did. They both felt it. As deep as the River Underground cut into the earth, this felt far deeper, almost primal.

D'Aargh wondered how much farther they'd have to climb the winding stone steps before they reached their destination, but he didn't have to wait long to find out. After one last turn, they stepped onto a twinkling, jewel-encrusted pathway illuminated by torches held by ornate metal holders placed at intervals along the wall. To his right, the path fell away into a vast chasm.

Numerous stairways lead into its depths, and a latticework of bridges, similar to the ones that crossed the Dūnhyldun-thîr (only much longer), connected the two sides of the underground canyon. They passed long assembly halls, shops, and meeting places. Everywhere D'Aargh and Mnoonge looked, dwarves moved about the ever-sparkling Ahîkehnn-dehln.

When Grunt stopped at a simple, unadorned room, D'Aargh peeked in. Rings of dwarves had arranged themselves around an open fire, the smoke from which floated through a hole in the ceiling. If it weren't for the sparkling walls and dwarves, it would have been similar to one of Gemini City's shelters.

The old tales had been right; stories were sacred to dwarves, and D'Aargh felt honored to be there. Not wanting to miss a single word, Mnoonge helped D'Aargh ask if they could sit in the front row, which Grunt agreed was a good idea. As they took their seats, an old dwarf who called himself Brunt prepared to speak.

Before beginning, they held a shimmering amber gem above their head, and as they turned, their eyes landed on D'Aargh. "Brethren! We have a Descendant among us today!" the dwarf announced.

Dwarfish whispers filled the cavern.

"They have the eyes!"

"A Descendant here?"

"I didn't realize any had survived the Great Fire."

"Right here in the Ahîkehnn-dehln!"

"I haven't seen the blue eyes since I was a child."

"What are they talking about?" D'Aargh's pocket asked Grunt, feeling self-conscious and shielding his face with his stout dwarven hand.

"You'll see," Grunt replied, smiling at the disguised wizard.

"*The Story!*" a dwarf shouted.

"Brunt, tell us *The Story!*"

"Yes, *The Story!*"

The old dwarf raised their hands, and everyone stopped talking. Then, they hummed.

"ohm...Ohm...OHM!" The low, discordant sound rose in a slow portamento. When they reached the same pitch, the dwarves lifted a hand above their heads as if holding a glass to make a toast.

D'Aargh was both in awe and terrified at the same time. "Grunt, what are they doing?" his pocket asked, Mnoonge's Aargh voice wavering.

"Listen. You might learn somethin'," Grunt growled.

"But they think I'm someone I'm not."

"Shush, you silly wizard. You ain't deceivin' nobody. Be quiet. They're raisin' a glass in honor of *The Story*."

D'Aargh became aware that the room had many more dwarves in it than before. The sound must have drawn more in, and there weren't enough seats. Dwarves stood along the walls, in the archways, and waited in long lines leading to the rest of the Ahîkehnn-dehln. What was going on?

Louder and louder. "OHM!"

"T'was hopin' you'd get to hear this," Grunt whispered.

Suddenly, the humming stopped, and the sound echoed into the distance.

The old dwarf spoke. "And now that we've raised a glass, I will tell...*The Story.*"

The sound of dwarves jostling for a place to sit filled the space.

"They were cast out!" Brunt shouted.

Shocked by the dwarf's outburst, D'Aargh almost fell off the bench.

"Shunned by their clan, they were. Banished by their people—our people, the Brethren—and forced to walk the long dark alone. You know of whom I speak: *The One with Blue Eyes*." Brunt said dramatically.

"They had blue eyes," the dwarf on D'Aargh's other side repeated.

Other whispers came from throughout the room. "Blue eyes. Blue eyes…"

"No dwarf had ever been born with blue eyes before," Brunt explained. "The Dark Wizard claimed their blood was tainted. Evil, he said, and the Brethren believed him."

"Why did they do that?" a dwarf standing against the wall asked.

"They shouldn't have listened!" another yelled, slamming their fist on the bench.

"The One with Blue Eyes was stripped of their name and cast out!" Brunt exclaimed.

The audience breathed in, stunned at how their ancient dwarven kith had been treated. It didn't matter how often they heard the story. It still shocked them that such a thing had ever happened.

"With no friends, no clan, and no home," Brunt continued, "they went to the only place a dwarf can go—deep into the earth from whence we originally came. But we mustn't get ahead of ourselves. Our story begins in the early days of Ancient Times.[14]

These were high times for the dwarves, mining under the great Ahrdylakkun-thūl, brought forth in the year of the

---

[14] Second Age of the Valley

Quivering Quake by the Dark Wizard of the North. But the Brethren weren't entirely deceived. They knew the Dark Wizard only helped the clans to meet his own goals—"

"What did he want?" one of the dwarves asked, followed by many others. "Yes, what did he want?" "What did he want?"

"Diamonds!" the storyteller bellowed.

The congregation gasped.

D'Aargh risked a glance behind him, and, unbelievably, more dwarves had squeezed into the room. They were practically sitting on top of each other, staring fixedly at the storyteller.

"The Dark Wizard knew diamonds were the purest and most dangerous gem in the world. Imbued with ancient power, they were capable of storing and reflecting magic upon the caster," the dwarf continued.

"Wait, that's similar to Holly-Mine's amulet," D'Aargh's pocket said.

"Sort of," Grunt grumbled, directing D'Aargh's attention back to the storyteller.

"But diamonds don't only reflect magic, do they?" Brunt asked.

"No," many dwarves answered.

"Diamonds amplify magic a thousandfold—even more when cut with many facets. It's why the art of diamond cutting began."

"I always thought it was to make them look pretty," Mnoonge commented for Aargh, though she'd never thought about it herself. The fact that they sparkled was enough for the small rat. "Wait, is that why wizards don't wear jewelry? Can they be dangerous for us?"

"Shut yer trap and listen," Grunt said. "And it's only diamonds."

"I've never seen a diamond in person. Not even at Thrairn's."

"Shhh!"

"Okay, okay. I'll listen," Mnoonge said, giving D'Aargh a funny look.

"Generations of dwarves toiled to perfect the cutting of diamonds, unaware of why the Dark Wizard was obsessed with creating the most beautiful gem in the world. First came the brilliant cut with its fifty-eight reflective facets. Then the most romantic cut of any gemstone, the hearts and arrows, but it wasn't until the golden ratio was used to create the fifty-seven facet diamond that true perfection was achieved."

Gasps filled the room. The possibility of storing that much magic terrified the dwarves!

"Deceived the Brethren were! They couldn't let the wizard get hold of such limitless power, could they?" Brunt asked.

"No!" came a chorus of answers.

"For if he did, he'd use the diamonds as a shield against other magic, and he'd be invincible!"

"We can't let that happen!" a dwarf cried out as if the tales of old were happening as they spoke.

"And we won't! Not then, not now, and not ever again!" the storyteller boomed. "This is why the creation of jewelry with diamonds has been outlawed. Let no dwarf cut a diamond except for…The Stores!"

The room exploded with cries of "Here, here!"

"What are The Stores?" D'Aargh's pocket asked.

"Never you mind," Grunt said.

"But–"

"Later!"

"Our forefolk devised a plan," Brunt continued. "While most of the clans worked for the wizard, groups of dwarves took shifts searching for diamonds in the deep. They weren't mining the diamonds for the Dark Wizard. No. They wanted to find them for their own protection. But no matter how far they mined, none were found. Though diamonds had never been plentiful, this seemed strange to the Brethren, almost as if Ahrdylakkun-thūl had decided to hide its greatest treasure."

"Where were they?" a dwarf with a high-pitched voice asked.

"They remained hidden until The One with Blue Eyes found them," Brunt explained.

"Blue eyes…blue eyes…"

"Alone and heartbroken—their spirit bound by grief—The One with Blue Eyes raised their axe to strike that solemn, final blow."

Brunt paused again, and the room became so quiet that D'Aargh felt the dwarves near him breathing.

"YAAAAAH! The One with Blue Eyes yelled!" the storyteller bellowed.

This time, D'Aargh did fall to the ground, and everyone in the room followed suit. Grunt pulled him back onto the bench, and the dwarves climbed back onto their seats, too.

"The One with Blue Eyes struck the wall instead, and the foot of the mountain cracked!"

"What did they find?" voices shouted. "Tell us what they found!"

"A diamond-encrusted cavern!" the storyteller answered.

"Oh, my!" Countless dwarves exclaimed. "They found the diamonds and saved the Brethren!"

"They did, indeed," Brunt said. "Climbing back up from the depths, The One with Blue Eyes returned to report what they'd found. At first, no one believed them, but The One with Blue Eyes produced a leather pouch filled with the stones."

The dwarf beside D'Aargh poked him in the side and, beaming a jaunty toothless grin, repeated what the storyteller had said, "They found the diamonds and saved us."

When D'Aargh didn't respond, Grunt gave him a stiff push, knocking his head into the dwarf's. Mnoonge forced herself not to yell.

"The dwarves didn't waste any time," Brunt continued, urgency filling his voice. "The Brethren devised a plan to create a prison for the Dark Wizard in case he betrayed them, which, of course, he did...You!"

Mnoonge yelped as D'Aargh cowered under the dwarf's thick indexing finger.

"Yes, you! We wouldn't be sitting here today if it weren't for your kin."

"No—" D'Aargh's pocket tried to correct.

"Quiet, Aargh. Let the dwarf speak," Grunt hissed.

"But Grunt, I can't let them believe something that isn't true."

"Aargh," Grunt said, taking D'Aargh by the shoulder, "I love you like a brother, that I do, but you can be daft at times. Why do you think yer so short? And have you ever seen anyone with those color eyes afore? The blue eyes I've ever seen are beauties—take my Gwynynn's, for example—but they're not like yers. Most are light. Yers are as rich as sapphires. There's only ever been one bloodline with that kinda blue afore. When we first met, I didn't say nothin', but I noticed 'em straight away. I imagine you was thinkin' of stuff you didn't ask me neither that day. I knew you was thinkin' about dwarves; yes, I did."

"Are you saying I'm part dwarf?" D'Aargh asked, jumping to his feet.

When he did, all of the dwarves in the room stood, raising their hands as if to toast him.

"Now yer catchin' on," Grunt said. "To The One with Blue Eyes!" he yelled.

"To the One with Blue Eyes!" everyone repeated, their voices echoing deep into the Ahîkehnn-dehln.

D'Aargh couldn't remember what happened next as it involved much knocking of heads. When he regained consciousness, he and Grunt were alone in the cavern.

"What happened?" Mnoonge asked, also trying to recover.

"Yer only part dwarf, remember?" Grunt said, grunting. "You took one too many knocks to the head and had to have a lie-down for a spell."

Grunt sat him up.

"Is it true? Am I really related to The One With Blue Eyes?" D'Aargh's pocket asked.

"That you are, my friend."

"But that can't be," Mnoonge said as D'Aargh took out the locket Dram had given him. "Neither of my parents were dwarves, and before that, no one had contact with the Brethren in an age of the world. Could it have been passed down that far?"

"Not likely. Yer too short, and those eyes are too blue."

"Then how?"

"You said yer mother was a wizard, right?" Grunt asked.

"Yes."

"Maybe that has somethin' to do with it. I mean, look at you all dwarf-like. It's not out of the realm of possibility that she made herself look human-ish."

That was way too much for Aargh to consider at the moment. It seemed impossible, but flying in airships and dwarves under the mountain had been fantasy until recently, too, so he left himself open to the possibility, no matter how remote. He'd have to work through that later when his head didn't feel like it was holding onto his body by a thread.

It took a while, but they made it to the river level in one piece. D'Aargh walked into the wall several times and almost took a header into the chasm, but Grunt helped him safely back to the ravine.

As they moved north, D'Aargh marveled at the dramatic colors of sunset visible between the dark rock walls. It was as if a giant had taken a paintbrush and drawn a jagged line across the sky. When they finally stopped, he noticed Grunt had a peculiar expression on his face.

"Why are you smiling?" D'Aargh's pocket asked.

"Turn around," Grunt said. "Whadaya think?"

The *Prosperity* was perched on an enormous rock outcropping!

"What? How did? I mean? Did you?" He was so surprised at the sight of the schooner sitting in the ravine that even the revelation that he was part dwarf almost left his mind. *"Acer saccharinum!* The *Prosperity's* an airship!"

CHAPTER 16

ONE PICKUP PENNY
THE WIZARDS' UNDERGROUND

Contrary to common sense, the farther Brindlewise and Paladand walked along the mysterious hidden passageway under the wizarding school, the fresher the air smelled. It was almost as if they'd left the basement and emerged above ground. Of course, this was impossible, but it felt that way, nevertheless.

When they reached a point where the tunnel turned sharply to the right, Nerah stopped to sniff the air. Paladand waited for her, not noticing that Brindlewise continued on without them.

When the young wizard realized this, he became alarmed. "Hey, wait up! Nerah, come," he said, pointing away from his body and back toward himself.

When he rounded the corner, he saw Brindlewise standing before a swirling mist...and the wizard's hand was trembling. Startled, Paladand motioned for Nerah to stay and cautiously approached the old wizard.

He'd never known the Spire Elder to be affected by anything. The heavens could be raining down around them, and Brindlewise might say, "I believe the sky is falling. Yes, yes, I do. It was inevitable, I guess," the same way a person might report that their bathwater was tepid. The young wizard admired Brindlewise's stoic nature. That's what *Remembering your C's* was all about, right? And he aspired to be that level-headed one day.

Stepping alongside the old wizard, Paladand looked into the mist. "It isn't possible. It simply isn't possible."

"Do you think it's a trick, young Paladand? If that's the case, it's pretty convincing. If I'm not mistaken, there's a light breeze rustling the leaves," Brindlewise stated, regaining control over his hand. "I'm wondering if that's Eastie and Westie Nort? In which case, this would be Old Middle-Forest Road."

"Middling Building Street North," the young wizard corrected.

"Ah, yes. Well remembered. That is what it used to be called."

At their backs, the dark, dank tunnels under the Spire receded into the gloom. Before them, a beautiful day blossomed under a golden autumn sun. The wide dirt road stretching out from where they stood was flanked by elegant two-story homes that stood at regular intervals as far as the eye could see. Its streets and sidestreets resembled Gemini City's grid-like layout. However, instead of streetlamps, the roads were lined with trees.

The most significant difference, however, was that the buildings were made of wood, not stone. Paladand thought their clapboards and shingles looked nice, painted with warm, earthy tones such as forest green, mahogany red, and burnt sienna. It gave them a homey look that resonated with the young wizard.

Most of the buildings had welcoming porches wrapped around their lowest levels and balconies outside their second-story windows. A few had railed spaces on their roofs where people could take in the summer sun or watch the stars creep by at night.

"I've seen buildings like these before," Brindlewise said. "In Annata'al. I once visited the hot springs there. They say the springs have healing properties. I had hoped the mineral-rich water would soothe my ailing knees."

"Did it help?" the young wizard asked.

"Not a bit. Shall we go?"

Once they passed into the mist, they turned around to see the stone doors of the Congregational House standing nobly behind them and the Once-Great Wall stretching out to the east and west.

"I do hope the school is still in there when we go back through those doors," Brindlewise commented. Paladand almost ran back to check, but the old wizard stopped him. "We can worry about that later."

"I'd prefer to worry about it now," Paladand said, his voice far more animated than usual.

"Suit yourself."

Brindlewise waited while the young wizard peeked his head through the doors. The way his shoulders relaxed told Brindlewise the school hadn't disappeared.

"Satisfied?" he asked.

Paladand let out an uncharacteristically nervous laugh. "Not by a long shot. There's a forest under the Spire."

"I wonder who put it here?" Brindlewise asked rhetorically.

"Don't ask me," Paladand said as they walked along the broad thoroughfare. "It doesn't make sense."

"Not to us, but it wouldn't be here if it didn't make sense to someone. The question is, who? Tarth? I doubt it. Tarth doesn't strike me as the kind of person who'd waste time creating a wondrous magical forest and then hide it from everyone. He's more of a show-*and*-tell kind of wizard."

Paladand agreed, adding, "But that doesn't mean he isn't here...or was."

"Exactly. That's the Paladand I know," Brindlewise said, sitting on a carved wooden bench.

The young wizard came to his senses enough to perceive Brindlewise's tiredness. The Spire Elder wore his weariness like a heavy mantle slung over his shoulders.

"Why don't I go ahead? I can scout it out and report back to you while you rest," he suggested.

"We should stick together. This place weighs on me," the sage old wizard explained.

"Yes, the air is heavy," Paladand observed. "Almost thick."

Brindlewise agreed. "That's an apt description. And the farther we go, the heavier it feels. The magic, I mean."

"Wait. Look!" Paladand exclaimed, directing Brindlewise's gaze ahead. "What's that?"

"A town square, perhaps? Give me your hand," Brindlewise asked, groaning as he stood. "Why don't we find out."

On either side of the green, there were large, official-looking buildings. The way they faced each other almost looked defiant.

"Town halls, maybe?" Brindlewise asked rhetorically, as neither building had a sign saying:

Eastie Nort Town Hall
KEEP OFF THE GRASS!

Transfixed by something hovering a few inches above the ground, Paladand said, "It's a 'pentce."

"It's my turn to correct you, my young friend. Penny is the correct term if I'm not mistaken. That's not a modern-day 'pentce. It doesn't have seven sides. It's round."

As the coin rotated, it caught the slanted autumn light and sparkled. Any other day, Paladand may have counted himself lucky to have found a happy penny, but there was nothing happy about their circumstances, and luck played no part in it.

"Not much unsettles me, but this does," Brindlewise observed.

As the younger wizard stared at the penny, the silly nursery rhyme he used to sing when playing skipskotch-hop popped into his head.

> *One pickup penny, lying in the wood.*
> *Two dark wizards, facing as they stood.*
> *Three was their number, magic cast in blood.*
> *Put the penny back, or the city's gone for good.*

Nerah crouched in a defensive pose, growling at the coin.

"Is this where the Spire's magic comes from?" Paladand asked.

Brindlewise thought about this for a moment before responding. "Possibly."

The young wizard shifted uneasily. He relied on Brindlewise to know these things. That's how he'd gotten his nickname, after all. Everyone at the Spire was familiar with the story of how the old wizard brokered a peace treaty with the Ildenbydders.

Inhabitants of the river city had stormed into the Congregational House, upset because runoff from the Lowland Wastes had contaminated their fishing grounds. The upper lords knew about the issue but had done nothing about it, which put them at a disadvantage.

With the two cities on the verge of war, Brindlewise had stepped in, successfully defusing the situation in such a way that satisfied the Ildenbydders and allowed the lords to save face (which was of paramount concern to the Congregational

House and the Spire). That's why people began calling him *Arften-brindle the Wise*, later shortening it to Brindlewise. Paladand hated nicknames, but the Spire Elder's seemed appropriate–though he still considered Arften-brindle a particularly beautiful name.

"Magic is all around us, of course," Brindlewise said, "but I'm confident there's a connection between this and the Spire. I imagine you're looking at the object drawing Aarghathlain's river of magic here from the Mounts of Ardilakk."

Paladand thought back to the night when the river had appeared in the sky. "When I first saw it, I thought it looked beautiful. And then we glowed, and it was exciting, but now, I'm not so sure. This feels wrong."

"Yes, it was beautiful, like a swirling current in the air, but air and water can also be dangerous. I imagine rivers of magic can be dangerous, too. There are forces at work here beyond anything we imagined."

Throughout his life, Paladand had always been the oldest person in the room, not in age but in other ways. Now, faced with unexplainable events and experiences, he felt young–almost childlike–frightened by the unknown. "Aargh must be told about this," he said, stepping away from the penny.

"He will. Yes, he will," Brindlewise agreed in a soothing voice, once again sitting and crossing his legs in quiet contemplation.

Paladand watched him. He'd been blinded by his desire to find the tunnel and had pushed the Spire Elder too hard.

Brindlewise chuckled. "Ah, there it is."

"What? What do you see?" Paladand asked, anxiously searching their surroundings.

"Pity," he replied, and the young wizard blushed. "Don't pity me. I'm an old man. There's nothing pitiable about that.

I may not have the energy I once did, but that doesn't mean it's time to put me out to pasture. I have a few surprises left in me, young Paladand. I can promise you that."

"I didn't mean–" Paladand started.

"Of course you did. It's only natural. Do you honestly think I can't see the looks the younger wizards give us, sitting outside conversations in the Observation Lounge? You'll be an elder one day. Then you'll understand," he said with a dry laugh.

"And when that day comes, it would be an honor if I have grown half as wise as you."

Brindlewise nodded and said, "Let's sort this out. It's our responsibility to remove the penny from here and hide it."

"What? No! We can't touch it. It's too dangerous," Paladand exclaimed, showing the older wizard his hands. "I got burned by a small amount of healer magic. I don't want to think what might happen if we were to touch that...that thing."

"I don't believe we have a choice. It's been compromised."

"By whom? We're the only wizards who know about it. We can keep it a secret. We won't tell anyone."

"You don't believe that. Everyone in Ardilakk Valley saw the river of magic. There will be many who come searching for what that means. And what about Tarth? I think we can assume this is what he was talking about when he said he had business at the Spire."

"But–"

"What if he retrieves the penny before we can get it to Aargh? What might happen then?"

Paladand remained unconvinced. "If we're lucky, the others have already discovered how Tarth made it off the grounds undetected. If that's the case, we can stop him from coming for the penny. Then we'd have nothing to worry about. Right?"

"The tone of your voice tells me you understand that no matter how hard we try, we can't protect it where it lies. We must act."

"Brindlewise, wait. The healer magic didn't just burn me. It tried to take control of my mind, and this feels far more powerful than healer's potion. If this is drawing Ardilakk's magic to it…"

Brindlewise took the young wizard's hand in his.

"Yes, Paladand, I believe you're right. Something bad *might* happen. However, if we don't take it, we can be reasonably sure something bad *will* happen. When it comes down to it, I know which risk I want to take if it means the penny is in Aargh's hands and not Tarth's or anyone else's. Perhaps, by removing it, we can break the spell that binds the Spire to Ardilakk. That would be a step in the right direction. Besides, I believe the danger lies in breaking the connection, not holding it. For example, Holly-Mine's amulet contains powerful magic, but it's safe to touch."

"This might be different."

"True, but don't underestimate Aargh's magic." Brindlewise let go of Paladand's hand as he continued speaking in his typically even tone. "I thought the stories about the fall of the northern cities were legend, but does this look like legend to you? Did this penny play a part in that? What if they disappeared instead of burning? I don't know, but I do know this: one of our tasks was to find out what Tarth wanted from the Spire. I believe we've found it. Let the others worry about the tunnel if there is one. Our job is to prevent Tarth from taking and using this magic. If I'm wrong, it's just a penny, and you can buy one of those warm buns at Bwain's. Get the honey butter with it. That's my favorite," Brindlewise chuckled, but the smile on his face didn't reach his eyes. "But if I'm right, this penny's power has caused great harm. And I'm not only speaking about Tarth trying to hurt Aargh and Holly-Mine. Power can make wizards behave strangely. I once had a friend who was obsessed with discovering magic, as he called it. I wonder if he did…"

The old wizard paused again, and Paladand nervously waited for him to continue.

"What if the same fate that befell the northern cities is waiting to take Gemini City, too?" Brindlewise asked. "I'm not going to let that happen. If I were to make an educated guess—and I'm good at those, as you know—I'd say we're at what Aargh might call *Step One: One pickup penny, lying in the wood.*"

In a rare display of deep personal feelings, Paladand said, "If that's true, and the rhyme is a prophecy, I'd rather not progress to step two. I've always thought there's a right way and a wrong way…good or bad…and this feels bad to me."

"You have a keen mind, Paladand. There can be no doubt about that, but you are young, and the world appears black and white to you. No, no. I'm not criticizing. Please, let me finish. As impossible as this may sound, one day, the division between right and wrong will no longer be a sharp black line but a wide and fuzzy gray one. You will see good people behave badly and bad people do good things. Do you understand?"

Paladand tried to follow what Brindlewise was saying, but his thoughts were consumed by the need to go for help. "But if we get Aarghathlain—"

"Take it from an old wizard. When you've gazed into the future, as long as I have, you sense things. I can't explain it, but we can't take the time to go back. If we do, we risk losing the penny. We're here now. We're here first. It's our responsibility to seize the opportunity before anyone else does."

"Then, let me do it with you," Paladand insisted. "I have experience working with enchantments. That's what our healer's potions are. If we take the penny together, we might have a better chance of controlling it."

"Control it? I doubt there's any way for us to control it, my young friend, and I have no intention of trying. Our job isn't to use the penny but rather to get it away from here to prevent Tarth from taking it. And no, we can't do it together. If the situation goes sideways, at least one of us has to be able to warn the others."

"I'm telling you, this is dangerous!" Paladand yelled, unable to contain his emotions any longer.

"You're right," the revered Spire Elder said flatly.

The way Brindlewise said the words made Paladand take another step back as if he'd been punched in the stomach.

As he did so, Brindlewise continued to press the issue. "Do you know what the third rule of wizarding means: *Be prepared to be remarkable?*"

After catching his breath, Paladand dutifully responded. "Yes. Trustworthy Wrudge taught us that lesson."

"Are you referring to the fact that he gave his life for Aargh and all of us?"

Paladand nodded slowly, realizing a *but* was coming.

"The look on your face tells me that you doubt that conclusion. Good. Dying doesn't make you great. We all die. It's as much a part of living as eating or breathing. There's no trick to dying, and it's no gift to anyone. Don't you think Aargh would be happier if Wrudge were with him? Of course, he would. It's not how Wrudge died that made him remarkable. It's how he lived. He lived his life so fully and devotedly that he and Aargh were one. That's why he was able to give away his glow." Brindlewise placed his hand over his heart and said, "You have the strength to do this. And when the time comes, you will bring order to wizarding in Ardilakk Valley."

"But Aarghathlain?"

Brindlewise sighed. "Aargh won't be returning to the Spire, and he knows this."

Paladand pondered the old wizard's words. Aarghathlain was great, in the truest sense of the word, and although the young wizard was confident in his own abilities, he wasn't ready to step into the ex-head wizard's shoes, at least not yet.

"Don't worry," Brindlewise said, knowing what the young wizard was thinking. "You'll have time to prepare for what lies ahead. Until then, Bee will guide you."

Paladand looked befuddled.

"I'm aware that you think he isn't serious enough, but Bartlebee is more than he appears. He's the best apprentice I ever taught. Try to look beyond the jokes. There's a thoughtful wizard in there who only ever thinks of others. I can't imagine a better role model."

The younger wizard protested, but Brindlewise knew what he was going to say before the words reached his lips.

"Gotharis did right by you, Paladand, but he won't be able to guide you through what is to come. Bee will protect you and everyone at the Spire, whatever the cost. It's Bartlebee whom you must look to for guidance. Listen to me. I've lived my life to the best of my ability. Have I made mistakes? Yes, but I've strived to atone for my wrongs. Honestly, the world hasn't been the same since I lost my Bruue. You never met her. She was before your time. Such a wise old owl. We made a great team."

As the old wizard spoke, Paladand petted Nerah, and she moved closer, purring gently and nuzzling his leg.

"Young Paladand, my time has come. I can hear Ardilakk calling, and is that Bruue? Yes. She calls to me. However, I must complete one last worldly task."

Before the young wizard could stop him, *Brindlewise, The Wizard Who Lived Remarkably,* stood and, with a wink, picked the penny up.

CHAPTER 17

PRIVATE SPIRE GARDEN
THE WIZARDS' UNDERGROUND

When the search assignments were handed out, Bartlebee attempted to swap places with Tassior and Onaveris. Tassior politely declined. O, being far less tactful, uttered a few choice tree names and flashed Bee his wizarding finger before storming off. Why? Because no one wanted to go near the southwest corner of the school's grounds.

Stuck where Dram had put him, Bee stood with his hands firmly planted on his hips, staring at a sign he'd promised never to disobey.

Private Spire Garden
KEEP OUT

And below that, for good measure, Groundsman Grimms had scrawled:

Or else!

Even from beyond the grave, Grimms frightened Bee, but of all the fantastic stories he'd been told, one, in particular, plagued him the most: *The Dwarven Ghost of Hyldun-dūln*. It didn't matter how many greenhouses he and Lan searched or how many plants his friend pointed out; nothing had the power to distract him from the danger waiting in that most haunted of places.

Wellspring Pond's constant gurgling set him on edge as he pondered the terrible things that might happen if they stepped beyond the garden's simple wrought iron gate. There were plenty of stories about the pond, too, but he was far too scared to think about them right now.

The sun's waning rays struck the sign, making it stand out against the darkening landscape, and Bee shivered. Unable to put it off any longer, he and Lan mounted the overpass that separated the garden from the main grounds. The otherworldly way the metal bridge amplified their footsteps, reflected by the water below, shattered what little composure Bee had left.

Boom.

Boom!

DOOM!

Postulant Bee hid under the covers as older boys told scary stories about ancient times in Ardilakk Valley. He felt his hot breath trapped under the sheet as Aargh shivered next to him.

"Centuries ago, before the great cities of Ardilakk Valley were built," a boy said, holding a candle below his chin. "there was a burial ground where the Private Spire Garden now sits—a place of ancient dwarven power."

Bee moved closer to Aargh, leaning against his friend as they listened.

"The wizards of the day longed to be near its magic. It enticed them, hinting at the possibility of great discoveries and wondrous deeds beyond speaking to trees. But the dwarves wouldn't allow it! They told the wizards that Hyl-dun-dūln was a sacred place that mustn't be disturbed, and

no matter what the wizards offered, the dwarves wouldn't budge, being more akin to rock than people.

"*Over the generations, more and more people flooded into Ardilakk Valley, and it wasn't long before the dwarves were forced to retreat under Mount Ardilakk. The wizards celebrated their victory by converting the dwarven temple on the site into the valley's first wizarding school and taking Hyldun-dūln for their own. If only they'd understood the dwarfish runes chiseled into the stones surrounding the burial ground, maybe the tragedy that unfolded could have been prevented. Instead, they foolishly ignored the warnings.*"

Aargh grabbed Bee's hand.

The boy passed the candle to someone else, who continued the story. "One night, a group of wizards decided it would be fun to tell ghost stories around a campfire, but not just any campfire. One in the exact center of the thirteen rune-covered monoliths. It was a pleasant evening, by all accounts. They toasted bread and apples while trying to scare each other into running away. Though several wizards twitched once or twice, in the end, everyone held their ground."

The candle was passed again. "When the moon rose high in the sky and one day prepared to turn into the next, the wizards decided to call it a night. As they gathered their belongings, one of their group pointed toward the darkness, warning that a figure had crept up behind them. Everyone laughed, thinking he was fooling around, but he wasn't. When the unluckiest of their party twisted to look, a dark shape blocked out the stars above him! Two shadowy arms grabbed the wizard and, with lightning speed, pulled him from the circle. The others rushed to help, but they couldn't find their friend. One of the searching wizards caught his foot on something jutting from the ground, causing them to stumble and fall. It was a hand!"

The candle was passed back to the first boy. "Everyone watched as it disappeared under the dirt, dragged into the earth by the Ghost of Hyldun-dūln! The next day, the entire school searched the ring of stones but found no sign of the wizard. The entire area was cleared, and a thick hedge was planted to keep people out. From that time on, no one has set foot—"

"Hey, Bee?" Alantus asked, jolting Bee back to the present. "Are you all right?"

"Uh, yeah."

"Do you remember that story? What was it? Um…*The Dwarven Ghost of Hyldun-dūln.*"

"Lan, you aren't saying you believe in ghost stories, are you?" Bee asked, feigning confidence.

"No, no, of course not," Lan said, but neither wizard moved.

There weren't any strange plants crawling along the ground at their feet or menacing fences or barbed wire. The space beyond the sign didn't even appear to be magical. It just looked like your average hedge and garden.

After adjusting the brown robes Dram had given him to hide the bright yellow of his usual attire, Bee suggested they check the perimeter first. That sounded like an excellent idea to Lan, so they moseyed along the path that led around the outside of the garden. No need to rush. Maybe they'd get lucky.

If he craned his neck, Bee could see plants peeking their heads above the carefully pruned hedge. Most of the flowers had closed for the night, but he could still detect the sweet aroma of their nectar wafting through the air. It made him reminisce about happier times, like when he and Aargh had snuck out of the school to visit the Portside Flower Extravaganza.

The smell of flowers had been so thick in the air that it felt like they had to push through it. Once the boys entered the main tent, they'd spent much of the afternoon hiding in an enormous honeysuckle display. They'd laughed and laughed as they plucked flowers from the bushes surrounding them. One at a time, they'd pull out the long style and taste the sweet nectar collected on its end, but their overindulgence came with a price. By dinnertime, the novices were doubled over with aching stomachs.

They knew they'd never make it uptown to 78Block hunched over the way they were. Luckily, a hay cart heading for the Spire stables passed, and they hitched a ride without the driver knowing. Flushed as they felt, they'd still managed to laugh the entire way uptown. Sadly, Bee rarely heard anyone laughing at the Spire anymore. Too much had happened, and wizarding wasn't as simple as it used to be.

The path was clear back then, when he'd first come to the school: study to achieve the three tiers of wizarding, graduate to Spire Wizard, and spend your days being wined and dined by the city's wealthy elite—all while following roots to the future. These days, wizards toiled day and night, designing spells to do all sorts of things, and Aargh had access to magic of incomprehensible power. Elemental power. Even so, Bee tried to hold onto the carefree youthfulness he'd always carried with him, but even he had to admit it was slipping away.

"It's called nyctinasty," Alantus offered, derailing Bartlebee's thoughts again.

Lan was standing on his tiptoes, also attempting to peer over the hedge, but he wasn't as tall as Bee, so he didn't see much.

"The flowers in there are called nyctinasty? Never heard of them," Bartlebee whispered as if waking them was a bad idea.

"No, no. Not the flowers. The behavior. I caught sight of a poppy through the gate and figured that's why you were scrunching your face. Isn't it fascinating? They close at night. People don't usually expect plants to do that, though many do."

Bee didn't bother explaining the real reason for his face-scrunching. The night was waning, and they needed to figure out how Tarth had evaded their watch. "Do you think there's anything poisonous in there?" he asked.

"I imagine so. Many plants are poisonous," Lan explained. "Then again, most of the time, you have to ingest the plant itself or get its oils on you to do any real damage. Of course, there's *Hippomane mancinella.* If rain drips onto you after falling on its leaves, it'll burn your skin. And most people know about *Toxicodendron radicans.* Its poison gets on everything. You can even inhale it if it's burned—"

"All right! All right! I get it. No offense, Buddy, but I don't need a botany lesson right now," Bee said sharply.

Lan's back hunched as if the Deputy Assistant Spire Grounds Keeper was attempting to climb back into his shell.

Bee regretted snapping. Deep down, he knew Lan was trying to be helpful.

"Sorry," he apologized. "I didn't mean anything by it. I'm pretty on edge. Once this is over, I promise that you can tell me all of the ways plants can kill me."

Alantus smiled meekly. "Thanks. That'd be nice. Not many people are interested in more than what's ripe."

Bee worried about his friend. Picked last for games and often left in the forest when groups went on field trips to practice speaking with trees, Lan never seemed to register in people's consciousness. There was that time when he was paired with Danee'all for the Wizards' Feast Pageant. It didn't go well. Bee tried to explain that Danee'all was the kind of wizard who never valued other people's contributions, no matter how hard they worked, but it hadn't made a difference. Lan still wound up spending a week under a planting table with his favorite dwarf lemon tree.

Of course, Lan didn't help things by frequently wandering off or getting distracted by an interesting vine or fungal growth, but that wasn't his fault. That was Lan, and Bee wanted to try harder to care about the things his friend found intriguing. After all, that's what friends were for.

"Truthfully," Lan added, "I've always assumed the plants in there were poisonous. Why else would it be forbidden for anyone to enter?"

He had a point.

"Wait a minute! How is it you've never been in there? Don't you take care of the Spire's gardens?" Bee asked.

"I do. Well, most of them. The Private Spire Garden is off-limits to everyone, even me."

"Not everyone," Bee said with a note of trepidation. "Someone must enter it. It's carefully tended. The hedge is perfect. Not a leaf out of place."

"That's what worries me," Lan mumbled.

Bee's scrunched face returned. "That's not a comforting thought. Not comforting at all." Lan and Bee had been friends since school days, but after seeing what Lan had done in the forest, Bee looked at him differently. It seemed his friend had an impressive hidden strength that he'd never acknowledged before.

As they stood there, Bee realized he was stroking Ermy's fur. She felt warm and soft, curled in his pocket. He enjoyed having a furry familiar, and a stoat fit the bill nicely. He couldn't imagine a lizard providing the same level of comfort.

Apparently, Lan relied on his familiar in a similar way because he had Pip in his arms, and he was petting the squirrel in long strokes that started between her ears and went all the way to her tail. Each time he lifted his hand to start over, her tail did a flip.

Screwing up his courage, Bee said, "Well, Buddy, we've been through a lot. I doubt the worst of it will be snooping around a garden filled with poppies."

Lan agreed, but that didn't remove the worry lines etched into his forehead. After putting Pip back into his pocket, Alantus sucked in the fragrant night air and reached for the gate.

It wasn't locked. Not only that, but it swung open without a sound. There was no warning or trap. It was only a gate. It didn't even creak, as every creepy gate should.

After stepping past the hedge, Bartlebee and Alantus were treated to the sight of a cozy cottage garden. Colorful delphiniums overflowed their beds while peonies and poppies slept. Along the borders, lavender cheerfully poked up from the ground, and flowers tumbled in that haphazard but beautiful way cottage gardens often did.

"It's amazing," Lan said, shuffling down the narrow path.

"Wait, no. It might be dangerous!" Bee said, but it was too late.

Lan dove headlong into a bed of flowers.

Bee ran after him. "C'mon, Buddy, I don't think this is a good idea."

"But isn't this heirloom iris beautiful?" Lan asked, surrounded by flowers. "I haven't seen one in ages. Besides, I don't see anything that dangerous in here. It's just a garden."

"Are you sure about that? I mean, most plants have changed colors or dropped their leaves. They don't call it the Fall of Autumn for nothing."

Lan didn't hear Bee because he was too busy inhaling the sweet fragrance emanating from the flowers.

"Lan!" he yelled.

"What? Oh...a...yes?"

"What's with you? We have work to do."

"I...I don't know. They're so pretty."

Bee took him by the hand. "I can see that, but are they supposed to be blooming?"

Lan surveyed the garden. "You're right. These plants bloom in the fall, but those over there don't. Do you think it's magic?"

"What do I think? That we should keep moving. This place gives me the creepy crawlies," Bee said, rubbing his arms. "Can't you feel it? I think we're being watched."

Lan shifted uneasily.

"Come on," Bee encouraged, putting an arm around his friend's shoulders.

"Sorry. I don't know what came over me."

"No problem. I wish we were here to enjoy the flowers, too."

After a while, Lan stopped short. The Private Spire Garden only occupied a corner of one of the ground's blocks, yet it felt like they'd walked a fair distance. "Is it me, or does this place seem big? Almost bigger on the inside than it looks from the outside."

Bee didn't answer. He was too focused on putting images of getting lost in a maze of magical paths out of his mind.

From where they stood, they could see a broad stone bird-bath in the center of the garden bubbling away as it over-flowed into a pond below, where waterlilies floated gently on the rippling water. One of the lanes ended in a small cul-de-sac where a stone bench sat nestled under a bountiful honeysuckle bush. Near the rear of the garden, there was a folly fashioned in the likeness of the Congregational House.

"That's strange," Bee said, pointing at the folly.

"Not really. It's common for people to model follies after famous buildings. It's probably where the garden tools are stored," Alantus explained.

"That's not what I mean. It looks like the new Congregational House, with leaves carved into it. Not the old building that had flat sides. I haven't heard of any work being done in here, have you?"

Lan fidgeted. "No."

The earth moved beneath their feet, and a loud boom broke the silence of the night.

"*Ostrya virginiana!* What was that?" Bee asked, turning toward the Spire.

Before Lan had a chance to answer, screams erupted from the school.

"Let's go!" Bee yelled, and they ran out of the Private Spire Garden to see what had happened.

Once they passed the hedge, a gnarled hand reached out of the shadows to close the gate behind them.

• • •

Terrified shrieks echoed through the stone hallways of the four Gemini City School of Wizarding buildings as people pushed and shoved their way outside. Everyone was convinced the Spire was collapsing on top of them. Once outside, the worst of their fears were confirmed as they watched the Spire lean farther and farther toward the Mounts of Ardilakk, pulled by some unseen force. Though invisible, they knew what it was: the river of magic.

Bee and Lan put their hands over their ears to block out the sound of wrenching metal as they dashed between greenhouses and raised planters. Everywhere they looked, students and wizards, were running for their lives.

"Quick!" Bee yelled. "We have to find the others."

"There's O and Tassior over there," Lan said, huffing and puffing as he tried to keep up.

"Yes, I see them, and there's Illbrahss and Afynn, too. Were Garth and Dram in there?"

"No. They were on the northern side of the grounds with Fizzbain and Pud. Brindlewise and Paladand were the ones searching the basement."

"Oh no," Bee gasped as they ran. "Oh no. Oh no. Oh no."

"We'll find them, I promise," Lan said, falling behind. He knew Bartlebee had a special bond with the old wizard, even beyond Brindlewise being his mentor.

"Over there!" Bee yelled. "There's Nerah. Hurry!"

The panther emerged from a darkened door, stopped, and looked back. Dirty and disheveled, Paladand appeared beside her.

"Pal! Hey Pal! Wait there. We're coming!"

Paladand stood there with a blank expression on his face.

Lan took one arm, and Bee grabbed the other. Then, the three of them moved as quickly as possible away from the school.

"You're safe now. I have you," Lan said in the same nurturing way he spoke to the plants in the greenhouses. "Come over here and have a seat."

Paladand's eyes looked glassy and vacant.

"Pal, are you okay? Where's Brindlewise?" Bee asked frantically.

The young wizard's head sagged, and his shoulders fell. Slowly, he pulled his hand out from deep within his robes.

"Is it your hand? Is your hand hurt? Talk to me, Pal! Tell me how I can help."

Paladand took hold of Bee's robes and brought the wizard so close that they were almost face to face. Then, he dropped something into Bee's upturned hand. It had no weight to speak of, but it felt warm. Electric.

Paladand closed Bee's fingers around it and held the older wizard's clenched fist. "Brindlewise named you protector of everything I hold dear. Therefore, I give this to you, Bartlebee of the Spire. This is the penny lying in the wood. Your mentor believed it was worth living for. We must get it to Aarghathlain before it's too late."

CHAPTER 18

A RIVER OF RATS
RATS

Throod gasped for air as she struggled to stay on top of the river of rats flowing through the Underoof. The undulating mass of animals crashed like waves against her, and the current threatened to drag her in the opposite direction from where she needed to go. She tried to move out of the stream, but a rat stepped on her broken tail, and she squealed, stopping her in her tracks.

"Get it together, Throod," she told herself. "You have a job to do."

Girding herself against the pain, she dove into the rat-wash, popping up every few feet and gasping for air. In this way, she swam the rest of the way to The Meeting Place.

If the chaos overtaking the Mischief was any indication, a lot had happened since she'd assumed her post in City Shelter 0Block3. She listened intently to the crisscrossing rats but couldn't make heads or tails of what they were saying. Rat conversations typically involve many speakers, each weaving their part of the story into the finished tapestry, and hearing small snippets as the groups slipped by wasn't enough to provide the whole picture.

She gleaned that there had been an accident at the school, but Wizard Aarghathlain wasn't there. He was in the ravine with dwarves, of all things!

"What next? Dragons?" Throod thought, much the same way Dram had when he'd first met Stump at the ruins of Marble House.

As bizarre as discovering unexplored dwarven tunnels under the city was–a revelation that caused quite a stir in the Underoof, being that rats prided themselves on knowing every last thing about the places where they lived–the next story she heard sounded downright impossible. If her ears weren't playing tricks on her, the Mischief was talking about stone people coming to life at the Spire!

After getting over the initial shock of hearing such an outlandish story, Throod began to worry. If that had happened, magic had–in her estimation–become far scarier because as undeniably awful as the Wizard of the Council was, that was more normal, for lack of a better way to describe it. People always fought with each other, burning each other's homes and waging war for one reason or another. Usually, the reasons behind what people did were utterly ridiculous as far as Throod and the Mischief were concerned. Didn't people understand that working together was the only way to survive? On the other hand, living stone was subtle magic. That kind of magic might appear anywhere, and you wouldn't realize what had happened until it was too late.

She looked over her shoulder in case magic had snuck behind her. Nope. At least not that she could tell. Then again, how would she know? And if that wasn't enough, she was in for another shock.

Rats are sensitive creatures, affected by the slightest change in their environment, and now, they were glowing. This, in and of itself, wasn't new, but until recently, it had been up to the rats when they did it. As she pushed through the crowded tunnel, Throod heard whispers of rats being whisked away to lesser-used places in case the phenomenon was contagious.

That didn't sound like the Underoof Collective she knew, and she quickened her pace.

Shockwaves of panic coursed through the tunnels around her. Gemini City's rats didn't know what to do. Many wanted to find Wizard Aarghathlain, while others wanted to run and hide or leave Ardilakk Valley altogether by hitching a ride on one of the many vessels docked in the Port Pier District. The most controversial suggestion involved electing a leader–a single rat to unify the Mischief and keep it from fracturing into factions the way people did. If that happened, it might mean the end of the Underoof Collective, or worse, because electing a leader was a radical idea for rats. Communal in every conceivable way, it wasn't in their nature to give that kind of power to one rat, and no one wanted the responsibility, either. Many passing voices steadfastly refused to step into such a role.

"Oh, no. Not me! Go ask your cousin."

"Are you kidding? I'd never!"

"Hold your tongue! I won't hear of such a thing!"

As Throod rounded the last corner, she passed out of the chaos and into one of the tunnels that led to The Meeting Place. It was eerily quiet compared to the mass of fur flowing behind her. Ahead, a solitary rat saluted her as she approached.

"Hello, friend Parsifal," Throod said through gritted teeth. The journey had taken a toll on the thin rat, and she needed to rest.

"Are you hurt?" he asked.

"It's nothing."

"That is not nothing!" Parsifal said, catching sight of her swollen tail. "Come here. I will assist you."

Parsifal gently lifted her tail off the ground so it wouldn't drag or bang on any pebbles.

"Sssss," Throod breathed in.

"Sorry."

"No, it's not you. I got caught in a trap."

"How did you get out?" he asked.

"A person released me."

"Really? That doesn't happen every day. It's kind of the point not to let you out if you get caught in one. You were very fortunate."

"I don't feel lucky, but I guess I was. Has the meeting of the Trust concluded?" she asked, noting how quiet the space was. "I've seen something unusual in a lower-block shelter."

Parsifal stopped when they reached the end of the tunnel. "There's no meeting today."

"But there's always a meeting," Throod insisted.

"It would be best if you came inside," he said, motioning for her to go first.

"This is very strange. I'm not comfortable with this," she said, hesitating.

"I'm sorry, Throod. It isn't for me to explain. All will become clear if you would be so kind as to join us in The Meeting Place."

"Who is *us?*"

When Throod peeked around the erudite rat, Buck noticed her and said, "Come in! I assume you bring news from the lower blocks."

The Dead of Night

CHAPTER 19

IT'S ALL FUN AND GAMES UNTIL...
HOLLY-MINE

Ralph's muffled voice called from behind the building's glass walls. "He said you'd come. He did! And you're here!"

"Who said we'd come?" Holly-Mine asked, but she was cut off by the cringe-worthy sound of metal on metal.

As the large plate glass window in front of her slid open, the firelight bursting from the Metal City's chimneys caught the glass, and she flinched. Gerald noticed and put a hand on her back.

Unwilling to wait for the wall to open fully, Ralph threw off his jacket, squeezed through the growing opening, and sprinted toward her. She stiffened when he wrapped his arms around her in a bear hug. Everything was wrong. They'd almost been killed. Ralph was wearing Norters' clothing and talking about them being expected.

The boy let go and reached for her hands.

"Ralph! Where are your marks?" she asked. The shameful brand street urchins carried with them, a tattoo of Gemini City's line and two stars, was gone!

The boy beamed, displaying his clean palms. "I took them off."

"But how? Why?" Holly-Mine asked, unable to conceal her shock.

Ralph curled his hands into fists. "I hated them."

"Hated them?" Holly-Mine repeated, moving away.

"I can take yours off, too," he said, back to being excited. "It'll be as if they were never there."

"What? No!" she said, hiding her hands under her arms. "I hate the marks, too, but erasing them won't make the pain go away. Of course, I want to forget, but I also want to remember, too. Don't you understand?"

"No," Ralph said, studying his unmarked hands. He didn't want to remember.

Gerald spoke in Holly-Mine's mind. "Your friend is a little erratic. Is this the way he always was?"

"No. Something is wrong," she answered in kind. "I don't know what's come over him."

Ralph looked up as if he'd remembered something important, and his facial expression changed again. He seized Holly-Mine's arm and pulled her toward the round building.

"Where are you taking me?" she asked, struggling to free herself.

"Come on! It's this way!" Ralph said, not letting go.

"Gerald!"

"Don't worry, Little One. I'm right here," he said, striding alongside her. "And I'm not going anywhere."

In front of them, the building loomed out of the darkness. Its resemblance to the Spire's Observation Lounge was unmistakable; only this room had been built directly on the ground.

Unsurprisingly, it was made of metal (metal beams, metal plates, and metal stays), but it wasn't elegant and polished like the Observation Lounge. The metal of this structure mimicked the weathered corridor walls and was constructed from a collection of pieces that fit together like an intricate puzzle. One might say the Spire's construction was focused predominantly on form, while this monstrosity concerned itself with function.

Holly-Mine pulled against Ralph's persistent grasp. She didn't like being forced to do things against her will—even by her friends—and she didn't want to go inside. "Please, Ralph," she begged, but the boy kept pulling.

Seconds later, they were in the room. The space felt as dead as the metal walls had, but she knew that wasn't the case. It could re-form and reshape itself at will like a wild beast changing to suit its needs. And the way the walls had slammed around them gave her the distinct impression that whoever was controlling it was very much alive...and malicious.

"Uh, Holly-Mine? Hellooooo?" Ralph asked, poking her arm when she didn't respond.

"Sorry, Ralph. I need a minute to catch my breath. I'm still shaken. We almost got hurt out there."

"No, you didn't. That was a game."

"A game?" Holly-Mine asked, shocked by the suggestion.

"That was no game, young man," Gerald said. "Games are fun, not dangerous. I'd think you'd be more concerned about your friend. She was terrified."

Ralph's demeanor changed again, and he started babbling. "I didn't mean...honestly...there's no way...I would never..."

The surprise in his voice revealed that Ralph had no idea what they'd been through, but Holly-Mine couldn't bring herself to comfort him. He was acting so strangely. One minute he was angry, the next happy, then embarrassed? It was as if his emotions were out of control, and, in her current state, Holly-Mine couldn't keep up.

"Does that mean you don't want to see the surprise?" Ralph asked, becoming agitated.

"I'm trying, Ralph, really, I am, but I'm not ready for more surprises. Can we go back outside for a minute? I need some air."

"Outside? Why? The surprise is in here. Let me show you. I promise you'll love it."

Ralph began to shake visibly, and Holly-Mine moved closer to Gerald.

"I'm afraid, Uncle Gerald," she said in his mind. "Ralph doesn't understand what I'm saying."

"Yes, I believe you're right. He's distraught."

When they turned, they saw Ralph had slipped back into his jacket and had pulled a pair of goggles over his eyes.

Scared that something terrible was about to happen, Holly-Mine asked, "Ralph, what are you doing?"

The boy beamed as he took hold of a lever sticking out of the floor.

"Wait! Stop!" she screamed.

When he pulled the lever, there was a loud CLANK! and the floor lurched under their feet. The frightful sound of metal scraping started again, and the room rose into the air. As it tilted and spun, Holly-Mine and Gerald were thrown to the ground, unable to withstand the forces pulling on their bodies. Around and around, it whirled, making their stomachs lurch and their heads dizzy. They attempted to hold onto each other, but it was no use, and Holly-Mine rolled away. In the center of it all, Ralph clung to the lever, cackling like a carnival barker at the Middling Street Fair.

When the wrenching and swirling finally ended, he pulled off his goggles and yelled, "Isn't it wonderful?"

Holly-Mine managed to stand, steadying herself against one of the many metal beams that held the room together. When her fingers touched it, she pulled her hand back, sickened by its deadness.

To her dismay, they were high above the Norters' camp. She could see the Mounts of Ardilakk looming against the starry sky to the north and far below to the south, lights flickered from the blockade floating on the River Wide.

Instinctively, she twisted to look at the wizarding school. "Oh no! What's happened to the Spire?"

Gerald put a hand to his face in shock.

"How did I not feel that when it happened?" she asked, reaching out to Sister Wind, but her connection to the world remained silent.

"Tarthanabelle says the Spire wizards broke it," Ralph explained.

Holly-Mine spun around at the sound of the wizard's name. "That's right! I'd almost forgotten. Ralph, listen to me. Tarth is a bad man. We need to get you out of here. Are you able to make this go back down?"

"That's not true. He helped me," Ralph said, becoming upset again.

"Helped you do what?" Gerald asked.

"Find you, of course…and to do magic."

"What?" The word exploded from Holly-Mine, and Ralph recoiled.

"I thought you'd be happy for me."

"What are you saying?" Holly-Mine asked, dreading the answer.

"Tarthanabelle gave me magic! Now, I'm special, too."

"You don't need magic for that. Don't you understand? You were already special."

"No, I wasn't. I was never special like you," Ralph said, hurt by her lack of enthusiasm.

"That's because everyone is unique. You're special in your own way. Ralph's way. Please, listen to me. Come with us. My father can help you," Holly-Mine pleaded.

"I don't need his help," the boy said, stunned by Holly-Mine's reaction to his big news. "Flinghower told me I have the greatest teacher in Ardilakk Valley to mentor me. I'm even going to have a familiar. I hope it's a duck."

Holly-Mine might have believed Ralph if not for the conflict in his face. Part of the boy wanted to stay with Tarth, but another part wanted to leave with her. Then she felt something for the first time since entering the camp. It wasn't the walls that had blocked her connection to the world...Ralph had! The pain of that realization emanated from Holly-Mine like a beacon in the night, calling to her sisters of the forest. With each heartbeat, the energy flowing from her intensified, making the barrier waver, and the boy's emotions were revealed.

Destructive anger.

Insatiable greed.

Incalculable danger!

"You must listen to me," she yelled, trying to make herself heard over the magic emanating from her friend. "When Papa tried to use elemental magic the first time, he got hurt."

"Are you saying I don't deserve to be a wizard?" Ralph asked, shaking more violently.

"No, of course not! I'd never suggest that. And being a wizard isn't bad, but—" She cut herself off. Holly-Mine knew magic wasn't inherently evil, but the consequences of using it often were. Changing tack, she said, "I don't want you to get hurt like Papa did."

Ralph's face flushed, and Holly-Mine felt something snap. Suddenly, the magic preventing her from connecting to the world shattered, and she was overwhelmed by his emotions.

"Oh, Ralph! What has Tarth done to you?"

His hair stuck out in every direction, and electricity sparked between his fingers. Elemental magic had infected his mind. It was taunting him...goading him on...thinking for him. But this wasn't the magic of the Earth Mother or the flowing magic of Sister Wind or Water. This magic was darker and far more dangerous, and it had taken hold of Ralph.

Holly-Mine forced herself to turn toward her friend. She needed to find out if what she thought was true. When she looked into his eyes, she saw—

FIRE!

Scenes of death and destruction flooded her mind...

The Wizard of the Council walked toward the upper lords cowering in a corner of Marble House's courtyard.

The sky lit on fire as the evil wizard exploded, igniting every tree in Ardilakk Valley.

A dark figure emerged from under the Mounts of Ardilakk. It was—

Gerald grabbed her, forcing her to look at him instead of Ralph. "Come back to me!" he screamed. "Don't let it in, Holly-Mine! Where are you? Come back now!"

With all her might, little Brown Eyes forced the fire from her mind.

It held on. It wanted her. It wanted to consume her. It wanted her power!

"YOU CAN'T HAVE ME!" she screamed, casting the fire out.

Ralph burst into tears, thinking she meant him, and a bolt of electricity struck the metal roof above their heads. Gerald watched as it raced down the structure toward the ground.

"He's lost control," Holly-Mine yelled.

"Come with me. I have to get you to safety," Gerald said, never taking his eyes off the boy.

Ralph's face contorted as electricity arced between his hands.

Holly-Mine pulled away. "I can't leave him. He needs me."

Tears streamed down Ralph's cheeks as he called out to her. "What's happening to me?"

Lightning shot in all directions, tearing apart the sleeves of his jacket and burning his arms.

Holly-Mine ducked to avoid being hit, yelling to her friend, "I'm here, Ralph! It's the magic. It wants to be set free."

The air hummed an ominous, high-pitched, angry sound that grated against Holly-Mine's teeth.

A terrible thought came into her mind. "Uncle Gerald, my amulet!"

Gerald understood.

If the boy lost control, Ralph's magic would be reflected back on him. What a terrible fate!

He frantically searched for a way to get the amulet out of harm's way, but they were far above the ground in a sealed room. Where could he take it? And even if he did, that would leave Holly-Mine vulnerable to injury, and he couldn't allow that either. Thanks to Tarth and his obsession with releasing elemental magic into the world, they were trapped in an impossible situation.

He watched as a violet haze enveloped the boy. The pungent smell of burning flesh filled the air, and he didn't hesitate.

Although it only took an instant to make the decision, Gerald had the time he needed to reflect on his life in Ardilakk Valley. He chided himself for the way he used to look down on everyone, and he hoped telling stories to children in his outlandishly colorful clothing had mitigated the pain he'd inflicted as head butler of Marble House, even if only in a small way.

To his surprise, he wished he had his little black books, or more specifically, he wished he had the *Tome of Triumphs*. It looked like he'd finally found one good entry to make on its pages.

Gerald looked at Holly-Mine and said, "I've always known, I guess, but now…I understand. And although I couldn't save Grandnanananny Oak, I can save you. I love you, Little One."

As he stepped in front of her, the last thought that crossed his mind was, *A bowl of tapioca pudding would have been nice.*

Light streamed out of the Norters' Tower for miles in every direction the way a lighthouse signals ships on a stormy night, warning the world that elemental magic was free to do as it pleased.

"NOOOOO!" Holly-Mine screamed as Gerald collapsed to the floor at her feet, having taken the full brunt of Ralph's magical explosion.

Her voice vibrated the windows, amplifying it and sending it out to every corner of Ardilakk Valley. The waters of the river rippled, and the mountains echoed with her suffering.

"What have I done?" Ralph whispered in a meek voice, his hands scorched by the wizard's fire.

No longer bound by the boy's magic, Holly-Mine reached out to the forest. "Sisters of the wood, find my father! I need him!"

CHAPTER 20

CAPTAIN AT THE HELM
AARGHATHLAIN

The *Prosperity* hovered above a stone outcropping, tethered to the ground by lengths of thick ropes. It was suspended by an enormous torpedo-shaped balloon in place of its majestic raked masts and billowing red sails. It still had a staysail that ran from the ship's long bowsprit to the point of the balloon, but instead of a foresail, mainsail, and mizzen, it had two immense propellers housed in round metal cages attached to the hull. The flying schooner shimmered and glowed like a vision out of a dream against the starry night sky, lit by the torches of Dahr Kahlahd-dîm.

D'Aargh stared in disbelief as Grunt rambled on, explaining how he and Gwynynn had converted the *Prosperity* into an airship. But it wasn't the flying schooner's construction that had captured the wizard's attention. "Bram!" he thought.

High above them, the young captain shouted orders to the crew.

"It's amazing, Grunt," D'Aargh's pocket said breathlessly. "You've outdone yourself this time."

The engineer grunted. "Wanna ride?"

"I thought you'd never ask!"

D'Aargh proceeded along the gangway, but after a few steps, he stopped short.

"What's the problem?" Grunt asked, almost running into him.

"What's he doing on board?"

There, standing on deck, was none other than Big G, Gemini City's dreaded footman! D'Aargh almost bolted back down the gangway before noticing Big G looked different. Where were his rope and whip? And was he smiling?

"Who, G? He's all right," Grunt said. "He's mighty strong but harmless. He begged Bram to give him a job. Said he'd dreamed of flyin' his entire life and wanted to come along. Happy as a clam, that one. No better hand on deck. Hey, you listenin' to me?"

Mnoonge poked her head out of the pocket, and both she and the wizard had troubled looks on their faces.

Grunt nudged D'Aargh's arm. "Are you gonna clue me in? What's goin' on?"

"Something's happened."

The wizard tried to make sense of the jumbled, disjunct images assailing his mind.

Lightning.

A strange metal tower.

Someone collapsed on the floor.

The last time he'd felt emotions this strong was when the forest had called for help during the Great Fire, but this time, the trees explicitly called to him. It was a message from his daughter.

"Holly-Mine's in trouble!" Mnoonge screamed. "She needs me!"

D'Aargh cast off his heavy dwarvish mantle and unsheathed Guildebrande. In a grand sweeping motion, he lifted the weapon above his head. When his hands met, light burst forth, dispelling the darkness that had settled into the chasm. Every dwarf stopped what they were doing, turned, watched, and waited.

Sucking in a deep breath, Mnoonge opened her mouth, and Aargh's voice commanded, "Earth Mother, the source of all things great and small, it is time!"

Grunt shielded his eyes as Guildebrande's light glowed brighter and brighter. Dwarves watched in awe as D'Aargh transformed into his One True Form...almost. He decided to keep the earring. He liked how it complimented his eyes.

With Mnoonge's help, Aargh's powerful voice resounded between the high stone walls. "I hear you, Sweet Girl. Papa's coming!" Then, *Aarghathlain, Keeper of the Precious Child*, and *Mnoonge, Voice of the Wizard*, said, "Where there is no road to meet me, may the wind be at my back. Where there is no ocean to ride upon, may I float on your river in the sky. Wind, child of the land and sister to the sea, take me to my daughter!"

Aargh shot into the sky, followed by a boom that echoed deep beneath the Dūnhyldun-thîr into the sparkling depths of the Ahîkehnn-dehln.

At first, the dwarves raised their shields, attempting to protect themselves from the magic they'd grown to loathe. But when they heard the wizard pledge to help his daughter–and word spread that he'd honored the dwarves by keeping his earring–cheers rose out of the chasm. It wasn't long before their voices were joined by the banging of axe handles and the stamping of feet. Magic had returned to Dahr Kahlahd-dîm!

Amidst the cheers, Bram's voice commanded from above. "Boatswain, are we ready to make way?"

"Aye, aye, Captain!" Sadie replied.

"Quartermaster, are all aboard?"

"All but Grunt, sir!"

"I'm a-comin'! You won't be leavin' without yer engineer!"

Bram scanned the horizon as he pulled a smooth blue-green stone from his pocket. He traced the delicate gold inlay in the shape of an arrow with his thumb and, holding it before him, asked, "Sister Wind, please show me the way to Aarghathlain."

The stone spun, hovering a few inches above his palm. It abruptly swung in the opposite direction, stopped, and pointed south-southeast, and he gave the order. "Release the gangway and prepare to cast off. We're headed to the highlands!"

At the last possible second, Grunt threw himself over the gunwale. A voice addressed him from above as he flopped onto the deck like a fish out of water.

"Ho there, Grunt," Bram said. "When this is over, you're going to tell me why you didn't alert your captain that Aarghathlain was in the ravine, isn't that right?"

"I surely will, Captain. I surely will."

Bram reached out a hand and pulled Grunt to his feet. "Good. Now, fire up Ebba. We have a wizard to catch!"

Prosperity's fans roared to life, and her tethers were released, allowing the bow to drift south as the ship lifted into the air.

As they rose up the ravine's forbidding stone walls, Gracie announced, "Captain at the helm!"

"Captain at the helm!" came the response from the crew.

When they cleared the gorge, Bram commanded, "All ahead full!"

"Aye, aye, Captain. All ahead full," Grunt responded, his metallic voice echoing out of a Talkie-No-Walkie tube.

"Ahoy, Captain!" Dag called from high above the deck. He was currently hanging off a rope ladder and signaling to something off the starboard beam.

"Quartermaster, you have the wheel," Bram said, pulling out his brass monocular.

"Quartermaster at the helm!" Gracie called out.

Bram looked west, across the city, and his breath caught in his throat. "What the..."

"What is it, sir?" Sadie asked, having appeared by his side.

"If I'm not mistaken, the Wizards' Spire is falling over!"

Sadie stopped writing on her tablet, and Bram handed her the spyglass. She raised it to her eye and gasped. "What does it mean?"

"That we have to find Aargh." Bram flipped open the brass cover on another one of Grunt's tubes and called to the ship's engineer. "Let'er rip, Grunt! There's no time to lose."

"But Captain, I'm already givin' you all she's got," Grunt's strained voice called from below.

"Grunt?"

"Yes, Captain."

"Give me more."

CHAPTER 21

A TERRIBLE REALIZATION
METAL CITY

Guildebrande sliced through the night sky, not paying any attention to the rows of lamps lining Gemini City's grid-like streets and sidestreets beneath him. He lived for this–defending his friends from harm's way–and he wouldn't let anything get in the way of the mission. Behind him, Aargh followed, gripping the sword's hilt as they flew toward the Highland Grasslands. Last, but certainly not least, Mnoonge poked out of her pocket. The wind whipped her fur and made her eyes water, but she didn't move, fixedly staring at the Metal City's tower.

Pointing at the circular glass structure, the small rat asked, "Guildebrande, can you pierce its walls?"

"It would be my pleasure, Wizard Aarghathlain."

"Then, take us to our Holly-Mine!" Mnoonge bellowed.

A shower of glass surrounded them as they burst into the room. Aargh landed on one knee, planting the sword's point onto the floor before him.

"Thank you, my friend," he said to Guildebrande in his mind.

"It is my honor," the enchanted blade replied.

When the window shattered, the last barrier to the outside world broke, and Holly-Mine gasped, breathing so deeply that Aargh thought she'd been suffocating.

"Sweet Girl, tell me what has happened," Mnoonge said as Aargh sheathed Guildebrande.

"They've come back to me," she explained.

"Who's come back?"

"My sisters. Oh, they've come back." A flash of terror passed across the girl's face, and Aargh heard her in his mind. "Hurry, Papa. Uncle Gerald's hurt! He stepped between us—me and Ralph. You must help him!"

"Are you saying Ralph's here, too?"

"Yes, Papa. He's over there, and he has magic."

Aargh came to the terrible realization that one of his deepest fears had been made real: a wizard had given magic to someone off the school grounds—unbound and ungrounded.

Across the dark room, he saw the boy silhouetted against bursts of fire from the Norter's many chimneys. Magic crackled in the air around them. It called to him. Enticing him to touch it...to explore its power...to seduce him.

Aargh recoiled.

Shaking off the sensation, he continued speaking to Holly-Mine in his mind. "How did Ralph get magic?"

"Tarth," Holly-Mine responded curtly, unable to hide the anger she felt at what the wizard had done.

"What? Tarth's here, too?"

Aargh and Mnoonge scanned the room for any sign of him.

Clearing her throat, Mnoonge spoke, using her rat voice. "I don't see him."

"I don't either," Holly-Mine said, "but I know he's here, somewhere."

"That may be so, but he isn't here right now, and that's a blessing," Aargh thought, kneeling beside her to check on Gerald. He did his best not to panic. The wizard's fire had blackened the ex-head butler's colorful clothing, but he was still breathing. "There's no point in me helping Gerald until we control Ralph's magic. Comfort him while I check on your friend. Can you do that for me?"

"Uncle Gerald can't hear me," Holly-Mine said, hopelessness filling her thoughts.

"It doesn't matter if he can or not. Wouldn't you want your friends near you if you were hurt? Be kind to him. Tell him nice things."

"But, Papa, I don't have any nice things left in me."

"Oh, Sweet Girl. I understand. Why don't you tell Gerald how much you care about him? You still have that, right?" he asked in her mind.

Holly-Mine nodded.

"There, there, Uncle Gerald, you'll be okay," she said. "Papa's here, and he'll take care of us. That's Papa's specialty."

Aargh's heart cracked. What if Gerald–and Ralph–were beyond help? And what about Tarth and the others? What if he wasn't able to put things right?

"Snap out of it, Aarghathlain!" Mnoonge's voice popped into his mind.

She scrambled out of the pocket and climbed to Aargh's shoulder. She was so close that he couldn't focus on her, but that didn't prevent him from seeing the stern look on her face.

Pointing directly between his eyes, Mnoonge cleared her throat and squeaked, "Pull yourself together. There's no time for dithering. Save that boy and get Gerald and Holly-Mine out of here!"

"Yes, ma'am," Aargh thought, getting to his feet.

Even from across the room, he could see the burns on Ralph's hands and arms. The only other time he'd heard about magic doing that was when the healers had mishaps enchanting their potions. The thought sent a shock through him.

"The healer's potions burn wizards if they use too much," Aargh told Mnoonge in her mind. "They're using fire! Do they know that's what they're doing? I have to warn them!"

"Absolutely, but what does that mean for poor Ralph?" Mnoonge asked, keeping Aargh's mind focused on the task at hand.

"The situation is much worse than I thought."

Aargh studied the boy's face. There was so much pain, but not from his hands. This pain went deeper.

How dare Tarth treat anyone this way, especially a child! Wasn't life challenging enough for kids like Holly-Mine's friend, forced to eke out a living on Gemini City's hard, stone streets?

Aargh spoke through Mnoonge. "Ralph?"

The boy's eyes cleared when they met the wizard's gaze. "I don't know what happened. I got upset, and it hurts!"

"I understand. Do you remember me?"

The boy looked at Mnoonge and then Aargh but didn't say anything.

"Ralph? I'm Holly-Mine's Papa. Will you allow me to help you?"

The boy held out his blackened hands.

"Did the magic do this to you?" Mnoonge asked.

The boy's demeanor changed in a flash. Panic-stricken, he babbled, "I'm not doing magic ever again! Magic is bad! Take it out of me. I don't want it anymore."

"It's okay. Calm down. I know magic is scary, but it isn't bad."

"Yes, it is! It hurt Holly-Mine," Ralph yelled, sounding like he was teetering on the edge of hysteria.

"Magic is part of you, and you aren't bad, right?" Mnoonge asked. "That means the magic isn't bad, either. Come with me. I'll help you, I promise, but it's time to leave. Do you understand? We have to go."

"You can't have him," a sinister voice growled from the shadows.

The sound of Tarth's voice triggered a series of memories in Aargh's fractured mind–encounters he'd brushed off at the time but didn't seem harmless anymore.

Sideways glances when the two passed in the school's hallways.

Tarth putting a hand on a wizard's shoulder to direct him away from Aargh.

Groups of wizards wearing dark cloaks instead of the order's traditional, brightly colored robes.

This moment had been a long time coming, and Aargh had chosen to ignore the warning signs.

Aargh remained focused on Ralph, not turning to face the wizard. "How could you give this boy elemental magic? He can't control it. It's too powerful."

"Oh, so you're the only person strong enough to control elemental magic in Ardilakk Valley? *Fusarium oxysporum,* you're arrogant, Aargh! Who do you think you are, taking elemental magic for yourself?"

Keeping his back turned, Mnoonge continued, "Look around! Ralph has proved how dangerous this kind of magic is. You can't go around releasing it into the world, especially for those who haven't been trained."

"Don't you remember? Commoners are the only people who can cast elemental magic. You made sure of that!" Tarth hissed menacingly.

Aargh spoke to Mnoonge in her mind. "This isn't the Tarth I grew up with. He's been corrupted."

"I understand how hard this is for you, Aarghathlain, but we must keep moving. I promise we'll deal with Tarth when the time is right."

"Thank you, Mnoonge. You're a voice of reason at a time when reason seems to have been lost."

Aargh rounded on Tarth, unsheathing Guildebrande and walking straight toward him. He almost didn't recognize the man who'd once worked with him to corral the familiars in the East Barn after a storm had blown open the doors. Gone were Tarth's beautiful crimson robes, replaced by a long, black leather coat that reached almost to the floor.

"You won't have Ralph!" Aargh's voice boomed from Mnoonge, shocking Tarth. "And, if I have anything to say about it, you will never have access to the Earth Mother's magic. Guildebrande, don't let him follow us!"

"As you wish, Wizard Aarghathlain," the sword replied, flying out of Aargh's hand.

Tarth threw up his arms to protect himself, but the blade stopped a few inches away from his chest. The wizard stared at it, floating menacingly in the air. When he took a step to the side, Guildebrande followed.

"Aargh!" he screamed. "You can't stop me! Ralph's not the only person in Ardilakk Valley hoping for more! Why can't you see the potential? With wizards that powerful, we can change the world! We can heal the sick and feed the hungry. Raze mountains and, in their place, raise cities. Don't you understand? WE WILL BE GODS!"

Aargh didn't know what to say. How many more friends would he lose to the allure of elemental magic?

Pointing out the window, Mnoonge squeaked, using her rat voice. "Look!"

The *Prosperity* was steaming toward the tower, illuminated by rows of running lanterns along her gunwales.

"Holly-Mine, help Ralph over to the window," Aargh said in her mind. "I'll carry Gerald."

With Tarth restrained, Holly-Mine put on the bravest face she could muster and went to help her friend. As they walked toward the window, she asked, "Will you show me your hands?"

"No," Ralph yelped, pulling back.

This triggered her fear again, and she jumped, but then she realized that although putting on a brave face may have been a facade, it helped her feel more in control, too. And even though she found it dreadfully hard, she forced herself to smile. "Don't worry. I won't touch them. I just want to look at them."

It worked, and Ralph relaxed, but when he lifted his blackened arms, she felt fear welling inside her again.

"Oh, Ralph," she said, casting about for the right thing to say. Then, she remembered where she liked to go when she didn't feel well. "I know how to make them feel better. Have you ever been to *Mother Mib's* cart on 13Block4? She has the best salty pretzels and shaved ice. I like boysenberry, but I'm sure she'd give us a little extra plain for your hands. That will cool them right off."

Flying while carrying someone sounded like a terrible idea, so Mnoonge asked Sister Wind to make Gerald float. As he lifted off the ground, Aargh guided him toward the shattered window.

The entire time, Tarth never stopped ranting. "What's happened to you, Aargh? Always doing whatever you want. Taking whatever you want. Taking whomever you want and doling out your own brand of false justice to anyone who doesn't fit your plans. Magic is for everyone!"

The *Prosperity's* gangway hit the floor with a clang, and Ralph, Holly-Mine, Gerald, Aargh, and Mnoonge made their escape.

As soon as they boarded the airship, Mnoonge command-ed, "Guildebrande to me!"

The sword flew out of the tower, right into Aargh's hand.

Free from the sword's restraint, Tarth dashed to the win-dow, grabbing the shattered edges of the opening. The wind tugged at his clothes as blood streamed along the casing from his sliced hands.

Realizing he was powerless to stop them, Tarth screamed, "Mother Tree, why have you forsaken me? Have I not worked as hard as Aargh? Have I not dedicated my entire life to wiz-ardly studies? What more do you want from me?" Blood ran down his arms as Tarth lifted his hands to the sky. "How can I prove myself worthy of your gift? HOW?" but the word came out more like a scream of anguish and fury than a ques-tion.

CRACK!

Lightning struck the ceiling, and fire sprung up around him...and inside him.

"Yes! Yes, I can feel it! I can feel everything!"

Tarth started sweating as the heat boiling inside him threatened to explode. He clenched his fists, trying to contain it. No, not contain it. Set it free!

"I see you," he said with a low, dangerous laugh. "No won-der Aargh wanted you for himself. You're beautiful!"

Tarth stood amidst the devastation, concentrating on the magic flowing through him. Powerful magic. Much more powerful than he'd imagined possible. Talking to trees was for children and wizard wannabes. This was real magic.

Everywhere he looked, he saw fire. Even with his eyes closed, he saw it erupting from the chimneys across the Northrim's city and in the static electricity playing about the clouds traversing the night sky.

Fire was all around him. It was in him. Or was he fire? He couldn't tell anymore. There was only fire.

CHAPTER 22

ONE HAND FOR THE BOAT
ABOARD THE *PROSPERITY*

"Permission to come aboard?" Mnoonge asked.

"Permission granted," Bram replied, amused by the rat. "I heard about your little friend here, but I guess I had to see her to believe it."

"Yes, this is Mnoonge," she said, bowing her head.

As soon as they stepped onto the deck, Sadie ensured everyone was properly outfitted for their voyage.

"Hello, Holly-Mine. Nice to see you again. What a fine corset. You'll have to tell me where you got it," she said, admiring the girl's Northrim attire. Then, turning to the crew, she shouted, "You there, find Holly-Mine a jacket. It's cold up here." When she saw Ralph's arms, she added, "Cutty, on the double!"

Anticipating the need, as any good ship's doctor would, he was already on the scene swathing the boy's arms with aloe vera-soaked bandages.

Pleased that the situation was under control, Sadie continued her work by placing a backpack at Ralph's feet and making a note on her whiteboard.

Small Boy: One Safetypack. Bandages for hands and arms. Additional care warranted.

Ralph stood there like a mannequin while Holly-Mine moved his arms and legs to put the pack on.

"What's this for?" she asked.

Bram kneeled and buckled one of the straps. "They're your safety net. Make sure they're nice and tight, but not too tight if you know what I mean. They can chafe but don't tell Gwynynn I said that," he added with a wink.

Holly-Mine tried to smile, but she'd used up her stores.

A crew member handed her a jacket, and she put it on, noting how similar it was to the Norters' attire. Then, she donned her pack as well.

When Sadie offered Aargh a safety pack, Mnoonge declined. "I'll be fine, Sadie. Give this to someone who needs it."

"So be it."

Wizard Aarghathlain: Refused safetypack at own risk.

Aargh and Mnoonge turned back to Bram. "Thank you for coming. And I'm sorry to ask more of you, but can the *Prosperity* take us to the Spire? It's imperative that we bring Ralph to the school."

"Already heading that way, but there's something you need to see. Quartermaster, take care of our guests."

"Aye, aye, Captain. Welcome aboard, Wizard Aarghathlain."

"Thank you, Gracie," Mnoonge responded.

"That's Quartermaster when I'm on duty, sailor!" she barked, but Aargh could see a twinkle in her eyes.

He was pleased to be back aboard the *Prosperity,* surrounded by friends. Well, not all friends. He noticed Otis glaring at him as he sat coiling a length of rope on the other side of the ship. There was a flash of light, and Aargh turned toward the Norters' tower.

Tarth!

Time slowed as Aargh moved to get a clearer view of what was happening. He didn't notice Gracie standing nearby, frozen in the midst of giving an order, or seagulls flying over-head, suspended motionless in midair.

Aargh's heart leapt into his throat. Tarth was standing in the shattered opening from which they'd just escaped, surrounded by jets of lightning. He had access to elemental magic, and considering how unchecked the wizard's emotions had been of late, there was no way he'd be able to control the power surging through him.

Like a phony-o-player revving up to speed, the world moved again, and Mnoonge screamed, "Bram, watch out!"

"Evasive maneuvers! Release the countermeasures!" Bram ordered without hesitating.

"Evasive maneuvers, Captain! Countermeasures released! All hands on deck!" Gracie ordered.

"All hands on deck!" many voices responded.

The *Prosperity* plummeted toward the ground as a bolt of lightning ripped through the sky above them.

Holly-Mine tore her amulet off and threw it to Aargh. "Here, Papa!"

"No, Holly-Mine, this is to protect you!" Mnoonge yelled over the wind.

"It's to protect all of us," she said.

Aargh looked at his daughter in amazement. The depths of her generosity knew no bounds. He couldn't remember a time when she'd been selfish or inconsiderate. Holly-Mine always put the welfare of others before her own. She was truly exceptional.

"I love you, too, Papa. Now, go!" she yelled.

Aargh jumped onto the gunwale, steadying himself by holding onto a stay. "I trust you, Sister Wind," Mnoonge said, and then he let go.

A hulking figure emerged from the pilothouse as Aargh fell.

When the brute caught sight of the man leaning out over the gunwale, he screamed, "Man overboard! Man overboard!"

But before he could grab the wizard, a girl with rich, honey-colored hair sticking out like the straw on top of a scarecrow's head stepped directly in front of him.

"Are you?" he asked.

"Don't worry. Papa's okay," the girl said in the man's mind.

G held out his arms to her, saying, "It can't be you. I've never been that lucky in my entire life."

"Yes, it's me, Mr. Footman," Holly-Mine whispered.

"Oh, you look so sad," he said, holding her close. "I'm sorry. That's my fault, isn't it? I know it is. You have to believe me when I say I'm not the person I once was. I've changed. I promise."

"I'm not so bad," she said, hugging him back. "And it has nothing to do with you."

G let go of the girl and bent down. That way, they could look eye to eye.

She rubbed his short-cut hair, smiled a careworn smile, and placed her hands on either side of his enormous face. "I have a gift for you."

"For me?" he asked, taken by surprise. Nobody had ever given G anything before, and he didn't know what to say.

"Yes, of course, for you. Is that okay?" she asked.

He nodded slowly.

Looking deep into his eyes, Holly-Mine said, "I forgive you."

G froze. Then, something inside of him–something he'd kept locked safely away–opened, and his face changed. A lifetime of ridicule released at once, and the pent-up emotions he'd been hiding poured out of him.

"Thank you, little girl. Thank you. I'm sorry, really I am. I didn't mean to scare you."

"You don't have to be sorry anymore," she explained. "You've remembered your lessons."

Aargh held his daughter's amulet before him, and the elements formed a shield to protect them from Tarth's magic, but it wasn't enough. He needed to make it bigger, and this time, Aargh didn't ask the elements for help. He demanded it, and they obeyed!

Aargh put his hand on Guildebrande, and Mnoonge said, "Powerful Earth Mother and Great Sisters Air and Water, shield this ship from those who would misuse your gift of magic!"

The wind swirled around them, drawing earth from the forest and water from the river. The amulet left his hand, spinning 'round and 'round, and the shield grew larger. Soon, the entire ship and balloon were enveloped by a sphere of earth, water, and wind, each distinct from the other but working together.

Aargh caught glimpses of Tarth through the undulating shield. "Brace yourself!" Mnoonge bellowed.

"One hand for the boat!" Bram commanded.

Tarth's lightning shot out in every direction. Screams came from the Metal Camp as bolts struck buildings. Then, the *Prosperity* was hit. The airship listed heavily to port, but the blast didn't penetrate the shield.

Aargh watched as the amulet reflected the magic toward the tower, taking the elements with it, and then it dropped back into his hand.

Tarth was knocked off his feet, and the tower's windows exploded outwards, showering the Metal City with glass, earth, and water.

Aargh stared at the tower. Was it over? Was Tarth going to stand up?

Yes.

Heaving with the excursion, the tattered wizard slowly pushed himself onto his hands and knees. When Tarth finally made it to his feet, he stood there, arms hanging limply at his sides.

Aargh could see that Tarth was lost, consumed by the magic he craved.

There was never a time Aargh didn't feel the draw, the allure, of elemental magic–pulling at him, gnawing away at his self-control. It was a constant battle to keep it at bay, similar to keeping emotions in check. Once in a while, the magic won, as it had in the Underoof, but Aargh would never willingly give in to it. Evidently, Tarth had, but how? Did Ralph give it to him?

"What if–" Mnoonge started to say before seeing that the footman had Holly-Mine! "Sweet Girl!"

"Don't worry, Papa. I'm fine," she said, nudging the hulking man.

The muscles in Aargh's body reflexively jumped as he contemplated running, but that was before he remembered G, as he was now called, had joined Bram's crew.

Towering over Aargh, the ex-Gemini City Footman said, "I'm sorry, Mr. Aarghathlain wizard, sir. I'm not proud of what I've done. Bram has given me a second chance, and I'm doing my best to do better."

G reached out a colossal arm, and Aargh stared at it. That was one big arm! Hesitantly, he reached out his arm too, worried G might break it, but G didn't, and they made a peace between them.

"How did Tarth do that, Papa?" Holly-Mine asked, taking her amulet from him and tying the ends of the broken chain around her neck.

"I don't know," Mnoonge said, but deep inside, he did. There was only one possible answer to that question. The binding spell he'd cast on the Spire had been broken.

"You'll find a way to stop it again. I know you will. Oh, and Papa?"

"Yes?"

"I love your earring. Can I have one, too?"

An image of Thrairn's gun popped into his mind, and Aargh felt bile rise in his throat. Thankfully, Bram interrupted their discussion by asking him to come to the forecastle deck.

"Can we discuss this later?" Mnoonge asked before he quickly turned and headed to the ship's bow.

"Look," Bram instructed, pointing toward the Spire.

"I must be seeing things," Mnoonge gasped.

Offering Aargh his monocular, Bram said, "Here, use this."

If Aargh had his voice, he would have gasped, too. The Spire was leaning over to such a degree that he was shocked it hadn't fallen to the ground yet. "What happened?"

"I have no idea. The lookout noticed it on our way to the Metal City, but we didn't have time to check it out. It must have collapsed while we were in the ravine because it wasn't that way when we arrived."

Countless questions assailed Aargh's mind. Did Tarth break the Spire? Did everyone make it out of the school safely? Were there any wizards left to heal Gerald?

"Hurry, Bram!" Mnoonge said urgently. "We have to get to the school!"

Bram flipped open the brass cap on one of the Talkie-No-Walkie tubes and yelled, "Grunt...now!"

"Aye, aye, Captain!" came the engineer's brassy response.

Ebba roared to life, and the *Prosperity* raced toward the Spire, leaving a long trail of white smoke dissipating in the breeze behind them.

CHAPTER 23

BROKEN

GEMINI CITY SCHOOL OF WIZARDING
& ABOARD THE *PROSPERITY*

The turbulent exhaust from *Prosperity's* giant fans whipped the Eastern Grazing Field's tall grasses as the ship landed along the Southeast Footpath. Dag, Cal, and a few other crewmembers rappelled down the sides while Gracie single-handedly lowered the gangway with her strong arm. The ship was secured in seconds, and the landing party disembarked into the chaos.

Bram tumbled across the ground as a blast of magic shot over his head. "Kill the lights!" he commanded. "And keep Ebba stoked. We might need to make a fast getaway."

"Aye, aye, Captain!" came Grunt's muffled response, already heading below.

Aargh scanned the crowd for Dramwitch and the others. He found it challenging to identify the dark silhouetted figures as frenzied wizards unleashed bursts of elemental magic. Fires dotted the school grounds, and flames leapt from deep within Wizardwood.

He passed dozens of injured students and teachers. Healers tried to work their magic, but most did more harm than good because their spell was magnified a hundredfold by their unbound emotions.

Catching up, Bram jogged alongside the wizard. "What can I do?"

"Take yourself and your crew and get as far away from here as possible," Mnoonge said, doing her level best to be heard over the mayhem.

"No. We want to help."

"What can you do? Look around. You can't let the *Prosperity* get caught in the middle of this."

"There must be something," the young captain insisted.

"Bram, what happens if this spreads throughout the city?"

"That can't happen, can it? They aren't wizards."

"Are you willing to take that risk? I'm not!" Mnoonge yelled. "Elemental magic has been set free. We have about as much chance of containing it as stopping the spread of the Postulant Pestilence every fall semester."

Bram didn't miss the note of panic in Aargh's voice.

"What if we keep the wizards behind the Spire Wall?" he asked. "That way, they can't infect anyone if it's catching."

"And what about your crew when you fly off? What if you take it with you? What if you bring elemental magic to other cities along the River Wide? No! You must go, but please take Gerald with you. There'll be no help for him here."

Not wanting to argue, Bram reluctantly agreed. "You'll find a way, but you probably aren't going to like what you have to do."

Bram was right, but Aargh didn't hear him because a thought had popped into his head. If Gerald could speak to the old oak, he must have visited Mother Tree, or maybe there were other ways to invite magic in. And if that was the case, all might already be lost.

"You fool!" Mnoonge said aloud. "How did you not notice that right away?"

"What's that?" Bram asked.

"Nothing. Go!" Mnoonge barked. "I'll call for you on the wind. And I'm sorry. I didn't mean to yell."

"I understand, my friend. Until we meet again," *Prosperity's* captain said, extending his arm.

Aargh pulled him into a hug. "Take care of yourself."

"Will do. All aboard!" Bram yelled, running toward the airship.

"All aboard!" came the response from the hands on deck.

"Get ready to make way. I want us airborne quicker than you can say, grandmamamama!"

"Aarghathlain?" Mnoonge squeaked, clearing her throat and using her rat voice.

"Yes," she heard herself say.

Surprisingly, Aargh didn't tell her that he was busy or ask if it could wait. Instead, he sat cross-legged on the ground to give her his full attention.

"I want to do my part, too," she said earnestly.

"You're more important than you know," Aargh replied in her mind. "The truth is, I need the entire Underoof Collective to help prevent wizards from leaving the grounds. But first, I must ask you a question. Do you know why I didn't make you my familiar?"

Mnoonge puzzled over the question. She must not be as special as Wrudge.

"Oh, no, that's not it," Aargh said in her mind.

Mnoonge was mortified! She'd overlooked the fact that they were still connected, and, at this point, they heard each other's thoughts nearly constantly. "I'm sorry. I didn't mean any offense!" she cried, putting her head in her hands.

Aargh chuckled. That happened to him all the time. "Mnoonge, I've given you something very important. Possibly greater than being a familiar."

"I'm thankful for the honor of speaking with your voice, but I can be more," she said, not understanding what he was getting at.

"I am aware of this. Truthfully, you remind me of Wrudge, and that alone is a gift beyond words, but that's not what I'm talking about. You aren't bound by the Familiar Oath. You see, familiars share their magic with their wizards but cannot perform it on their own. You can."

Mnoonge tilted her head to the side. "I'm not sure I follow."

"Obviously, I've shared my magic with you, but haven't you felt magic passing from you to me, too?"

Mnoonge had noticed the connection moved in both directions, but she'd written it off as a side effect of the spell. Was it more than that?

"Mnoonge?" Aargh asked in her mind.

"Yes?"

"This is my gift to you," he told her, reaching into his pocket and pulling out an acorn.

The small rat started to say, "No thank you, I'm not hungry," but stopped herself, remembering Aargh's conversation with Dramwitch in the tunnels.

"In a way," he continued, "I'm giving you what we already share, but I'd rather you had it with Mother Tree's blessing."

"No, I couldn't!" Mnoonge said, shocked and scared but also honored beyond words.

Aargh smiled. "You have, and you can."

He held the acorn close to her. She reached out her tiny hand, stopped, and pulled it back to look at it. She studied its four tiny pink fingers. So small. Even for a rat.

Then, her mother spoke to her in her mind, *You may be small, but you are mighty!*, and she placed her hand on the acorn. When she did, a shudder ran through her body.

"Elemental magic is yours," Aargh said in her mind. "You, Mnoonge, are a wizard!"

She bowed low as rats do, but Aargh wouldn't allow it. "I told you when we met; you must never bow to me. You are my equal."

Remaining bent at the waist, she said, "You honor me, Wizard Aarghathlain, but I don't deserve this gift. I've seen the evil elemental magic can cause, and I'm not sure that I'm strong enough to control it."

Aargh unsheathed Guildebrande and got to his feet, towering over her, which was not how the shortest wizard at the school was often described, and his voice filled the small rat's mind.

"Thirteenth daughter of the seventh son of Clan Oon, rise. Did you not come in the name of Wrudge?" he asked in her mind, holding the glowing sword before him.

"Yes, Wizard Aarghathlain, I did, but–"

"And did you not do so willingly."

"Yes."

"And did you not accept my gift of magic?"

"I did, without reservation."

"And most importantly, did you not pledge to be remarkable?"

"Of course I did," she squeaked proudly. "and I'd do it again!"

"You didn't seal this covenant at the Spire, and you've never set foot on these grounds before now; therefore, the spell between us remains intact. Elemental magic cannot be taken from you until the end of your days. But, Mnoonge, you mustn't abuse this gift. There are limits. Even I don't understand the full extent of the power we wield, but if you are calm of heart and keep a clear mind, the Earth Mother will guide you. Most importantly, you may never use your magic to hurt anyone or for evil purposes. Understanding what I've said, Daughter of Oon, do you pledge to be bound by these rules, forsaking all others?"

"I do," Mnoonge replied.

"Then you are protected."

Guildebrande glowed brightly and then faded as Aargh sheathed the sword.

"And Mnoonge," he said in her mind, less formally. "I'll guide you if you'll let me."

"May I ask Mentor a question?"

"You may."

"If it's possible to cast such a spell and protect me from the dangers of elemental magic, why don't you cast it on Ardilakk Valley and free us from Tarth's madness?"

"You know the answer to that question. I cannot force such a binding on anyone, and I cannot take what isn't mine using magic. A wizard must accept being bound of their own free will. Tarth would never agree to that. He'd only agreed to the Wizarding Oath because he was already bound by it. You see, I didn't cast a new spell. I simply changed the old one, if that is the correct way to put it. But now it's broken, and he wants to release elemental magic, unbound, into the world. We can't let that happen. That is the responsibility and burden we bear."

"It frightens you, doesn't it, Mentor Aarghathlain?" she asked, astutely reading the worry lines on his face.

"Yes, it frightens me."

"I will shoulder that burden with you," she offered, touching his leg, not unlike Wrudge did the night of the Great Fire.

Feeling her touch made Aargh question if he was doing the right thing, but it was too late to change that now. They could only move forward, and he was glad to have Wizard Mnoonge by his side.

Mnoonge addressed her mentor using her rat voice. "I will keep my word and honor the oaths to which I have sworn allegiance. I accept these gifts and all that entails of my own accord and of my own free will," she squeaked. "Tell me what I must do."

"Mobilize the Collective. Have the Mischief surround the Spire grounds and prevent anyone from entering or leaving."

"But how? Teach me, Mentor."

"There isn't time. I trust you to do what you feel is right. But before you go, I must ask for one last sacrifice."

"Tell me, and it will be done," she said, stepping back.

"I'm sorry to have to ask this of you," Aargh said in her mind, "but may I please have my voice back?"

Mnoonge hadn't expected this, and she involuntarily recoiled, suddenly realizing how much speaking for Aargh meant to her—far more than she'd thought. Breaking the spell would most certainly result in her losing a part of their relationship that she'd grown to love.

"I'm sorry," he said, sensing how difficult his request was for her. "Our connection means a lot to me, too. When I first gave you my voice, I'd hoped for you to be my representative, allowing me to be in more than one place at the same time, but I couldn't exist as a human and a rat simultaneously. However, in time, my failure transformed into a blessing. You became my friend, confidant, and, much to my surprise, my teacher. I'm grateful for what we've shared, but we must go our separate ways. You cannot grow into the great wizard I know you can be, tied to me in this way. And I must resume my duties, unshielded by your presence."

Mnoonge understood, but that didn't mean she had to be happy about it. "Will you lift me to your shoulder, Mentor?"

Aargh bent over and picked her up. She took hold of his ear with her tiny hands and whispered the same words he'd spoken to her in the tunnels.

He breathed in a long breath, and his voice was restored! "Thank you."

"You're welcome," and she kissed him on the cheek. "I must go now. I have a job to do."

Aargh placed his new apprentice on the ground, and she scurried off to gather the Mischief.

• • •

As Bram reached for the rope ladder that had been lowered to him, heavy footsteps approached from behind, but he didn't turn around. "Why aren't you on board, Quartermaster?"

"Captain, I formally request reassignment," Gracie stated, standing at attention.

Looking over his shoulder, he asked, "Can't this wait? We need to get out of here."

"You do," she said, "but I need to stay. I'm askin' to be reassigned to the Spire."

Bram took his foot off the ladder and faced her. "Gracie, the *Prosperity* needs you. I can't imagine running the ship without you."

"They need me more," she explained, still standing at attention.

"At ease, Quartermaster, and if you're jumping ship, you can call me Bram."

"I was hopin' to have permission, sir. They ain't goin' to make it without my help. I can do this. It's what I've trained for my whole life."

"I said, call me Bram. That's an order," he corrected, and she relaxed. "Is this really what you want?"

"It's not a matter of want. I have to do this."

Bram knew that when Gracie set her mind to something, not even the wind could change her course, so he said, "A-ten-hut!"

She snapped back to attention.

"It has come to my attention that the Quartermaster has asked to be reassigned to the Wizards' Spire. Is this correct, Quartermaster?"

"Yes, sir! It is, sir!" she responded crisply.

"Then let it be made known that on the first day of the ninth week of the year, three hundred and thirty-three, Quartermaster Gracie Thourabear is hereby assigned to the Gemini City School of Wizarding, accepting all of the responsibilities therein. May you serve the Spire as admirably as you've served aboard the *Prosperity.*"

They saluted, and she said, "Thank you, Bram. I won't let you down."

"See that you don't, Gracie. Gemini City is counting on you."

Bram climbed onto the ladder, and the ship rose into the air. Gracie returned many salutes along the length of Prosperity's gunwale. When they were high in the sky, she abruptly did an about-face and got to work.

CHAPTER 24

BRINDLEWISE THE REMARKABLE
GEMINI CITY SCHOOL OF WIZARDING

Bartlebee's robes flapped wildly as he sprinted across the Spire Grounds. "Aargh! Aargh! Over here!"

"I've never been so happy to see that yellow of yours!" Aargh exclaimed, embracing his friend.

"Hey, you have your voice back!" Bee gasped, bending over and putting his hands on his knees. "Hold on a sec'. I need to catch my breath."

Aargh fought back strong emotions. He hadn't anticipated how much seeing his best friend would affect him after being apart for so long.

It must have been evident on his face because Bee said, "Save your breath. I feel the same way."

"Where is everyone? Are they safe?"

"We haven't seen Dram or Garth yet," Lan explained, joining the conversation. "They were at the lake when it happened."

Aargh greeted the rotund wizard by clasping his arm. "I hope they're okay. It's anarchy around here. Can you tell me what's going on? Is the Spire lost?"

"That's his department," Lan said, pointing at Bee.

"I'll do my best, but I honestly don't know where to start."

"Tell him about the penny," Lan suggested as more of their friends joined them.

"Yes, the penny. Uh, Brindlewise, I mean Pal, well, both of them, really, picked it up. It was under the school, and we think it has to do with your river of magic." Bee shook his head. "Wow, I'm not doing a good job of explaining this."

Aargh looked puzzled. "What's so important about this penny?"

Just as he asked the question, Paladand arrived, assisted by Fizzbain and Tassior. Aargh almost didn't recognize him because the hunched and shivering young wizard had Dram's old robes draped over his shoulders.

"Are you sure you're up for this?" Bee asked, helping Paladand sit on a stump.

"I'm fine," he said, pulling the robes tighter. "Aargh, what Bartlebee is trying to say is that the nursery rhyme is true."

"You mean the one about the lost cities? *One pickup penny, lying in the wood?*" Aargh asked.

Paladand nodded. "That's the one."

Holly-Mine slipped her hand into Aargh's, having snaked her way through the group with Ralph in tow. Bee winked at her, and Lan moved his hand a little. Holly-Mine waved back, but it wasn't her usual happy wave. This wave looked heavy and slow.

"We were searching for Tarth's tunnel when Paladand and Brindlewise found a penny under the school," Bee said, trying again. "You won't believe this, but they stumbled on an underground forest...a city down there."

"Hold on a minute. That's impossible," Aargh interjected, but the look on Paladand's face told him it was the truth. "Where's Brindlewise? I'm sure he can sort this out."

The wizards' faces dropped.

Paladand pushed himself forward. "I'm sorry, Aarghathlain. Brindlewise is gone."

Aargh collapsed onto one knee, and the others kneeled with him. Holly-Mine let go of Ralph and hugged her father. "How?" he asked.

Bee looked at Paladand and nodded as if to say, *Tell him what happened. He needs to know.*

Taking a slow, calming breath, the young wizard said, "As you know, Brindlewise and I were tasked with searching the old school. We looked for hours but didn't find any tunnels. Instead, we discovered a secret door that appeared to lead outside, though we knew we were deep underground. We left the school and followed a wide road through a town that reminded us of Gemini City...possibly Eastie and Westie Nort. It sounds bizarre when I say it, but there's no other way to describe it. And right in the middle of the town green, a shiny penny floated above the ground. I told Brindlewise not to touch it, but he wouldn't listen. He kept saying it was compromised, and we had to prevent it from falling into the wrong hands. Then, he did it. He took it. Just like that."

Pausing to collect himself, Paladand gestured with his hand to demonstrate how Brindlewise plucked the penny out of the air.

Forcing the words out of his throat, he said, "I couldn't save him. I tried, but the magic was too strong. There was this thunderous sound–like pulling the plug out of your bathtub, only much louder–and it took everything. The roads, the trees, the buildings...the whole town."

Tassior hugged Paladand as he wept with all-consuming grief. Though they were surrounded by a chaotic scene, no one moved–transfixed by the young wizard's story.

When Paladand regained his composure, he continued. "Brindlewise got trapped in the magic. I held his hand so hard...so very hard...but I wasn't strong enough. I'll never forget the feeling of his fingers slipping out of mine. I told him to hold on, but it was no use. Do you know what he did then?"

Aargh shook his head.

"He smiled. Can you believe it? Brindlewise, of all people, smiled at me. Then, he was gone."

Choking back tears, Bee whispered, "Lan and I were in the Private Spire Garden when it happened. Right, Lan?"

"Yeah," Alantus said half-heartedly. "We felt the ground shake."

"We're pretty sure it sucked up more than the underground city," Bee added. "We think the river of magic was pulled back to the Mounts of Ardilakk, and it almost took the Spire, too."

More in control now, Paladand finished his story. "I don't know why the magic left Nerah and me there. Maybe it was because we hadn't touched it."

"No one will ever know," Illbrahss said under his breath.

"I tried to leave but found myself rooted to the spot, blankly staring into the darkness. Brindlewise was lost. The town was lost. Everything was lost...except the penny. There it was, lying on the ground. Without thinking, I bent down and picked it up. Isn't that ridiculous? Like it was a happy penny that I found on the street. What a foolish thing to do."

"At least you're here to talk about it. Things could have been worse," O said. He sounded irritated, but they knew he meant well.

"I guess you're right. Thankfully, nothing happened. I woke from my stupor when parts of the ceiling started falling around us, and we bolted for the doorway. And, well, you know the rest. I'm sorry. We shouldn't have left him."

"You couldn't have done anything more. Brindlewise was already gone," Tassior consoled the young wizard.

Catching everyone off guard, Paladand sat bolt upright and grabbed Aargh's arm. "Brindlewise was convinced that Tarth knew about the penny. That's why he sacrificed himself, to make sure you had it...not Tarth and his followers. He said you'd protect it. I didn't know when I'd see you again, so I gave it to Bartlebee. I hope that was okay. I would never go against a wizard's wish."[15]

"Yes, of course," Aargh said rigidly, shocked by Paladand's sudden emotional outburst.

Tassior defused the situation by helping the young wizard let go of Aargh's arm while Bartlebee produced the penny.

Bee had always carried a youthful air about him, but Aargh sensed it was fading. He wished they were skipping along the high pass or trying to out-toss each other at the Middling Street Fair, but those days were gone.

"Relax, Papa. Breathe," Holly-Mine said, leaning her head against his.

Aargh took the penny from his friend and looked at it. It had no heaviness to speak of, but he sensed the weight of its power. Holly-Mine did, too.

"Don't use it. It's dangerous," she said. "Darkness made that penny. Put it away and never think about it."

Aargh agreed, slipping it between the pages of *Holly-Mine's Diary* for safekeeping.

The wizards' faces surrounding him looked drawn and tired as Alantus helped him to his feet.

---

[15] Although wizards have never been able to see their own fate, legend has it that before a wizard's passing, they are granted one last glimpse into the future—a look at how their life shaped the world and what it will be like without them. This is known as the *wizard's wish*, but the term has been adopted by Geminians and all peoples of the River Wide to refer to any person's dying request.

In a brief moment of clarity, Aargh realized the nursery rhyme might be a prophecy. "One pickup penny, lying in the wood!"

Bee nodded.

"Does that mean all we have to do is put it back, and everything will return to normal?" Aargh asked. "That's what the rhyme says; *put the penny back, or the city's gone for good.*"

"I tried," Paladand explained. "It didn't work, and I'm beginning to think there's more to the rhyme than we know. Besides, Brindlewise was adamant that I not leave it there. He didn't think it was possible to protect it in that place."

"Papa? Where's Ralph?" Holly-Mine asked, searching the crowd.

"I haven't seen him," Aargh answered absently, focused on the discussion about the penny.

"But he was right here a minute ago."

The atmosphere around them changed as a wave of concern emanated from Aargh's daughter. Her gaze locked on something, and everyone turned to see what she was looking at.

About a dozen paces away, Ralph stood alone, reaching toward the sky. And, as if drawn to him, countless wizards and students converged on the boy from every direction, also grasping at the air.

"Take me with you!" they pleaded.

"Come back!"

"Don't leave us here!"

Aargh watched as their combined emotions condensed into a purple haze. As the crowd grew, the magic coalesced and moved with them.

It gathered into a vast, purple swirling mass, writhing and spinning with the strength of hundreds of panic-stricken wizards, novices, and postulants. Terrified faces poked out of the mist, wailing or screaming–reflecting the emotions that had created it.

As Aargh watched, the magic transformed into a mass of hands, and without warning, it shot toward the *Prosperity*.

"Bram, look out!" Aargh called on the wind, and the airship veered off course.

The hands followed.

He watched as the magic arced across the sky toward his friends. It tore at the ship's lines, searching for a place to hold in an attempt to pull it back to the school.

Just as the *Prosperity* reached the River wide, the magic overwhelmed the vessel. The balloon caught fire, and the airship plummeted toward the earth, leaving a long streak of black smoke hanging in the sky.

"Nooooo!" Holly-Mine cried out, and Aargh grabbed her as a fireball rose from where it crash-landed. She wriggled out of his arms, screaming at the sky. "Uncle Gerald! Bram! Grunt! Sadie! G!"

Holly-Mine spun around, and Aargh saw that she had changed. Her hair and skin had become much darker, like amber maple syrup harvested at the end of the season.

"Sweet Girl, are you okay?" Aargh asked, not knowing what else to say.

"No, I am not okay!" she screamed. "This has to stop! Stop it now! No more! It is time for this to end!"

The raw, ancient power of Holly-Mine's emotions exploded, and everyone grabbed whatever they could to keep from being knocked over or blown away. The sky warped, and Sister Wind spun in circles, creating a vortex in the middle of the Eastern Grazing Field, sucking up the excess magic that had gathered over the school.

"AAAAAH!" Holly-Mine screamed.

The trees of the forest swayed to and fro as tornado-like winds spun faster and faster around her.

Unable to stand, Aargh crawled along the ground. The closer he got, the more the winds ripped at his face and clothing, but he made no attempt to protect himself. He didn't care what happened to him. Holly-Mine was all that mattered.

Aargh slipped his arms around his daughter and sang her favorite song, though he changed the words...

Sacrifice is given by a heart that's true,
and the earth rewards hearts where love once grew.
There above the river,
Standing here with me,
The Earth Mother will return a life to thee.

Comforted by his voice, Holly-Mine stopped screaming, and the winds diminished.

Everyone looked scared, but many of the fires had gone out, and the excess magic and purple haze had dissipated.

"Talk to me, Sweet Girl."

"I don't have any talk left in me, Papa."

"I know."

"It's that..."

"Yes?" Aargh encouraged her.

"Ralph!"

"Ralph?"

Aargh saw the boy running toward the 67th Sidestreet exit. He turned back to his daughter, and their eyes locked for an instant. Then, she took off.

"No, Holly-Mine. Wait!"

"I have to do this, Papa."

"Let me help you," Aargh pleaded.

Holly-Mine turned and said, "Not this time."

Aargh was stunned. She looked so grown up, almost–

"And Papa?"

"Yes?"

"I love you."

Then, she was gone…and so was Aargh.

• • •

No one noticed that amidst the mayhem, thousands–no, tens of thousands–of puffed-up rats had encircled the grounds at Wizard Mnoonge's command. Once they were in place, she gave the signal, and they started to glow. Gradually, their glows melded together, illuminating the buildings that faced the school with its shimmering light.

Frightened wizards and students rushed the exits or climbed the Spire wall, throwing themselves against the barrier. Every time one did, the wall wavered, but it didn't collapse–at least, not yet. However, the strength of rats wouldn't last forever.

"Wizard Aarghathlain, where are you?" she asked, but her mentor didn't respond. She was on her own. "What would he want me to do? Probably, tell everyone to stay calm. But how? I don't have his voice anymore."

Once again, the small rat's mother spoke from her memories, *But you have* your *voice.*

Mnoonge thought back to when she was a pup. Being the runt of the litter, she'd had to fight for everything because she'd never be as big and strong as her brothers and sisters.

However, her mother had always insisted that strength came from within. *Don't let anyone judge you by your size, Daughter Mnoonge. Your voice is as strong as any.*

"Yes, mama," she said under her breath.

Then, Mnoonge raised her eyes to the starlit sky.

"Sister Wind, I have heard the great Wizard Aarghathlain call to you, and you have answered. I ask that you hear me now. Please, fill my lungs and make my voice heard by all who stand on the broken Spire's grounds."

The air curled around the small rat, and Mnoonge spoke.

"The great Wizard Aarghathlain commands you to be calm! We must stay at the school until magic is under control and those who are hurt are cared for. When the time is right, Aarghathlain will return."

She'd stretched the truth a bit, considering she had no idea where Aargh was or if he planned on coming back, but it seemed like the prudent thing to say.

The trouble was, it only worked for an uncomfortably brief time. Almost immediately, magic started building up again, and people returned to throwing themselves against the magical rat-wall.

"Now what?" she wondered.

CHAPTER 25

PITCHFORKS AND SHOVELS
THE WIZARDS' UNDERGROUND

Trapped by one of the Congregational House's metal chairs, Bee nervously tapped the armrest. Its broad, curved back prevented him from sitting how he wanted to, which added to his aggravation.

In an extremely frustrating move, the school's administration had decided they needed the city's support to deal with recent events. That was a laugh. If wizards didn't know how to deal with the breaking of Aargh's spell, how could a bunch of bureaucrats help? They couldn't. That's how, but there Bee sat, nevertheless.

The only good thing that had happened was they'd found Garth and Dram waiting at the Congregational House when they arrived. Unsurprisingly, neither had taken the news about Brindlewise and the Spire well, but that was to be expected. It had been a difficult night for everyone. At least, now, they knew how Tarth had slipped off the grounds undetected, which was valuable information, indeed.

Bee should have been happy to hear this news, but he wasn't. He'd been forced to search the one place in the entire world that genuinely terrified him, the Spire had collapsed, he'd lost his mentor, and to top it off, they'd had to leave Lan behind.

Before making their way up the Congregational Footpath, The Wizards' Underground had gathered outside the sculpture garden—not in it. None of them had any intention of setting foot between those statues again.

"I think we're good," Bee said, clapping his hands together. "As long as we keep anyone who's used elemental magic from leaving, we should be safe enough."

Tassior, the gentlest of wizards, politely suggested that they doublecheck.

"All right. Has anyone here used elemental magic?" Bee asked.

"Ahem."

"Who's that?"

The wizards parted, leaving Alantus standing alone with his hand raised, if it could be called that. His arm was tight to his body, and his fingertips barely made it past his collarbone.

Bee shook his head. "Lan, are you raising your hand again? We've been through this. Say what you need to say. We're in a bit of a rush."

Lan wasn't a natural public speaker, and his face blossomed into a bright shade of red, not unlike the Cardinal Glory roses he tended in the gardens. "It was unwell."

"Who's unwell?" Paladand asked. "Do they need a healer?"

"No, that's not what I meant. Before this started, it wasn't doing well, and I left it on the bench. I meant to return to it, but then we had to search the grounds."

Bee lost his patience. "Lan! Spit it out. We're on the clock!"

"I used magic to save my *Hyoscyamus niger* plant, but it didn't work. It burned up in my hands, and I'm worried I might hurt someone. I'm really, really sorry."

"Oh, Lan," Bee said, giving him a hug.

The others gasped, worried Bee was about to explode into flames.

"What in the world did you do that for?" Onaveris asked, throwing his hands in the air.

"Have a heart, O. I'd do the same for you if you needed a hug. Besides, if Lan were going to go haywire, wouldn't he have done it already? Right, Lan? You're not going off the deep end, are you?"

Lan shrugged.

"See. It's fine. Everything's fine."

"I've never needed a hug in my life," O grumbled.

Bee chuckled at the ornery wizard. "Listen. What if the situation just got out of hand when the floodgates opened? Don't get me wrong. I'm not telling everyone to start using magic the way Aargh does–he has a lot more experience–but it can't be all bad. He did save us from the Great Fire, remember?"

It took a while to get everyone on the same page, but in the end, they voted to appoint Lan Spire Pacifier–a job he took seriously. If elemental magic reacted to emotions, Lan planned to go with happy, not scared or angry. That mostly meant he spent the rest of the evening reminding wizards and students to practice their C's…and he smiled a lot. Smiling is the best medicine, he told everyone, and he was right.

For Bee, it was a lonely walk along the Congregational Footpath without his friend. Of course, he considered all of the wizards in their group friends, but after hearing what happened to Brindlewise, he had an overwhelming desire to keep everyone close.

"That's far enough!" a squeaky voice commanded.

The rat-wall loomed before them, but it wasn't the only barrier blocking their way. Mnoonge was standing in the middle of the exit with her hands on her hips. "Aarghathlain said: No one is to leave the grounds. No one," she explained. "Not until we get magic under control."

Although the look on her face was enough to stop them dead, the tapping toe confirmed there'd be no talking their way out of this one. Even so, Bee had to try.

"Yes, I understand that, but I'm Aargh's best friend, Bartlebee. He must have mentioned me. And I'm sure he'd let me out if he were here."

"I don't remember Aarghathlain saying, *Mnoonge, I want you to keep everyone here except Bartlebee. He's my best bud. That means the rules don't apply to him*," she responded, crossing her arms and staring fixedly at the wizard.

"Tenacious little bugger, isn't she," Bee muttered.

"What's that?" Mnoonge asked, raising an eyebrow.

"Oh, sorry, I was–"

Bee didn't get to finish before a heavy hand landed on his shoulder. He almost fainted when he turned around. An extraordinarily stern-looking woman towered over him, and she had a metal arm!

"Name's Gracie. Former Quartermaster of the *Prosperity,* and I'm in no mood for standin' around. I just watched my ship go down over the river and have no idea if my friends survived. So, make room. I have some conversatin' to do."

To their amazement, Gracie's legs shrank until she was practically sitting on the ground.

"Hello, Noble Mnoonge. Do you remember me from the *Prosperity?*"

"I do indeed, Quartermaster. You were second in command. I'm very sorry for your loss," the rat said, bowing her head.

"That's kind of you to say. They was a good crew, and I shoulda been with 'em. T'was foolish of me to stay behind, but I ain't no longer Quartermaster. Call me Gracie," she said, her stern voice wavering slightly.

"Of course, Gracie. You did what you thought was best."

"That's correct, and now, I must be doin' somethin' else I believe's right. These gentlemen have to accompany me to the Congregational House. We're goin' to gather support for the Spire and restore order to this here city. We cain't do this trapped here, on the school's grounds. It's a risk, there's no doubt. Especially considerin' we know nothin' about this magic we're dealin' with, but it's a risk we're goin' to have to take. Do you understand, Noble Mnoonge?"

"Although I appreciate the respect you have shown me, my title is *Wizard*. I am Wizard Mnoonge, apprentice to the Great Aarghathlain at your service."

The wizards gasped.

Gracie shot them a glance Sadie would have been proud of, as if to say, *Show some respect, boys! You need to get out more. The world's full of wonders.* Then, the ex-quartermaster continued speaking, focusing her attention on the small rat. "Pardon me, Wizard Mnoonge. I didn't realize there were rat wizards in the world, and it's pretty clear none of them knew neither," she said, throwing a thumb over her shoulder.

"I believe I'm the only one."

"Impressive. My apologies for my forwardness, but will you let us pass?"

"Yes, I will let you pass. May the wind fill your sails, and the strong currents of the River Wide take you where you want to go."

"Thank you," Gracie said, nodding her head in deference to the rat.

Mnoonge touched her hand and said, "Save us, Gracie. Save us all."

Gracie saluted as she clicked and whirred back to her normal height.

"As for the rest of you," Mnoonge added, "Don't make me regret allowing you to pass. Wizard Aarghathlain trusted me with one responsibility, and although I'm going against my word, I believe he would have agreed with your mission."

Bee and the other wizards stood there speechless.

"I thought wizards had manners," Gracie said. "Say thank you to the little lady, and let's go. And if any of you step outta line, you'll be havin' me to deal with!"

One by one, the remaining members of The Wizards' Underground–Bartlebee, Fizzbain, Tassior, Onaveris, Pud, Afynn, Illbrahss, and Paladand–thanked Mnoonge and followed Gracie off the Spire grounds.

Once they were outside, Gracie turned to Bee. "You seem to be the one these folks look to, so it'll be you who's in charge while I'm away. I've got somethin' to do."

Then, she stole into the night, leaving Bee and the others to face what awaited them at the Congregational House without her dominating presence.

Stuck between the curvy chair's arms, Bee's shoulders slumped as he thought about Mnoonge, Lan, and Gracie.

"Bee, I'm worried about Aargh."

"Uh, what's that? Oh, Dram, sorry. I was thinking and didn't see you there."

"No problem. I said, I'm worried about Aargh."

"Oh. He's probably fine. I bet he's off hiding the penny."

"I guess, but it doesn't feel right," Dram explained, drumming his fingers nervously on the chair's armrest. "Aargh is many things, but the most important is: he's a planner. He wouldn't disappear without leaving instructions."

Dram wasn't wrong.

"Great. One more thing to worry about," Bee mumbled.

The sound of a latch clanking echoed off the room's curved walls, and everyone sat up. They watched as the representatives entered, taking their places around the oak tree

Aarghathlain had planted years before at the rotunda's rededication ceremony. She was responsible for recording what happened in the Congregational House and already had many roots.

The Chairperson's gavel came down with a resounding boom, and the room exploded with voices talking at once. People were out of their chairs, pacing, arguing face to face, and gesticulating in frustration. Their voices bounced around the rotunda, amplified by the triangular glass panels of the Capam Speculo.

In the midst of it all, Paladand stood silently, admiring the tree. Putting his hand on her thin trunk, he asked, "Young Oak, I know you aren't ready to foretell the future and that you are preparing for winter, but you have heard many conversations held within this building's walls. Please, share with me what lies in the hearts of Geminians."

"Smart, Pal. Very smart," Bee said, watching him from across the room.

The young wizard's face fell as he listened. Many of the meetings she'd overheard were filled with dire predictions and heated arguments over how to defend the city from what the representatives believed was an inevitable conflict with the Norters. When she was finished, he thanked the tree for her help and scanned the room, locking eyes with Bee. The older wizard pointed to Fizzbain.

Paladand nodded before walking over to the only wizard who wore different colored socks. Usually, that kind of thing (not following the wizarding dress code) would have bothered him, but just as he wore the crescent sun in honor of his past, Fizz donned different colored socks for a particular reason, and Paladand respected that.

"I believe we could use a little FizzBit if you don't mind," he said. "But try not to bring the ceiling down on us, okay?"

Fizz smiled and yelled, "Hippopotomonstros-esquippedaliophobia!"

Paladand looked at the wizard for a few seconds before real-izing the room had gone completely silent.

Bee stifled a laugh.

Shaking off the surprise of hearing the most frightening word he'd ever heard (If it was actually a real word. He'd have to check later.), he took advantage of the stillness. "My dear assembled representatives and esteemed wizard colleagues. I completely agree that there is much to talk about. However, we have pressing matters that we must attend to immediately. I don't doubt Gemini City is frightened by what happened at the school. Aarghathlain's spell has been broken, and elemen-tal magic has been released into our city."

Mumbles around the room grew louder and louder until Fizz pulled out Bit again. Immediately, a hush fell over the crowd.

"You and your toad are surprisingly persuasive," Paladand said.

Fizz smiled.

"It's important to consider that our sisters and brothers on the highlands didn't experience the destruction the Wizard of the Council wrought on our fair city," Paladand continued. "They have no memory of the Great Fire and do not view elemental magic with the same reservations as we do. And more troubling, if accounts are to be believed, Tarthanabelle– yes, one of our own–is mobilizing their forces to take Ardi-lakk's magic. We can't let that happen. Not only must we pre-vent any one group from controlling magic in Ardilakk Val-ley, but we must also find a more permanent way to prevent its use altogether."

Several representatives balked at this, suggesting Gemini City deserved to retain sole control, but a chorus of reminders about the Great Fire silenced them.

"Dram has spoken with his mentor, and he's trying to create a new spell to ground wizards. No, don't get too excited. We don't know if it'll work yet, but he's doing his best. Also, Aarghathlain is missing, which adds to the challenges we face."

A loud knock on the rotunda's south-facing door echoed through the hall, interrupting the young wizard. An attendant opened the door and in paraded a delegation of farmers carrying pitchforks and shovels.

The chairperson banged her gavel and stood. "I'm sorry. This is a closed meeting between Spire Wizards and Gemini City representatives. Whatever you have come to speak about will have to wait until we are finished."

"Hmm. Madam Chairperson," an old farmer said, slurring his words. "We apologize for interrupting your important meeting, but we are from Old Eastie Sowtown. We've heard what the Norters are planning, and we won't sit idly by and watch our city taken from us. We have come to tell you that we are marching to the Mounts of Ardilakk to stop them."

"Excellent!" Bee said under his breath, catching sight of Gracie standing behind the delegation.

"Your offer is welcomed, but it is not for one square alone to defend our city," the chairperson explained. "We must stand together to defeat this threat, magical or otherwise. Furthermore, we have not yet chosen a leader for this endeavor. I assume you have a suggestion from within your ranks?"

A woman dressed in allovers and heavy work boots stepped forward. "No, ma'am. We do not. That's not how we townies run things, but we are good at getting work done when the need arises. And right now, I can assure you there is a need to get work done."

"Be that as it may," the chairperson said politely, "if we intend to gather our forces, we'll need a strong leader. Do the wizards have a suggestion?"

"We do," Bee said, getting to his feet. "Sorry, Pal. Don't mean to step on your toes."

Paladand was unperturbed.

"Who is this person?" another representative asked. "And are they here to speak on their own behalf?"

"Hold on a second. She's right over there. Gracie, would you mind joining us up front?"

CHAPTER 26

THE WORLD BETWEEN
AARGHATHLAIN

Aargh let the sun's warm rays caress his skin, filling him with a sense of tranquility. The world around him was quiet, save for the occasional rustling of leaves and the trickle of water as it played about the pebbles in a nearby stream. In this moment...this singular moment...all was right with the world, and Aargh felt a deep sense of peace and contentment.

He inhaled the rich autumn air. Mmm. Apples and cinnamon–a personal favorite. He wondered if, somewhere, a grandmamamama had put pies on the windowsill to cool.

Looking around, he noticed that he was standing in the center of a large clearing, possibly a town green. Around the edges, one-level homes painted warm, earthy colors sat under wisps of smoke rising from their chimneys. They were built of wood and mud with domed tops to help the rain run off, and all of them were nestled between deciduous trees covered with beautiful orange and red leaves.

Aargh lifted a hand to brush the hair away from his face. "Oh, a journal."

The One True Book of Spells
by
Aldenthwaine the Incipient

"That's right. Aldenthwaine's spellbook," Aargh said distantly. "I don't understand what all the fuss is about."

Yes, you do! Your father warned you! It's dangerous! Put it away!

Although, like most wizards, Aargh often talked to himself, the separation of his voices this time was more akin to being split in two than the casual discourse of inner thoughts.

The Aargh standing in town was far from the troubles plaguing Ardilakk Valley. That Aargh didn't remember the pain and suffering he'd left behind, only the joy and tranquility of a peaceful autumn day.

The other Aargh frantically tried to be heard, having been hidden away. Silenced.

"Which tree will I sit beneath to read my book?" he wondered aloud. "There are so many to pick from."

Aargh spied stands of oaks and maples, an ancient ginkgo tree with its fan-shaped leaves, stunning crape myrtles, and a black tupelo displaying an array of colors from yellow to red to purple, all on the same tree!

"What a glorious way to spend the afternoon. I can't believe my luck to have come on such a perfect day."

Aargh, get a hold of yourself! Don't be deceived! Can't you tell this is wrong?

He felt a slight twinge. It was hard to imagine anything unpleasant on such a delightful day, but yet, a thought nagged at the back of his mind.

"Ah, Gerald's belt," he said, absently unbuckling from around the journal and letting it fall to the ground.

A circular seating area framed by fall flowers caught his attention. The planting beds were filled with yellow coreopsis and vintage orange and red marigolds, adding a nostalgic touch to the scene. Bountiful chrysanthemums, with their varying hues, from white and light yellow to deep burgundies and purples, completed the picture, providing a stunning display of nature's beauty.

"I think I'll sit here a while. I wish I'd remembered to bring a basket. This is such a lovely place for a picnic. Oh, look! I did remember!"

Aargh's favorite picnic basket had been placed beside a small, red and white checkered tablecloth. On top was a plate of berry fritters and a tall glass of iced cider.

"And are those pickled apples? How delightful!"

Aargh picked up the jar of fruit. He loved it when they had a little cloth tied around the top. It made them look so homey. He pulled on the string holding it in place, and a note dropped onto his lap.

> *We think you'll agree; our pickled apples are*
> *just as good as your great auntilee's...maybe better!*
> *(Not satisfied? Stop by our store to try some free samples.*
> *We're sure we have something you'll like!)*

"Look at that. They sound like such nice people. I'll have to stop by sometime. I do love samples."

Aargh sat himself down and opened the jar.

"You know, the only thing better than a picnic is sharing your pickled apples with someone else. I wonder where everyone is."

He hadn't seen a single person strolling along on the road or beating out a rug in their backyard. No birds sang overhead, and he didn't hear any dogs barking. Strange.

"It must be Sattersday morning, and everyone is sleeping in."

He used a small fork to fish around the jar for the juiciest apple slice but paused before he got one. The spellbook was open on his lap.

"What's this? That's funny. I don't remember opening my journal. Oh, yes, silly me. It isn't mine. This is Aldenthwaine's book."

Get rid of it, Aargh! Don't read a single word on its pages! Throw it away and forget about it.

Aargh shifted uncomfortably as an image appeared in his mind. Marble House. Yes, he'd recently visited the ruin of Marble House.

"What did my parents mean? What spell could be so dangerous? Is it to hurt people? Is it the spell the Wizard of the Council used to steal Mother Tree's magic or bring down lightning onto Middling Street? Why go to such lengths to hide it from me but not destroy it? That doesn't make sense. If they didn't want me to have it, why didn't they throw it into the fire and be done with it? There must have been a reason for keeping it."

They told you. Don't you remember? They couldn't destroy it! No one can. It's too powerful. Please wake up!

Beneath it all, Aargh struggled with the possibility that his beloved mentor would write down anything so egregious. That didn't sound like his teacher and friend, at least, not the Aldenthwaine that had, for all intents and purposes, raised him from boyhood.

Aargh, what are you doing? You can't rationalize this! This is beyond you!

Maybe they didn't understand, he tried to convince himself. Then again, his mother should have. She'd mastered elemental magic, after all. However, *master* might be too strong a word for it. Give it a go, and hope for the best would be far more accurate in his experience.

Aargh, are you out of your mind? Holly-Mine needs you! The city needs you! Leave this place!

Without any idea of what he was doing, Aargh uttered a series of incomprehensible words–completely oblivious to their significance or meaning.

Countless words.

Streams of words uncontrollably poured out of his mouth.

Brighter and brighter, the sun shone above him, burning his skin and singeing his robes. Suddenly, a pain drove its way into his mind, piercing his thoughts and jolting him out of his magical stupor. Holly-Mine's voice called to him. Gone were her gentle whispers, replaced by screams that forced him to put his hands over his ears.

"No, Papa! Stop. You promised you'd listen to me. You mustn't! It's forbidden!"

"Holly-Mine, where are you? What's going on?" Aargh asked, realizing he'd been reciting a spell. "This isn't possible. Wizards can't be bound without their consent. Where am I? Who brought me here?"

More pain.

More magic.

He could see it! There was lightning in his fingers! And it was traveling through his hand. Aargh threw the spellbook away, but it didn't stop! Farther up his arm, it crept.

"No!"

The magic clawed its way toward his mind.

"You can't! I won't let you! I am the Earth Mother's and the Earth Mother's alone!" he screamed.

It almost had him.

The pain changed. It became sinewy...poking and prob-ing...searching for a way to break through his defenses. Not succeeding, it changed again into long, sharp daggers stabbing at his mind. It was in his ear; the ache was unbearable, pushing harder and harder. It wouldn't be long now.

Aargh recklessly grabbed Guildebrande's grip, drawing the sword. His other hand slipped off the scabbard, and the blade's edge sliced into the flesh, cutting his fingers to the bone. Wincing in pain, Aargh stifled a yell, trying to keep control.

"Guildebrande," he called to his familiar. "Guildebrande, are you there?"

Of course, he was there. They were linked, but the sword struggled to answer, assailed by the magic threatening to overwhelm them. Aargh and his familiar's connection was their strength and their weakness!

Far away, the blade's voice shimmered at the edges of Aargh's mind. "Friend Aarghathlain, place my cross-guard over your heart."

The magic resisted, making Aargh's arms heavy as he struggled to lift the sword. Intertwining his fingers to get a better grip, he pulled the hilt nearer to his chest. The pain was excruciating, but it worked. The magic put more energy into stopping Aargh from casting his spell than trying to enter his mind.

Aargh's blood flowed along the sword's razor-sharp edge, dripping to the ground at their feet. "We're doing it, Guildebrande. We're doing it!" he said through gritted teeth.

"Memenumdnwil," the sword replied, unable to form words.

Aargh made one last effort to draw the blade close to his breast. When the sword made contact with his body, Aargh's hand healed, and Guildebrande's light burst forth again.

Speaking with the same voice, they bellowed, "We are of the earth, and of the sky, and of the water! We are one, wizard and familiar! We are not defeated!"

The spell cracked.

The ground warped and churned. Trees toppled over, and buildings tumbled. The good feeling was gone, as was the park. Aargh watched as the sky grew dark and the town faded until they were alone, standing in inky blackness. The only light came from Guildebrande's blade.

His mind restored, Aargh moaned. "Poor Bram. Oh, Gerald and Grunt and the others. And Ralph, too. Guildebrande, we must find a way to return to Holly-Mine. But how? Where are we?"

The sensation of being watched made him look around. They weren't alone.

"Hello, Aarghathlain," a familiar voice spoke from the darkness. "It's been a while, hasn't it?"

A tall man wearing elegant purple robes with gold embroidery emerged from the nothingness.

"Aldenthwaine?"

WINTER IS COMING
RATS, DWARVES, ODARAPHRIM & TARTHANABELLE
In the moments, days, and weeks
after Aargh's disappearance.

Rats are practical creatures, which means they usually reach a consensus on virtually any topic with little fuss, but not this time.

"Absolutely not!" Wrulde said, pacing around the Meeting Place.

Buck puffed his chest, making himself look bigger than he already was. "Do you have a better idea?"

"Let's take a step back," Parsifal interjected, trying to squeeze between the other rats before the situation became untenable.

For hours, Throod had sat patiently listening to Buck, Wrulde, and Parsifal try to agree on what to do next, and she'd reached her limit. She jumped to her feet, startling the other rats.

"Listen! I've had it up to here with all of you. Quit your bickering and sit."

The other three rats stood frozen in mid-argument, staring at her.

"Now!"

They scrambled to arrange themselves in a neat line facing her.

Parsifal cleared his throat and said, "I'd like to make clear that I had nothing–"

"Zip it!" Throod said, cutting him off and cringing at the pain in her tail. "I've been here the entire time without saying a word. Now it's my turn to talk."

There was a loud crash as a pile of rats tumbled out of a tunnel and into the circular space.

"Hey,"

"did you hear?"

"Mnoonge is a wizard!"

"Most of the Mischief…"

"is at the Spire,"

"helping Wizard Aarghathlain."

"Can you believe it?"

"A rat wizard!"

Throod, Buck, Wrulde, and Parsifal stared at each other in disbelief. Then, without saying another word, they ran as fast as possible to find out what had happened.

● ● ●

Hammers and chisels echoed from the depths of Dahr Kahlahd-dîm. Dwarves were carving long staircases from the Dūnhyldun-thîr to the valley floor. It had been an age of the world since the chasm had seen dwarven craftsmanship re-shaping its visage, but watching Aargh transform and fly out of the ravine had stoked a fire that had been smoldering for generations.

For far too long, the Brethren had sat idly by, waiting for fortune to come their way. Wizards had been gifted to the world at their request, so why had dwarves shunned them? Only magic could reopen their halls under the Mounts of Ardilakk, and they intended to take back what was rightfully theirs. From this time forward, magic would once again serve dwarves and restore the glory of old!

Never before in its long history had the hidden city chosen to reveal itself to the world. Now, the Brethren were on the move.

• • •

Phrim and his Northrim companions packed their belongings—not forgetting what was left of the figs—and headed to the cliffs of False Hope Bluff. It was a challenging hike up steep embankments through rocky terrain. More than once, they had to stop and catch their breath or put out a hand to keep one of their group from slipping back toward Old Eastie Sowtown.

During one of their breaks, Phrim had contemplated walking away from wizarding and leaving Aargh and Tarth to their own devices. He could be happy working the earth and singing songs around an open fire at night. The only square without straight roads had community, precisely what Phrim had always longed for, but it wasn't to be. If he didn't see his plans through, Old Eastie Sowtown might not exist if Tarth got his way, and Phrim couldn't let that happen—especially now that there'd been an unnatural event, as the townies put it.

A battle had raged in the sky over the Metal City. Phrim had missed it, being so exhausted from picking vegetables that he must have slept right through it all. From the sound of it, the aerial display had been pretty impressive, with bright lights, explosions, and an airship that had gone down in the river. Afraid what they'd been trying to avoid was happening, Lank, Pawd, Chpader, and Malba had remained hidden in one of the domed huts. The townies, however, had watched from their tree houses and planned to head to the Congregational House for the first time in generations to make their voices heard. Phrim knew that was the last place he and his companions should show their faces, so they'd said their goodbyes and began their trek to the cliff's edge. From there, they planned to watch the river for any sign of a way to get into the camp by water.

When he'd turned to wave goodbye, Phrim had no idea that he'd never lay eyes on Bud, Elsie, or their farming community ever again.

When they finally reached False Hope Bluff, Phrim and the band of Northrim outcasts pitched camp on the southern tip of False Hope Bluff. Malba pointed out the ship where her cousin lived, and they took turns watching for its dories to be launched. Phrim planned to map the dories' routes and try to rendezvous with her cousin the next time he went out.

Thankfully, they didn't have long to wait, but a problem immediately presented itself. Hundreds of dories launched at once, and their paths crisscrossed so much that Phrim had no hope of charting their courses. He was about to give up when he noticed something peculiar.

One of the dories broke away from the fleet by sneaking behind a passing steamer. Phrim never took his eyes off it, watching as it slowly but surely floated toward the opposite bank.

"That's it! That's our way in. Some of the Northrim are slipping away from the fleet," he said, slapping the rock beneath him. When he did, his mind filled with a buzzing sensation that prevented him from seeing straight.

A surge of energy burst from his hand, and the rock cracked along a vein of quartz. Shocked by the magic, he slipped off and landed hard on the stony ground. Even though he was in pain, he didn't move, focusing all of his thoughts on regaining control of his senses.

"Did you do that?" Chpader asked.

"I...I think I did," he answered, rubbing his temples. The buzzing was gone, but it had left him with a splitting headache.

"How?"

"Trust me. I'd like to know the answer to that question myself. The only thing I can think of is that Aargh's spell has been broken. That must be what happened at the Spire. You know what this means, right?"

Chpader and the others looked at each other questioningly.

"If I have it, so does—"

● ● ●

"AAAAARGH!" Tarth bellowed as lightning shot out of him in every direction. Confused and entirely overwhelmed by elemental magic, he struggled to understand what was happening.

RAGE!

FIRE!

DESIRE!

People on the ground ran for cover as a massive magical discharge traveled down the Metal City's tower, leaping to surrounding buildings and burrowing deep into the earth.

Every time Tarth moved, lightning shot out of his hands, and when he opened his mouth, fire belched from him like a banshee's scream. When he looked at something, anything, it dematerialized into a heap of molten metal.

Frustrated, he slammed his bloody fists on the floor only to find himself flung across the room and landing hard on his back. Gasping for air, he tried to turn over but was too exhausted to move.

The door flew open.

Tarth opened his eyes to see who'd been foolish enough to come into the room, and the bursts of magic started again.

"It's me!" Flinghower yelled, diving behind a twisted metal plate to protect himself.

Through sheer force of will, Tarth made it to his feet. "Stay where you are if you know what's good for you," he said through gritted teeth, not willing to open his mouth.

Much to the chagrin of students and teachers alike, the one thing Fling had never been able to do was keep from sticking his long nose where it didn't belong. This time, however, peering over the barrier to see what his mentor was doing turned out to be a near-fatal mistake.

Tarth's outburst was so powerful that the entire tower shook, and several buildings in the city collapsed.

When Fling came to, he found that Tarth had dragged his bruised and battered body to the center of the room.

"I told you to stay hidden," Tarth growled. "Have you forgotten how to listen to your mentor?"

Fling tried to roll onto his side, but Tarth growled again, and he stayed where he was. "What's going on? Did Aargh do this?" he asked.

"Who else? He must have realized that I'd figure out how to access elemental magic sooner or later, so he poisoned it against us."

"But it looks like you've gotten it under control."

"DOES THIS LOOK LIKE CONTROL?" Tarth roared, moving his arm and blasting a jet of magic so intense it singed their clothing.

After a few minutes, Fling risked looking at Tarth again. Despite the obvious danger and the strain on his mentor's face, he couldn't help but be excited. Tarth had done it. He had magic!

"This is nothing to smile about," Tarth snapped. "Magic is useless to us if we can't control it."

"But there must be a way. Maybe instead of using it, we can harness its power. Contain it somehow and only let it out when we need it?"

Tarth's demeanor changed, and he seemed to calm down a little. "Yes. Capture it like a wild animal. Keep it on a leash, as it were. What an excellent idea."

"Do you think that's possible? How would we do that?"

A flash of anger made Fling recoil again, but Tarth didn't explode this time. Instead, his mentor's face curled into a wicked smile. "How, indeed?"

REFERENCE

CALENDAR

Ardilakk Valley's calendar is divided into four seasons: autumn (weeks 1 through 13), winter (weeks 14 through 26), spring (weeks 27 through 39), and Summer (weeks 40 through 52). All cities on the River Wide have followed this calendar since the beginning of Ancient Times (a.k.a. the Second Age of the World).

The new year is marked by the Fall of Autumn Celebration, which is considered the most important holiday of the year as it marks the end of the bountiful seasons of spring and summer and the beginning of leaner times.

The calendar year's fifty-two weeks each contain nine days numbered according to the week in which they fall. Therefore, if Mundsday the 9th is the first day of the ninth week, all of the other days in that week are also referred to as the 9th (Toodlesday the 9th, Wendingsday the 9th, and so on). Additionally, each day holds special meaning in Ardilakk Valley (for example, Wendingsday is known as the *Day of Wanderings*).

Although no scientific correlation has ever been proven, it is surprising how frequently this lore coincides with actual events. For example, you would never hear of a Geminian intentionally leaving for vacation on Landingsday or cleaning the water closet on Sattersday.

DAYS OF THE WEEK

Mundsday (MU)
The Day of Beginnings

Toodlesday (TO)
The Day of Leavings

Wendingsday (WE)
The Day of Wanderings

Landingsday (LA)
The Day of Returnings

Middlingsday (MI)
The Day of Questionings

Thrundsday (TH)
The Day of Longings

Frittersday (FR)
The Day of Distractions

Sattersday (SA)
The Day of Resting

Sundsday (J)
The Day of Cleanings
(Originally All Suds Day)

EVENTS AND HOLIDAYS

Mundsday the 1st
Autumnal Equinox/New Year's Day

wk1
Fall of Autumn Celebration

Mundsday the 14th
Winter Solstice

wk20
Midswinterfest

Mundsday the 27th
Vernal Equinox

wk27
Middling Street Fair

Thrundsday the 33rd
Day of Rain Celebration

Mundsday the 40th
Summer Solstice

wk46
Midsummerfest

Sunday the 52nd
New Year's Eve

MAP: ARDILAKK VALLEY

(West)

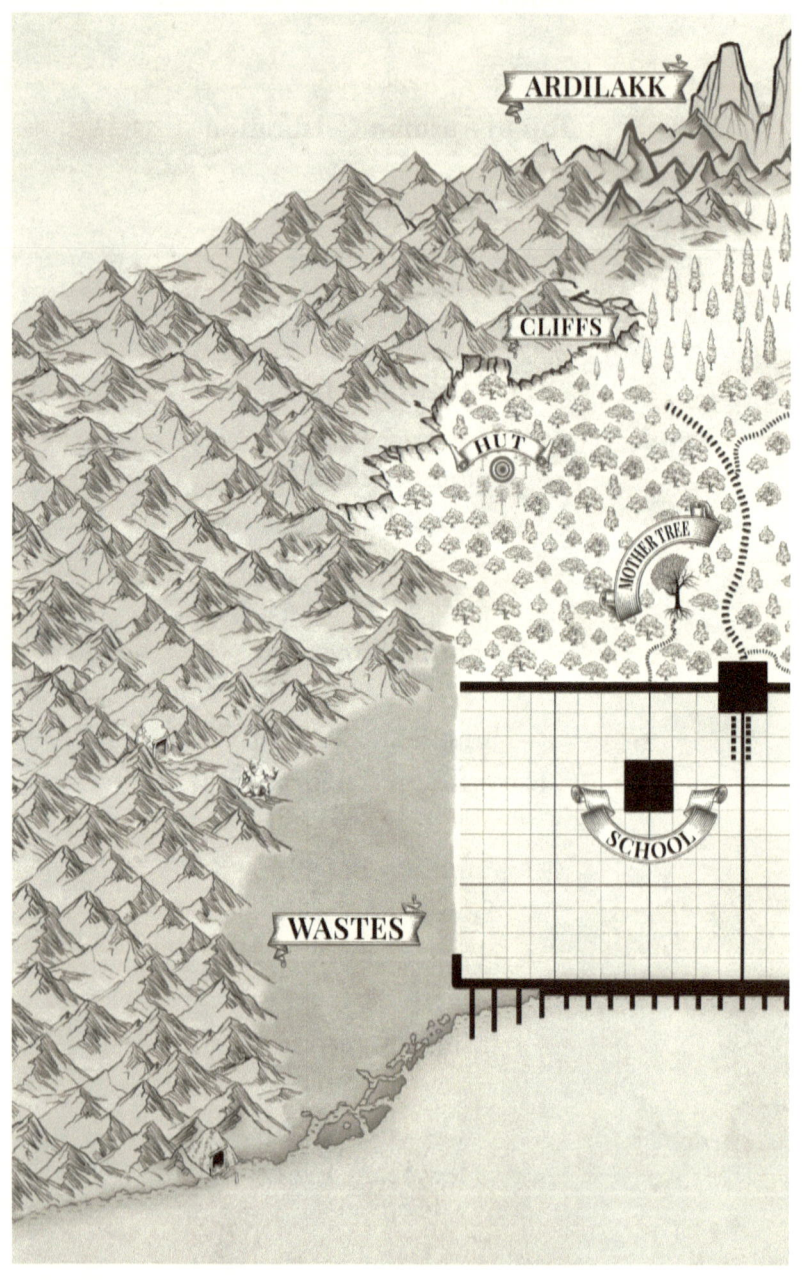

(East)

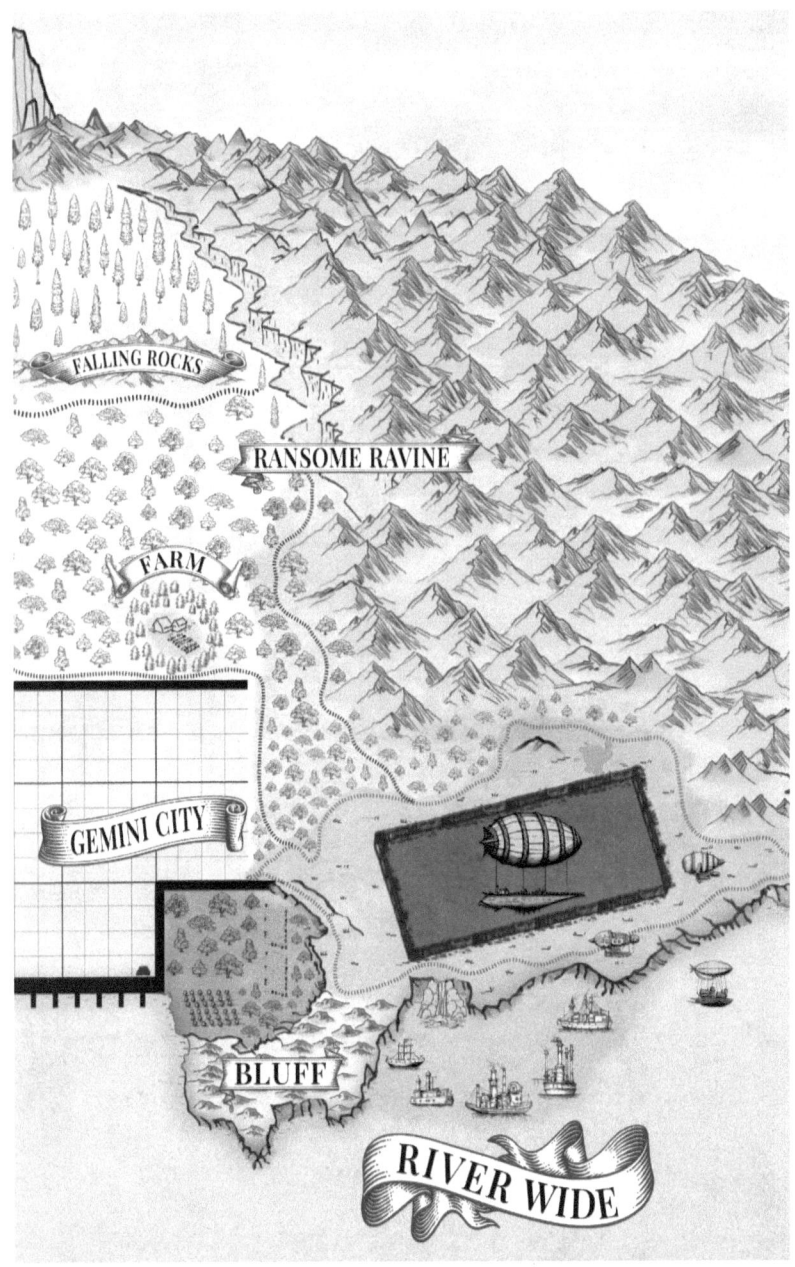

FALLING ROCKS

RANSOME RAVINE

FARM

GEMINI CITY

BLUFF

RIVER WIDE

MAP: GEMINI CITY
(West)

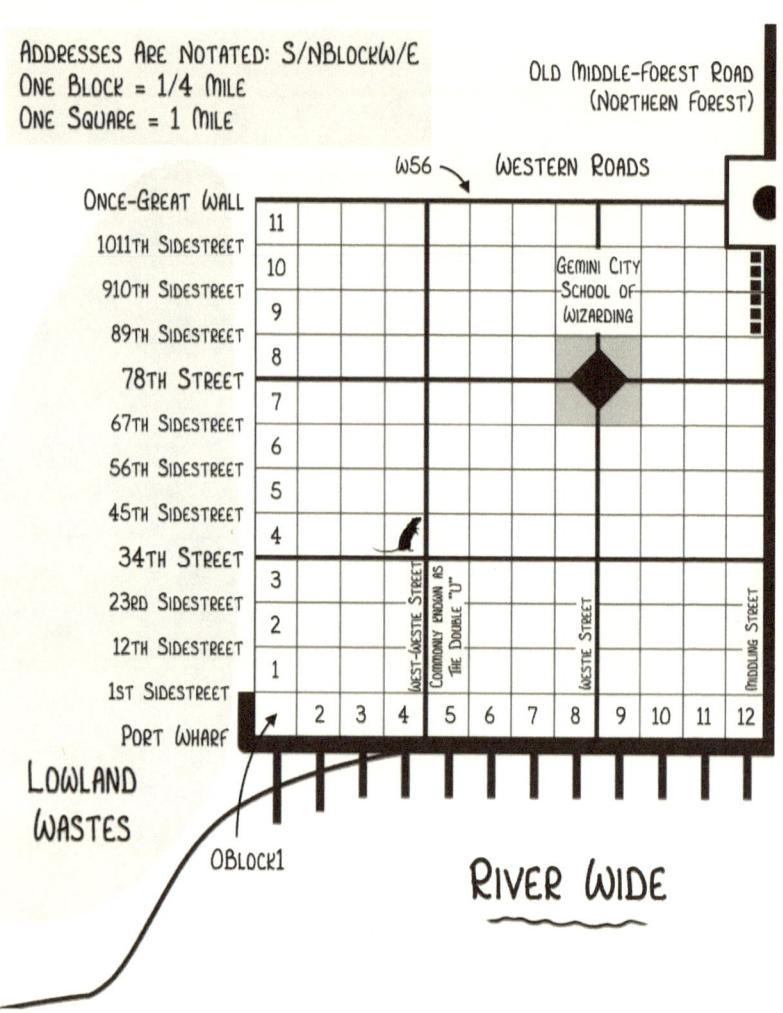

ADDRESSES ARE NOTATED: S/NBLOCKW/E
ONE BLOCK = 1/4 MILE
ONE SQUARE = 1 MILE

OLD MIDDLE-FOREST ROAD
(NORTHERN FOREST)

W56 → WESTERN ROADS

ONCE-GREAT WALL

1011TH SIDESTREET

910TH SIDESTREET

89TH SIDESTREET

78TH STREET

67TH SIDESTREET

56TH SIDESTREET

45TH SIDESTREET

34TH STREET

23RD SIDESTREET

12TH SIDESTREET

1ST SIDESTREET

PORT WHARF

GEMINI CITY
SCHOOL OF
WIZARDING

WEST-WESTIE STREET
COMMONLY KNOWN AS
THE DOUBLE "U"

WESTIE STREET

MIDDLING STREET

LOWLAND
WASTES

OBLOCK1

RIVER WIDE

(East)

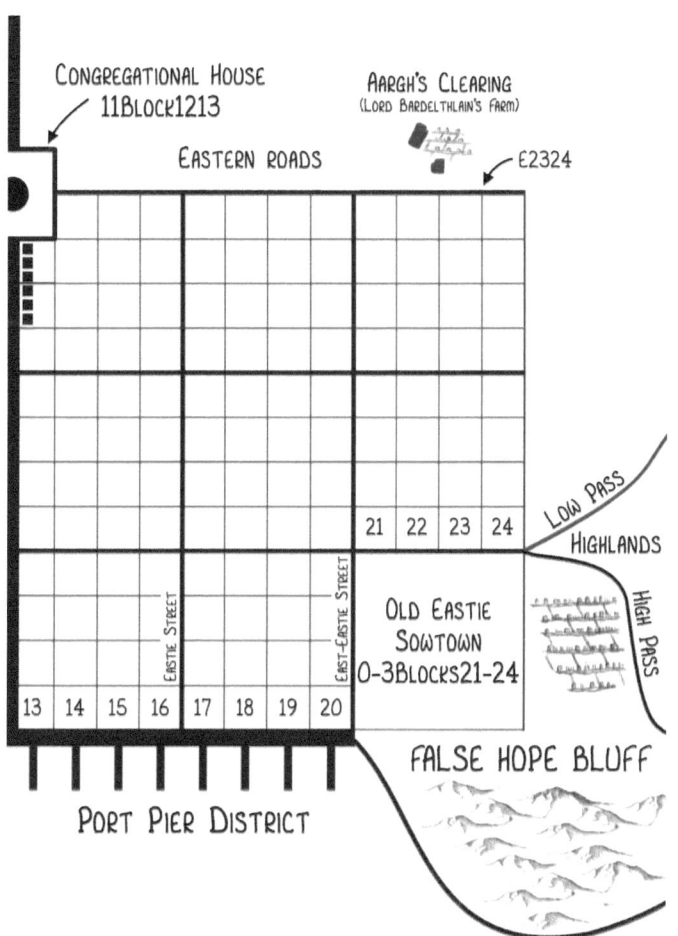

CONGREGATIONAL HOUSE
11Block1213

AARGH'S CLEARING
(LORD BARDELTHLAIN'S FARM)

EASTERN ROADS

E2324

LOW PASS

HIGHLANDS

21 22 23 24

EASTIE STREET

EAST-EASTIE STREET

OLD EASTIE
SOWTOWN
O-3BLOCKS21-24

HIGH PASS

13 14 15 16 17 18 19 20

FALSE HOPE BLUFF

PORT PIER DISTRICT

MAP: WIZARDING SCHOOL GROUNDS

(West)

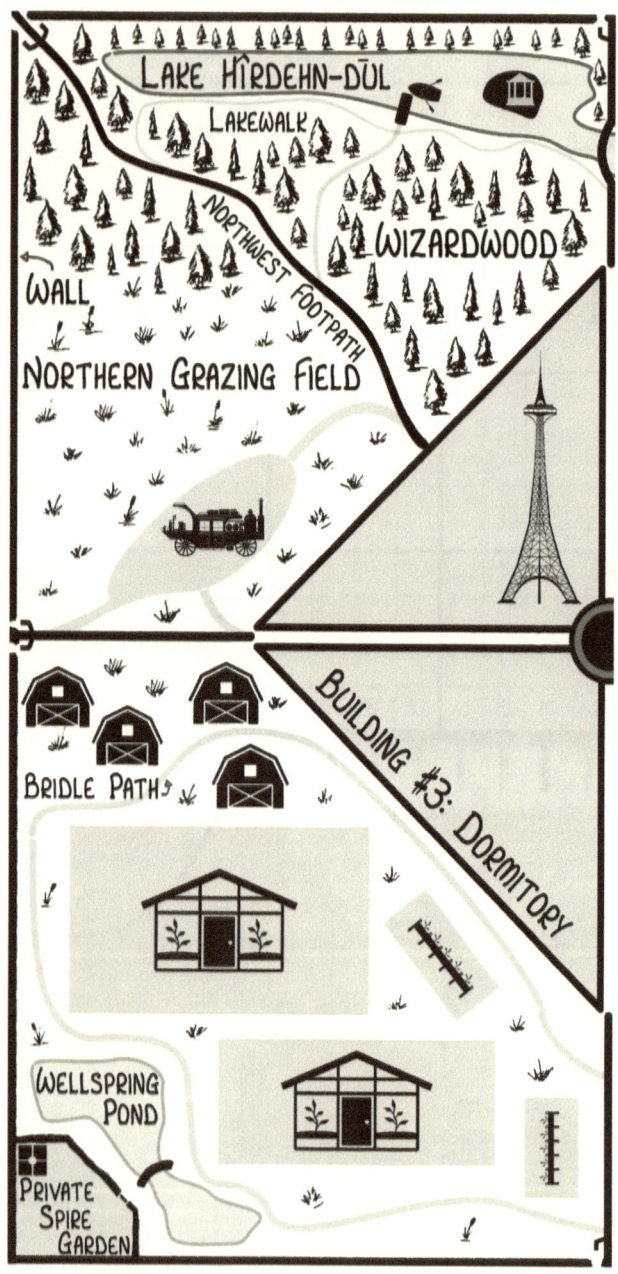

MAP: MARBLE HOUSE

(First Floor)

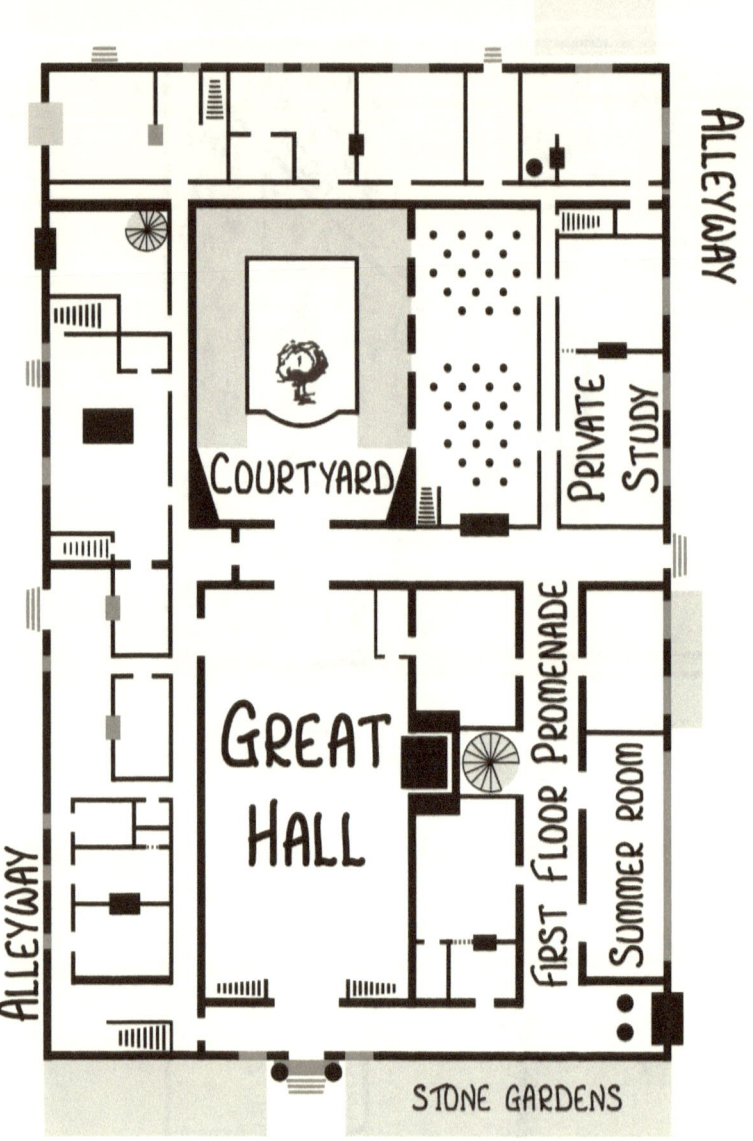

ALLEYWAY

COURTYARD

PRIVATE STUDY

GREAT HALL

FIRST FLOOR PROMENADE

SUMMER ROOM

ALLEYWAY

STONE GARDENS

(Second Floor)

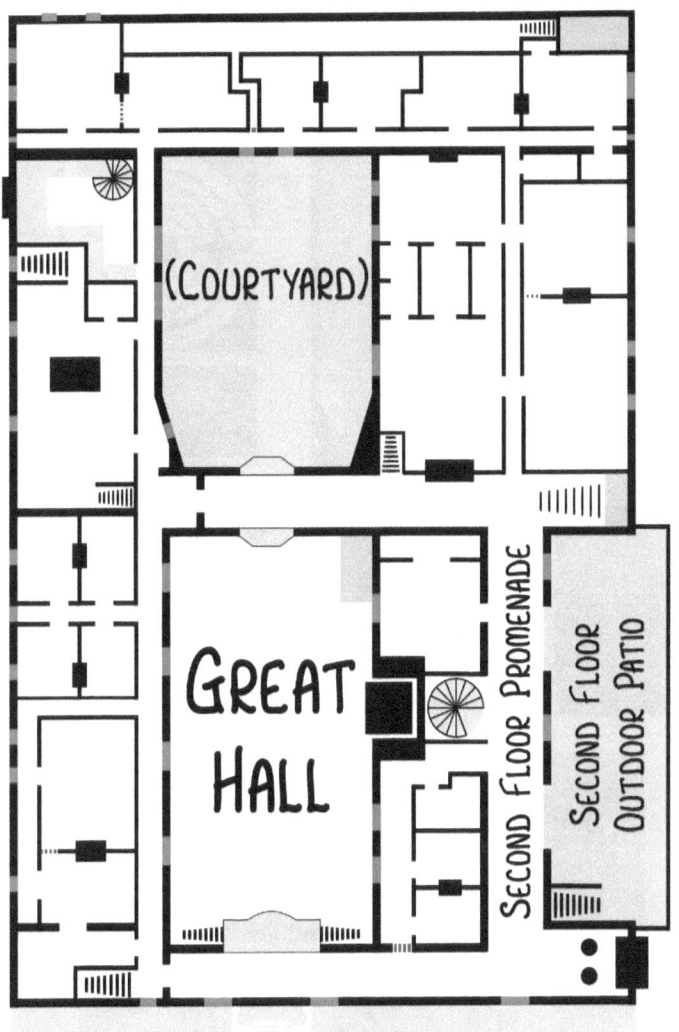

(Roof)

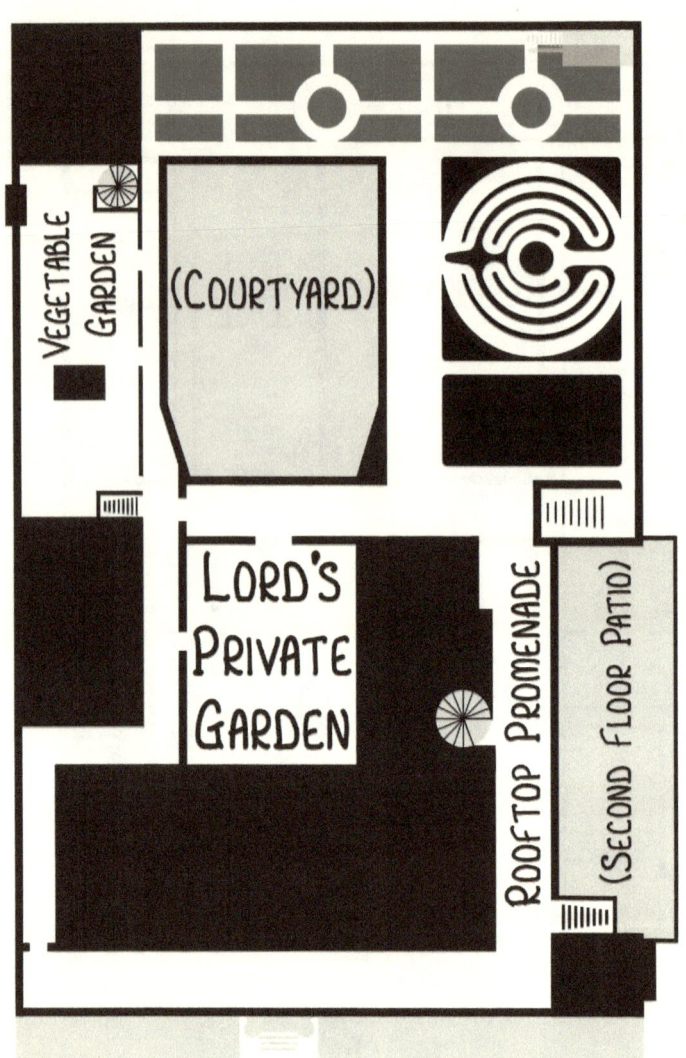

VEGETABLE GARDEN

(COURTYARD)

LORD'S PRIVATE GARDEN

ROOFTOP PROMENADE

(SECOND FLOOR PATIO)

(Basement)

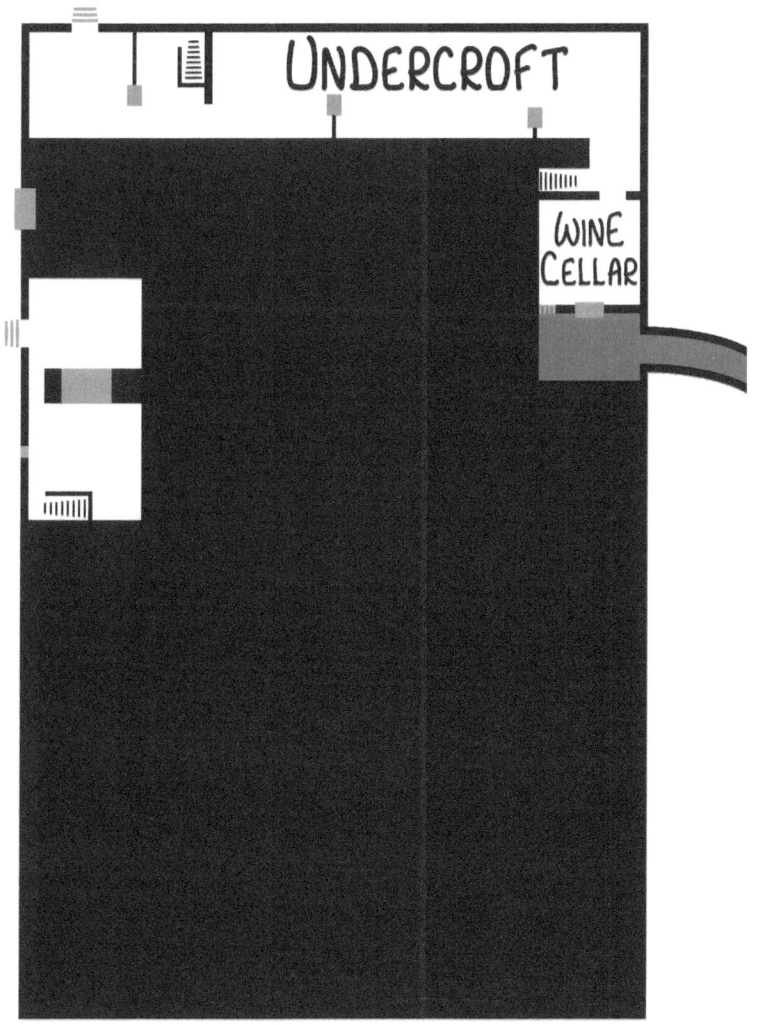

UNDERCROFT

WINE CELLAR

MAP: ANCIENT QUADROPOLIS

(West)

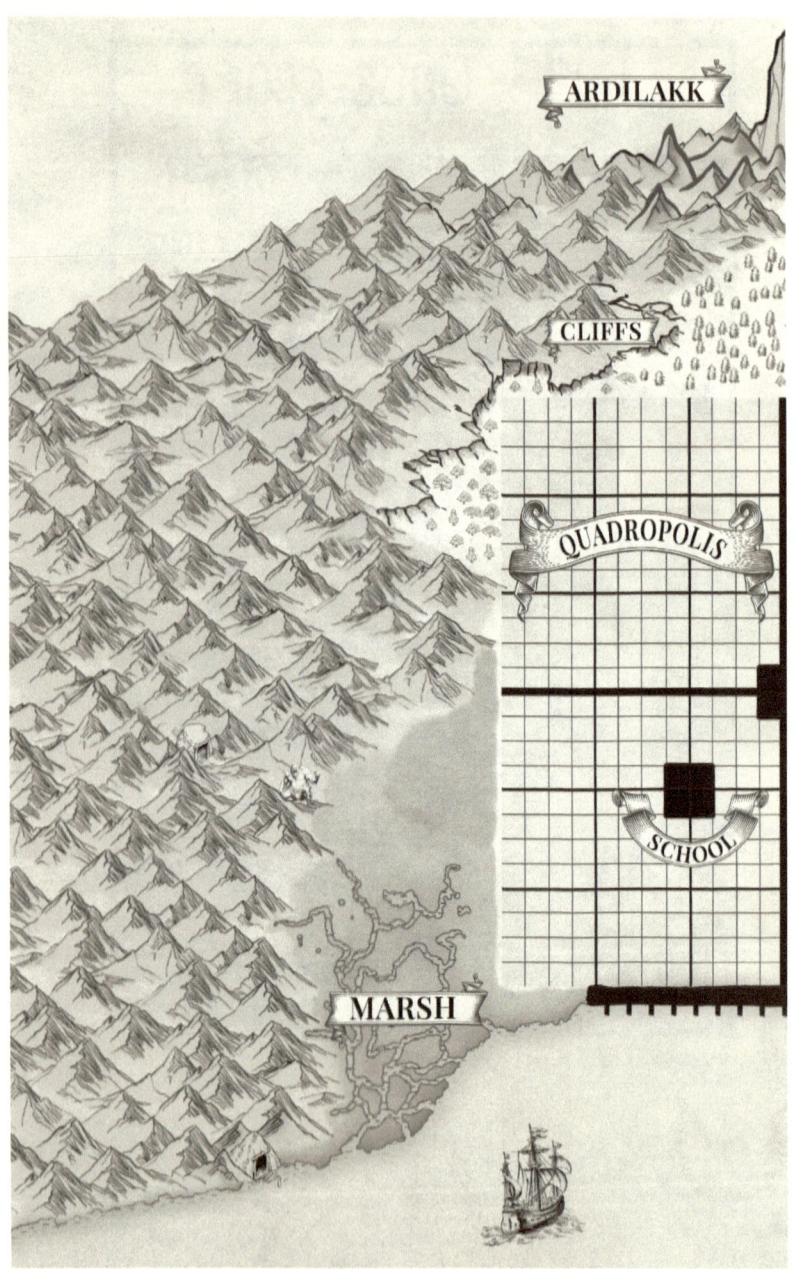

(East)

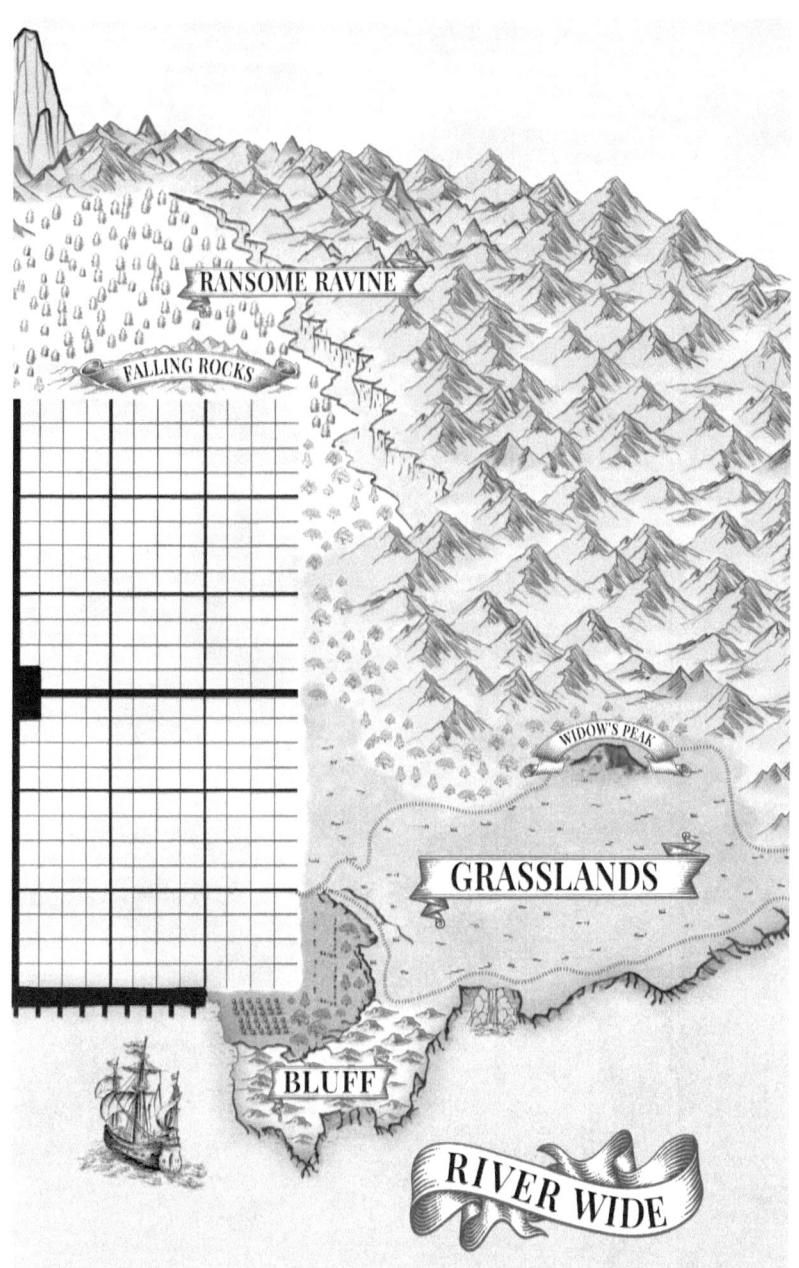

THE ADVENTURE CONTINUES!

for more information, please visit:

www.wizardsdiary.com

ABOUT THE AUTHOR

ROBERT J. BRADSHAW finds inspiration on the rocky shores of Cape Ann, Massachusetts, though putting pen to paper doesn't always mean writing books. His musical compositions have been heard on concert stages worldwide, from Lincoln Center to Thailand, Europe to Australia (where his opera ".Gabriel" was premiered courtesy of Opera Australia). When concert halls fell silent in 2020, and the intensity of isolation weighed heavily on his family, Rob suggested they workshop an epic fantasy tale for fun–yes, this is the kind of thing his family does for fun! So, every night after dinner, they sat in the living room (on the couch, on the floor with the dog, crawling up the stairs, even sitting in his wife's spinning office chair going 'round and 'round and 'round…) dissecting every aspect of what would become Aargh and Holly-Mine's adventures in Ardilakk Valley. Little did Rob know how joyful (and how much work!) the project would be, and he is thrilled to be able to share *The Wizard's Diary* with fantasy readers like himself.

For more information about Rob and his creative endeavors, please visit www.robertjbradshaw.com.

THE WIZARD'S DIARY

BOOK ONE
THE WIZARD'S DIARY
(PARTS I & II)

BOOK TWO
AN UNWIZARDLY SILENCE
(PARTS III & IV)

BOOK THREE
A THOUSAND EYES BY NIGHT
(PARTS V & VI)

BOOK FOUR
THE ONE TRUE ROOT
(PARTS VII & VIII)

COMPANION TO
THE WIZARD'S DIARY
ARDILAKK THROUGH THE AGES
(TERMINOLOGY, FOLKLORE, MAPS,
HISTORIES, AND SONGS)

www.ingramcontent.com/pod-product-compliance
Lightning Source LLC
Chambersburg PA
CBHW022203030726
47494CB00019B/47

9 7 9 8 9 9 0 6 0 9 6 8 6